# REVIEWER COMMENTS

### Praise for an early draft of
### "The Sound Chaser Versus the Thunder God"
### (Originally titled: *"The Seeker in Forever"*)

"Highly recommended . . . to be given high praise for an originality and cleverness that is as entertaining as it is thought-provoking."
— Small Press Bookwatch, Midwest Book Review

"A mind-bending world . . . This flight through the imagination requires a full and complete appreciation for the raw, elemental beauty of the human experience."
— Miranda Orso, The Electric Review

"A turbulent whirlwind of passion that takes the reader on a rollercoaster without a safety harness. Fox's unique, beautiful and unforgettable manner of storytelling means that readers will need to be prepared for their minds to bend quite erratically if they are to fully comprehend and take pleasure in the experience."
— Catherine Tuckwell, BlogCritics.org

"This book will take you on a wild ride . . . A definite read for anyone looking for a rare adventure of violence, insanity, and power struggles."
— Adreann Stephens, SLUG Magazine

"The prose is visceral and emotive. . . . The book felt like it was begging to be read aloud or turned into a performance piece. . . . A mindbender . . . I'm glad that I had the opportunity to read it."
— Ash Brown, Experiments in Reading

"The reader should be forewarned that this is not your mother's political satire, but instead a whole new animal altogether. . . . Prepare yourself for a bit of joyride the open-minded will undertake with gusto."
— Sylvia Cochran, Roundtable Reviews

"An entertaining book that is a great read for anyone who enjoys a fast-paced, well-written political satire."
—Cherie Fisher, Reader Views

# *The* FIRE BOOK

## *of* Scenes and Stories

## First Edition

---

# Alan Fox

StoryFocus™ Communications
New York
www.storyfocus.com

The Fire Book of Scenes and Stories (First Edition)
Copyright © 2013 by Alan Sean Fox

StoryFocus™ Communications
New York City
Tel (718) 775-5540
www.storyfocus.com

Printed in the United States of America

ISBN-13: 978-0-9762276-3-2


Publisher's Reference: 0210_Fin_03_Storm_Edition

## Dedication

This book is dedicated to you

And I hope it helps you to know
My love goes with you wherever you go

## Acknowledgements

Stories frame our world. When we walk the world, we all go down our own road, but we start where the old roads leave off. I'd like to thank the following for their poetic inspiration.

*Patricia Barber, Jack Bruce/Pete Brown, Vinicius de Moraes, Dick Gregory, Frank Herbert, Bill Hicks, Michael Hutchence, k.d. lang, James Douglas Morrison, Roland Orzabal, Joan Osborne, Cole Porter, Socrates, H.G. Wells, Brian Wilson* and many others.

# Contents

# The Sound Chaser
## Versus
# The Thunder God

# Her Scorching Beauty
# and
# His Wicked, Wicked Sidewinding Ways

## The Violent World

ONCE UPON A TIME, in a dark expanse of life, in the age of stars, along the arm of a spiral galaxy, there came a world that *peopled*, violently.

*Oh Violent World, Set Amid the Brutal All, of Life!*

Here, in the soft revolutions of darkness, there came roaring, violent themes calling, and there came: *Life, reality,* and *the mirror of life.*

Here there came a world to tread amid the mighty violence of a cosmos, and the absolutes of brutality.

Here there came a world to overthrow chaos and to forge being, and strong presence, to call into the universe *the will to beauty.*

Lights calling it home, it rose forth. . . . to burn with mighty and curved intent. Here the darkness was made to yield by the violent world calling itself home, amid the light and age of stars.

It emerged from fires.

And its motions rippled outward, upward, onward, roundward. And conspired a strange armor of rock and blue sheen—The world turned onto itself, heating to a warm stone and iron form, rounded. It's armor, cooling to a coat of basalt and granite—And here, onto its outer works, onto its hostile-featured outer realms, onto the lands floating on its rippling mantle, there came wildernesses and forests, reaching out to sun and sky, stretching to coastal waters, and to blue-green dreams of oceans vast & deep & wide.

All along the Earth and its seasons, the ripples turned and spread within themselves.

The motions, once started, did not stop. There was only the moving forward—motions leading on to motions.

Seasons leading onto seasons. Journeys to journeys. Echoes to echoes.

The world rippled, and the ripples *peopled*. Just as the rippling of a tree forms *leaves*, so too the world rippled and formed *people*.

The people, emerging, found that time stretched out before them and called them to journey across the world.

They came to birth and death, and to feeling the flow of the world.

They came alive, and marched to death in bands, schemes, and winds of yesterdays, todays, and tomorrows.

Reckless and hungered, they coursed. Murders by the roadside, spoke of their progress, as they sowed a brave new world. As they peopled a brave, strange flowing world.

And found themselves flowing in mighty currents.

The people, struggled and strove, and broke each other.

The motions rippled.

Creating—while the world was young—a he-being, *Miles Roark,* and a she-being named *Daphne Fox,* a woman who swam in mystery.

Her mystery groped out at he-beings and drove them to grow hot. And bothered. And to long achingly for her motions.

In the course of the timeline, in the slipstream of the now, in a tavern, her mystery groped out at two he-men—the team of *Mahoney and McSmithers*—who had emerged from a duststorm on the horizon and retreated into the establishment's dark shades for a round of drinks.

Outside, the sun was fled and gone.

Nightfall covered the realm.

The ground rhythm rippled onward, outward and upward.

Wildfire, ran wild in the wilderness.

The motions suggested the he-being, *Miles Roark.* He, that would one day encounter the she-being, *Daphne Fox,* that swam in mystery.

He, was a seething burning fire.

She, was a princess, queen of the byways.

They were in a strange night of stone and heated iron mists.

She, was steeped in mirth. He, seething.

Their motions would extend into the furthermore.

Into the recesses and reaches of forever.

But first, there would be great barriers, which were quite a consideration. What difficulties lay before the onward motion? What was there to halt the forwarding?

The world, and its gold. A force red, and its might.

But, these lay in the storms of the futureflow. Out there. In the looming moving storms of the futureflow.

In the here and now ... which when you get down to it, is all we ever have, had or will have ... there is a region ...

And in the region of the now, there lies *the tavern*—and within the hollow tavern's recessed dark shades sit the two *he-men*—the team of Mahoney and McSmithers—applying themselves seriously to getting rotten, stinking drunk. And warming themselves on a feeling ... of the embrace of her warm, wet mystery. Or more particularly by visions of her warm, wet inner being.

The thought trails spreading out into the tavern, speak of the team at work, rendering, forming the philosophical stylings of Mahoney and McSmithers.

# A Tavern, "The Caveman's Grotto & Grill"

IT WAS A DANGEROUS WORLD filled with overrated treasures and underrated pleasures, mainly to be gotten through hunting, murdering, destroying and devouring. And this tavern was a retreat, but it had a kind of calm that verged on violence.

A dark center gave out dark motions, which streamed outward to a shore of walls that buffeted them back. The walls were made of granite and stone, of bedrock and boulders.

Lying on the shorewalls—adorning them, lending them dignity—were wooden deathclubs, dark face masks, flaked flint arms, and ground stone weapons. The place had the look, and charm of the good old days, of the Stone Age! . . . and the outdoor life. It was filled with the haunting remnants of happy days spent under the sun hunting, struggling, fielding, dying and murdering.

This was the backdrop.

And in the spotlight, the team was at work.

Mahoney drank his whiskey.

"In books . . . the hero's a superstar," said Mahoney. "The hero is a firebrand. In books, the hero is a freaking firestorm running wild. He's a secret service agent. He's a swashuckler, buccaneer, you know what I mean? A 'firestorm cocktail'—burning with feeling, baby. You following me?—"

"Oh aye, that's correct," said McSmithers.

"He's outside the field," said Mahoney, "outside the grid—The hero is a big burning question and we have to hang in for the answer—See that's the hook, that's what pulls us, the audience, into it . . ."

"That's the fantastic thing always," McSmithers said.

"And he's in a big game—Secret service double agent, maybe," said Mahoney. "Commander turning a war, maybe. Commando being chased, maybe. That kind of bull mud thing. That level of frickin' cosmic happening, okay."

"That's right, a proper game," said McSmithers.

"The hero is a mystery and he's in a mysterious game. That's what I'm getting at there. Okay, now."

"Yes, that's fantastic," McSmithers said. "Tells you a bit of something it does."

"Fantastic," said Mahoney, "that's right it's always fantastic—If not a commando, then a former commando. If not on Her Majesty's Secret

Service, then formerly with Her service. Can speak any langugage, true?—Can speak Anglo-Saxon, Middle English, and American English—Expert with any weapon. Can chop his hand through a wooden trunk the size of an elephant."

"Oh aye, that's a marvelous thing," said McSmithers.

"His hands are weapons. More dangerous than my mouth. You know the kind of guy I mean?"

McSmithers saw the profit in being a hero: "That's for sure. Very cool—Has all these magnificent women around."

The man drank his whiskey. "Yup, and he's always in the game, always a player. Never looks around—wait a goddamn minute—'Goddamn hell, what am I doing here?' Like any normal person.

"Well . . ." the man swung around to the trail he had been carving, "this girl is just like that . . . *Daphne Fox*. . . . Oh . . . fashionably lean. And, ah! . . . no drag on her. You watch the way she walks—no fears. Wild with the power. Wild as can be."

The man drank his whiskey.

This was the straight shoot, the hard hit, and the knowing sit of the team of Mahoney and McSmithers.

Outside, a siren blared and it began to rain in the deep forest.

# Scorching Beauty in the Rain, in a Lemon Yellow Dress

DAPHNE FOX LAUGHED—spring always brought the rain.

*And she liked the way that rainy days brought out the color in everything.*

She was moving through the crackling rains. Crystal teardrops drenched her. She was floating on water and air, and wind and sky.

She was wearing a yellow sun dress. Bright lemon yellow. Sexy yellow.

She walked naked, in her clothing. This was the feeling she always gave people. Particularly he-beings.

She laughed, at what had been and what was to come. At life. At the explosive sky above, at the storm, at the clouds around her.

She fancied the shape of schemes drifting in the dark echoes there, the rumblings of a sky crying, the drops tracing pictures of the past in the spring rains, singing of what was and what now will be.

She knew this was a moment between battles. She was on an island floating on nothing, nothing more than her life force, which was a force like a whirlwind.

The earth opened wide as she soared. She rose and left it all behind.

The drops drenched her body, making love to it.

And the mystery of life and youth swirled around her.

She did not know that she was in enormous danger, and might be murdered in a few minutes.

Yet, it was there. Much was being given unto her. *She was about to have a chance to die.*

She returned to her hotel, and the cabin amid blue and black shadows in the woods on the outside of town—And she approached her door, gliding through the rain, just as the thunder began to really rumble.

As she passed through the door, on the other side, a man waited, in a chair, sleepy-eyed, probably just having taken a nap, holding a gun.

Daphne entered, unaware of the man concealed further in the room.

Daphne spun to slam the door with her leg. As she turned, she spotted the man with the gun. She froze with her left leg raised in the air.

She looked at the intruder. He was huge. Nearly seven feet tall. *And, she thought, he has the coiled killer look.*

She peered at him through a sexy squint.

Her left leg stayed up there, where it had just closed the door. And her body was now set in a T-shape. She looked at him and smiled.

"Hello," she said.

"How are you?" the giant said.

"Fair to middlin'. How are you?" she said.

"Better and better," the giant said. "How's the weather out there?"

"Whoa! What a party going on out there. People splishing and a-splashing and a-reeling with the feeling. Splish splash—why don't you go on out there and jump into the bath?"

He laughed. "Maybe later."...They were getting into it. Let the good times roll...."I'm here for something."

"What?"

"You don't know."

"I have no idea."

"Oh, it's going to be like that, is it?" he said.

"Like what?" she said.

He smiled. And, oh my, what big teeth he had.

Now her leg came down, the one that had been raised in the air at the door. "Are you looking for me? I wasn't expecting anyone with a gun."

"Yes, you and a guy that was very rude to some friends of mine a few days ago. When do you expect the gentleman?"

"I don't know who you're talking about," she said.

"When do you expect him?"

"I don't know who you're talking about. You've got the wrong room," she said deadpan. "You really do have the wrong room."

He laughed. He wasn't going anywhere.

"You're talking bull mud," he said. "This is total bull mud."

"Are you here by yourself?" she said. And she swept her gaze across the room.

"Look at you sizing up the situation. You're a smart girl, aren't you? Are you sure you're not a professional? ...I have some friends nearby. When do you expect the gentleman?"

"Should we invite them in? Will they be carrying pistols? Can they bring cocktails? Maybe they can bring their friends. And their friends can bring their friends. Everybody can bring guns."

The giant was courteous as he moved toward her. "You want to play some games? Let's play some games. What the hell, you want to try a little of this?"

*Pow!* He punched her. She tumbled.

"How is that?" he said. Now, his objective in this game was *'to be popular.'* He felt that you should do your best to be popular with your victim. This was what he was about. This meant for her to think that he was wonderful and terrific and entertaining. And also to be popular when he went home and solved the case for the boss. To be popular . . . okay . . . And now he was feeling it, giving this thing an emotion that suited him. *Hey, isn't this fun?* he thought. *I mean waiting for these things is a pain in the ass but when they turn up . . . then you get to play! Okay . . . okay . . .*

"Was that a good thing?" he said. "Did you like that?"

"Very solid," Daphne said. "I can see why you would be proud of it." She rose to her feet. "I'd like to study that when we have the time."

"Why don't we make the time?"

"Let's do that," she said. And smiled.

Now he hit her in the head. He belted her. With enormous feeling and conviction. He felt that it would have to be a hit that threw her head—one that threw her head so hard that she would fly across the room—*Bam!*—Her head went flying across the room. And as this thing was happening what he needed from her, in order to feel his full manhood, was he had to hear a yell of pain that was unbelievable.

He listened for it. But she didn't scream—*ah, it was all right, he decided*—he liked the ones that didn't scream.

He liked her wet clothes. He liked that he could see her breasts. He liked that she didn't carry an umbrella.

*Little yellow riding hood in the dark room.* Very sexy. With the rain outside. Very nice. They were alone. The giant and the girl in the yellow dress.

He liked her. There was something innocent about her and her yellow dress. He liked innocent girls.

Now he was looking at her soaking wet yellow dress.

He went to her, and tore away part of her yellow dress. Part of the front.

She looked at him. He hit her again. Hard. It sent her crashing.

Now she was writhing on the floor, groaning, her face buried.

Once the agony subsided, she came up laughing. It was as though he had played a terrible joke on her by belting her.

"Okay," she said, "you won that one."

She crawled over and tapped his foot.

"Ahh, tag, you're it," she said.

He kicked her hard. She screamed with the pain. Then started laughing.

She pulled herself up by using the table. She was in bad shape. *She grabbed a thing off the table.*

The giant aimed his gun at her.

She revealed that the thing she was holding was *an army knife*, the smallish kind you fit into your pocket. The blade was in its case. A lemon yellow case that matched her yellow dress.

*What was that about?* he thought. *Where the hell did she get a yellow knife? Son of a bitch.* She was fashionably lean. No drag on her. You watched the way she walked. *Scorching Beauty in a Yellow Dress.*

Daphne winked at him.

She held herself in place and spoke to him. "I knew a loan shark," she said, "who knew people better than any psychiatrist. A woman came to him to borrow money ..."

The giant held his gun completely still. He held it high in the air, with a bead on her; his hand was steady; he didn't move a muscle except to breath.

"This loan shark asked this woman how much she needed," Daphne said, "and she told him. The man took the money out, without counting it—this loan shark knew how much money he had—and he put the stack on the table. *'Shall I wrap it for you?'* he asked. *'No,'* she said taking the stack and putting it in her bag. She thanked him and started for the door. He stopped her. *'Give me the money back!'* he said. *'But why?'* she said—*'Because you don't intend to repay the loan—you didn't count the money.'*"

The giant was fascinated. "You didn't count the money, huh. Hah! I like that! That's hot!"

"You're not here to use the gun," Daphne said.

"One never knows, do one?"

"You're here to do some damage but not to kill anyone."

She started using her femininity to enthrall him.

"What if I fought back?" she said. She raised the *yellow army knife* in an ineffectual, harmless way. She pulled open the blade. She turned her eyes from the blade to him. She smiled with great sexuality. *She had great red lips.* "What if I fought back? Would you like that?"

"You're a marvelous girl. Listen little girl, don't you know I'm dangerous?"

"Why are you dangerous?" she said. She was an actress now. You could never tell why someone might think he was dangerous.

"Because I have a gun," he explained. "Because I'm paid to beat people. If your man walks in, I'll beat him worse than you."

"Nah-nah na-na-na. I'm a killer too. I can be just as dangerous as you."

"Is that so?" he said.

She smiled. "Would you like me to fight back?" she asked.

"What could you do little girl?"

Now holding the blade out, she began to move toward him. She stumbled. She could barely walk.

The giant brought his eyes to the blade. It was a slim, and slender thing, not much of a blade at all. She was charming, he thought. Nobody, that he ever came to beat the hell out of, ever did a thing like this. There had been other beautiful women he had beaten and normally the women cried, some tried to defend themselves; but no woman ever came at him with nothing. This blade she was brandishing was nothing.

"You're going to stab me with the knife?" he said. "You'd never make it. And what could you make of it?"

He showed her how he would knock her back. As he extended his gun hand, she flew at him.

She bit his wrist while stabbing the knife into his abdomen. You never saw a woman stab anything harder. But it was really a feint. What she was really doing was what she did next. She quickly got the gun from him, backed out of his reach, and fired into his chest.

He tumbled back. Then began to rise toward her.

"Enough little girl," he said, "now you shot me, are you happy?"

And now he was on his feet. He was coming at her, shrugging off the bullet wound.

She took hold of the gun by the barrel and attacked him. *Bam!* Her blow sent him to the floor. And now what she did was to beat him, hard. It was a little of this, and a little of that, and before long she was finished beating him with the gun.

She pulled herself up. She was bruised and bloody from what this man had just done to her.

Now she jumped up into the air. "Wwhheeeee!" she yelled. And as she came down, she landed on his ribs.

She stepped to the floor.

Then she sat on the giant.

Instead of crying with relief, she was laughing.

"I won the game," she said softly and studied him for a reaction.

She took hold of his nose in her fist. The whole nose, and gave it a good hard twist. His lights seemed to be out. He didn't seem to be feeling a whole hell of a lot at the moment. Or was he? Did she see a trace of something?

Now she grabbed his ears. She twisted both of his ears as hard as she could.

Pull.

Pull.

She fell back laughing.

Poor giant.

Sadly for him, he had stepped into the wrong room. Such things did happen in this crazy world.

And he had stepped into a nice dark room where a nice girl in a yellow dress was spending the night on her way to visit her grandmother in the woods. And alas for him, little yellow riding hood had big teeth and ate the big bad wolf.

At first, it had all seemed so nice. So right. Such a beautiful evening.

She was a girl filled with modern cool, and scorching beauty.

Little did he know he had stepped into his own *Twilight Zone,* where a nice girl named Daphne Fox—who wore a soaking wet lemon yellow dress—would kill him, and sit on his body. Then compose herself. And calmly call the police.

The police were very kind to her when they came. They thought she was terribly sexy.

What the giant didn't understand was that *she way sexy*—most men thought she had a perfect face, perfect breasts, a perfect body, a perfect walk, and a perfect smile—*and being sexy* in a *dangerous, hostile, brutal world,* was dangerous. This girl knew that and she was not one to let the world rough her up. To push her around. To belt her. To tear her yellow dress from her fulsome breasts. No.

She always fought back, fought even against indestructible giants with guns.

She swam in mystery and dove out of it at surprising moments. Moments she chose to take and to make sing in her own way, always in her way, and *only in her way.*

# House Crimson

IN THE SAVAGE FOREST CITY there was a center, and in that center, a skyscraper, and within—a charged core, where a group was rallying.

At the flare point, of the large gathering, stood their leader—*Cinjun Khan S'mythe!*

He stood on a stage, firing up his people.

The audience was a crowd of young people. The faces—pretty and handsome. The bodies—supple, strong, and sexy.

And what these young people saw in Cinjun Smythe was an enormous thing. It began with his very look. Cinjun Smythe had the look of a great being. His features seemed to be the work of a master sculptor. His eyes blazed with rapid and deep energies. His body ran wide in frame and seemed built of only lean, sinewy muscle. As these young people looked at him, they imagined him leading men onto a battlefield. This would be his proper setting. They imagined him aiming a gun. This would be his proper setting. They imagined him directing forces from a command chamber. They imagined him leading a troop of horseback riders into a rugged mountain wilderness. They imagined him living within an enormous estate. Living within *The Great American Whyte Stone Mansion Under the Big Sky.* These things were his proper setting.

This man was barrel-chested, and when he spoke, his voice rose like a thundering boom from some great depth of emotion and power.

As they gazed at him now, he was taking control of the atmosphere and producing enormous charges of feeling. He was creating, with his presence, one of those times when every little movement stood in significance; where every movement became distinct and vastly important; where every movement seemed to ring into an eternity of emotional feeling.

Now Cinjun drew in the charged moment he was producing and hurled its energies, like some big generator, back into and across the reaches of the chamber.

He stood before them and he did not speak.

He was drawing out the dimensions of time and space.

He moved with no hurry. He stood calm before a riotous crowd.

They wanted him to speak. They couldn't wait for him to speak. They wanted to hear him.

He stood still at the center of the stage and he did not move. Nor did he speak.

They began to cheer. They were getting the message.

He was saying much beyond words.

*Him standing there*—that was the message.

People began to laugh, and scream, and give themselves to the moment with joyful abandon.

He was amazing. Cinjun Smythe was just standing there.

And they were getting it.

*He was here.* That was the message.

He stood before them.

And, goodness oh goodness, boy oh boy, wow oh wow.

This man was an amazing sensation.

*The Big Red One*—was what they called him. The sensation of an experience. A big sensation.

And he continued to stand there.

He smiled.

They cheered and cheered him, the rising of the *Big Red One*, and then slowly, ever so slowly they went quiet.

They all went quiet.

You never heard such thick silence cast in such folds of deep, rapid energies.

Now Cinjun held the moment still. He held it still longer. And longer still. In the quiet, you could hear the people breathe. And then rising from it—a pure, true beautiful note that became him, and larger than him.

*"This is the greatest country in the history of life on this world!"* Cinjun said.

The reaction was cheers. They loved hearing him say this. It sent them into a roar.

The line held deep meaning. You could think about it all day and still find something new in it.

He left it there, holding the moment in a state of extreme charge. He produced a hell of an effect on the audience. His confidence seized their attention entirely.

"This is big sky country. We are the greatest country on the planet.

"We are the greatest!"

They applauded.

*"Your country, your country, your country*—is not as it is normally perceived by us. *Your country, your country, your country*—is all of the universe focused at the point you call here and now.

"We are a moment in time and space. And tonight it is our time to rise."

"This is our country.

*"We rise into the air now."*

They ate up every moment of it.

It was so good that it felt like sin.

It felt like a dream, and now, with him to lead them, they were stepping into the dream.

The night filled with magic and there was magic all around them.

Now he stood there, holding himself still, feeding the silence.

The energy in the place quickened.

A follower howled, detonating a round of cheers.

This ignited more clapping.

Cinjun was setting the night on fire. This was the way it was meant to be. This was the energy you needed to change lives.

He then drew them to silence and now Cinjun began to thunder.

And now Cinjun 'Big Red' Smythe spoke:

*"Tonight, I bring us out of the darkness! Tonight, I bring us into the light!"* Cinjun said, and he formed a perfect design, as he began riding the waves of a vast people ocean.

"Tonight we bring fire into the world, and raise high the flames into the air."

The waves rippled to the outward reaches of the hall.

Now he spoke in thundering but heartfelt human tones.

"Tonight, I bring you a journey song. I bring you *The Promise of Great Journey*.

"Tonight, I bring you the ship of unity. I bring you the craft of unity. I bring you *The Crystal Craft of State*.

"Tonight, I will bend the shape of our existence into the force and song of a people perfectly cast and curved into the shape of a mighty and bold union. I bring you *The Force-Song of a People Boldly United*.

This sent them into a roar.

*"I take you into the air now!"* Cinjun said.

They pounded. Stomped. Beat the floor. The firestorm ran wild in the wilderness.

"We will set sail in *The Craft of State*. To cross the ranges and seas of *Big Sky Country*.

"We must take the helm. I intend to take the helm of the command deck," Cinjun said.

"Tonight we turn our light and features upward. And we defy gravity to bring us down. We move up into the air now. We must steady the controls. We must set a course. We must fly with steely resolve. We must travel. We must make our bold voyage. Oh, we must journey, my friends. The furies cry. Dear hearts burn with it. We must reach our glide path. We must fly our craft as steady as she goes. Our destination is *The Whyte House Under the Big Sky*. And the command deck at the bridge of *Big Sky Country*.

"We must be ambitious for the hard choices of government!

*"We are up in the air now!"*

They roared. And he stood before them.

"I bring you from out of the cold. I bring you from out of the dark. Tonight we shine. Tonight we move the tides. We ride the air currents.

*"We are up in the air now!*

"Gravity will yield. Gravity will not conspire to bring us down.

"We are up in the air now!

"We all have wings now. We rise over walls. We form bold union. We form a perfect design.

"We are up in the air now!

"We will not fall into darkness. The air will not thin. Plane up and farewell. Farewell to those who will not risk. Farewell to those who will not use their fist.

"We are up in the air now!

"We will make the shape of reality. We will push into great risks.

"We are up in the air now!

"The color of our purpose will begin to sing and play. The color of our mission will carry into day. We will take our purpose, we will take our journey . . . to all the frontiers of our country. This world and this journey will bend to our will.

*"We are up in the air now!"*

They grew wild. The place exploded. They were on the verge of leaping into the air.

They applauded with all the force of their being.

The place was filling with bone-shattering noise and a sonic boom.

Now he sang softly, amid these mighty engines. His words began to form smooth, cool rings.

His words began to weigh.

"Let us speak tonight of the color of our mighty purpose."

In an easy steady state he forged his next thought into being.

"I will lead you through the wilderness to *Eden Estates*, to *The Whyte House Under the Big Sky*."

Now he pounded the beat. And made the rhythm dance.

And brought them deeper and deeper into temptation.

He built the road with simple stones.

*They will not be able to resist this journey,* Cinjun thought. *Now I will take them into the moment.*

"The Federation is about blue, the blue of the sea. It's about white, the white of the true pure open, and the light of the big sky that hovers above our frontier land. But it is also about—*Red!*

"Red-shifted and red-framed must be our stance.

"We must never forget the beautiful promise of red. We must not forget the force of life, the beauty and life-breath of what red is, what it stands for and about.

"We must make bold meaning and raise it to great heights.

"We must strengthen the red; we must heighten it.

"We must make it a deep, rich red. A beautiful red."

Now he took them into the moment:

*"Tonight, we launch House Crimson!"*

Red flags went up.

The flag of House Crimson was a stark splash of red.

It was nothing but pure, bright red.

Now, red flags went up everywhere in House Crimson.

"There is the blue and white of peace, but there must also be the red of war. The red of a united front. The red of beauty. And the red of a people moving into bold union, into new life and new being. Peace, war, love, life. Raise the red lantern. Raise the red lifeglow. Raise the sceptor of fire high, and breathe now your life and being into this bold union, into the people and force of—*a House Crimson!"* Cinjun said, and raised his fist high into the air. "Tonight we rise above them all—We move into the air now!—Tonight we climb the wave and rise away from them all!"

In a sweeping gesture, he brought his fist down in a wide arc, and continuing, in a great wide arching motion of his entire body, he then once more raised his fist high, higher, and higher still, as he shouted:

*"Up, up and away—from them all!"*

Now these people filled the place with cheers! They began to chant and stomp and fill the great chamber with their beating force, and crimson screams.

Now these aroused men and women were feeling the possibilities. All the *possibilities.*

No one in the place would see any sleep tonight.

# The Sidewinder

IN THIS FOREST SOCIETY, there was a cocktail party, held at night. And within, there was a woman—a Daphne Fox being—who strode and shimmered and lit up the night.

She was a rip current that drew in all full-blooded men. That pulled them toward her gravitational center. They came at her from all directions— men in suits.

Alone and apart, stood: *He*.

Now, he was *Miles Roark*. At this party, he brought a touch of madness into the mix.

He, stood on the far side of the room, swimming in mystery.

There was something about him that appealed to some of the room's beautiful young ladies. For some of the young ladies, he sparked thoughts of soft warm bedrooms; lingering touches, bodies confused—swims in satin silks and strange senses. He, was sexual imagination and a cure for unhappy girls locked in prisons of solitaire—He tore traps away, he broke through barriers, and flew fast away—He swam in mystery.

He stood, in a long upward surge. He was wild-eyed with tousled hair. And there was something savage about him. He had the look of a young lion.

A friend appeared before him, saying:

"How would you like to meet a girl—who is *wild with the power, wild as can be?* Everybody loves this baby."

It was this, that lured Miles into action—

And Miles moved in the way winter springs into summer, and summer falls into winter. He was a living force, moving forward, a set of changes making changes go round.

It was as if he were a man stepping out of a whirlwind. This was the way he moved. He emerged from a storm. Around Miles's features you imagined the tempest, and the savage wildman.

He, had the thing! The charm of the insane. The jungle was his setting, the wilderness—he was realization—he emerged from a thunder.

A thundering Earth.

A savage night.

A brooding sky.

And in this way, . . . he moved, . . . a tempest, moving with gentle mood.

And in this gentle way, Miles gently entered Daphne's awareness.

"Hello Daphne," he said, and she turned to him. "My name is Miles," he said, as if she were asking.

She looked at him. Her eyes, a frontier swirl.

"Miles, . . . Miles, . . . Miles, . . ." she said, binding him in coils.

She looked at him.

"What do you do?" she asked.

"I grow old," he said. "What do you do?"

"I grow young," she said. "And I kill men. I killed a very big one once, when I grew very young—with a knife."

"That's good training," he said.

"What do you do while you grow old?" she said. "At parties like this one? There are so many beautiful women here. There must be a lot for you to do."

"I talk to people," he said.

"What are these talks about? Maybe you could go talk to one of the ladies here."

He held her look.

"I talk to people about love," he said.

"Oh my," she said.

"And wonder," he said.

"Ah," she said.

"And questioning," he said.

"*Questioning* what I *wonder,* and should *love* to know," she said. "What is there to question? Questioning reality? This moment here, is this real? Are you real? . . . What is it we live in? What is this place, that's all around us? . . . Is this the solid in the empty, or is it the empty in the solid? Questions like those. How do the ladies react?"

Miles smiled.

She held his look. *"Love* and *wonder* and *questioning?"* she asked.

Miles beamed. "Oh, how they do fit together," Miles said. "And, oh my, the places they will take you." His smile held some charm for her she noticed. "Simple. The great in the simple. Do you like simple pleasures? Do you like the absolute? Do you like spirited talk?"

"How are the talks going with the ladies?" she asked.

"Dreamy," he said.

"I see," she said.

She looked around the room. There were many beautiful woman here. She returned her eyes to him.

"Miles, . . . do you like to travel?" she said.

"I do . . ."

She smiled teasingly.

"Do you like to have sex?"

"I do . . ."

"Then why don't you go fuck off, dear boy?" she said.

She looked at him.

"How was that?" She asked. "There was *love* and *wonder* and *questioning* in that. I made it all fit together and showed you how it would take you to places—To a place of the absolute. To fuckoff land. I send a lot of men there. They never come back."

"Until now," he said.

"Oh," she said.

He looked at her. He liked her. She had gotten him to say, "I do!" Twice. Within a moment of meeting. Suddenly, they were taking marriage vows. Well, how do you like that? He recognized this. This was a love storm.

He was enthralled by the nature of her femininity. She revealed many dimensions in every aspect of her being; she produced an amazing presence. She was a woman who was not afraid to use the language of adulthood, to use industrial-grade language, to use the hottest kind of language—to open her show with *"Fuck off, dear boy."* He sensed that in her cursing, she was saying there is nothing wrong with the language. She felt free to use the entire language. Even words that some people separated off—because they were normal, and filled with nasty inhibitions that she did not have. A lot of people escaped direct language. To her this was a source of great sadness. There was nothing more useful in communications, than making your point and getting to it. It showed a high regard for Miles when she said to him, "Fuck off." She placed them immediately on a level of direct communication. She was making a human-to-human connection. She was forging a lovely bond  and now she continued.

"Why are you squinting?" she said. "Do you think it makes you look sexy? How do the ladies react to that look of yours?"

She locked eyes with him. Her eyes, were shimmering. . . . On a whim, she adopted his squint. And made some improvements on it—it made her look sexy as all hell.

Miles grinned.

She raised her lovely face high and looked at him.

Then she lowered her face. And now *Tygers* crouched in jungles in her shimmering dark green blue eyes.

He looked at her.

They stood a long moment staring into each other.

She drew a breath.

She parted her lips. And now she spoke softly, ever so softly:

"*I need perfection,*" she said to him.

"*I need perfect intent, perfectly cast.*

"*I need wicked perfection,*" she said.

She stayed perfectly still and continued to speak softly to him.

"*I need wicked perfection, some twisted heart that can entangle me.*

"*. . . To keep me alive. . . .*"

Now he was looking into her eyes. So many twists and turns in those eyes, he thought, those twisted, twisted eyes. Dark green and blue, and filled with dangerous turns. He felt himself assailed by huge grips of emotions that came flooding out of her eyes. *Tygers* of feeling, raging. Abruptly, she became turbulent waves of feeling moving into everything. He saw her moving about him, heaving with violent disturbances, and yet staying perfectly still. She made him see misty streets of blue. And an immense feeling for him, among other feelings. Now, bolts of feeling crackling and surging through the all of her. She said this thing and many things softly but he felt himself torn by the immense feelings bursting out of her. She was shattering his world and yet the only physical signs of the great emotions she was displaying to him were—the *Tygers* springing wildly from those mad eyes of hers; those mad, mad eyes.

"*Hmmm,*" she said eyeing him through those mad, mad eyes.

"If that's you, . . ." she said.

"If you're wicked perfection, . . .

"If you're a tangled heart, . . .

"If you're a chill divine, . . .

"*If that's you, then mystify me,*" she said.

"*I dare you, Miles. Mystify me,*" she said again.

Then she held herself and him in silence.

The silken moment went on forever.

And now she moved away from him. She walked away, carving through these people with no effort. She walked away, into streets, true and blue, . . . she, was rise and fall. She, was delirium, promises, . . . ways to try, and ways to fly.

Miles stood there a moment, holding his gaze outward. She was slipping in and out of sight on the far side of the room.

Miles rejoined his friend. "She is wild with the power, wild as can be."

"That, she is," the friend said.

*Wild!*—Miles thought—*Wild with the power to make every moment come alive.*

*None has her beauty!* Miles thought.

Fascination with no limits, deeper and deeper it went.

Scorching beauty bearing a name—Daphne.

In this night, . . . white light everywhere, but he couldn't see a thing. She filled his night, with blinding light. And everything that she was. Everything was broken up in dances, . . . dancing rhythm. And all that she was.

Style and rhythm. Substance and purpose. Force and sway.

He was losing his mind, she was causing the world to vanish around him. Leaving only her, and eternity.

Leaving only *a bright eternity!* and her.

Her glaring sun streaks . . .

Her glare and glory . . .

All this, as he gazed on her sun-streaked looks.

She, was her orchestration and her precision. And here and there, she was a glimpse of her thigh. She was a cool wind in a hot summer.

Outside, the night was laughing.

At the ebb and flow, of her.

At her form and spell. It felt the ebb and flow, of her.

She was doing it to the night as well. Maybe this night, was a man. Or a woman, admiring. The night felt itself carried. It felt the ebb and flow, of her.

She was doing to the night, what she did to men—the stars cried for her kisses.

# I Am the Sky God

IN THE GATHERING HALL, Cinjun was taking his people to a feverish high.

Cinjun was now taking them deep into a very ancient, primitive scene. One that had repeated many times along the corridors of ancient galleries.

He had now become the great, ancient leader. He was prying something open for them. Something important. Something incredibly deep and wide. He was bringing them to a great, big whalloping, secret from the ancient gallery. Now they could touch it for themselves:

*There are good people and there are bad people.* Cinjun was helping them sort out which they were.

It was appealing. He spoke in simple words. From which, he illuminated something for them. Something elusive. Some huge thing.

The people, of bold union, adored him. He illuminated something for them. Something very important. It was this great, big thing.

He was giving them something fleeting—that they desperately needed.

'We are good. They are bad.' . . . 'They shall lose. And we will win.' . . . He was singing a very popular song. A song of cheer, 'All Will Be Well.' Quite a classic. And what a hell of a rendition. Ferocious.

No more complicated order to tear at certainty and confidence, and to weaken you in the night. He willed them into a raw, cheerful state.

*They were good, others were bad.*

Ah, now it all made sense at last. And Cinjun continued to make sense for them.

They would no longer feel cold in the night.

They ate every moment of his slow moving.

They were desperate to come into power. And he was bringing them into raw primitive forces that could move the times.

He was writing history, standing on his feet.

This was an extreme sense of showmanship.

"Our charge is to take hold of the world," Cinjun said.

"We must see the color of our purpose. And raise the day.

"I'm going to *The Whyte Stone House Under the Big Sky.* I'm there already; it's only a matter of time. I know the shots, I have mastered the shots, and I breathe victory.

"I'm going to be the *Theater Commander*, here in *Big Sky Country*.

"There's nobody who can stop me. And I'm taking all of you with me!

*"We are up in the air now!"*

Fists flew into the air. It was a promising beginning. They were off to another planet.

And Cinjun—he was their thunder god. He made the skies crackle—as he launched and hurled thunderbolts into the distance, across the ranges and dreamscapes of the night.

# Nothing

NOTHING HAPPENED ... for a while ...
   And then change sprang from the void.

# The Stone Cold Attack

MILES WAS MEETING with the stone man-being who was his stone boss-being—commander of his field and realm.

And the stone boss-being was forcing into the world a scene from the ancient gallery!—He was seizing upon the midnight day and explaining to Miles how now seemed it rich to die.

He commanded Miles: To seize upon the midnight! and die with no pain! Miles had a big, round fulsome difficulty here; he was not the dying type.

The boss-being and Miles were met in a high office within a mighty skyscraper in the great forest city.

The boss-being was known as: *Mister Dean Deacon D'rke D'rth Dar.* This was the side of his being he was showing now.

He was Mister Dean Deacon D'rke D'rth Dar also known as Dean Deacon Muerte. He had many sides to his being. He went by many names. He had many missions, many things to do. Much to put down. And this life so short—he had little time to put it all in order.

They sat in the place, both men imprisoned in suits.

"God damn it!" said Deacon. "I've just about had it with you. All you have to do is follow some basic rules. Repeat some basic messages. You follow some basic principles, and you follow some basic thoughts, and that's all you do—Can you understand that?"

Miles felt the wind shout like a drum; it had come. The black thing was risen here.

"I do things my way," Miles said.

*"Do things your way?"* Deacon said. *"Why should anybody let you do things your way?"*

... They were moving into the hardest fall there ever was. ...

"You're asking a broad question," Miles said. "Can I give you a broad answer?"

"Go ahead, but don't take all day," Deacon said. "I'm not here to listen to you. You're here to listen to me. Remember me, I'm your boss?"

"I remember," Miles said.

*"There isn't much time in life, and the time is always gathering darkness,"* Miles said.

"What does that have to do with it? Life is short," Deacon said.

"There isn't time to lose," Miles said, "on being somebody else."

"Ah-hungh," Deacon said.

"No matter how far you go, you always come back to being you," Miles said.

"I see," Deacon said. "You're going to lose here. This is not one you're going to win."

"Why?" Miles said.

"Because you're not meant to win this one," Deacon said.

*"There's a trail to being you, and you have to follow it. Or you never get there,"* Miles said.

"What an idea," Deacon said. "That's an idea. . . . And let that idea *die.* . . . It's not real. And that's not what's happening here. It's got nothing to do with it. That I can tell you. . . . I know what's going on here."

"What?"

"A rebel yell," Deacon said.

"The way to be a star, is to burn," Miles said. "Everybody is a star, and everybody burns."

"That's a good one," Deacon said without a trace of joy.

"Life is a song. You sing it into the air . . . that you breathe . . . around you," Miles said. "Life is not far away. It's here and now. And you sing it in your own voice."

"Oh, how about that? That's another good one. The good ones keep coming," Deacon said, not at all pleased by where this was going.

"Thinking is about looking closer at life," Miles said. "You don't come at life with answers. Life comes at you. . . . You come at it with questions. And you find answers.

"Can you be right even if no one believes you?" Miles said.

He went on. "You have to be *an awakened thinker.* A here and now thinker. A standalone thinker. You question. And you find answers.

"I work at a clean approach to the target. And I work at bringing sense into my thinking. . . . I work in my way. I don't go into other people's messages. I live my life. I understand what I understand. I don't live other people's messages. I do what I do. I am who I am. I speak with my own words," Miles said.

"You're rambling," Deacon said.

"Maybe it's all well and good that I do things my way," Miles said.

"Thinking," Miles said, "is about looking at *tangling weaves* and *mysterious angles,* and seeing how to move into *the tangle of the mystery.* It's moving into the here and now. It's questioning. It's finding answers. Answers that stand the test of reality. . . . It's about testing reality."

Deacon loved that. He clenched his hands into fists.

Deacon stopped. He thought about it, and thought about it. And then he spoke, with new mildness and calm.

*"You're a test."* Deacon said. *"That's what I see. You're a test of me. You're a goddamned test of reality."*

Miles smiled, and became entirely charming.

They were charming with each other, just as charming as two people could be while attacking each other with long swords.

"Isn't it nice to have a good test?" Miles asked.

Deacon rubbed his forehead. Gathering himself.

*"Do things your way. Why should anybody let you do things your way?"* Deacon said, coming at it again.

*"They let you,"* Miles said, *"because you're a wind and sky thinker.* A land and sea thinker. A grass, tree, and forest thinker."

"A storm and season thinker," Miles continued.

"A wonder thinker. A keep on wondering thinker," Miles said. "You question. And you find answers. . . . You question . . . because . . . *that's where the wonder is."*

And here Miles went on——

"And like ships in the night, the answers come, . . . riding the waves of questions, . . . of questions whirling fast and devil furious.

"Sometimes the wave answers are startling. But sometimes those startling wave answers are the right answers.

"In the end, the right answer takes down everything.

". . . It conquers all. . . .

"The right answer stands tall over the wrong answer.

"If you're on an answer journey, don't you want to find the right answer? No matter where it comes from? And sometimes the right answer comes—a-barreling out of the night—leaping at you from unusual places.

"The answer comes at your from weird and hidden places.

"Sometimes the right answer doesn't look like the answer you want. It doesn't look like anything at all.

"When reality speaks sometimes it has a strange sound.

"The right answer has reality. And reality can't be crushed. It can't be warped. It can't be destroyed. Reality *is* what *is*. And it's absolute. There's no bending it into another thing.

"The right answer takes down the wrong answer.

"You go with what you feel to be right. And it might not be what people are asking for.

"You do things your way, to learn what your way is.

"You do things your way. You learn what your way is. You do it and you believe in it, because there's nothing else you can ever truly know.... There's no other blue ocean like it, where you can in the end become the ocean. ... And the ocean is always beckoning in the night.

"The most beautiful thing in another human being is attitude and confidence. The attitude that says this is my life. The *'attitude of fire,'* which comes from heat and power and the force of being you, in your own way. That's the *Way of Ways.*"

Miles said, "That's where to sail your ship into, when the night gathers."

Miles looked at Deacon.

And Miles said, quietly, ever so softly, *". . . Maybe you'll win . . . . maybe you'll lose . . . who ever knows? . . ."*

Deacon looked at this, and *saw* what he was *seeing*.

And Deacon felt the touch of a volcano, flowing.

*Deacon was so angry, he could murder. He was lonesome in his mind.*

"You're going to give me the right answer?" Deacon said.

"Yes," Miles said.

"What if I don't want the right answer?"

"I don't stock wrong answers."

"Don't get wise with me," Deacon said.

"What's wrong with wisdom?" Miles said.

"Just because you thought it, doesn't mean it's wise," Deacon said.

"And just because I thought it, doesn't mean it's wrong," Miles said.

"We're back to the wrong answer and the right answer," Deacon said.

"Who's on the right answer?" Miles said.

"You're not," Deacon said.

"What if I am?"

"I'd know it."

"How would you know it?"

"Because it would seem right."

"What if the right answer seems wrong?" Miles said.

"What if the wrong answer seems right?" Deacon said.

"Then you test it against reality and it breaks down."

"How do you test reality?"

"By looking at it, and asking it questions."

"Questions?"

"Yes, every wrong answer falls apart under questions."

"What if they're the wrong questions?"

"Then ask more questions. You hit the wrong answer with enough questions and it doesn't stand a chance."

"Who comes up with the questions?"

"Everyone."

"So in your reality, everybody is throwing questions out there and coming up with the answers they like. They're flying questons around the room and coming with the answers they like. Oh, yes! Isn't that nice? Everybody gets their answer that fits their day. How fantastic is that?"

Miles said, "You can't create answers for reality. . . . Reality *is*. . . . The answers *are*. . . . You can't fight the answers."

"You don't know what you're talking about," Deacon said.

"Why?"

"Because you're not talking naturally."

"Why?"

"Does this sound like a natural conversation to you? Does this sound like a conversation people have?"

"I don't know. Are we people?"

"I don't care."

"Why?"

"You haven't said anything to me yet."

"I'm not mixing up anything."

"What are you doing?"

"I'm talking about what we're talking about?"

"I know what we're talking about."

"What is it?"

"This is a sound chase."

Miles smiled.

"Is that what you know?" Miles said.

"I'm dead sure," Deacon said.

"You don't like it?"

"I don't like sound chasers."

"They say that's what wrong with you," Deacon said.

"Who?" Miles said.

"All the people here."

"How do you find the answers?" Miles said.

"You don't," Deacon said.

"Why?"

"They find you. You don't go to the answers. The answers come to you."

"Is that what this is about?"

Deacon paused. Gave it thought. Moved on. "I'm going to give you a chance. This is your lucky day. . . . You can tell yourself that and believe it."

Mister Dean Deacon D'rke D'rth Dar continued. "Let's get to the heart of the matter."

Miles centered his attention.

Deacon was forcing a scene into the world. And now they came to it.

A chorus cried beneath Deacon to accompany him. And what came out of him was a wall of sound. A piercing, forceful wall of sound.

Wrought with charm, and grace, and mighty force.

They were just a shot away form it now. And they moved with a fiery motion.

This was now *a red train.*

This was the risen Mister Dean Deacon D'rke D'rth Dar.

And here there came broad, roundhouse blows.

"The point of life is to do things your way," Miles said.

*"Why should anybody let you do things your way?"* Deacon said.

"Why should anybody stand in your way?"

"What are we talking about here?"

"Life."

"This isn't about life."

"Why?"

"This is about the order of things. Can you stand the world order? And can you take the world's orders?"

"Why should I?"

"Did you just say, *'Why should I?'* Who the bloody hell do you think you are?"

"I'm me. Who else should I be?"

"You work for me."

"Shouldn't you want my best, that's what I aim to give you."

"Your best?"

"What else is there worth giving?"

"You ask a lot of questions."

"That's how you find a lot of answers. And how you find where the answers are hidden. How else do you find answers?"

Deacon harumphed. This was going nowhere. Just going in these mysterious circles that Miles blazed. There was something strange about Miles Roark. Something otherworldly and strange.

"Where are we going?" Deacon said.

"The only place we can go," Miles said.

"Then let's get there."

"How do I use you?" Deacon said.

"As much as you can," Miles said.

"I'm going to show you how. And I'm going to show you how *to get right*. In your soul. You're going to get hit in your soul."

"You're running wild," Deacon said. "We're going to tighten up on your reins."

"I don't have reins," Miles said.

"Did you just tell me you're bulletproof? You're indomitable. You're invincible!"

"I'm telling you I'm in my right mind. And I'm all here."

"What does that mean! What are you saying to me!" Deacon said.

"I'm telling you I'm not a horse," Miles said.

"You sound mighty arrogant to me. What is this?" Deacon said.

"What it is, is. This is what it is," Miles said.

Deacon became very quiet.

"Here we are in this precisely now," Miles said. "How amazing is this life."

"Did you just tell me, '*What it is, is*'?" Deacon said.

"And this is what it is," Miles said.

"Who the hell do you thing you are! You better damn well get your emotions under control."

"I'll control my emotions."

"Good!" Deacon said. He didn't know what else to say.

"I'm going to let that be," Deacon said. "We're going to move on to the coast."

"It should be a nice view. I always liked the coast," Miles said.

"Here's where we're going," Deacon said. "To answerland. To the end of the road. No more circling in the mountains."

Deacon looked at Miles.

"I'm going to want to see you produce some beautiful answers."

"I'll do my best."

"Good."

"You're a fucking kid—some people around here think you're arrogant." Deacon breathed deeply. "Some of the people here feel that you talk like a *Sound Chaser.*"

He looked at Miles, and paused for a reaction.

"They say you throw Sound Chaser chords out there. That's what they say about you."

Miles gave him no reaction.

"Now they treat you the way they do because they feel you're *insane.*"

Deacon paused. Received no reaction.

"Do you understand where we are? They look at you and they see a person who is totally insane—"

"—All the best people are—" Miles said.

"—I," Deacons said, "don't have room in my life for this sort of thing. We do not have room in our lives for this sort of thing. *You* do not have room in *your* life for this sort of thing. Do you understand? So I'm going to help you become a better person. You will fix your entire being, right now. You will no longer act like some goddamned Sound Chaser. Do you understand? Are we clear?"

They were moving into deserted streets, and into retreat from light. A place where hearts drowned.

"Are we clear?" Deacon said.

Miles brought in some light.

*"Not all who wander are lost,"* Miles said.

"What a thing to say." Deacon came out of his chair. "I think it's very interesting. Who said that, *Scofield Morefield?* That damn *Sound Chaser.* You're going to feed me lines from that maniac?" He was moving slowly but this was indeed the risen Deacon D'rke D'rth Dar. "You're going to talk like this when I'm doing my darndest to help you become a better person?"

On this dark street the sun was black. Time had died; the wind had died. Deacon had set sail to catch something—*in his teeth.* Deacon had set them wheeling across this landscape. They were on the way. The street was cold; it's trees were gone. He assaulted Miles, slowly with iron determination.

"I have never been talked to like this." Deacon held still. "You have right now to straighten out. Show me that you can fall in line. And show it to me now."

There was something here Deacon did not like seeing, he would break this man! It was absolutely necessary. And for his own damn good. He would teach Miles. Make him obedient. Crush him, and stamp out the menace in this young madman.

*Not all who wander are lost?* Deacon raged! He was a night without day.

Deacon was king of the highway.

Miles would fall on this road.

Miles stayed very even and spoke simply.

"A man doesn't borrow other people's arms and legs, so why should he borrow other people's brains? I think my way, and I say what I think."

Dean Deacon D'rke D'rth Dar harumphed.

Deacon leaned forward and said something very clearly and distinctly.

"We're going to take a look at reality together," Deacon said.

"And you're going to pick your favorite theme. Your absolutely favorite theme in life. A theme for a picture.

"And you're going to pick anything at all you like, as long as you pick a red theme—a red sun.

"Do you follow? Do you understand?"

Deacon looked at Miles, and looked into his mind.

"Now, what would you like to be your favorite theme? The greatest theme in all the frontier western world! You're free to pick any theme you want, as long as you pick a red sun."

"I understand," Miles said.

*"Pick a theme."* Deacon said.

Miles held his look firmly on Deacon.

Deacon held his position, and kept his eyes locked on Miles.

"I want you to pick your favorite theme for me now."

And now Deacon smiled charmingly; he was ready to be Miles's friend.

"I hear red is your favorite. A red what? Go on, a red what?"

Deacon's smile became marvelously warm; everything was going to be all right; they were going to live in the same world and be friends; and it was going to be a beautiful world filled with happy trails.

"Red is a marvelous color. Isn't red your favorite color? Go ahead. Tell me—What is your favorite color?"

"Go on, what's your favorite theme?

"I hear it's a red sun. How about a red sun going down over a horizon, how about a red sun down over a city, over a desert, over a country town? A red sun down over a frontier wagon train?

"What's your beauty? What's your favorite theme?"

Deacon looked at Miles.

He kept it there, waiting for Miles to give it to him.

Miles looked at Deacon.

Miles turned away and then slowly turned back to Deacon.

*"A green forest,"* Miles said, *"over an ocean."*

He had cast it in sincerity.

Miles had opened his mouth, poured his heart out.

It went heart to heart.

Deacon was looking to Miles for an answer. And what Miles drew was: sincerity. A view of a human soul.

Miles had answered plainly; green happened to be his favorite; truly it was, and some things were forever.

They were going down into it now.

"...Damn...," Deacon said. He took a deep wistful breath and looked at Miles with lament.

"I thought we were getting somewhere." Deacon continued to look at Miles, a sort of slow peer.... He was looking into Miles....

"Why," Deacon said.

"...why?..." deacon said softly..." ...why green hills ..."

Miles looked at him.

*"The hills are where love greens,"* Miles said.

". . . You're . . . fired," Deacon said.

"You're fired today.

"You've gone dark. You've turned dark. There's no one else but you that did it.

"You are fired and you're gone. We will see no more of you now.

"You're fired," he said, coming at it again. "We're finished with you. Wrong picture."

"Remember one thing. Don't paint any pictures. Don't chase any sounds. You're finished.

"Let's hope you enjoy a fine ruin.

"Enjoy the wayside. Enjoy the ruin. Enjoy the end.

"Your end is now," Deacon said.

*There*, Miles thought, *it had to be.* Here on this stage, the time had come. They were going to drive a while . . . down into the scenic drive of the below . . . and spend a while observing the black all around, counting the hours to a rendezvous . . . Dark cool waters of pain dying beneath a sky without stars would pass their long while before time would see life move into the song. For now, there was annihilation, and a black thickening cloud.

The moment would cost Miles many things, things extremely dear to him. A heavy price, but the moment had a rightness—and a great goodness—to it. The darkness could not be helped—there was no avoiding it; Miles dove into the dangers to be found below, before him, and all around him.

The danger loomed, a horrible menace, describing itself as a reflection in Miles's eyes. Miles took his heart and let the melody of his heart play his song. Miles's song was dark and rich and deep; and, there was a tenderness, that lay there; and found emergence; tumbling up, a bursting, exploding fiery light that took on startling shapes. And there was something else— Tygers crouched in jungles in Miles's dark eyes.

Miles loosened his tie. It was such a pleasure to have it sit askew that he did not want to forego the pleasure for an instant longer.

He would drive a long while into distance . . . lonely distance, away from bitter time.

Dark winds crying. He would find the sun at the rendezvous.

# Into the Wild Blue Yonder

IT WAS A MOMENT OF GREAT ACTIVITY in Miles's office, within the high office company, within the high skyscraper.

*Skyler Larkin Malloy*—the he-being that had been a shadow beneath the light of the she-being Daphne Fox—he, . . . that lucky, lucky Skyler Larkin Malloy, he was here.

Skyler and Miles worked in the same place, *The Agency.*

Skyler was skilled and mighty in the stone cold way.

He was a stone friend being, practiced in the stone cold way. Hollow eyed, but burning with black fire. Black flashes of darkness. He moved in his way. Of raised slow eyelids, and beautiful curly mouth. He was lucky— lucky in fortune—and lucky in love . . . the beautiful women many a time being upon his bed. Skyler took his luck as his due and boasted about it in bars, where the beautiful women lay. And his stone cold thoughts, he presented as mighty works from on high, lavishments from his high and abutted place. He loved watching them descend upon the day.

"Miles, you're the darndest bastard in the world!" Skyler said. "Why would you blow a good time like this!"

Miles turned to Skyler. "I do things my way."

"Why should anybody let you do things your way!" Skyler said.

"Sometimes I bring a better way—" Miles said.

"Have you heard the expression '*You're a fool boy*'?" Skyler asked.

"No, what does it mean?" Miles said. "Explain it to me. How do you say it in English?"

"That is English."

"What's a fool?"

"A person who puts himself above others. Who doesn't know his place in the scheme of life."

"Like a prophet."

"No, a prophet isn't a fool."

"Why not? Can a fool be wise?"

"Laugh it up Miles—You're a fool boy."

*"Not all who wander are lost."*

"Where have I heard that one?"

"Ah, wow, is that a Scofield Morefield line!" Skyler said. "What the hell is it with you? Are you another Scofield Morefield?"

"No," Miles said.

"A goddamn Sound Chaser," Skyler said. "You're going to give me the talk of some goddamn Sound Chaser?" Skyler turned to Miles. "Why would you build a ship and then when it's ready, sink it?"

"I'm going to study with him," Miles said. Miles wasn't looking at Skyler.

"With who?" Skyler said.

"Scofield Morefield," Miles said.

"You can't. He's dead," Skyler said.

"Not yet," Miles said.

"Too bad. He's insane," Skyler said.

"That's the best way to be. You can see farther that way."

"For a talented guy," Skyler said, "you've got to be the lousiest fool I ever met. You heard what he did with his career? You get involved with him and you're finished. What could you possibly hope to get from that lunatic?"

"To see a few things," Miles said.

## Tearing Away From . . .
## The Stone Cold Black Hold

HE WAS HURTLING out of the place. Not fleeing into sadness.

He was rising into the wild blue yonder.

Here on the stage, the time had come. Under the strains of horrible rumblings and cold surroundings.

The song was going to be played—*or he would die attempting it.*

Miles would never rest, never tire, never stop. He would pick up honesty, the best of himself, and then let it go, into time and space.

Come what may. Let stone cold attacks come.

Many there had been, many there would be. Growing in force and menace.

Threatening colds.

Cold cold cold.

Smothering light, smothering warm being.

Biting biting biting.

Cold cold cold.

Let it come, he would fight.

It had come and was coming and was yet to come.

The stone cold attacks.

Here on the stage.

"You need to stop where you are! And bury this thing you've been carrying around." Voices aching, the sounds they were making were cold. So cold. Played so wrong.

Screaming, blaming.

*Get some honesty, and take the best, the rest let go,* Miles thought.

Not this thing they came to him with, a cage. A cold cage.

An icy future.

Pain, was their goodnight song. Played so wrong.

And they screamed so loud, so long. Blaming. Screaming so loud, so long.

"Welcome to the real world!" they said. Welcome to the *We* world! was their song.

Welcome to the *Real World.*

We are the real world.

Enter the real world.
*The Goodbye World.*
And the *Goodnight Song.*
Walk into the Real World. The We World.
We own it, and you're staying here for a while.
If you don't straighten out, the time will be all too short.
These were the sounds they were making.
Cold death,
in the form of friendship.
O *get some honesty,* . . .
*take the best,* . . .
*and then the rest* . . .
*let go.*
He was thrown onto the stage, thrown into this world. He would make it bright and fill it with sun streaks.

He was thrown into it, and he would make much of it, before the end came.

If he was to sing his swan song, it would be sweet and mighty and brave.

Light and flowing, soaring and easy.


*The Stone Cold Players* do come!
The dangerous people do come to you, here, as friends. Always, they come.
*The Doom Patrol.*
*The Stone Cold Marauders.*
They lay it all out for you. Follow the We way and you can do great things. Follow this, the worldly way and the woven war, this thing, leveled in late lament, and with this thing you can go high to do great things. For surely this is greatness! A greatness come to the kingdom.

They lay it out for you.
*The Stone Cold Friends.*
Cold
& the Stone Cold Friends.
Cold
& the Stone Cold Goodnight Song.

Here on the stage. . . .
Listen to the sound. . . .

Here on the stage. . . .
Playing their song. . . .

The sounds they are making . . . are . . .
so stone cold, . . .
screaming so loud, so long, . . .
sweet song . . . sung so wrong.

The moves they are making are so stone cold.
The path they lay is so cold, . . . shaped in cobbled stone. They lay it all out for you. Follow the We way. Enter the Real World.
They attack with swift stone screams. The Feel Real World.
"Welcome to the free world. Go on, rush in. Dive, plunge, swim, and flow, and do not stop."
Do not cease to enjoy the peace.
Do not stop, do not halt, do not falter.
Do not miss your chance to lie on the stone altar.
Welcome to the We World.
Welcome to the Real World.
"Go on, go on, come in.
"Here in this place, in here, we are all friend and kin."
They suppose their greatness into being. And all must yield to its immense icy Earthen involution. Welcome to the revolution.
"We're here to help you." You do believe we're here to help you?
Show that you like us, . . . .
Show that you are us, and move thus. . . .
Show that you can be guided in our image.
Show that you hold strong in the stone visage.
Show that you can be pushed. . . .
Show that you can be hushed, and rushed, and crushed.
Wear the beautiful stone face,
And you will win the race. In beautiful pace.
"Here is how we need you to be." Here is how we need you to live your life. Here is how you must be.

So beautiful, once you are become We.
Oh, so beautiful to be,
We and we and we.
Ever beautiful to see, just
We and we and we.

Welcome. To a warm world of warming We.
Oh, To See
Oh, Beautiful World
of We and we and we
  of we & we & we
Did you ever see anything as beautiful as we & we & we?


Blood in the streets.
 When you don't go with We. When you bring danger to the We World.
You must vanish from the Real World.
 This is the big it.
 It's your new year's resolution. Welcome to the revolution.
 Revolve revolve revolve.
 Be sure. . . . Be here. . . . These days it's the revolution.
 Blood in the streets in the stone cold friends.
 Blood in the streets in the stone cold players.
 Blood in the streets in the chilling blows.
 Danger, pounding a beat.
 Hideous, wretched and sad. Stone cold.
 The stone cold damners.
 Cold cold cold.
 Biting biting biting.
 Howl howl howl.
 Shriek shriek shriek.
 The shrieking madness.
 The shrieking musts.
 Ashen ashen ashen.
 Murder murder murder.
 Devouring devouring devouring.
 Frozen to the bone.
 Sinking like a stone.
 Lone lone lone.
 Alone alone alone.
 Nothing more, nothing more, nothing more.
 Don't let your heart do anything new. Enter the prison. Enter the dead
stone prison, there's a lot of joy to be found here.
 *Don't they know what life is worth?*
 What it is to rise?
 "No!—You will not rise! You will not rise! You will not rise!"
 Fear fear fear.

Shivering shrill sentences.

He, would not let it end there. There were fine vistas beyond. Much to be found in the beyond. Much beauty, and truth.

They break you down. Fears. Break you to pieces.


Oh, Stand Tall, Headstrong Like a World!


There is much light out there.

Dark dank cold, was a little too short on love for Miles's taste.

He liked more tropical climes.

Fresh light, fresh being. Free and strong.

Tigerish walks, and flowing struts.

Expanding ribs, extending spines, he liked growing taller and stronger. That was more his *Way*.

Let their revolution of blood eat their bones and bring them into the cold earth.

Miles was going to spread his wings, and take to the skies. He was going to find *The Wăoynde*.

No more cold sleep, no more stone cold being under stone cold bites from stone cold scavengers.

Time waits for no man. Time slipping. Creating the future. An open future.

It was there for you.

No more cold daggers,

No more icy daggers, and cold knives.

He was going to flame, and take to the skies.

The great way was out there. *The Wăoynde* that rose into the skies.

That tore free of the ground, escaped from, sailed free of gravity and tyranny.

Opened and opened and opened.

Proceeded in twisting curving motions.

A flight clothed in the colors of light.

A purpose and a might, a soaring light.

A flight.

Life.


Chew chew chew.

Go, go, go, go, go. Chew chew chew.

Stone cold dogs.

Hyenas in the form of jackals in the form of dogs, in the form of friends. Dear friends, there to help. Dear and near.

And chew chew chew.

The stone cold compassionate ones.

Laughing at the sun.

Chew chew chew.

Cold cold cold.

Abyss abyss abyss.

Nothing to be made, nothing to be seen, nothing to be known. They know all. And they will show all to you.

The brutal All that there is.

Chew chew chew.

Bite!

Cold cold cold.

The stone cold end.

It's beautiful, try it, you'll like it.

The stone cold end.

Death clothed in a warm sun blanket.

This was the offer.

Accept it or die!

This was the mighty engine
This was the soft parade
This was the picture of life
This was the system.
    Believe in it or die!
This was the load,
    Believe in it or die.
This was the trail,
    Walk it or die.
This was the race,
    And the race was already run,
Welcome to the Real World.

Really, there is a lot of good in it.

Miles would have none of it. All right then, he would be damned.

Maybe there was something improper in Miles's upbringing. Some deadly flaw in his mind. A flaw in his character to bring on ruin. But Miles was on a hurtling hunt, for a sweet dream known—and known only to himself—as—*The Whirlwind Wāoynde*.

. . . This dream, . . . known only to himself.

## Out in the Fields, Scofield Morefield

MILES WAS KNOCKING on the front door but not getting a response. He could hear the soft strains of music coming from the back yard.

"Scofield Morefield!"

In yelling the name, Miles stretched out every vowel.

"Scofield Morefield!"

Scofield Morefield, a handsome old man came to the door, stark naked, and holding a "dirty martini," one mixed with extra olive brine.

"Hello, I'm Scofield Morefield."

"I'm Miles Roark."

"Ah, magnificent! Tell me now, who the bloody, piss-besotted hell is Miles Roark!"

He yelled this one past Miles, playing to the neighborhood—It was standard theatricality.

Miles said, "Let's put your drink down. We've got work to do."

# The Big Red One

THE STREET BOARDS PROMOTING House Crimson were abstract. Big red splashes. And occasionally—you might find—filling the frame . . . an image of *Cinjun "Big Red" Smythe*. He was 'Big Red' in the sense of a big red dawn.

A *light*vision reporter was questioning Cinjun in front of one big red splash. He asked Cinjun, "Why do they call you the Big Red One?"— The cover of a leading magazine presently available featured—in banner writing—a fascinating story about *"The Big Red One,"* filled with every praise known to man.

Cinjun looked into the light with an iron gaze that missed nothing.

He filled his setting; his presence seemed to be a massive life force emerging from the deep, streaming background splash of red. And the life force was smiling warmly. As warm and charming as anything you ever saw in your life.

"Why do they call you the Big Red One?" the interviewer had asked.

"I'm a message that is beyond words," Cinjun said.

"I'm an experience."

He was the awakened one. In an enlightened state. With the "up, up and away"story.

"I'm here to talk about reality," Cinjun said.

"What is reality?" the reporter asked.

"Reality is the fundamental 'what there is,'" Cinjun said. He pounded the table. Thwak. Boom! "That is reality. It's beyond words.

"Reality is the absolute."

He held his gaze. He stood quiet.

He stood in *reality*.

# Start It All Over Again

A NAKED WOMAN WAS BATHING in Scofield's hot springs bath, and sipping an apple martini.

Scofield had slipped on a robe and was walking Miles through his garden—and you could not help but notice that this was the strangest garden you ever saw . . . a meadow beauty filled with greenery and fertile flowers . . . and soaring, flowing, exploding shapes cast in marble and bronze.

Miles swept his gaze across this place, took in the entire immense expanse . . . and in a gently streaming movement lifted his gaze from the beautyscape . . . and now aimed it at Scofield.

"I'm here for training," Miles said. "I'm here to learn what you learned and pick up where you left off."

Miles's eyes were locked on Scofield. They were doing something, Scofield observed; producing and radiating beams of a joy-splashed kind of fire.

Scofield felt a wave of savage energy radiating from this young man.

Scofield had seen this before—

"I don't train sound chasers anymore," Scofield said.

Scofield was going to shift this world into its true orbit.

"Listen kid," Scofield said. "You want to get girls, to make a little money, to make people laugh. There's nothing wrong with that. You want what I had. I still want it myself. Buy yourself a little jokebook, try them out on your friends, and the ones that work, you stick with. Now let me get on with my day. I was in the middle of a very important love affair when you walked into town."

Miles held himself entirely still. His eyes were on fire.

"Let's hold it now, old man," Miles said, blazing back brightly, "we're wasting precious time. I'm going to travel over ground you've covered."

Miles continued to hold himself entirely still. His voice came softly. And now Miles again came to his terrible purpose, "You're going to train me. It's time to start it all over again."

Miles's eyes were on fire. And now Scofield saw *Tygers* crouched in jungles in Miles's dark eyes.

Scofield stood and wondered what he might make of this young man.

"I'm not going to help you," Scofield said. "You can't know what you're asking for. I do. Slow down. Think with me here."

"There's a bright future for me in the blood, pain and sand," Miles said. "If that's the trip, that's the trip. Get your saddle, let's ride."

"They will beat you and break you," Scofield said.

"You had it rough," Miles said, bounding along cheerfully. "No denying it. Some will slip, some will fall. When your chin hits the ground, you pick yourself up, dust yourself off, start all over again. If seven times you fall, then eight times you rise."

"You can't know," Scofield said. "How do I make it clear to you? They will tear you in half. It's their world. Don't make the mistake I made. Don't imagine there's a way to win. It's a no-win from start to finish."

"I only know about winning," Miles said, "you're the expert on not winning."

Scofield held his look. "Will you listen to me and not answer?"

"Yes. For a moment. Speak."

"I'd be committing a crime if I kept you here. You need to recover. I would make you worse."

"Perfect."

"The path looks fine to you at your age. The air smells of spring. But I've seen where it goes."

"It's the same old story, a fight for love and glory," Miles said. "Let's start it all over again."

"I don't train sound chasers anymore."

"Is that so? An interesting statement. You might want to write it down. It sounds like something to put on your gravestone," Miles said.

"I . . . do not . . . train . . . sound chasers, . . . anymore."

"If I were you, I would say it until I believe it. There's no substitute for persistence in learning a thing."

Scofield was looking at Miles now with eyes that missed nothing. *Danger!* Scofield thought. *This man comes loaded to bear with danger.* Scofield liked that about him,

"I don't teach you how to be a sound chaser, anymore. But I do have a class for some of the simpler *hots* in life. How would you like to learn how to get pretty darn hot—even if it doesn't make you a sound chaser?"

Miles was determined to get where he was going—Bring him hell or high waters. Bring him pain or anguish. You see, the problem was that the weather cycle was running a little too low for him. He liked it right around *'Too darn hot!'* He was on his way—such a way—and the destination of his journey was *Too darn hot!* No low cycles. Only one place. A place by the name of *Too darn hot!*

Scofield scrutinized Miles.

"I teach a class," Scofield said at last. "You may join. How would you like that?"

"Yes. It'll be an honor for you to have me. I'll shake you out of your rut," Miles said.

## Her Stormy Lover

HE HAD THOUGHT much of her. Now he called her to journey.

He had reached her on the call instrument. As the signal had called out to her, Miles had gazed out his window.

Daphne had picked it up at her end and spoke politely with him. He seemed to have caught her interest. This was his hope.

He asked if he might see her; if he might come around to her place; and take her out to ride on a whirlwind. And his thoughts went to her eyes as he talked to her. Her eyes, and their frontier swirl.

"No," Daphne said, "I can't see you Friday. You see," Daphne now spoke softly but with great conviction, revealing a terrible predicament, "my old fiancé from years ago returned from the Peace Corps on Sunday." She drew a deep breath, and produced a sigh that shook her with great emotion. "What can I tell you?" she said. "I'm sorry. But the flame rekindled. Hotter. Than ever." She sounded sorry as all hell.

"I'll be a perfect gentleman," Miles said, "and make great dinner conversation."

"You're very sweet," she said, and then she was struck by a thought of importance. "You would make someone else a very good husband."

Now he beamed, "You're going to have a delightful time."

"Oh my," she said, with a sexy, girlish cry. And then grew alert to the enormous danger. She said softly, "What about my stormy lover from the Peace Corps?" She spoke with great concern. She was in dire straits. This was a hell of a perilous situation.

"We can talk all about him," Miles said. "We'll have a lovely, brilliant time."

"Friday night," she said, "meet me here at sunset." She said this thing almost in a whisper. She was taking a great chance.

"What should I wear?" Miles said.

"Clothing!" she explained. Didn't he know?

"Where are we going?" he opened wide her imagination.

She closed it with a sexy whisper and a silky tone, "Why don't we pretend that you're the man in the relationship. You pick the place. I'm longing for a man to surprise me, in the right way."

"Where's your flat?" Miles said.

"Oh now," Daphne said, "you got my call exchange. I'm sure you'll be able to track down my flat. I have enormous confidence in your abilities. And now I'll reveal nothing more." She broke off the connection.

## Pure, Bright Red

HOUSE CRIMSON HELD its red flag up to the world, with its beautiful mark of pure, bright red.

And there were red flags up everywhere in House Crimson.

Here on 'House Crimson Lane,' there was much great activity and much talk of great crimson purpose.

"Red is our fire symbol," Jack said.

"Red is our heat shield," Bill said. "Red is our posture. Redshifted is our stance."

"We're part of big red," Susan said. "Go big red."

"We're going to take 'Big Red' out from Reality Valley, up into the mountain of the gods, and from there we're going to change the world," said Smackwater Jack.

"Red is the color of the fire department," said Big Jim. "Red is the color of emergency teams. Red is the color of the fight."

"Let's look at what the future holds. What does the future look like?" Brick Bullwinkle asked. "In the American century, it's a red sky at morning. That's where it begins."

"Once you stop straining and just listen, you'll get the message," Amelia said.

"We're giving people something to dream about—tomorrow," said Emily.

These people were fighting for the color they believed in. And they didn't give a damn who knew it.

"You have to see 'inside' the color," Irene said. "Not just look from color to color."

"Red is bold. Red dominates the visual field," Karen said. "Red catches the eye."

"We have to learn our colors. Once we gain the ability to truly see them, we are surprised," Jeffrey said.

"Each color has a sense of life," Dale said. "Red has a long wavelength and a slow frequency. It has a presence to it, a sustain. It's a brilliant, a brave color. Seeing red is a special experience. It's a cultured, refined perception."

"It owns the base of the spectrum," Jill said. "Listen to it. Listen to the quality of its tone. It's very different from all the others. And there's a lesson in that, for us. A lesson on how to be, . . . strong and pure. And bright."

And Eleanor said, "It's such an amazing experience, seeing red—truly seeing it, for the first time—*red*."

"And once you see it, it will stay that way," Colin said. "Throughout all time—past and present—it will have that pitch. Call it what you will. But the pitch is it."

"That's the beautiful experience. Seeing the pitch of red," Big Jim intoned.

"Seeing what we call *'Force Red'*—Seeing pure, bright red—

"Red is our strike symbol. You must strike the enemy to fight the enemy.

"*The Crimson Leaves Strike* is a symbol for a strike that takes apart your enemy both mentally and physically.

"*The Crimson Leaves Strike* is about attacking the enemy from a higher attitude, from higher ground.

"You must look down on the enemy, and take up your attitude on higher places."

Cinjun had taught them the *Way*.

Cinjun Khan Smythe, the warlord, might very well be feeling it now. The feeling in this place was now growing so very vast, reaching so far and rising so high that it had to be reaching and touching others. Reaching Cinjun in his command chamber astride House Crimson. High atop this forest city.

And in his high chamber, Cinjun was being interviewed.

"Why do they call you the *Thunder God?*" the interviewer asked.

"They call me the thunder god, because I strike from above. I strike down on the enemy from the sky—"

"From the sky? From a higher center?" the interviewer asked.

"From a higher plane . . . of *reality.*" Cinjun said.

"Wow," the interviewer found himself saying softly, before he realized it.

Cinjun looked at him. And held his gaze. Nothing moved.

# The First Ground of Being: The Fire Attitude

SCOFIELD WAS TEACHING his class in a vast acoustic solarium. He was sitting a distance from the stage. At the moment, a student stood on the stage, and a line of students waited to file onto the stage.

"You can't make a direct appeal," Scofield said, "You can't do what everybody else does.

"If you see a guy come on the stage and the first thing he says is, 'Hello, how are you folks doing tonight?' Ask your date—'Do you want to go see a show after this?' Because this particular happening cat already proved he isn't worth watching. Say to yourself, what would everybody else do? And then don't do it. Next!"

Miles walked onto the stage. He was about to open his mouth, when he saw Scofield sigh.

Miles walked off the stage and proceeded to the rear of the solarium. Scofield and the other students watched this.

Now Miles ran down the center aisle and leapt onto the stage.

He landed gracefully, and stood poised, his legs spread wide, his weight held low, entirely still, with his back to them all.

The people in the place held their eyes on him.

Miles turned, slowly. And walked toward them, but you wouldn't really call it a walk. A prowl, is what it happened to be.

The people breathed. This was all they did.

Now Miles lunged a pace forward, drove his body into a graceful upward surge, and let loose something.

"Rrrraaarrgh!" Miles hollered, sending a terrible cry into all the reaches of the night.

He roared, his voice crackling with a bellowing rumble coming from deep in the gut. He was feeling the lion. And it affected him, he seemed taken by a madness that reached from the ground and surged through his entire being.

He produced a deep and vast reaction in the people. One young lady felt a chill travel her spine.

Miles prowled the grounds. Like a lion driven mad in a wilderness of pain.

"Aaarrrgh! Yarghhh! Yeh! Oh yeah!" He seemed overpowered by some crazy feeling.

Scofield studied him. Just studied him. Scofield revealed nothing. Nor did he show any intention of reacting any time soon. He seemed made of stone, but a stone in a state where it is fired to an extreme heat, and is casting off a red orange glow.

Now Miles—in a staccato burst—shot his gaze to the other wing of the place, catching the eye of one of the young ladies in the class. "Rargh!" he told her. She shrieked.

Now the people made noises.

"Hold it—" Scofield said, "hold it down everybody—"

The place became silent.

Miles turned to Scofield and observed that the old man was studying him with great intensity. So Miles reflected the intensity and studied Scofield with just as enormous an intensity. It didn't happen to be intense enough to produce a reaction in Scofield. Scofield was heated, burning, stone—that revealed nothing.

There was no talk, no noise, anywhere in the place.

"Now," Scofield said slowly but very deliberately, "out with what you took the stage to say!"

Miles broke away from his penetrating study of Scofield. Abruptly, Miles became laid back and exuded an easy charm. "I," Miles said, "don't have anything to say—yet."

"You mean to tell me," Scofield said, "you don't have anything at all?"

"Not yet," Miles said. "Important to get a good start though, don't you think?"

"Get the hell off my stage," Scofield said. "Next!"

# Force Red

---

CINJUN AND ANOTHER REPORTER WERE STANDING before a big red splash. The reporter repeated the fashionable question, *"Why do they call you 'The Big Red One'?"*

Cinjun smiled warmly, efficiently radiating charm and energy. He seemed to radiate the big red dawn they spoke of.

"I am a force in motion. People name me for what they see in me. And in themselves," Cinjun said. "In me, they see a center and a force."

*"What is 'Force Red'?"* the reporter asked.
"We're entering the era of design," Cinjun said.
"And 'Force Red' is a force of design.
"It's a design force. It's big.
"Bigger than ourselves. Bigger than our time.
"It's a forward arrow-force moving us through an unfolding design.
"Leading us to a more perfect design, and to a modern reality.
"It's taking us to a real place.

"It's about edging," Cinjun continued.
"We're exploring the edges of a force.
"Something vastly bigger than ourselves.
"The force driving to the new reality.
"It's about edging into a new reality.
"Moving from the old world to the new world.
"From the old reality to the new reality.
"From the classical reality to the modern.

"Force Red is a fighting force," Cinjun said.
"The force driving to the new reality.
"We have to move from the old world to the new world.
"It's the forward arrow-force of struggle."

Oh hear it now, fine gentlemen and gentlest ladies.
*Force Red,* this was in the ancient tradition of power expressed. One person in charge. Society control flowing outward from a person of power, an architect of dreams. This was the way to rise—for *all* to rise. A man has to become ruler. We need it. It's absolutely essential.

*Wanted: A good man. A new strongman.*

And he was here.

*New strongman for sale!*

A man emerging with his cousins, sons, and daughters. *His lovely daughters,* Cinjun thought. *Beautiful, sexy.* One-ruler leadership, being the subject on his mind and elsewhere regions of his bodily form.

*What does your vision tell you about the future of this country?*

One-person rule and immense people force.

*Oh, sweet strong man in charge.*

This place needed it. . . . It had always had a strong man to hold the country together, to guide the people force along the civilized path. It needed it now again. Oh, sweet new strongman for sale!

Let the poets pipe of love in their childish way—

Let them pipe of peace, of cosmic awe, and wonder in their childish way—

Who's prepared to pay the price for a trip to paradise?

New strongman for sale!

Who will buy? Who will sample his supply?

Let the poets pipe of love in their childish way—He knows every type of love better by far than they—New strongman for sale!

If you want the thrill of love, you've got to go through the mill of love.

New strongman for sale!

*"Follow me, and climb the stairs."* New strongman for sale!

If you want the thrill of life, you've got to go through the mill of life.

Who's prepared to pay the price for a trip to paradise?—New strongman for sale!

Old life, new life, any life that is true life.

You need to pay the price of the through-life, of the through-strife—

*"Follow me and climb the stairs"*—New strongman for sale!

Cinjun would move in his people force, soon. Take the battle on the wind.

Scenarios forging, beautiful options developing. This was where to find hope.

He conditioned himself and his forces to advance his works. His great, good, noble works.

He was going to make the crooked places straight, lay the mountains low, exalt and raise the valleys, . . . and melt all turmoil into gold.

Tough times demanded a sweeping style.

In this world that *peopled,* the greatest gun was *people.*

Fit, strong, ready men . . . and women. Cooperative women. His vision remained on the subject of women for some time.

And then he would turn to the world. He would be hard, hitting, savage, but manly.

He was forging fearsome being. And that meant producing different sides to his character. To everything turn, turn, turn. To every season a purpose.

This season was for opening wide the promise of House Crimson.

His thoughts traveled into distance. He turned his memory lives and inner fires to the difficulties of future days. He would have to forge fearsome being; and from that being what wonders might come.

He entered a thinkstorm of wonders.

He would be absolutely wonderful, and would wield people force, sunbeams and moonbeams to great effect, to produce marvelous life change.

He was forging fearsome being.

He would ascend the imperial path and take the seat of power in the imperium through deeds, the deeds of a god emperor.

He was forging fearsome being.

Oh architect emperor.

Oh marshall emperor.

Oh Cinjun Khan S'mythe.

New strongman for sale.

Bringing form to his being of Cinjun Khan who would take the imperial path, and in good season, who would produce fearsome wonderful life change for the people of this good world, of this goodly world.

He was setting up the dimensions of the things to come.

Large scale things.

To save the people.

New strongman gathering energies and forging the fearsome being, with violent dimensions.

*Vrooom. Thrak. B'Boom.* He was forging fearsome being.

He felt himself to be an architect emperor. People force could be shaped in the way an architect shaped a building.

He would shape a people dream.

He had crafted the dream. And now—to bring the dream into reality. To shape this mighty people force that stretched out before him.

Now an architect pounded and forged into being.

*Vrooom. Thrak. B'Boom.* He was forging fearsome being.

What mattered heavily in his high office were the challenges of the violence that needed to come. The architect was readying himself.

He will unleash the dream. He will set the dream on the world; unleash its power; and take the world into its golden designs. All would be set to order; and held rigidly in place by supporting beams that could sustain enormous force. They all had a friend in Cinjun Smythe.

He would be a friend to the just and a fearsome being to the evil ones.

Those who would not get friendly would get dead.

Cinjun would be gentle and compassionate in murder, as a true gentleman should be. When he killed there would be nothing personal in it; this was extremely important to him. He would never murder out of a personal struggle. You could only murder as a swordmaster, quietly feeling the mighty purposes of the dream.

Cinjun's dream was beautiful, and now he bit hard on the beauty.

Unfortunate, but you would always have the damned—*Enemies be damned*. Keep them from creature comforts. Bring them low. Freedoms were nice things. But you could not afford to give everybody freedoms. The price was too high.

Beauty could be made real. So that beauty could shine all throughout the land. Purple mountain majesties. And no one would stop the goddamned beauty from having its beautiful way. Don't you dare get in the way of the beauty. This was the idea. Brilliant? Of course it was.

His thoughts were ever of beauty, and brilliance, and life wonder. And paradise. And goodness all the days of his life.

Beautiful things to see, playing misty visions. Beautiful things to see. Wandering through this wonderland.

That spoke of warm progress under the stars.

# Darkness and the Dark Nothing

NOTHING HAPPENED, DARKNESS GATHERED.
Darkness settled over the following nights and days.
Nights slipped into days, days slipped into nights.
Nights faded into the darkness.
Nights faded. Days faded.
Time went a-slipping into the past.

Then came a long day's journey into night.
And then came a now,
a dark now,
and
the darkness gathering.

Now,
Night nighting,
Dark darkening,
Time fading.

# The Mainspring of the Brutal All That There Is

MILES OVERCAME a hornswoggle from Scofield and wrangled him—out to a tavern, "The Caveman's Grotto and Grill," perhaps you've heard of it. The team of Mahoney and McSmithers performs here, and yes, many top flight entertainers work this room, many performers, and drunks.

Miles wanted an answer to the burning question. Sometimes, the secret is not in the mountains, it's under your feet, or across the table. *How do you do it?* Was the burning question.

He wanted to manifest the players.

*The Grounds and the Ground Rhythm.*

The rhythm and the motion.

The grounds were the episodes.

The ground rhythm led to and became the motion.

Ground rhythm to . . . motion.

The question was burning.

He saw the motion. He sensed the ground rhythm. But what lay between? *Where did the rhythm meet the motion?* he needed to know.

He wanted to create ground rhythm. You see he wanted rhythm to be his business—when he grew up, and went out into that wild wilderness world known as America.

And to create *story trains* with his ground rhythm that could carry thundering motions across the frontiers, all the way across the rocky mountains and coastal ranges, to the far waters, high surf, and blue-green seas on the outer reaches of the country.

*He was looking for the ground rhythm.*

You went through it all day without thinking about it. The beat that made the ground rhythm. That established the feeling and then changed the way you felt it.

Now in the train he was looking for: The drum was the centerpiece of what in music they called "the rhythm section," the bass walked it, and the piano accompanied it. Just as in an old wild west iron train, taken together, they pushed, pulled, tugged, and moved the band. They were: the engine, the wheels and the body—Power from the engine; roll from the wheels; and form from the body.

Roll from its "strut"—The "strutting," created the rhythmic feeling. And then the attitude coming in; giving it shape, and the shape was what the jazz players called 'comping,' . . . accompaniment.

Then came the loose hit!

*That's what I'm looking for,* Miles thought. That thing. The looseness. The unfit, the offbeat. The thing that gives it its tigerish strut.

The syncopation. The thing that plays against the rhythm. The other rhythm. The outside rhythm. The partner rhythm.

The thing that goes against the rhythm.

The place to derail the train of thought.

Miles drew in the mystery swirling all around him and aimed it at Scofield. He held Scofield in a steady gaze and spoke.

The question was:

"*How do you do it*"?" Miles said. "How do you get to it? *How do you do it when you know how to do it?*"

Scofield took in a deep breath—it was a kind of expansion. And he met Miles's gaze.

Scofield said, "You want . . . the secret . . . of *everything.*"

"Yes. . . . Call it out, I'd like to have a look. I've been looking for that damn secret everywhere."

Scofield smiled, and his face was the wall of all time.

"You . . . want . . . the secret . . . of everything."

"Ah," Miles said, "it wouldn't be a bad way to spend the evening— Taken all in all, *infinity* is not a bad night's work."

And then Scofield leapt—He dove into it, with all he was.

Scofield pulled away the curtain and threw it aside.

And Scofield showed him the changes that shape the song.

He charted the harmonies, laid bare the arrangement.

What he said was:

"The . . . secret . . . of . . . it . . . all . . . is . . . *opposites.*"

## The Melody of Scofield's Heart

Let's move in visions, let's fly in pictures, let's dance in sights, to glimpses of fleeting purposes—This was what he was saying to Miles.

He was saying it with his feelings, which flowed from him and took to the air, charging everything they touched.

In back and under Scofield were crystal ships and crystal visions and great whirling motions.

This was what he was giving Miles.

The words, they didn't matter much. Oh, they didn't matter much at all.

The notes just played and played. The song was rich and deep, set in a deep blue. It was the melody of Scofield's heart—you know—that the notes obeyed.

Scofield said, . . . some more. He said words and called them by name. What matter of it?

Ah, but the feelings.

It was the evening of the world, and Scofield began to play—a song, rich and dark and deep blue.

He was breathing a feeling, a deep and rich feeling, an insanity, a madness.

It was all set in a deep blue. Scofield continued to flow.

And, to let imaginary forces work on the words to rend them with feeling.

He was feeding Miles enough to produce a feeling. A sympathetic reaction. A resonant chord—an off center, off beat, off-the-wall stepping out of time and space, and present place.

Something that could build to the heights and match the intensity of Scofield's feeling.

From there, expand to fill a world, and an *All*.

What he was giving to Miles was a view and a feeling for *the world that peopled*.

"Hmm, let's see now, *opposites,*" Miles said. "Day, night, man, woman. Light and shadow."

Scofield said, "Most people stop there. I'm talking about something that is both. Can you picture a light that is a shadow? That would get interesting, wouldn't it?"

"Those kinds of opposites exist?"

Scofield said, "Everywhere."

## The Stone Age

"Let's come at it from another direction," Scofield said. "Let's strip away the modern world. Strip away everything that is not essential. Go back to the Stone Age. Make it stories about cave people."

They lurched forward into it. Scofield had tossed it into the air, and as it moved—away they went. He moved in great throttles forward. He ignited the booster rocket. And sailed across the sky.

Miles felt the chill, divine.

And moved into sun streaks.

Lately, he had begun to see a thing . . . and Scofield was giving it life and words.

In flares and ricochets, they progressed.

The blue sky called to seduce—and bewitch—and to give them the wings of their fate.

This was the slant of the pitch.

This was the hitch, they fastened on, and climbed onto eternity.

Lately, Miles had begun to feel things. He followed the feelings. Scofield set them to words. Together they riffed in rhythms.

The old man, and the young man, now become one, in the riffing, the mad riffing.

Bounds away! And anchors away!

Scofield climbed past the sea, onto land, and then flared into some certain sky streaks.

And flew on by! The destination, *Sun Rains*; the territory of *Go Insane*; and the *Look of Love*. Yes, joined below and above, a certain look, the look of love. Such was the nature of the place. Shimmering in glowing passion and all that lay beyond.

Scofield took his heart, and let the notes just play. This was the thing Scofield cared most about in the world. He rent it with feelings, hurled it, with mad passions.

It's dark sometimes, but surely this was light. And not the light of the world. This was the light of the *All*.

To most, it was not a fit subject.

To the wise, it was a cool wind from the edge of a cliff.

It was not something most people cared to waste their time on—And don't you waste their time on it either. That would be a nasty and ugly thing to do. And a most wicked sin. The work of an unforgivable sidewinder.

Scofield sidewound unforgivably, incorrigibly, devastatingly. Like he was doing no wrong! He was just a-sidewinding and a-sidwinding along, like he could get away with it, get away with anything he damn well pleased.

He flared.

He was a-reeling with the feeling. A-zapatoo, zapatoo, zapatoo. A-rapatoo, rapatoo, rapatoo—

Woooh! Flaring, baby, flaring!

Hurtling into the void.

He would drive this thing all over town. Hell, yes!

Don't get in his way, this was his being.

He knew what to want and where to go.

He flashed and flared.

And took them away.

Beneath him a drum kicked, a bass boomed, the whole Earth opened wide, as he soared. And exploded his being.

Miles was cool with it. This was the force of endless search. It was cool. He got into the beat. Crazy rhythm! . . . he liked it . . .

Yes, this was cool. And he swam, glided, and surfed with it, across the spaceways.

Way over yonder, that's where they were bound.

Run, and not to touch the ground.

Run in waves in the stratosphere, where the air was thin, but space was near. Where you felt the touch of eternity, and the wide expanse, . . . beyond.

They were on their way.

And moved in the way.

To way over yonder.

They came upon such a grand view, that they journeyed into the further realm. Into mindbending, into reality warping. And beyond.

Scofield continued, . . . making changes go round:

"There was the caveman who came to the other caveman's place and stayed too long. He made himself at home in someone else's home—We're talking—the Unwelcome Houseguest!—*Opposites* . . ."

*And, images were upon the waters:*

*The caveman* lounging with his feet on a boulder in another caveman's place . . .

. . . And the changes were going round, and round, and round, to . . .

*The cave people* wading across a river at night. And from the shore—the caveman wading in to help; knowing what he was doing; taking the torch from the clan; and then—oh oh, tripping; dropping it in the water. And then it was a-splooshing in the water—not much good to anyone—

Presently, colors were turning the world around again.

Too-doop, too-doop, too-doo doo-doo doo roop.

Scofield continued:

"The caveman who acted like he knew everything but actually knew nothing—the Bumbling Expert!—*Opposites* . . .

"The little kid caveman who knew more than the big adult caveman!—*Opposites* . . .

"The confidence-man-caveman who sold a sucker a cave that leaked in the winter—the Confidence Man and the Sucker!—*Opposites . . .*"

The images continued to roll across the waters.

To-do-doop, do-doop, doo-doo-doo doo roop.

Scofield said—"The caveman who got the cavegirl pregnant and had to marry her to make peace with her daddy caveman—the Shotgun Wedding—*Opposites.*

"The little cave mouse who roared at the lions—Mice Behaving Like Lions—*Opposites.*

"The caveman who told his wife, 'What are you getting upset about? All I did was rape your sister'—the Innocent Tyrant—*Opposites.*"

*The images rolled across the timeflow,* repeating themselves in the corridors, again and again performing the same movements.

The young blood-savage "erect" caveman hollering at his wife.

The many cave men & women. The people of the world, all the people in the whole damn world—ah, whole wide world.

Ah, the story of the *World*—deep and great and wide—and opening wider into rooms of strangers, and strange nights, strange days drifting in strange sins and wishes. Strangers in strange lands. And here, to this place, comes . . . the *Clown!* His face is a wall, the wall of all time. And the face, . . . is haunting . . . haunting . . . haunting, across the realms of lately, presently and soon, and all that you could see, feel or be.

Thumpa, thump a thumpa. Doom, doom, doomp, doompt.

Scofield continued:

"If you were giving me this talk instead of me giving it to you, we'd have another one—the Master Being Outdone by the Apprentice—*Opposites.*"

Miles said, ". . . *Opposites,* . . ."

Miles held himself still, ". . . and all the people in this whole wide world . . ."

"Opposites that attack logic," said Scofield. "The opposites have to be a violent assault on common sense. Those are the ones you want."

### The Experience

Miles, he felt the wind shout like a drum.

It set his breath on fire, it had come.

Rending his heart with fire.

The waves of fire. Streets and avenues alight with flames, setting sail, catching stars, and on and on and on going so, so far.

He felt it come, it was come.

Fire. And . . .

The road to, the road to, *the Road to Dreams.*

Wind shouting like a drum.

It couldn't last; it had to stop. But in the wave, time had died. There was only drowning; his heart drowning in love's dreams. Swirling eddies of love dreams; pulling him under. Mighty forces rending and throttling, down and around, whipping motions, of drowning.

Whipping tails of love dreams.

All whipping tails, it formed roads.

Roads to dreams, and dreams that went on and on.

You could build time on, you could build life on. The lovers of the stars—oh, if you would watch them go.

The winds of life!

Winds of life wiping away the cold of time that died.

His heart was drowning in love dreams, so deep, so rich, and blue.

And then . . .

He was setting sail for a dream so far. And the way, the leading, was all, it was all . . . tenderness . . . how dark had won, and the light was come.

The winds of life were coming on.

The winds of life were coming through.

Taking him:

. . . into *Cool Rapidity.* Cool, cool, cool; . . . rapidity . . .

The avenues cried. The winds of life swept through. On their way, to love dreams.

The seas were cold; the streets were dark, all going so far.

The winds of life swept through.

Whipping tails spinning in a dance. Dancing barefoot; some strange music drove them on; through strange fields of dreams. Whipping winds of life on dark streets.

He entered streets where time had died.

His heart was drowning in love dreams. All the scenes that had to fail because they were too far.

Suffering, difficulty, desire, . . . will to beauty—and a heart drowning in love dreams—

Oh, This Was the Experience! He was being, being:

. . . experienced.

*The Pacifica Love Dream Experience!*

The shout the drum the dark street the winds of life the no retreat the way the road of dreams.

Man, this had been worth the trip! What an experience! And now coming out of it through a tumbling up, he streamed and expanded to fill the avenues of the *All*. All the colors of the wind that shouted like a drum.

All this was on the way to the path of dreams.

All this was on the way.

Away he went.

Way leading on to way.

This was the way. Way leading on to way. Swirling, whipping ways.

Echoing in corridors, repeating the same movements.

Way leading on to way. All was way.

No retreat. Time had died, and it was all there at once.

And the one thing Miles thought was:

How beautiful!

*How Beautiful It All Was!*

He had the feeling. And you don't give up the feeling when you've finally got it down—you keep it hot and squeeling when you take her on the town.

Opening wide, rending apart the time that had died, Miles said:

"*Opposites*—leading on to opposites, all is opposites."

And this was how he emerged from the *Pacifica Love Dream Experience*. Way leading on to way, all was way.

Scofield's old dream, long forgotten, whipped forward suddenly—leaped— and grabbed at Scofield.

*Tygers* crouched in jungles in Scofield's dark eyes.

Scofield, waited in this place.

Chains broke; sounds tumbled down. Amid falling leaves and tangling weaves; he tumbled into this place. . . . Oh, hear it now, here and now. Truth seemed this day, not far away. And happiness lay, not far away.

"You're a mad old man," Miles said.

"Not all who wander are lost," Scofield said.

Miles smiled.

"You have it," Scofield said. "Well, I'll be a son of a bitch. You do have it."

"I know," Miles said. "I have it."

He was a breeze that burned in knowing, and in knowing more, burned more.

"Let's give it a go, Sco"—Miles liked this—This was cool—"Let's riff on it."

Scofield said, "Now?"

"There's not a moment to lose," Miles said.

"You don't want to think about it?" Scofield said.

"I've thought about it. I'm better when I don't think. It slows me down. Throws me off my game."

Miles was raring to go. "Let's hit it!"

Let's go. Watch it, watch it.

Watch out now! In, we go!

Watch out now! We're going into it!

When you hit the dance floor, you've got to be jumping.

A skidalong bim tang,

A skid om bop!

That wild swing, you just can't stop it.

Woah, watch it, watch it, you just can't stop it!

A thoom doom doomp! Oh, watch it, watch it.

A poo doo doomp!

A skidalong dim dãome, a skid ohm bãome!

## Working to the Riff

Scofield felt the flaring sensation and continued.

Miles felt the ease of it. It had its own motion. He rode it.

Like cloud working with sky, they worked in the natural way, making changes go round.

The splendor of nature all around.

## Riffing

They entered an air of spring.

Riffing.

They riffed together:

"Where is *The Scraper* . . ." Scofield said.

". . . in the sky," Miles said

"Where is *The Friend* . . ." Scofield said.

". . . in the girl and the boy," Miles said.

"How is *The Judge* . . ."

". . . crooked."

There was wonder here, Scofield thought.

And went on.

They were near something. As near as you could go. They continued along the edge.

"What do you know about *The Hero* . . ." Scofield said.

". . . cowardly," Miles said.

*"The Reformer?"* Scofield said.

"Sinful," Miles said.

*"The Prude?"* Scofield said.

"Over-sexed," Miles said.

*"The Identity?"* Scofield said.

"Mistaken," Miles said.

"How did *The Dope* become a dope?" Scofield said.

"Education," Miles said.

"What do they do with *The Other?*" Scofield said.

"Each faults," Miles said.

"Who is *The Animal that Roars?*" Scofield said.

"The mouse," Miles said.

Who suffers?

The wrong person.

Who is in charge.

The wrong person.

Who is getting the medals?

The wrong person.

Where is the wrong person?

Driving.

Who is in charge?

The underling.

Who is outdoing the master?

The apprentice.


Where is the up?

In the beat.

Where is the down?

In the town.

Where is the good?

In the night.

Where is the bad?

In the break.

Where is the turn?
 In the road.
 Where is the weight?
 In the train.
 Where is the depth?
 In the sea.
 Where is the lightning?
 Before the thunder.

Where is the hint?
 In the lie.
 Where is the poet?
 On holiday.
 Where is the mystic?
 In the words.
 Where is the truth?
 In the thoughts.

Where is the sense?
 In the common.
 Where is the non?
 In the sense.

Where is life?
 In the madness.
 Where is the world?
 In the story.
 Where is the star?
 In the picture.
 What's getting talked away?
 The night.

Where is the lead?
 In the escape.
 Where is the beginning?
 In the end.
 *What* is the secret *of it all?*
 Opposites.
 And what is the secret *of everything?*
 Opposites leading to opposites. All is opposites.

Where are the opposites?
    In the pieces.
    Where are the pieces?
    Lost in the everywhere.

Where is the turnaround?
    In the twelve-bar blues?
    Where is the end?
    In the song?
    Where is the secret?
    In the opposites?
    Where is the everything?
    In *The All.*

Where do you build the sense?
    In the nonsense?
    Where is the wisdom?
    In the madness.
    Where is the truth?
    In the insanity.
    Where is the voyage?
    In the wandering?
    And where is *the wandering?*
    In the wonder?
    And where is *the wonder?*
    In the love dream.
    And where is *the love dream?*
    In the world.

They went silent.
    That was where it ended.
    In the sharp of the point, and the twist of the word—And in the turn of the world.

# The Blue Night, the Field & From In to Out

NIGHT PASSED to darkest night.

And Miles went out into the blue night.

Into the blue field, amid the dark green, the violet earth and the astral yellow. To find the wicked, wicked sidewinding.

To find the sidewinding to meet the cold emptiness.

And, the stone cold players.

To fight the stone cold death.

That was coming for him.

Tonight was the night, Miles thought. This was the night, there was no other night.

This was his moment—from a star so warm he was going to ride across the dark.

To the people of the sky, to the people of *The Way*.

Tomorrow called to seduce and bewitch—to give him the wings of his fate, and lure him with her cosmic kiss.

His memory brought him to the day he had walked into this field with Scofield Morefield.

He remembered the day that Scofield had shown him the vast and radiant field—

*"You will need to fill this field with feeling,"* Scofield had said—

He had extended his hands.

"Find the feeling. Fill your life and being with it."

That was the lesson from Scofield. Radiate feeling.

Use your imagination to light a fire, and radiate it in waves.

*How*—that Miles would have to discover for himself.

Radiate the attitude.

They had walked into the field during that day.

*"Fill the field with feeling,"* Scofield had said. "That's what we do. . . . We fill a place with feeling, with emotion. . . . And it's not something we do with our *bodies*. We do it with our *spirits*."

Miles had looked around the field that day. Scofield was right.

"You have to be able to turn it on and turn it off at will," Scofield had said. "You have to be able to fire up the attitude and turn it off whenever you want. You have to be the master of the attitude.

"When the moment calls for the attitude, you give it to the moment.

You bring it on. And then when the moment is over, you end it.

*"You have to be the master of your own body, the master of your own feelings—and the master of the moment."*

"Show me," Miles had said to Scofield. "Show me how it's done."

"Ha, ha, ha. . . . You want me to show you how it's done," Scofield had said.

And then Scofield smiled. Why the hell not?

The morning passed a long moment.

And then—Time slipping. Time slipping.

Scofield stood in the center of the field, surrounded by distance.

Around him lay a garden of trees and wilderness.

Above, the sun sat high in a sapphire sky.

Scofield stood a long moment in that sunlit garden.

Then Scofield threw himself into a surging form, and whirled to the sky. To the blue sky.

*"Oh, let it rain!"* Scofield cried.

He could not stand a life of blue sky one more day.

"Oh, let it rain!" Scofield cried to the heavens.

Take away the empty shape of the day.

He wanted mood and motion.

"Damn it all, let it rain!"

Oh, bring on the night and bring on the rain. A pelting, powerful rain, palpable, sensual. Insane.

*A Liquid Flight.* Of slips and slides.

The sun made him feel like a fool, it did not much his mood. Oh, let it rain.

Let the thunder crack, and the lightning snap the tension.

Washing away the times.

*"C'mon, bring on the rain!"*

Bring on the rain. Pelting rain, palpable, sensual. Insane.

And Scofield ended it there.

He went skidding out of the moment.

In full control, he returned to what he had been just a few moments ago.

He left no trail behind.

Scofield returned from the moment—and turned to Miles.

He looked at Miles.

"A rain song—was my song, . . . today.

"Your song will be different.

"The song changes every day, and every moment.

"A fool chases the song.

"The song doesn't matter.

"The attitude is everything.

"Find the attitude—And ride it.

"Use your spirit—Nothing else can help you.

"Because there's nothing else to it—The attitude is *you.*"

## The Blue Field

Now Miles spread his hands wide and gave himself to the place.

He began to walk into the cool, radiant field.

There was no thinking your way there—

To the attitude he was looking for. The emotional attitude.

*The Whirlwind Wāoynde.*

The one that existed only in his head.

Each person was a different shape of nature, and focused the world in a different way, into the here and now.

And each life force took on different dimensions.

His life lay out there, to be found—in the *Whirlwind Wāoynde.*

## Into Insanity and Outer Reaches, He Was Come

He was leaving behind the sea of faces that told him to stop.

They said, "Stop!" The enemies of his endless search.

He defied them, one and all. The enemies of his endless search, were just dust blowing along the brown windswept Earth, singing the same old song. Stop! You cannot do this! You cannot be this way!—Damn them all to hell, and damn him—yes, he would be damned, everything would be damned. All right then, everything would be damned. There was no stopping him.

No hanging on. No slipping away slowly day by day.

He was going to rend the night, and, tonight, be everything he was to be. He would will the enemies to vanish. He would destroy their song, and deliver himself, out of his sadness, out of his pain, and move into outer madness.

He would will himself into insanity.

Ramp it up.

*Who is a good man does not try.* The love that wants to it, well it is. Who says much that goes, does not go. As well as it does not go, does not come. Who inside of itself does not leave, goes to die without loving nobody.

Keep it up.

His courage would be the only thing to guide him. The strength from inside would be all, all else would be forgotten.

He was pulling himself through.

He couldn't remember the sea of faces that told him to stop.

He couldn't recall all the things that had tried to stop him. All the cold things burning thru the void.

Now it was time for the people of the sun, people of the sky.

Time to get lost in a mission of outsiders and mavericks.

And maverick outside, to outer seas, outer skies, outer spaces, outer reaches, to outer madness. He was come.

### The Ride, the Fire & the Wicked, Wicked Sidewinding

Ride the fire.

The fire is the ride.

The *fire!* sparked, sparked to flame.

The becoming, he was making it happen.

No! No stopping, damn it Miles! This is the night! Go!

### Move Into the Groove

Move! You will never, ever ever think your way there.

There is no think to there.

You will never, ever ever walk there, in the cold dawn.

There is no way to walk there from where you are, from anywhere, there is no walking there. The long line of years? Of walking. And going there. That was preparation. From here, you leap! You have to take to the skies.

There is no human way to do it. You have to imagine it.

You have to play the game; you know the game it means; a little game, called *"Go insane."* The falling leaf pleads, and the way up, leads.

Go! Move!

Out, to outer space, outer reaches.

Find yourself lost, inside a song.

Play crazy games, jump from the top of a tower.
And dive up, head straight up.
Take to the skies.
Damn it, take to the skies!
C'mon.
C'mon.
C'mon.
Fire fire fire.
Burn burn burn.
Run run run.
*Wind blew.*
And he blew in the wind.
He took to it.
He took to the wind.
C'mon, bring it on home! Hit it! . . . Bring it on, sweet baby, bring it
on!
C'mon burn.
Burn burn burn.
Miles felt the fire, flaming.
It grew, until it took over his world. Until it filled his entire world.
*Now ride it!* Miles thought.
Ride it, and damn it all do not chart a course!
Hurtle. And boom.
That's all.

## Break On Thru

His mind wanted to cry out loud—Yes, his mind wanted to cry out loud!
   "I returned, and saw under the sun
      all is opposites.
   "Opposites leading on to opposites,
   "All is opposites.
   "Enter the dream
   "Enter the dreamscape
   "Enter the scape
   "Enter the escape
   "Enter the bender
   "Enter the mindbender!"
His mind cried out loud!
   "Oh you crackling winds! Bring me giants!

"I feel too strong to war with mortals! Bring me giants!"

Oh you crackling winds!

Bring him giants. Mad, dangerous, cunning, ferocious giants.

Yes! He was a-reeling with the feeling! He yearned to wrestle with *Tygers* in the night!

He wanted force and sway—*The Wilde Whirlwind Wāoynding Wild!* Screaming wild!

He was looking for *The Wāoynde*—he yearned for *The Wāoynde*—she, the *Wāoynde*—a mighty lady of force and swirl . . . a girl that looked quite like Daphne.

## The Blue Field

He stepped deeper into the blue field, the vast, cool, radiant blue field.

## Astral Fields Come Away!

Radiate in waves. Pulse On! Keep it up.

And a-sidewinding we will go!

Sidewinding leading on to sidewinding, all is sidewinding.

Travel in sunbursts.

Travel into a sunburst, and emerge, into another sunburst.

Way leading on to way, all is way.

Astral fields come away!

Wheels within wheels; circles from circles; motions from motions; waves on to waves.

Time slipping.

Mind bending.

To the heart of the sunrise; to the mainspring; to the great everything— *To The All!* . . . He was come.

Of mainsprings and opposites, of wheels and elementals.

Oh elemental beauty!

Sidewinding to sidewinding, wheeling in sidewinding

To outer space, to extreme madness . . . He was come.

## The Mindbender

Opposites jolting about.

Shaking and forming, spheres, and, round go a-rounds.

Wheeling, spinning; . . . emerging . . . Wheels within wheels. Motions

from motions. Escape! Surge and charge. Light and rumbling thunder.
Thundering grooves—grooving and smashing—smashing and thrashing—
thwarting and cavorting, rending and trending, slipping and a-sliding, into
way.

## The Blue Field

He stood in the center of the vast blue field now.

## Ripple Breathing

Hit it! and let it go
    Hit it, and let it go
    Ascent!
    Spread out.
    Take it all in.
    Spread out, take more in.
    Breathing.
    Ripple breathing.
    Filling, spreading out.
    Breathing,
    Breath pulse.
    Brave weddings of summer mornings.
    And, *Gardens,* grinding out forms.
    Elemental shapes and elemental beauty.
    And he was into it . . .
    Somewhere a *Barker* spoke . . .

## The Blue Field

He began to walk the blue field.

## The Barker

Somewhere a strange carnival barker cried: "Step right up! Step right up!
To the realm of strange riches!

    "The name of the realm? Oh, you know the name. Don't you know the
name?

    "It has a pretty name.
    "And it has it all.

"Deliver yourself.

"Ah, there you are, and you are here. Now that you're here, have a look, a look around."

Crystal ships sailing on the winds of life. Gems and rubies in the hold.

Mighty captains and mighty passengers. Looking to a rainbow, and hills and streams. Following to the place beautiful.

People and passages.

Crystal visions journeying on the rainbow bridge to Asgard, Valhalla, Olympus, and the other paradises to found in the realms of mind.

To Thor, Odin, Loki, Athena, Aphrodite, sea of faces.

And shooting, burning across the void . . .

He saw a *Seeker Hurtling in Forever,* a *Sound Chaser.*

Hurtling and rending.

All boom.

## The Thing Was . . .

The thing was a *Capoeira,* a dancing burning fighter hurtling across the sky.

Bathed in symphonies, hurling colors in exploding sunbursts.

Hurtling to hurtle. Burning to burn.

Burn burn burn.

Run run run.

It was a thing red and crimson, a thing green and emerald, blue and azure, indigo and violet.

Burn burn burn.

Run run run.

. . . in mad, furious motions.

Azure and forever, yellow and startling.

Hurtling across the history of human emotion.

Carving futures, haunting pasts, playing in the fields of space.

Red and fiery, green and forest, azure and forever, yellow and startling.

And it was soaring, gliding upward.

Leaving the barren land for the green yonder.

Leaving dusty spaces for dark green forests. And the emerald realms of life.

It exploded through winters, pushed through rivers, across springs, through skies, blazed through summers and forest mountains, raced through autumns and cool serenades, forming motions within motions and sending out wheels within wheels. All spiraling. Motions wheeling and wheeling motions. And all was moving upward.

*The Wāoynde.*

Forming motions from motions and wheels from wheels.

## The Blue Field

It was forming a *mad wilde whirlwind wāoynde.*

Taking in the field.

Surrounding it in the whipping tails of a *wāoynde.*

*A wāoynde* that rose high into the air, to dance among the clouds.

And now—rise—speed—*and away!*

## Becoming

It was beautiful.

And so easy.

So light and easy. It was lightness and ease, and . . .

. . . its shapes, its elemental shapes, . . .

Well, I'll be a son of a bitch! Miles thought. It had always been there.

It was in the shape of all his days that had come before and all his days that were to come.

The damn thing has been here all along. Well, old friend, here we go.

Do you know why I recognize you, old friend? You're me.

And your name is Miles Roark.

The cosmic kiss was on Miles. And he laughed. It was such a grand kiss.

It moved away from Miles.

The thing was a-reeling with a-feeling and flowing into way, Miles thought. Elusive whisp! Whispering wind! Windsprinting spring!

It had disappeared over the horizon.

## Argh!—The Bright Blue Chase

Miles gave chase—Moonlight smiled on the chase.

Then there was only exertion, and blood flooding through the channels of his being. His mind knew effort. "Ah! Argh! Yeargh!"

His mind cried out loud.

Exertion, and blood pumping. "Ah! Arrgh! Aaaaaarrrrrrgh!" Miles was racing, . . . this was the fastest he had ever gone. Oh furious race! A madman chasing his madness.

Miles chased it down. Aimed himself right for it. And hurtled into it.

Headlong into mad insanity.

The world exploded all around.

Miles, was in a state of perfect calm. A state of perfect pulsing grace. The moment went on forever.

Gentle, gentlest all. Moving in *The Way*, he broke on thru, to the other side.

It moved inside of Miles.

Miles moved inside of it.

Red and fire, yellow and light. He was in the heart of the sunrise.

And they moved. In one world, one place, one being.

The becoming of one, Miles was making it happen.

*They were become one.*

He took himself into it. *He was become it.*

He allowed it to take over everything, while he took it over.

The person and the force, were become one.

Miles Roark, the *Seeker in Forever,* the *Sound Chaser,* hurtled into the futureflow.

And he was in it, a fire to ascend the *'brightest heaven of invention,'* a *Whirlwind Wāoynde,* of his own spinning emotions.

He had plunged into his own maelstrom.

He was making it happen—and now it was taking him—into space.

He was dancing through space—the space of a cool, vast, radiant blue field.

## The Blue Field

Now Miles was running through the hills and dales of the blue field.

Oh, witness here—an American boy—running through the blue field chasing and catching his own feelings.

Sending them out into the blue field. The trees, clouds, and stars, as his audience.

He was running and running through the blue field at midnight.

Wouldn't you call that mad? Yes, most would call it insane.

Hmm, where was this madness leading? Where could it go?

This was far from very strange wandering. He must be lost.

Miles continued a while longer.

It was the deep blue of the Pacific Ocean and a young man carrying the *Pacifica Love Dream*. Into the world, the violent, brutal world. Into the wild, wicked, naughty and strange world.

And then he began to dance. Stomping in that blue field at night, he did *a blue ocean dance*.

A good old-fashioned under the moon in the big city blue ocean dance.

Oh strange attitude in a strange night of iron mist.

Now clouds circled about in the blue night and gazed down on a young American boy, in the center of a great field dancing.

There he was leaping and dancing in a field at midnight.

Surely he was insane. He was dancing to songs inside his head, and to rhythms that beat deep in his body.

The boy was a little crazy—That you could see.

He was a young man and this was the sort of thing young men did.

This was new. And that was the job of young people. To bring in the new.

Sometimes it looked strange, very strange to the naked eye.

On that blue night—
In the midnight hour—
In a field—
In the middle of the park—
*There was a young man dancing*
*& moving into way.*

## All Passing and All to Pass

It was all done lightly—oh, sure, with vast effort involved—but done lightly in his moving on. And on he went. To more fun. To fantasia.

To waking up lost in the throes of life, to not knowing exactly where he was, it would all be part of his moving on.

He was a living force moving forward.

## Dangerous

And he returned to the morning of the world.

Oh, dangerous, he was, he was dangerous now.

The notes were playing, and the melody of his heart, was what the notes obeyed. Warm and true, the heart was describing itself. It was a clear sound, rich and dark, set in a deep blue.

Now, heaven help him, he was dangerous. And to be dangerous in this world was to be in danger.

Now, he would meet opposition. Now, he would meet the things that would try to stop him—The things that always stopped people like him.

Yes, now, things would try to stop him. Things would get hot and ferocious.

He had purpose and force. And there were many people who did not like that at all, not one lick. They would stop him! They would try. In the end, they would succeed, he knew. It had never gone any other way. But Miles chuckled, he could go pretty damn far before they stopped him.

So let them do their mighty work. There was a deep menace in the world, and Miles was going to punch it in the chest. If the blow got through! Then, a fight, a battle, a deadly combat. And then what? Then what? Would he be killed?

Miles laughed, shrugged, and kept moving forward.

# The Young Ladies . . . To Be Enfolded

CINJUN WAS MEETING with a group of new people. Enfolding the new young ladies.

The setting was the gymnasium, and the group had the feel of a team assembled.

"Who are you? . . . Who are you? . . ." Cinjun said.
    "Where are you from? What do you want?
    "Who are you?
    "Are you afraid? What do you want?
    "Who are you?
    "What is your purpose? Why are you here?
    "Who are you?"

"What is your center?
    "What is your core?
    "What drives you?
    "Everyone lives in their own reality. Who are you? What reality are you living in?
    "What is your sense of reality?"

"What is your center?
    "Everyone lives in their own reality.
    "Who are you? What reality are you living in?
    "Here you will find the center of reality."
    *He was giving them a center for their reality.*
    "Here you will find drive.
    "Here you will find heart.
    "Here you will find soul.
    "Here you will find the path.
    "Here you will find the way outward,
    "The way to drive dreams through the changes.
    "Here you will raise the sun into the sky,
    "And soar into . . . the new world."

He spoke to them,
Making moments come alive.

Perfection was very near,
And none else had her beauty.

He walked through the ranks, passing one beautiful young lady after another.

"This is the true joy in life, being used for a purpose recognized by yourself as a mighty one. To be burned up in the pursuit of it."

"You must enter a state of awareness.
"True awareness."
"Here, you must move between two worlds."
"You have talents hidden inside you that you have yet to discover. Here you'll find one that is the key to many others.
"There's a vast difference from the way you are now to the way you will be on the other side of this."
"It will happen in your awareness.
"We're going to open up incredible abilities in you."

## Amelia

In an alcove of House Crimson, Amelia talked about joy to the new recruits.
Amelia said, "You enter a secret laboratory. It's like crossing the border into a different universe.
"It's exciting. It's like being on another planet, it's us against all of them.
"It's wonderful to be a part of living, breathing history!"

## The Young Ladies

In the gymnasium, Cinjun continued along the line of young recruits, moving from one red-cheeked young woman to the next beaming young femme who was living in the pink and rosy.
"Who are you? What do you want?
"You want this purpose. To be deep in this purpose."
"Feel it . . . Opening up power and ability in you.
"To give you body awareness, power awareness and reality awareness.
"To give you "color awareness"—that means a scale of awarenesses.
"To give you *body awareness, power awareness and reality awareness.*"

"You must become a force of nature."
"You relax and soon naturally you begin to notice little differences.
"It's an abstract experience.
"It puts you on a different level of perception.
"You already have this ability in you.
"It's inner workings are delicate.
"It's lives on a perceptual level. It's a richness of perception."
"It's not something that is far from us.
"We just have to know how to bring it out."
"It's an expansion of awareness.
"At first, very faint. Very abstract."
"You discover that each color has a sound, and each sound a color.
"We're going to open up incredible abilities in you."
"To discover new being."

"You move to the *New World*.
*"The Western Frontier Nation."*

"Believe in the promise of the *West*.
"A western frontier country."

"Set yourself on a course. Try to reach something that is out of reach."

"Over the horizon ... chase the sun ... to America."

## The Fine Battle of a Him and Her

IT WAS ANOTHER NIGHT. And Scofield was teaching in a woodland amphitheater set in the hills outside the city.

The students were seated along the slope of the ancient hills, observing Scofield, who was directing his attention to the stage below.

On the stage, lying in a rehearsal bed, were a sexy young woman and a handsome man—Sarah and Jack—who were playing out a scene of a married couple.

Up above the stage and the sloping hills, there was a grove of trees, that along with the students had stopped by to see this night-time presentation of a wilderness story and wilderness thoughts.

Attentions turned here, to the stage, to the scene that had just been played out, and was now slipping into the past.

The trees stood sentinel. The students observed with interest. And Scofield spoke with his full resonant voice, about what had played out here, and what now was swiftly a-timeslipping away, and he spoke in an intimate tone, invoked to share primal thoughts—with friends.

Scofield was not a lecturer. He was simply an old and wind-aged gentleman who had been to some certain places in time and space before others had; he was simply a traveling man talking about what he knew—about where mighty truths lay, out in the wilderness open, along the landed range, for all to see.

Here in this place, the land held the scene; underneath the students, there were boulders, there was stone, there was ground, and there were leaves of grass.

Amid the sloping hills, and the low stone steps, sat Scofield in a director's field chair, . . . but he was traveling far, to strange lands, . . . he was the traveling man, he was a kind of butterfly, he was changing right before their eyes.

Scofield turned and cast his gaze along the sweeping line of the students. "The picture that this scene is from, . . . this scene that we just saw played out," Scofield said to the students, "is a picture called *'The Fine Battle of a Him and Her.'*

'The story is about a couple who are incompatible.

"It's about the reality of a connection between two people. Two people who are involved with each other in a strange way.

"They fall in love. They move apart. And in time they come to an end.

"But before they get divorced they absolutely destroy each other. Not only destroy each other; they wreck the entire house; break all the furniture; they destroy the property; and finally there's nothing left.

"*Odd bedfellows* should not be in the same bed together, that's what this is about.

"Now . . . how do we *physicalize* that? . . . Considering that *you must always physicalize every conflict.*

"You must physicalize every scene of battle. Remember the principle. A scene is not conversation, a scene is a battle of wills."

Strange bedfellows make strange days.

This is a battle in the war between the sexes. This is an episode in that war.

It's two people going wrong together and loving it. They love this wrong love.

A man and woman going wrong together and loving the journey, . . . *living for the journey.* This journey that is going wrong and more wrong.

And it's thrilling. It's exciting. It's new and lovely.

They can't get enough and can't go deep enough. There is no end to it.

It's dangerous and brutal and it's love. Weird. It's very weird.

But it's a strange world. And this is a strange love between two people.

Sometimes love is strange, and weird, and warped.

It becomes a mystery within a mystery within a mystery.

And the people in it can't understand it.

It's like being trapped inside an absurd poem and you love the poem but it doesn't make sense—and that's what you love about it.

That you have to find the sense in it. That it's you and her. And this weird thing is all yours.

It's a reality, a connection, between two people that is totally mysterious from the outside.

Two people drowning inside each other's love dreams—that's weird, isn't it? Does it get any more weird than that?

It's like they're on a Greek island in the blue of the Mediterranean Sea, and nothing else matters but what's on this island.

They're carving ripples in each other.

We watch it and we think—oh my god—'I've been there. I've felt like that about somebody. I wish I could feel that way again about somebody.'

His relationship to her body. Her relationship to his body.

It's a weird connection of two frames. It's a dance, a partnered dance. But a crazy, distorted dance.

It's the fine battle of a him and her.

You have to turn a story into a physical scene.

The story is the war between the sexes. How do you make that physical theater? With the audience sitting above the scene of combat. Because that's what we like. To sit back and watch others in pain. To see people suffering through greater problems than our own.

Every story has to be about a theme.

And you have to physicalize that theme.

You have to make the theme real.

You make the words flesh. And you make the people act.

You make the questions real. And you make the questions into scenes.

This is a love story about a theme of battle.

Every story has to breathe life. Life has to breathe themes. Themes have to breathe purpose.

You must make the purpose into flesh.

You must make the themes into people,

. . . and scenes of conflict,

. . . and stories of combating wills.

The lesson is about mighty themes calling.

Flames and love—live only for a little while.

It's a story about a flaming love. And how the fire dies.

Along the way love burns and burns.

Dying embers of love.

It's about love themes, fire, and battle.

The ache of love and lost things.

About when life was beautiful, and love was young, and then how twilight comes and darkness gathers.

It's a school of love story.

Not all love stories end happily in storybooks.

Not all love stories end in a place that makes sense.

Some end weird, and strange, and brutal.
They end with hearts aching.

This is about how love is the burning point of life. And since all life is sorrowful, love is agony.
Love is pain. Beauty is truth, truth be beauty.

It's haunting and weird.
It's something we've all gone through. And we recognize parts of our own love lives in it.
Who we loved and how it went wrong.
It's about battle wounds and love thrills. Love wounds and battle thrills.
It's about love times and love thrills.

Every good story is about more than the story. It's about the mirror of life. Each good story is a mirror of life. And the big themes of life.
How the themes come and go. And here how they come and go in love stories.
Lies and truths in love. Cheers and losses in love. The glow and darkness of love.
Bitter love—that's what this is about.

One acts independent, haughty. The other needs her.
But both need each other.

Do you ever *hate the person you love and love the person you hate?*
That's what this story is about—those kinds of crazy, mysterious realms.
These are the feelings we struggle with.

This is the blues.
It's what one man said, "It's a pain you can't live with, and a woman you can't live without."
It's the hardland of the winter of love. This is a tale from the badlands of love.
These are the distant sands of love. The lands of sirens sweetly singing.

Images played across the screens of the students' minds, pouring into their awareness, with remembrances of sights they had seen in their own lives, of men and women locked in mortal combat—

The fine mismatings of a him and her—

The strains of the old song, ringing low in a lonely distance:

"... *The sleepless nights, the daily fights ... I miss the kisses, and I miss the bites ... The lovely loving, the hateful hates, the conversation with the flying plates, I wish I were in love again.*"

Oh, to be in love ... In the throes of love. Ah, love.

And now Scofield was the butterfly, swimming in the sky, changing right before their eyes.

He was forming wind trails, by and by.

Scofield said, "The problem with these two people is they are madly in love with each other but can't get along. You could not possibly have as much passion as has to be generated for this story to work—I mean by the end it's the ultimate battle, they reach the ultimate end that two people in this kind of love can reach—it's devastation—it's an emotional carnage ... that has to be—and this story could not work if they did not have an enormous emotional response to one another.

"Well, I always say that the people who quarrel best, are the people who love each other the most. Egh, it's ... it's, ... ah, it's, uh ... it's the old dictum: *The opposite of love is indifference, not hatred.*"

He continued———

If you really are involved with somebody, if they get under your skin, if they bother you, if they irritate you, it's *a connection,* even though it's a negative connection.

The problem with the scene as you played it is that you made them both dislike each other. That's not what the story is about.

The story is about two people who are crazy in love with each other, who just can't get along. That's where the root of the basic joke lies. The joke lies in *incompatibility.*

Now incompatibility doesn't mean two people aren't nuts about each other. They could be absolutely insane about each other but they're *incompatible!* Whatever the hell one says, causes disturbance in the other. You understand? Everything that you try to do leads to dissension. But if you weren't getting a bang out of the arguments, *they would not continue.*

So your problem is how to argue interestingly, with a lot of variety, for three acts?

And how to physicalize it all.

"Where are you in the story?" Scofield asked.

Sarah said "He goes to the hospital and I never show up."

"It's the end of act one?" Scofield asked.

"Right," Sarah said.

"He gets rushed to the hospital and they think it's a heart attack. It turns out it's indigestion," Scofield said. ". . . And now you go into the next part of it; you're home again."

"Right."

"Okay." Scofield held his look————

Now you're in act one. All right in act one, you haven't reached the point yet where you've been breaking furniture or hitting each other on the head, right? You've only reached the point of violence where you shove him off the bed. That's only the beginning.

Later it gets to where you throw things at each other. Where you wreck the house. Right? You threaten each other, right?

And the audience is sitting there saying, vicariously, boy would I love to do that. Would I . . . I get so pissed off at my wife that I would love to have the freedom to do that, except God knows it would cost a lot of money. I mean you could wind up with a divorce, and lawyers, . . . and big . . . trouble; and then worst of all, you could *lose* the other person, who you *need* very much. The idea being that for there to be a murderer, you need a murderee. If you have a masochist, you need a sadist. It's got to be a partnership.

Whatever he says to you, Sarah, causes you to get disturbed.

Now, if somebody could sit the two of you down and say, 'How do you feel about her?' you would have to admit that you're crazy about her, Jack; you need her.

Somebody once said that *the most important thing in life is to have a worthy antagonist.*

If you don't have a worthy antagonist, you don't have spice in your life. You've got to have somebody you can't stand; it's very essential. It keeps your vibes going. If everything is all goddamn peaceful it's like death. But if you can't stand somebody . . . I have *Cinjun Khan Smythe.* As soon as I see him, he bothers me. The minute I see his picture, he irritates me. He disturbs me. Drives me crazy. So this is politically a very happy time for me. When it's all nice and groovy, there's no excitement, you understand?

Okay.

Now, for that to work you have to play the basic joke, which is . . .

Both of you are trying to get along. You are *trying . . . to . . . make it work,* you follow?

Sarah, when you say I want a divorce, it's convince me to *not* get a divorce. 'You need me. Don't be such a drip.' She tries to be good to him.

Her emotion is guilt, because she has had secret longings that he were gone. But if he died, you'd grieve like crazy. You'd be the biggest mourner at the funeral. You understand what I'm getting at?

There are people you can't stand who you are terribly *involved* with. Her objective is: To not have an argument. His is: To get an explanation. What's wrong? Why doesn't our marriage work. She can't give you an explanation. You're as much wrong with the marriage as she is.

Pick emotions that will irritate each other.

Sarah, your emotion is guilt. He was in the hospital, right, and he was supposed to be deathly ill, and it turns out he only had indigestion.

But, Sarah, you behaved terribly—you were awful! You were *glad* he was suffering. You have to be pleased at the thought that he was dead.

In other words, he deserves the suffering because he doesn't love you enough to forgive your faults, and to stop arguing. Okay?

And what emotion can you choose for *him?* His emotion is fear. 'If she doesn't love me, I'm lost. Because she's the one person in the world I need to have love me.' He's in constant torment.

She keeps saying to herself, *to not have a quarrel, to not have a quarrel, to not have a quarrel.* Try to get along. Put an ice pack on his head. Make it better but nothing can make it better.

They're *Odd Bedfellows.* They should not be in the same bed together. Tuck him in, put the blanket over him. Make him comfortable. Be a nurse. Adjust his pillows.

And him—You like the attention.

Now her—switch pillows; you want the pillow for yourself. Don't hold his head, let his head fall."

*Bang!* His head hits the board—

"That's it," Scofield said.

"That's two people who shouldn't be together.

"Climb into bed right over him, step on him a little.

"Pull the blanket over yourself, so he's left with no blanket. That's an incompatible marriage.

"He says, *'What's going on?'* Now she gets out of the bed. Pace. Be much more disturbed. Your guilt is overwhelming. You can't sleep. You can't rest. You're always on the edge of a quarrel. Pick up the chair, slam it down. Tell yourself to not quarrel. Now sit down.

"Now, Jack, watch every sign of her behavior. Does she love me, doesn't she love me? Why is she mad at me, what did I do?

"Okay, I'll give you another for instance . . . go to where you're in the bathroom . . ." Scofield said.

It's morning, they're standing at the bathroom sink, both holding their gaze on the mirror. They're brushing their teeth and fighting for the spout.

"He wants control of the sink," Scofield says. "She wants control. Shove each other a little."

They do. Then, next, he's shaving in front of the mirror. She's putting on her make-up.

"Get in her way with your shaving."

He does.

"Now be disturbed. Cut yourself shaving."

Jack does.

"No!" Scoield said. "A man who cuts his nose is not funny. Accidentally cut your throat! She enjoys that."

They turn back to the mirror.

"She can't see. Get to the mirror by climbing over his back!"

She climbs onto his back and continues putting on make-up.

He throws her off.

"He stands there. Puffs himself up. How does she like that?"

"Now go to the next part where Jack is back in the bedroom . . .

"She locks him out of the bathroom, and tells him she wants a divorce through the door.

"He's thrown from fear into hysteria.

"He shouts through the door. She comes out, knocks him over, when the door swings open. She marches right over him to get dressed.

"Go to the next encounter. They both start getting dressed. They head in opposite directions. They collide. He finally lifts her up—out of his way.

"They continue the arguments.

"Okay, I'll give you another for instance . . . We see, the marriage bed is right in the middle and no one's in it.

"They're speaking. She grabs a pillow off the bed. She punches the pillow. It's 'him.'

"While she talks, she punches 'him.'

"*Pow!* She belts the pillow." Scofield says. "Now go to where she says she wants to smash his face in."

Sarah says, *"When I look at you, when I see you, lately, I want to smash your face in."*

Jack says, *"You want to smash my face? Go ahead, smash my face in. Come on, smash my face in."*

"She belts him," Scofield says.

*Pow!* She punches him. He goes flying. He meets the floor.

He opens his eyes. He blacked out for a second there, but he's okay now, it was nothing. He puts his jaw back on his face. And he's back in top form. He jumps up—Springs up. *Boing!*

He says, *"How would you like to try that again—smarty pants—"*

*Bam!* She belts him. Apparently she would.

He goes down. The carpet thuds. He dances cheek to cheek with the floor for the second time. Only this time, it's not so easy for him to get up—She made sure she meant it this time. But, up he goes.

He gets to his feet, barely but squarely. And now, they're ready to face off—'Into the next round, dear?'—What do you say, shall we dance?

"That's two people who love fighting!" Scofield said.

"Now you've shown this couple to us. That's an incompatible couple. And that's two people who love fighting. They're madly in love with each other. They need each other. Two people who love fighting—*The most important thing in life is to have a worthy antagonist.* That's the whole point of it. You need someone to keep your vibes going."

Miles was in the audience, watching. Observing with eyes that missed nothing.

Out beyond the amphitheater, high on the hill, the trees stood. And moved in the wind. They did not say a word. There was only the wind. The *winding* wind of time. Moving through a night passage. Through a beautiful spring evening.

# The Lay of the Land
*The Lightvision, the Netways, the Syndicates, and the Pulsing Newsfeeds*

"CROSSING OVER IN STYLE, how do you do it?" Miles said.

He sat in The Caveman's Grotto and Grill, directing his attention to Scofield Morefield.

"A drifter, *off to the see the world*—how should he do it, my huckleberry friend?" Miles said.

"If a dream maker is going off to see the world, where should he go? There's an awful lot of world to see out there—to what end should the dream-maker drift?

"How do you get to *Dreamsville?* How do you get to the *Pleasuredome?*"

*"The three great lessons of the Sound Chaser* are: the story, the attitude, and the audience," Miles said.

He continued. "We've done the story—the story of opposites.

"The attitude—the attitude of being you. The attitude is you.

"The third great lesson—is the audience.

"What's the lesson of the audience?" Miles said

"That one is the question-and-answer game," Scofield said.

"How does that go?" Miles said.

"You find the questions that are out there. You find the questions that lead to trouble—Trouble is our business—And then you give them a new answer to the troubles that are out there," Scofield said. "You find the questions hidden in the world. And couple them with opposite answers— It's a game of opposites again."

"Why are there three lessons?"

"Opposites," Scofield said.

"How is three an opposite?"

"Three is the dimensionality of space—and *Sound Chasers* work in the natural way. Pick some sticks off the ground. Turn them in *opposite* directions. You can only get to three *opposites*—high, wide, and deep.

"High—is the story.

"Wide—is the attitude.

"Deep—is the answer," Scofield said.

Miles looked at him. "There's a war craze in the world," Miles said.

"What's the answer?"

"The answer is easy," Scofield said.

"Love—is the answer," Miles said.

"Love is the answer," Scofield echoed him. "You've heard this one before. Everyone has—It's an easy opposite."

"How is this hard?" Miles said.

"The hard part is—the question. Finding the question can take forever. Most people don't question. They just walk thru life."

"People question all the time," Miles said.

"Not the deep questioning—Not the deep *quest*-ing of life to find awareness beyond themselves—Normal people don't think about these things—They don't go after the rainbow's end raging around the bend, my huckleberry friend."

"Where are the questions hiding?" Miles said.

"In plain sight. Where else would they be hiding? The questions are there in front of us—Most of us don't see them. Most of us will never see them."

"Why?"

"That's a good question—Find me an answer. That's how the game goes."

Miles laughed. "Ha! This is great. I love this lesson."

"Here's the question—How do you *cross over in style?* How do you get to *Dreamsville?*" Miles said. "I come back to it—

"A drifter, *off to the see the world*—how should he do it?

"There's an awful lot of world to see.

"To what end should the dream-maker drift?"

"Let's talk, about what a nice, young man has to do, to break on thru," Miles said to Scofield.

From in to out, we go; how do you step on out? . . . While summer is in the world.

How do you get past the gate to the stage? . . . While you still have the strength to do it.

*The Gates of Wealth;* the portal to *Eden Estates.* And the problem of how to break on thru.

He was speaking to Scofield of the ways and byways to:

*The Light of the World.*

Of *The Light,* haunting, spreading out through the canyons of this vast forest all.

Outside, across the vast realm, the people gathered.

Where did they gather but before the *light*tanks. For surely they were the light of the world. Where did they gather but before the *light*vision, for surely it was the light of the world. All the people. All the people in this whole wide world.

The image of the great society assaulted Miles. And the force shaping its contours. *The great gravitational pull of society.*

The gravitational pull of society, forced the form.

You could see it. *The force* pulled all things to the center and built a form moving outward.

The gravitational pull of society pulled all things to the center; all people to the center. All the ways, and doings, of all the people in the world that peopled, were pulled to the gravitational core, to *Eden Estates,* and in the core of *Eden Estates,* was the *light*vision.

The *light*vision cast its formlight upon the day.

Its great and mighty spotlight.

Everybody wanted to be in the center, and everybody wanted to be on the *light*vision.

Miles broke further into this dream of: the *light*vision. And turned his thoughts to the *newsfeeds.* . . . Lately his thoughts had turned to the newsfeeds and the newsrooms that lay under and behind, . . . in back of the *light*vision. Rooms full of newspeople, peopling the power stations.

At Miles's side, a raging thought. A clown and a strange face, along the wall of all time. . . . In the night, haunting Miles. . . . Miles, wishing he were closer to the answer—He had to get there—He would wish and will his way there. Make his way there at all costs. No matter who rose to stop him.

How could he get onto the *light*vision, for surely that was the light of the world?

The *light*vision was the *Pleasuredome* of *Eden Estates;* the heart and soul of the world-striding *Federation.* All roads led to the *light*vision; it was the times. It was everything.

And in the center ring, standing in the spotlight, *The Star of the Show*— "Ladies and Gentleman, let's give him a warm welcome; please give a nice, big hand to:

"*Cinjun Khan S'mythe.*"

Cheers!

Cheers, and people.

People and portals.

Portals and *The Gates of Wealth.*

Outside and all around, *The Moneyflow Mountains.*

Screaming winds. *The Wilderness of the Moneyflow Mountain Range.*

Inside ... *The Garden Party.*

Spreading outside and beyond, lay the canyons of the *All.*

And out there the people wanting, wanting, wanting. . . . Demanding in dark streets where time had died, . . . demanding raw, full existence.

Singing, 'How do I get to the *Pleasuredome?*' 'How do I get to the *Pleasuredome?*' 'How do I get to the *Pleasuredome?*'

*The gravitational pull urged all things to the center,* Miles thought. For in the center, was a great party! . . . For some special people. And it was very hard to get into the party. The special people didn't want you there; the world was their palace, and you were there to do the yard work, that was all. No partying for you.

Now, when you got to the spotlight, well, they had a champion standing there to meet you, Cinjun Khan Smythe. With a charming smile.

The look in Miles's eyes—of *Tygers* crouched in jungles—spoke of his thoughts.

The *light*vision cast the spotlight, which was the light of the world.

Cinjun stood in the spotlight, flare point of the lightank, which the *light*vision beamed to the world.

His power was great and beautiful to see, radiating, . . . people and money. And all the good works under the sun that money and people could force into *your* world.

*The Moneyflow,* shifted and slipped, . . . assaulted Miles, . . . it was what fueled the *light*vision and the newsfeeds.

Moneyflow, shook Miles's thoughts and took him into quick sensation.

*Money was an idea, abstract—money was a great structured symbol for balancing and healing and growing closer.*

It was the total structure that dazzled you to death.

The way it moved—like a terrific, fearsome hurricane force making landfall and bringing in vast, towering ocean surges. Scattering. Spreading across the land. Rampaging. Recasting the Earth. Smashing. Trampling. Changing the shape of the world.

Money flowing. Money forming a mountain. Up and up, . . . the mountain would go. And then another mountain. And another. And another. Rising. Rising. Money forming shapes in the void, a landscape, and mighty waters, mighty rapids.

In the distant void, in the void, a *Cash Flow.*

In the void, the *talents* of gold flowed in streams. The cash and wealth of nations flowed. The soostones, the gems.

And there was a red flow. The talents of red flowed.

And there was a hunter—leading other hunters—traveling along the amber plains.

Amid the purple sage, the hunters attacked. There was a marauding and slaughter of vestal virgins under the shining blue sky.

The coin of realms, the silvered streaks of color, papers and wafers and stacks and stones, the colored, streaming *talents* that amounted to the wealth of the world.

And the stream flowed. The *talents* streamed. The stream flowed.

Like snow drifting. Like sand duning. It formed a mountain. High and mighty.

And at the peak of the mountain, stood Cinjun Khan Smythe. And he spoke to the assembled host in crimson words.

Bringing almost a sexual release.

*Freeing the Moneyflow.*

Allowing it to gush. To shoot. Allowing the *Moneyflow* to ejaculate. To give it to *Mother Earth* in a big way. With penetrating force.

Oh, what his heart has heard!

Good people—coming out of his being—witness the glory of tomorrow and: *A Beautiful Sermon on the Mount.*

Witness, in the wild breeze . . . *Moneyflow,* in orgasm. *Moneyflow,* realized.

"He does wonders with his menu," Miles said. "He serves all of the classics. *'This is the promised land.' 'We are the chosen people.' 'Home, home on the range.'*"

"If you watch him," Scofield said. "You see a man that knows how to hit all of the marks. He knows that the key is to get on the newfeeds. The newsfeeds fuel the news programs."

*Ah, the Pulsing Newsfeeds. And the central newsfeed.*

## The Wayfinder

*"The Wayfinder* is the pulse you want to reach," Scofield said. "That's the master of the newsfeeds. That's the giant."

It was the main line of the great *All.*

In the great society of the world-striding *Federation,* the great networks all operated off the grace of their newsfeeds. Which in turn looked for enlightenment to *The Great, Majestic Feed—The Wayfinder.* In shifts throughout the day, *the Rundowns,* came forth. Transmitted from the central cores of the *Wayfinder,* they instructed each station and outlet as to how it should wage the battles of the day, and where *The Wayfinder* was going with the day. Where it shone its light, revealed what was the *'news of record'* for that day. The rest, was the filler business. Filling the patches, and holes, and open spaces.

The core of cores, the great central body and central news line was *The Wayfinder.*

Even the man in *The Whyte Stone House Under the Big Sky* trembled before its might.

A channel into that, was what Miles needed.

The truth was plain to see. What Miles needed was a channel into that great body.

That was the great colossus that had to be ridden.

Oh, to enter the ring and ride the great bull.

This was what Miles proposed doing. He thought it would be fun.

And why not. He had all the time in the world. What was there to stop him? Until his intent was discovered. Until the bull noticed him. Then the weather forecaster predicted clouds of pain, and beatings. Majestic, soaring beatings.

*The Netways,* assaulted Miles next, in the hour of his need, the world trembling around him.

*The Netways* springing outward from *The Wayfinder,* depending on the core.

All roads led to Rome, and this was the Rome that ruled the world.

*The 'Roman' Feed. The Grand Feed.*

Miles would get to it from a neighboring less sheltered newsfeed, perhaps that was the way on.

*Newsfeeds, News Organizations, News Syndicates.*

*The Post Syndicate.*

*The Times Syndicate.*

These were the forms and bodies that played across his mind.

And *The Light of the World.*

For where did they gather, but before the *light*vision.

Its sound and fury, many a times signifying nothing. Yet—here and there—emerged truth and purpose, the form and pressure of the times!

Beaming truth and purpose, and emerging there, the form and pressure of the times.

The *light*tank, surely it was the light of the world, the motion of the field.

The gravitational pull of society assaulted Miles's thoughts.

"How do I get to the *light*vision party?"—This was the question for Miles.

The gravitational pull of society—everybody wanted to be in the center.

"How do you get to the center? How do you take center stage?"

## The Golden Gods Riff

Scofield drew a breath. "They go through *Golden Gods,*" Scofield said, "Their current golden god is *Cinjun Smythe.* And their current magic operation is *House Crimson.*

"They always have to have a flavor of the month and an enemy of the month.

"A flavor of the season, and an enemy of the season.

"The flavor this season is: Cinjun Smythe. The enemy this season: is *you and you and you*—all the people that do not go along with the *Cinjun Smythe Group Thinking Machine.*

"*The Cinjun Smythe Think Tank.* You have to join it; because if you don't, you reveal yourself to be an ally of the great enemy.

"The *light*vision eats; it eats waves. It always needs a *new* wave, a *new* age, a *new* thing. They call it news, right? To keep the *light*vision going properly, you always need a *movement wave*, a *question-and-answer wave,* and an *enemy wave. The Golden God* riding the movement wave right now is Cinjun Smythe.

"They need the *Star of the Season,* who gives you the *Movement of the Season.* And the *Star*—to make him interesting—is always fighting the *Enemy of the Season.* Presently it's Cinjun Smythe and House Crimson fighting . . . what? What is the great evil?—You and you and you, because you're not part of them."

Miles spoke, almost to himself: ". . . To get onto the newsfeeds . . . you have to be dressed for the party."

"And what do you wear?" Scofield said.

"Money." Miles stayed the course, pushing further along the path. "So the question is, what do I have that is stronger than money?—"

Miles directed his attention outward, to take in the world. To take the world into his grasp. The whole, wide world. And what he would give the world.

"*Energy,*" Miles said. "I'll give them an energy story. I'll give them a *fire story* and a *fire book of stories.*" He slapped the wall. "An *energy wave*—I'll give them a *love wave.*"

Scofield laughed—Hell, he had to laugh at that one—*"A love wave."* He looked at Miles. "Tighten up your act. And do it. Give them a love wave."

*Energy*—You fire up the great engine. Step back. And listen to the engine hum. And you take it into the danger lurking all around, the danger to be found, the danger everywhere within *The Soft Parade.*

Miles was on his way.

Off Miles would go, with his energy.

Miles was on his way.

To a dark encounter. To a place . . . where waited Cinjun Smythe, . . . with his *death gift* . . . To a place where waited Cinjun Smythe, . . . ready to give Miles the gift that would absolutely last forever.

# On the Air

THE GATEKEEPER.

News director Ripkin Kabob walked a young businessman around his newsroom.

"The wisdom of the common man," Ripkin said.

"Hah," his listener laughed at the very thought.

"Play to that and see where you end up!" Ripkin said.

"That'd be a fine business," the listening businessman said.

"The average man is a dimwit," Ripkin said. "That's not your audience in the news business."

"Who's your audience?"

"I'll tell you who your audience is. Picture a ten-year old boy. Now picture a ten-year old girl. Write for them. That's your news audience. And give them good pictures. They like picture stories."

"Good pictures win out over substance every time," the man said.

"It's not even a contest," Ripkin said. "Will people ever change? We don't know," Ripkin declared.

"Hmm," his listener said, "yes, we don't know if people will ever change."

"What will become of it all?" Ripkin said.

"That's a tough one," the listener said.

"That's the mystic," Ripkin said. "Life is mystical. But we're used to it."

"Hmm," his listener responded.

"What can we do?" Ripkin said.

"We're in the news busines," the man said. "We can do what we can do," he added.

"Listen here, this is where you take your stand," Ripkin said. "Talk to *the level of the people*. Talk at the level they want to know. . . . The evening comes . . . they turn on the news program . . . you give them the attack picture. Pictures and attacks." Ripkin echoed Cinjun Smythe.

"Pictures and attacks," the listening businessman said. "That's how you lay out a news story for them."

"We have to bring people into reality. We have to draw their attention," Ripkin said.

"And bring them into reality?" the listener asked.

Ripkin looked at him. Was this real, he wondered.

"The reality picture is an attack picture," Ripkin said. "Pictures and attacks—we're showing people what's out there. In the great 'out there.'"

"That's the outside," the man said.

"That's the outside," said Ripkin. "So many roads out there. Show them the attack pictures along the roads of life."

"We're showing them horizons," the man said.

"Horizons?" Ripkin asked. "Yes, horizons. We're showing them life, and what lies, for them, in the life ahead."

"And then we put it on the air," the man said.

Ripkin clapped his hands together with a loud smack. "And it's there for . . . *the people,*" Ripkin said.

The evening was coming. And soon another news program would come on the air to open wide its views of the world—its views set in simple attack pictures.

Its views told to a ten-year old boy, and a ten-year old girl.

The truth glided in strange flight in this violent, brutal world . . . when the evening came over the world.

# The Crosstalk Show

CINJUN SMYTHE WAS on a program.

The anchor said, *"Tell us about House Crimson."*

"Well, people are afraid of the world." Cinjun spoke with charm and a strange elegance. "We're showing them we can take hold of the world."

"We really need to take a look at a reality revolution.

"Let's take a look at reality."

"I want everyone out there to take a look at reality."

*He was running on reality!*

"To see the future in ways others have not," Cinjun said.

"It's a new day, a new theater, a new age."

"We have to move from the old country to the new world.

"We have to shift the reality."

"We have to slingshot ourselves into the future."

"We're breaking apart reality illusions.

"It's about shifting your center. Shifting the 'Who are you?'"

"Your center lies in the new reality. 'Who are you?' lies in the modern reality.

"We're moving out of the *Ancient World*.

"The ancient reality.

"It's about reality and getting to a *higher plane of reality*.

"There is classical reality. But there is also modern reality.

"We have to send ourselves into the future. Into the future reality. To step into the warlord reality. The fight reality.

"The heightened state of reality."

*"You want to step out of the past?"* the anchor asked Cinjun.

"We call that old reality and this new reality," Cinjun said.

"Classic reality and modern reality.

"Old reality, new reality.

"Mirror reality.

"We cannot live in a mirror of the old."

"It's a new day," Cinjun said.

"We're entering a new theater.

"It's a new world.
"We're reality testing and reality shifting
"We're testing reality. Testing character and testing reality.
"We're testing for truth. Is this truth?
"Reality—is the fundamental 'what there is.'
"Let's look at the noble truths of reality."

You could see him, you could feel him, in the interview.
The great Cinjun Smythe.

"I'm taking people on spiritual journey—to modern reality. At the end, everyone will be real?" Cinjun said.
"You're not going to live outside your world. You're going to live in your world. You will be real."

Along the way would be *fighting*. And the *fight reality*.
He told them we had to move through the fight reality to get there. Moving from classical reality to modern reality, the difficulty lay in moving through the fight reality.
The dream at the end would be the modern reality.
The struggle was where the fight reality took us against the sidewinders and the sound chasers.
"We must be travelers and fighters," Cinjun had told them.

He was taking them on an *Answer Journey*.
He was answering questions: Who are you? What is this thing you're doing, this force?
What is the dream? Where is this going?
He was answering questions.
He was moving people on a journey.
Be centered in what you believe, in your principles.
Be centered. Be centered in reality.
Know who you are. Know where you're going.
"We are a people boldly united. Forming a perfect design," Cinjun had told them.

Cinjun felt it! It was time to cross the Rubicon and take Rome. The Federation needed him. The Royal Thunder God Emperor Cinjun Khan Smythe was a necessary step. In order for them all to grow.
This was the purpose of the foundation.

He was a man of matter and strength.

And it worked.

People ate it up and asked him for more.

He offered mission, and purpose.

Dark, but most people were not looking for light.

They had their *light*vision, and surely that was the light of the world.

And everywhere it featured, Cinjun Khan Smythe.

## Enemies Everywhere

Everywhere, enemies of the endless search.

Tricks, full of tricks. And bitter tears. You have to see your way.

And the way is enemies everywhere.

Push back, fight back, kill!

Kill softly, kill hard, kill quietly, kill truly, kill with a long sword. Kill your fears. And your bitter tears will turn sweet.

. . . with *meaning* and *peace war.*

Cinjun was making it clear, perfectly clear for the masses.

They were too comfortable. Fat on the riches of *Peace!* What about the enemies? What about them? Lying in wait.

Cinjun's selfish ways had disappeared with the realization of the new age. And its promises.

Hear that sound!

Glory! But also enemies all around!

The time has come, children.

My children, my women and my men.

Perhaps he would start an army of women.

Full-bosomed women with long hair, long legs.

It was something to consider.

He would have to spend some time with some beautiful women and explore what could be done with them.

Some possibilities immediately came to mind.

*Merrily, merrily, merrily, we roll along.*

*Life is but a dream,* Cinjun thought.

What does he hear?

About war and peace.

What does he hear?

About love and sex.

He was going to reap a hex of love, and he was going to war for peace.

Ah-hum!

He was man enough to take it where it had to go.

A force of ripe fighting women; it was fitting.

Women in riot gear.

He would have to remove unnecessary clothing.

And dress them with his hand.

## In a Dark Room

THREE MEN WERE STANDING on one side of the room. Cinjun was standing on the other side.

He stepped into their midst.

They surrounded him.

It was a test of Cinjun's will. He must prove to be invincible.

No assault must be allowed to get through.

*Press on. Move forward.* This was how Cinjun operated.

One man moved in. Cinjun dodged his blow and punched him in the jaw sending him flying.

Cinjun had no problem receiving their blows; he either blocked them or took the pain of any blows that got through.

He slowly obliterated the three men.

When he was finished, he kicked a body aside and stepped on another's chest.

Cinjun stood tall, and said, "Gentleman, tonight you have seen power. Go forth and tell the tale. Be not ashamed; what you've seen is beauty, with a fist."

# Dance the Night Away

MILES WAS SITTING with Scofield in the tavern.

Miles said, "I'm going after Cinjun Smythe."

"What?"

"I'm going to fight Cinjun Smythe."

Scofield said, "We're talking."

"You're talking, I'm planning." Miles said.

Miles looked Scofield in the eye.

*"It's time that the hunter became the hunted,"* Miles said. *"He's a great hunter. It's time he met a greater hunter."*

They left the tavern, and walked to Scofield's house.

*No more teaching, no more training—I'm ready to fight, only fight,* Miles thought. Warden, warden, warden! Won't you break your lock and key. Let this poor boy be.

They came to Scofield's door. Miles stopped and gazed at Scofield with a grin.

"Sco," Miles said, "have you noticed how beautiful the summer is this year?"

"I have," Scofield said.

"Now is a good time, for me to do it!" Miles said. "Now, is the time!"

Scofield held his look. "Why, because the trees are green, and the sky is blue?"

"No," Miles said, "because now I'm young."

Do not schedule a thing for him. He was on his way, and he would arrange his own meetings. Fine meetings that would call forth finer days.

"So tonight, I'll leave you where I found you Sco," Miles said.

Scofield looked at his front door, and Scofield grinned.

"Don't you have a dirty martini," Miles said, "and an urgent love affair you have to get back to?"

Scofield looked at him.

"While you're young, get on the *Wayfinder,*" Scofield said. "Go where the audience is waiting for you.... Get on the *Wayfinder.* ... Get on the bloody, piss-besotted goddamned *Wayfinder.* Do you hear me?"

Scofield continued.

"The Wayfinder—is a newsfeed.... And it's more," Scofield said. "So goddamn much more.... It's the home of the supreme being. The ancients used to feel the mountaintops were the homes of greater beings.... That's what we've come to today.... *The Wayfinder* is the biggest newsfeed. Today it's what passes for the home of the supreme being.

"That's the one you want to come to. That's the one to run to. That's the one. That's the place to sing your song—and sing your heart out. That's where you give it all you've got."

Miles said, "And it answers the other question I've had—The one that worried you so much when it came time for us to sing, '*Let's Start It All Over Again.*'"

"How to save your life?" Scofield said.

Miles smiled. "Yes, to save my life—Where can I do that?—After all, I would like to live through this experience—That's the problem—The escape. The turn at the end of this road—Where can the hunted turn on the hunter?—And live to tell about it?"

"Where the odds are even," Scofield said. "Where the powers are equal—On the *Wayfinder*. Get to the *Wayfinder*. Get your story on the *Wayfinder*. One story is as good as another there. The audience calls the shots in that place.... That's where you can find surprise turns.... Hell, no one knows how the turns will go there. It's a free for all. And a game of anything goes."

Scofield continued. "The story is everything there—And you have the best story."

"I have the story of the world," Miles said.

"Who's going to beat that story?" Scofield said.

"Hah! That's where the story wins. I have to get on the *Wayfinder*."

"If you do—that'll be something."

"That's the place to fight the fight."

"That's the place to fight," Scofield said. "There's no finer way to die and no finer way to win. If you win—you'll knock them all back. They'll be a long while killing that. It's hard to kill a goddamned *love wave*. Once they get started, they go forever—the gift that lasts forever."

"I like it."

"Give the audience the gift that'll last forever."

"And that's what the world needs the most of all things."

"Love," Scofield said.

"True love," Miles said.

"You're all set—to go drifting, my huckleberry friend. Write me when you get to the rainbow's end. . . . Hasta la vista, my friend," Scofield said.

"Hasta la vista, my friend," Miles said.

Miles leapt into the air, into the strange days, and the fortunes to be found, out over the moon, and a little beyond tomorrow.

Lovers of the stars, could watch his trails, lonely in their huts.

While Miles, well, he, was raising a smile.

Oh don't you know the truth of it, my huckleberry friend?—*While summer is in the world, you must seize it.*

And this happened to be the summer of his life.

Perhaps the summer for us all—All of us huckleberry friends—all of us off in the fields of life picking huckleberries together, crossing over in style, and here and there raising the smile.

All of us thinking about the world and what we're all after at the rainbow's end.

*Oh, there's such an awful lot of world to see, and so many place to go.*

So many places to find other huckleberry friends—while crossing over in style.

And somewhere out there—telling the biggest stories in the world—set amidst the futureflow—guiding the fields of the *light*vision—lay the *Wayfinder.*

And out there lay the *possibilities.* All of the world's possibilities.

And also out there—lay some talk of love. And some talk of a world reshaped and reforged by a *love wave.*

# The Inner Circle at House Crimson

IN CINJUN'S INNER CIRCLE, he presided at a horseshoe table. He was a kind of king, and his people were knights and barons of the realm.

"We need your time and energy," Cinjun said. "We need you *to put your sword on the table.*"

He walked around the seated group.

"We must purge the bad energy," Cinjun said. He turned to a tough, rugged man and looked him dead in the eye. "Rise."

Cinjun willed the man to step forward.

The man rose. Straightened himself with a great, tough kind of dignity. And then proudly and gladly brought himself down to a kneeling position before Cinjun.

The man said, *"Cinjun Smythe is the greatest man that has ever lived or ever shall live. . . . He is the best there ever was."*

Cinjun held his look.

"Are you ready to make your statement?" Cinjun asked. "Are you ready to make your *Oath of Kin?*"

"I am," the man said.

"Do you want it?" Cinjun asked. "Do you believe you want it?"

"I do," he said. "I believe in that which is before me."

He was braced to take his oath of kinship in reality. His oath of virtue and kin.

This was the *Inner Circle Reality Oath.*

The oath to the journey. The oath to the reality journey. To the fight reality.

The oath to the *Big Red One* and the *Force Red* forward arrow-force.

To the force red, the house crimson—and the big red one.

The big red centered one. The enlightened one in an awakened state. Cinjun Khan S'mythe.

Everything here, in this moment, was about giving yourself to the journey.

To hear the journey calling.

To set foot on the path.

To hurtle forward.

To touch reality.

To become part of the modern world.

Presently, the inner circle of young people stood gathered before a dais.

The rugged man took hold of a sword, planted its tip into the ground, propped it straight up, and clasped the handle with his hands. Then Cinjun surrounded the hands with his own hands.

"I promise," the man said, "on my faith that I will, in the future, be faithful and will observe my homage completely against all persons in good faith, and without deceit."

Now the man looked Cinjun in the eye and continued:

*"I will love what you love, I will hate what you hate.*
*"Your friends will be my friends, your enemies my enemies."*

Cinjun looked down at the man.

Cinjun turned to the others and scanned his gaze across them.

"You each . . . can learn from him . . . and the beauty . . . with which he took . . . his oath . . . of kin."

He turned back to the man.

He released the man's hands, and raised him to his feet.

Cinjun looked into the man's eyes.

And Cinjun softly said, "Welcome right honorable gentleman—to the modern world."

A royal thunder god emperor—needed people who held him in their heart. It was a handsome trait.

It was a message you had to applaud.

And the people around Cinjun and this man now did indeed applaud.

It was a moment that spoke of beautiful, mighty, lordly love within the walls of House Crimson.

# Rendezvous

MILES WAS PICKING Daphne up at her flat.

"Hello stranger," she said.

"What do you do for work?" he said.

"Karate," she said. "I'm practicing to be a husband beater. Are you interested in a partnership?—Where are we going?"

"A political fundraiser," Miles said.

"Will they let me make a speech? Why are we going?"

"My nemesis will be there."

"You have a nemesis. Very cool. You'll have to point him out to me. I have about ninety-six nemeses. We'll see who has the more fashionable nemesis."

And she walked on by.

"You're wild with the power, young lady. Wild as can be," Miles said, as she passed him by.

"You've got a little wilderness in you too, young man," Daphne said. "Shall we march off to an enchanting evening?" she said and continued walking away, onward, into great bounding distance.

# High Society and the Acrobats in the Ballroom

MILES ESCORTED Daphne to the gala. She saw Skyler, who was there with a beautiful woman, Mimi Sutton.

Skyler said, "Daphne, how are you?"

"Hello Skyler," Daphne said.

"Daphne, I'd like you to meet my *wife*, Mimi. Mimi, this is my *sister's friend* Daphne."

"Congratulations," Daphne said. "When did you marry?"

"A few days ago."

"Amazing," Daphne said.

"What have you been doing?" Skyler asked, as an accusation.

Daphne held herself still. "Thanks for asking," she said. "And you?"

*"House Crimson,"* Skyler said. "I'm sure you've heard about it . . . all over the place."

"Isn't that splendid?" Daphne said. "What is *House Crimson?*"

"We'd love to talk with you," Skyler said, "but we're here with *Cinjun Smythe*—I'm sure you understand. . . . It was great seeing you."

Daphne held herself still. She watched Skyler and Mimi move away, and through a great effort of will, she did not hit him.

In the great hall, the party attendees were gathered at tables listening to Cinjun Smythe who was astride the platform putting on a good show. A strong show. Filled with very powerful stuff.

"We need a greater America," Cinjun said.

"Everyone thinks the future is somewhere else. The future is here."

"We're part of the American story. Your story is my story. We share the same American story."

"We are the greater story of Greater America."

"We're all here in America, to experience the character of America."

"I'm here tonight to talk about rescue from danger. . . .

"I'm not part of the cheering section. I'm here to rescue people from danger.

"I'm here to talk . . . about the nature . . . of reality," Cinjun said. "We stand all square in the *Great American Reality Experience.*"

"We must lift the load into the air, the load that we call *America.*"

He fired up the mass of people, speaking at some length, introducing them to reality and to their world.

And to the new age.
He voyaged into the future.
All the while his heart stayed with them.
Then Cinjun stepped off the platform into the crowd of people.
A supporter said, "What a privilege to hear a man who will one day stand for us use words like sinner and repent."
Cinjun showed himself grateful, and moved into the thick of the crowd.

Presently, Cinjun found himself breaking into a spur-of-the-moment floor speech, before a small band of people, who were gathered in rapt attention in a circle around him.
The crowd of faces kept wearing a smile as he spoke.
*"America is the country of the endless frontier,"* Cinjun said with quaint intimacy to his small throng of devoted listeners.
"Of the big sky, . . . of manifest destiny. . . ."
How inspired he sounded—And Cinjun pressed his rhythm to greater heights.

"We are *the nation of the western frontier*—
"We live in *big sky country*—
"We are *the country of 'can do' enterprise*—
"We are *the nation of the big sky.*

"Unlimited resources,
"Opportunity for all,
"Ragged forms—
"Turned to replete riches.

"Ascent through courage,
"Mass-production scales,
"Nothing-to-fear hearts,
"All-will-be-well minds,

"Clear-eyed people,
"With scientific know-how,
"Working men and women,
"The envy of the world.

"Gung ho—

"And can do.
"One,
"And all.

"Oh, now—this is our history,
"And this is the place we form our bold vision—
"Oh, now—do you hear our history, in our voices!
"We live out here in the wilderness . . . in the *Big Sky Country.*"

Yes, thought Cinjun, it was a fine finish. A high.

He held himself silent.

In response to his performance, there now came: applause and cheers. The people were shaking with a sonic boom.

Cinjun was an efficient door-to-door politician. Always, he played for effect, always he was precise, and always he proved winningly effective.

Cinjun Khan Smythe was a golden god to the people he encountered. And, also—you couldn't help but notice—a man heartbreakingly handsome. Always, the girls cried, *"Come to my arms. Forevermore stay in my arms."* Always, the men, drawn in by his chiseled looks, felt themselves lured into a comfortable underling existence, felt his inner violence, felt themselves moved to cheers, and felt themselves become determined to join his assault force. Always it was the same, . . . the crowd ate him up.

Cinjun would fire them up, and then all too soon, with great measured charm, walk on by, careful to leave them feeling that he wished he could linger.

Always they gazed as he walked on by. Always, they saw his royal heading, *The Great Sunset*—to which, they each, then found themselves drawn with longing hearts.

Always, in this manner, Cinjun strode through the crowd. And the look—the look set deeply in his eyes—was the look of the thunder god marching to victories soon to be blessed with names. Yes, his godhood's soaring look was come upon the land. He allowed it to work its magic and allowed it to join with his song of sweet tomorrows. Oh, how sweet the promises he gave to every man and woman in the place, particularly to every women, and how sweet the future he held, lying for them softly there, just a little ways out over the moon and past tomorrow.

They each saw it, reflected in his eyes. And each reached for his thrilling promises.

Pulses quickened. The energy and the hearts in the place quickened.

Cinjun was determined to make sure that everything tonight would absolutely go his way. He would make this grand party an absolute victory.

Cinjun felt certain of his powers, felt he could glad-hand everybody in the place. And he just might. He decided he would. After all, he was here to save each one of these souls. He moved rapidly. He advanced on tomorrow. He grabbed everybody's hand. This moment in time was a monument to the way he operated all his days.

*He grabbed Miles's hand and shook it. Firmly.* In so doing, he was saying, 'I control you.'

"Good of you to come," Cinjun said. "Thanks for your support."

Abruptly, Cinjun stopped. Thunderstruck. He felt something disturb his mood suddenly. What was it? he wondered. Was he catching something in *Miles's eyes?*

Cinjun paused. Time died.

Something in Miles's face, his casting, his aura, his persona, something vibrated.

Cinjun was immediately thrown into a different key.

Cinjun realized that he had to assume a different manner than his usual manner, that he could not speak as he had spoken moments ago.

This was: strange sensation. And bounding force. Cinjun went on extreme alert.

Miles said, "Cinjun, I'm Miles Roark."

He looked at Miles—*Tygers* crouched in jungles in Miles's dark eyes.

"You say it as though I know that name," Cinjun said.

"The name is not important," Miles said. "You're selling happy endings. I'll give you something to talk about in a speech."

"Give it to me fast. I have to go," Cinjun said.

"In the whole history of mankind—and that has now included billions of lives—not one life has ended happily."

"Where do you get your research?"

"Would you be interested in looking at my research?" Miles said.

"No," Cinjun said.

"People are barbarians. That's my contention. I can prove it. Give me a piece of a paper and a pen. I'll show it to you: the proof, the facts, the findings. You can check my work. I'll lay out the case for you."

"Thanks for your suggestion. We have a lot of good talks coming up."

"I've got an idea for a talk. Can I give it to you?"

"Give it to me quick."

Cinjun recognized this. Here at this mighty party, amid these mighty engines, in this place of certain victory, Miles was throwing madness into the mix.

Now Miles said to Cinjun:

"How about giving a talk on *love?*"

"*On love?*"

"We live in a wild world. We live in a violent world. We live in a world that's trying to kill us every day. People are barbarians. People are savages—And nothing has changed in a 100,000 years.

"We're still those cave people. We still have the same minds. And we still have the same problems.

"Every day when we walk out of our caves in the morning, we may get eaten by *Tygers.*

"I'm a *Tyger*—Did you know that Cinjun?—Oh, *Tyger, Tyger,* burning bright, in the forests of the night—I'm your *Tyger,* Cinjun. And I'm here to introduce myself and tell you my story.

"The story I have for you is an old fire story. An old sound chaser story.

"You can use it in your act. Make it a talk—about the way of love.

"How about it?—*Love.*

"When you're in a fierce, brutal, strange and wicked world—of suffering, struggle, and confict—where every last scene is about a combat of wills—and of *tygers* crouched in dark jungles—how about talking to us about finding rhythm and blues, finding heart and soul, finding love and wonder."

Now Miles said to Cinjun, with all the charm and poise in the world: "Do a speech on love. I think you could be great. Make that your biggest speech—talk about love. . . . Teach our hearts how to smile. Talk to us about love."

Miles spoke with a look that said more than words could ever say—it was there, shimmering in his eyes, the look of love.

The look of love radiated from Miles's face—and in his eyes, there was the start of something, something that seemed . . . like it could go to forever.

Miles showered Cinjun with his look of love.

"So for your next talk: Love is the way, . . . until the sky falls down. How about it?" Miles said. "I can prove that one to you too. I'll show you my work. Then you can use it."

*Wouldn't that be lovely?*—Miles's look of love said.

"What would we do with love?" Cinjun said.

"Start *a love wave,*" Mile said. "A wave of peace, love and wonder across the national scene—*A love wave.*"

"Walk away," Cinjun said. "Walk away."

Miles stood there.

"Are you a *Sound Chaser?*" Cinjun said.

Miles looked at him.

He looked like a goddamn *Sound Chaser,* Cinjun thought.

"Roark, Miles Roark, is my name," Miles said. "And I come from the offices of Miles Roark International."

"Go chase something else," Cinjun said. "You're in the wrong room. Walk away."

Miles smiled. "If you were truly a *Thunder God,* you wouldn't be afraid of *Sound Chasers,*" Miles said.

"Thank you for the talk. Now walk away." Cinjun smiled charmingly. "I'm going to watch you walk away now."

Cinjun left it there.

There was something shocking about this man that Cinjun couldn't place. Miles seemed to have some kind of unexpressed ability to close down the town.

Cinjun held Miles in his look.

Miles didn't give the least bit of a damn. Miles held Cinjun with the look of love. And then, Miles, was raising the smile. All the while, looking at Cinjun, with eyes that missed nothing.

*Miles turned*—

*& Miles went away.*

With a smiling heart.

A heart full of love.

A heart so true.

Rich and dark and blue.

Singing of a *Pacifica Love Dream.*

And of the turning of a world.

Cinjun didn't like what he had seen—He had seen *Tygers* crouched in jungles in Miles's dark eyes. Cinjun knew it was crazy—why, it was madness—but he had suddenly caught raging glimpses of strong forces— horrible, deadly things—standing between himself and the moon of the forest city. Forces strong enough to defeat Cinjun. They, well they, had crouched in Miles's dark eyes.

It disturbed Cinjun all to hell. He was a long moment recovering.

Time passed . . . and then Cinjun moved away, . . . and greeted Skyler . . . who was standing with some people.

*Oh Cinjun.*

*One sad goodbye, doesn't mean we can't love again. Our love will last. You'll remain in my heart.*

As the strains of the love song slipped into the haunting past, Cinjun felt himself drawn into the present moment.

*An Old Rich Man* appeared before Cinjun, saying to him:

"Just stand there so, and let me *look* at you. Just *look* at him! Look at him! Ain't it just good to *look at him!* Ain't it now? Ain't he just a picture! Some call him a picture; I call him a *panorama!* That's what he is—an entire *panorama.*

"Oh, I am so glad to see you! Oh my soul, the sight of you is such a comfort to my eyes!"

This old man had come to this place, this evening, to line Cinjun's pockets with gold; to load Cinjun's war chest. He was one among a vast many who loved Cinjun so.

*Oh Cinjun.*

*One sad goodbye, doesn't mean we can't love again. Our love will last. You'll remain in my heart.*

The strains continued to haunt Cinjun as he moved deeper into his pure and true, and suddenly dark evening.

The world rippled around him—and outside the dark blue night spoke of a love wave.

And of *Sound Chasers* cast in madness.

And of:

*Tygers, Tygers, burning bright, in the forests of the night.*

## The Love Affair

MILES AND DAPHNE left the party.

He asked her about her history. "Skyler Malloy—how did you meet him?"

"Parachuting into enemy grounds, skiing on an alpine slope, then I saw him on a military trip in the desert. We got into a scrape in an Arabian bazaar," Daphne said.

And she continued. "We worked together to defeat the forces of evil. But he turned out to be a double agent. . . . He belongs to the dark side, and the dark arts. Stay away from him."

"I worked with him too," Miles said. "So you don't care for him, do you?"

"No more or less than I care for death, typhoons, tempests, tornadoes and earthquakes," Daphne said. "I got lucky a few years ago, and got a chance to belt him one in the jaw. I sure would like to give him another shot of my good swinging arm one day."

"Maybe your day will come," Miles said. "What did he do, to bring out your fist?"

"I don't remember." She thought back on it. " *'What a strong arm on that girl!'*—Skyler had said—I remember him saying that. . . . He learned that some girls do have a good pitching arm. It's nice when you can teach men about women. . . . Especially men like Skyler, about women, and about a woman's place in the world—And where a woman's fist is liable to go, . . . when his face is nearby."

She turned to Miles. "I have super-strength, did you know that?"

"That must come in handy."

"I'll show you." She flexed her arm. "Go ahead touch it."

He gently touched her arm. "Wow. That is an amazing arm."

"That muscle is like steel," she said. "Coiled steel. . . . Honed to perfection."

"To do what?" he said.

"Well, it's a man's world," she said. "And with men, a girl sometimes needs a little more than her wits."

"Men are that bad?" he said.

"Oh, you'd be surprised how *bad* some *bad men* can get?" She smiled. "Luckily I got early training from a very *good man* about what to do when you meet some *bad men* in the woods, on a dark and stormy night."

"From who," Miles said.

"From my daddy," she said. "My father mated with a *Tygress* to have me—He was a hell of a fighter. My mother liked that about him—He was a great lover, and he loved her truly."

"You don't say. That is a nice thing," Miles said.

"And don't you worry about a thing Miles," she said. "If any bad men attack us, I'll protect you."

"Well, now, I might be a fighter too," Miles said.

"Oh, is that so?" she said.

"Yes," he said. "My mother mated with a *Tyger* to have me—She taught me how to fight in the *Weirding Way* from a very early age. She was a killer. And a great lover. She loved my father very much."

"How cozy," she said. and turned to him—

"Raarrghh!" she said—And what a roar it was.

"You make every moment come alive," Miles said.

"I know!" she said. And she walked on by. . . . Now as she passed beyond him, she said with lips devil red, "All the stars that shine upon me, want to kiss me every night."

*I don't want them,* she thought, *I don't want the moon, don't want the sun . . . a little love will do.*

She wanted to turn winter into spring. Spring into summer. And keep a little summer forever. With a plain golden wedding ring.

The only thing she didn't want to let get away from her . . . was a little love.

They went to Daphne's apartment where they sat in her living room. She parted one of her veils to reveal one of the great secrets of her inner life—

"I have super strength!" she said.

"Yes, I've heard about that," said Miles.

"It's true," Daphne said. "You've beheld my arm and my fist. Do you want to see one of my great feats of strength?"

She cleared the table.

And set her arm into the starting position for *an arm-wrestling session.*

She sat there before him in an arm-wrestling position.

Miles smiled. He looked at her. And moved closer.

Now Miles grasped her arm.

And they wrestled.

They struggled mightily.

Miles prevailed.

And once the deed was done, Daphne walked away.

"I prove my point!" she said.

"You lost?" Miles said. And grinned.

"Oh, you're a sore loser," Daphne said.

"We arm-wrestled. I brought your arm down. I won. I remember that part of it. I brought your arm down. I won. I did."

"You can't; I have super strength," she said. "I'll prove it again."

And, . . . presently . . .

They grasped arms over the table and again locked wills. It was a ferocious battle. They started sweating.

Miles brought her arm down and won again.

She walked away.

Daphne said, "I won again."

Miles looked at her. "Are you going to stay with that story? I brought your arm down. I won."

"You can't; I have super strength."

Miles demonstrated on the table. "When I take this arm, grab your arm, overcome your arm, and bring it down to the table, I win. How can you deny it?"

"It's true," Daphne said. "If you could do something like that you would win. If you had anywhere near my strength you could."

She grabbed Miles's arm. "Go ahead prove it."

They battled again. They struggled like demons.

Daphne said, "See you can't bring me down."

Miles said, "You can't bring me down either."

She said, "Maybe I don't need to show off my super strength."

"Are you insane?"

At that moment, Miles relaxed his grip ever so slightly. That was all Daphne needed—She slammed his arm into the table—Slammed it so hard that it broke through the table—Knocking him out of his chair—And spilling him onto the carpeted floor.

She looked down at him on the floor.

She joined him on that carpeted floor, and said. "You're going to tell me again that you won?"

She met his eyes. "Do you know the key to victory?" she said.

"What?" he said.

"Take all the quit out of you—Intend to win," she said. "Then move in for the kill."

The night passed into darkest night. And they moved into her bedroom.

Now Miles was lying on top of Daphne. He kissed her.

He was passionate, she was curious. She observed him. That was all. Observed him.

He stopped. Gave her a rueful grin. He only did duets.

Miles and Daphne stepped out of the bedroom.

As Miles passed her, he said, "Thanks for the evening."

"I'm glad you enjoyed it," she said to his back.

Miles turned to her. "Tell me supergirl, what turns you on? What charges you up?"

"You're not my type. I like talking with you."

"What makes a guy your type?"

"Danger."

"Couldn't I be dangerous? You don't know me."

Daphne stood in the center of the room.

She told him, "Slap me!"

Miles stared at her.

She insisted, "Come on. Slap me!"

Miles stared at her.

"No. You're not dangerous." She had his full measure now.

She slapped Miles—*Whoosh! Slap!*

She was wild with the power, to make every moment come alive.

Wild with the power, she was young, and looking for a worthy opponent.

To make every moment come alive. Her specialty: explosions of feeling.

He did not move. She told him, "Go ahead slap me."

He grabbed one of her wrists, then the other. Brought them around to her back, while keeping her face to him.

He brought both wrists into one hand. He leaned her up against the wall. His mouth was practically touching her lips.

She felt his breath on her face, his body close to her.

Wild color lit up her face.

The silken moment went on forever.

Miles said, "I'll slap you on our second date.

"If I slapped you on our first date, we'd have nowhere to go.

"I'm neat, clean, shaved, and sober, and I don't care who knows it.

"I'm everything that a well-dressed young man should be. I'm dating you. Good night Daphne."

He left.

The gift he would give her, would last forever! But that change, would come further down the river.

# Seasonflow

SEASONFOW.

Seasonflow produced the waves of nothing that were the setting. And the movements of nature that emerged from the setting.

And the flowing of the world that peopled.

The actions of nature.

The duning, the sand duning. The mountains mountaining. The light lighting. The sky skying. The ocean oceaning. The stars shining on the world that peopled. And the people feeling the way.

Violent flow. Violenceflow.

Murderflow, moved across the face of the world.

And suddenly—abruptly—out of nowhere and out of nothing—posing great and sudden menace to the world order—what rose into eruption? *A Peace Craze.* Yikes!

Killing.

Murder.

Blood in the streets.

And now all might lose to *Peace. The Peace Craze* threatened the natural flow.

It was haunting. Who knew where the *Peace* might lead; what kind of chaos it might sow in a world that peopled. Hell, it might stop everything. It might stop absolutely everything. That was always the danger with *Peace.* It stilled the mighty rivers. *Peaceflow* was still and *Peaceflow* was deep.

The people girded up their loins and called for a savior. Who would save the world?

*Peace* might settle on the works of man—and then what? Who wanted to live in a world so troubled by *Peace,* so different, so horribly changed, so altered and warped from this world that peopled?

And there was more—the still more dangerous threat was the force that *Peace* brought into the world—beware the shadow of the craze—its shadow cast itself deep and wide—its shadow fell so soft—it produced the dark hellish shadow—the ancient evil seducer known only as *Love.* Now the people could allow much into the world but *Love* was out of the question. It was very hard to do business when you were suffering from love for your enemy.

The night fell upon the land.

Nightfall covered the realm. Night fell upon the realm, making all things vulnerable to *Love.* Softening hearts, lighting candles, opening bottles of wine, whispering sweet nothings. *Love* descended on the helpless world.

Help! they screamed. Help! We're drowning in love dreams!

*The Love Storm* tossed the tiny ship of the world that peopled. If not for the courage of the fearless few, the tiny ship would have been lost. All hope would have been abandoned to—*Love Hell.* . . . But now hope sang its cry.

The people girded up their loins—and cried out—into—the night—they searched out—they searched out—a strongman—Night so dark—where are you—come back—so dark—so dark—come back—oh strongman and let us feel the ease of strong empire.

Life was easy in a strong empire. In a world that empired.

Oh, strongman—return now to the people of the fair and strong.

And Cinjun Khan Smythe came upon the land. Bringing the Song of Unity . . . to lead them to a House Crimson.

The god emperor savior. The thunder god of their dreams. *Be not afraid, for I am with you*—He used this thought and shaped it into words; this being his greatest appeal. A sexy and strong appeal it was.

---

# Peace

---

THERE WAS A PEACE CRAZE in the nation. A love craze in the nation. And other such deadly dangers.

There were rogues and scoundrels who were deliberately taking steps toward *Peace!* And they didn't care who knew it.

---

# Peace . . . and Love . . .

---

THE PEACE CRAZE WAS STRONG. The Love Craze was strong. Cinjun felt it assaulting the nation. Who knew where such a craze might lead.

He girded his loins.

The people were sore afraid. They needed a god emperor to enter their dreams. A thunder god.

Cinjun looked all through the country, and tried to find a man who was more of a god emperor, more of a thunder god, than himself. And his fear grew great, deep and wide—No such man existed, but for him. No other man held the qualities. No other man was everything—only Cinjun was everything. And all would have to submit to everything.

Cinjun—well, he girded his loins.

Push and shove, might be necessary. Invasion and penetration might be necessary.

He was ready and practicing on some of the more beautiful young ladies within the mighty walls of House Crimson. Giving them the gift that would last forever.

Nothing happened.

The season crossed the world.

The sun traveled the sky.

The world stayed in its orbit. And the night sun continued to burn, an inferno in the void. Giving life and love and peace and the gift that would last forever.

He viewed the sun. The world was in his favorite moment of the day ... when the sun was crimson ... sending red into the world. The red was traveling across the forest city.

He felt nature; nature filled with purpose. Filled with crimson purpose.

And he bathed in possibilities. All the possibilities.

There was a peace craze in the nation. He turned his thoughts to this.

Some grew violent. Did things to their people. Made nature grow red in tooth and claw. It helped—to stop the dangerous thing that was threatening the nation.

*The Peace Craze* was taking the nation into its grip, but luckily there were some people who kept their wits about them in the face of threatening peace.

*The Love Craze* was wreaking havoc. Fortunately some stayed with the traditional way ... making nature grow red in tooth and claw. They were not seduceable. They were not the tramps and whores of love, and never would be. They maintained the ancient honorable way of nature red in tooth and claw.

In this way crimson purpose survived among the people of right and might. And held out hope for a bright future in which the country would be saved and taken into a House Crimson.

A savior rose among the people ... a thunder god in form and spirit and power ... and he was righteous among them. He was righteous among the men. And righteous among the women. Especially the women.

He gave them attention, and the gift that would last forever. He gave them Cinjun Khan Smythe. And he held no part of his body back from the women.

He gave them the bodily gift of the god emperor. He was Cinjun Khan Smythe. The most important man that lived, ever had lived or ever shall live.

And the women—many in number—said, 'Come to my arms. Forevermore stay in my arms.'

He did what he could for their need.

And he gave to them in a mighty way . . . often helping them to experience life change in satin beds among silk sheets. And flowing warmth. Taking them on a ride. Getting on the inside. Getting it on the inside.

He was the thunder god. And most giving of his godhead, of his godhood.

He was warm sensation. And he was warming them.

He was connection. And he was connecting with them.


*The Peace Craze* loosed itself in the world.

*We just have to hold society together until this peace craze dies down,* the wise men said. And they girded up their loins. And the people were sore afraid. And there was a great gnashing of teeth.

*The Peace Craze* crept into reaches of the forest society and exploded itself into being in the most unexpected places.


Soon some people who you might have thought were fine and good people turned out to be peace savages, love brutes, who threw aside all modern manners and joined the *Peace Craze.*

They threw aside noble anger and softened themselves to this deadly inferno of peace taking shape. *Peace* taking the changes. Taking over the life changes. Turning good and proper life changes to sordid affairs of peace. And love.


*The Love Craze* loosed itself in the world.

*We just have to hold it together until this love craze dies down,* the wise men said. And they girded up their loins. And the people were sore afraid. And there was a great gnashing of teeth.

*The Love Craze* crept into reaches of the forest society and exploded itself into being in the most unexpected places.

Soon there was even talk of love among assassins and worse yet—among pleasure seekers, sinners—Hell and damnation, was no one safe when love and peace reared its deadly blood ship on the high seas of good living?

And they girded up their loins. And hardened their hearts.

And called for a god emperor to come deliver them. A mighty god emperor who could stand with the people of might and right.

Cinjun Smythe happened to be available. And perfectly presentable. He was the perfect one. And the perfect one moved to seal his perfect destiny.

He would smite any who got crazy. He would deal with the wicked. And the wicked would get dead.

He would put the world in order. And get to any who chose to be crazy—Oh, to be crazy, was a sin. There could be no forgiving the sin of madness.

He would show no mercy. He would produce destiny. And they would get dead.

He would take them to the place beautiful—House Crimson.

He would carry the world that peopled out of orbit and take it to the place beautiful—to the promised realm?—a House Crimson.

He would save them from evil. And he would not be gentle to the evil.

Pity the evil. Cinjun Smythe was come. And the evil would be made nothing.

Cinjun Smythe thought much of evil. Evil filled his thoughts and gave him no rest.

He looked on all the works of evil. And became expert in evil. So that he might reap good with a mighty sword and a stout heart.

Good would be worth the murder.

Paradise would be worth the slaughter.

Paradise was a bloody business. Which he happened to be in.

Happiness for sale. This was his business.

Happiness for sale. Happiness that's fresh and bold. Happiness that's only several days old.

Who would like to sample his supply? Happiness for sale.

Happiness was bloody expensive to produce. This he knew.

He was producing loads and loads of happiness.

For purposes of mass production, he was raising money on the most massive scale in history.

True happiness broke sales records. The proof was in the revenues and receipts.

And this was why he was raising money. Filling a war chest that like some other-world fuel tank seemed incapable of topping off. The more money he put in it, the more there was to get for his war chest.

He raised loads and loads of money. Boatloads of money.

*Happiness for sale*—He ran a prosperous business.

He found it a prosperous business.

Perfect happiness for sale.

Who would like to sample his supply? How about you?—Might you be able to use some happiness? I'd like to show you some happiness.

His "sell" was particularly effective with women. His happiness operation worked wonders with them. He seemed to be hell with the women. . . . Maybe it had something to do with his good looks, his charming smile, his worldly manners. . . . Why you could go on . . . Cinjun Smythe was plainly and simply perfect. The most perfect man that lived, ever had lived, or ever shall live.

Ask him yourself, he'll tell you. He's perfect and loaded to bear with happiness.

Who could ask for anything more from a man? What else could there be out there other than the gifts Cinjun Smythe gave?—These gifts that could last forever.

In the weaving flow of the timeslip, *Happiness* made him strong.

The people made him strong.

Everything made him strong.

And every day made him stronger.

Every night made him happier, particularly the nights he spent helping women experience his happiness.

In this way he moved into his full destiny, which he carved one *day'night* across the *night'sun'sky*.

He carved his destiny and writ it large—as it is written so shall it be—

*Strongman for sale.*

New strongman for sale. A strongman that's fresh and bold, a strongman who would boldly go where no strongman had gone before.

New strongman for sale.

He was perfect. And moved perfectly to a perfect destiny, and everything was perfect around him.

What could possibly disturb his great destiny—nothing. He knew there was no man out there to equal him.

He was a god emperor. He felt his role in the course of human history. Accepted his responsibility to rule humanity. And to rule the world that peopled.

It was a wild world but he would make it tame.

He was a thunder god. And the thunder god would tame the world.

Cinjun Smythe was filled with such humble thoughts. They never left him. He carried his truth everywhere.

He filled the *All* with his truth. And saw everything through his *All*.

The *All* was his to command. And command it he would.

He would make the world . . . His violence would be absolute. He would beat "nothing" into form. And then he would beat the form into shapes that would suit his powerful destiny.

And he would beat any man out there who dared take him from his world beating and happiness ruling.

He was good. That which opposed him was evil.

He would destroy and murder evil. The thoughts filled his head and gave him no peace.

*Peace*—Ah—Cinjun's thoughts went to—the goddamn *Peace Craze* that was threatening the world. *The Peace Craze*—that Cinjun had to smash violently in order to save the world.

He had to take the world into true *Peace*—the kind of peace that came from bloody slaughter.

*The Peace* and *Paradise* you earned and gained through: murder.

The kind they had been searching for throughout all of history. True peace was elusive. But he was about to show them the way to it.

And so he raised his mighty blood sword and strode into the futureflow.

This was the way some people looked at Cinjun Smythe and how he operated—Cinjun saw it as far more beautiful.

Murder worked wonders. Beautiful wonders.

He was off to perform beautiful life-saving miraculous murders.

He had nothing to fear.

## Nothing Forming

A MEADOW OF *NOTHING*, in the mist.

A valley green with nothing.

Nothing was in the world. And nothing happened.

Nothing struck. Nothing happened.

The music in the night—faint—nothing. Nothing sang its song and produced nothing making nothing happen.

Nothing was new under the sun.

For a time . . . nothing filled the void . . . and then change came into the world . . .

It came out of nothing at all, you might say.

*The Nothing Daze* moved, and slipped into Miles Roark, producing an effect.

*Nothing Daze, all in my mind. Lately things just don't seem the same— Nothing Daze all in my brain, acting funny but I don't know why, excuse me while I kiss the sky.*

Nothing was happening, and happening in a big way.

And amid nothing, a *War Path*.

Cinjun carved a *War Path*.

He beat nothing into form, turned absolutely nothing into form—a beautiful *War Path*.

*Come see the view along the trail,* Cinjun Khan Smythe cried, *broken trail so long.*

Leading into distance, a distance that seemed about the size of forever. But probably went beyond.

Come see the *Violenceflow River*, the *Violenceflow Mountains* and all the great land of *Violence*.

The land of the fair and the brave and the stout and the noble, and Cinjun Khan Smythe.

# Cinjun on the War Path

CINJUN WAS ON THE *LIGHT*VISION.

"Let's bomb them into the Stone Age," Cinjun said.

"Take out the buildings. Take out everything. That's the only language they understand. *That's the only reality they understand.*"

Cinjun was rolling and rolling along. Sorting it all out for the good people. Putting everything into its right and proper place. He seemed unaware of danger to his designs.

But there was danger on the edge of town . . . Miles Roark.

That's where you found Miles, out there. . . . To get there, what you did was you rode the highway, to the end of the road, to the edge of the forest society, to the *Outskirts of the City.*

That's where he was. Just bring your gun, and you would be safe.

You went to the edge, all the damn way, out past everything.

To the outskirts of the city.

In a far recess—in the place Miles knew as home—Miles was watching the *light*vision fascinated, for surely it was the light of the world.

And he did so enjoy watching Cinjun on there. Speaking with such profound wisdom that you found it hard to contain your joy. At the fact that Cinjun Smythe lived in this world. Such a good guy.

Miles spoke to the *light,* and its flickering *Cinjun-bringing.*

"Cinjun, I'm amazed. Let's bomb them into the Stone Age. Wow! What an idea. Where do you go to get an idea like that? Where else has there ever been an idea like that?"

# The Sky God Calls for a Modern Debate

FURTHER IN THE TIMEFLOW—at a tavern, The Caveman's Grotto and Grill—Miles was watching Cinjun on the house *light*vision. As were others, for surely it was the light of the world.

Miles was standing beside a man, who was saying, "That Cinjun sure is a great thing to come along."

The patron had a head like unto a *hammerhead shark.*

Yes, he was standing beside a man, who had a head, oh, such a head—and a wisdom? Like unto a napkin.

The man had understanding, like unto a lowlife, like unto a gathering of stones.

"Hey, keep it down," Miles said. "Let me hear what the great man has to say. Let Cinjun be heard"

Cinjun had threatened to make a major announcement. Of earth-shaking importance. And now he moved to spring it on the world.

Cinjun moved into it, in a slow measured tone.

"I feel we are living in a very important time," Cinjun said. "And I feel we are coming into a very important moment. And this is why I have decided to do something revolutionary. It is time for me to step up, and start something altogether new.

"It's time for—*A Modern Debate*—" Cinjun said.

—The Hammerhead cut in—"The man makes the most sense of any man I ever heard!"

Miles tried to ignore him—but the Hammerhead was going to talk through Cinjun's words.

Miles turned.

"Hey, shush!" Miles said. "Give the singer some! Is that any way to behave while the thunder god is speaking?"

"How about I hammer your teeth into your nose?" the hammerhead man said. The hammerhead man was, possibly—*high strung*. All the signs were there.

On the *light*vision Cinjun said:

"—We must get into a debate of the *Big Questions*. I think we need it, which is why I'm calling for a series of debates in which we will look at the issues of the every man.

"A Modern Reality Debate—" Cinjun said "—not among politicians . . . but among the people on the street.

"Not insiders, we have to let the outsiders get into the ring. It's absolutely essential. I'm a come-from-nowhere guy, and a lot of people dismissed me. But I think I proved that sometimes the come-from-nowhere guy has the most important things to say. The most important questions to ask.

"What I'm saying is: Let's ask the *Big Questions*——

"Is this the country it should be?

"Do we have the society we need?

"Is the economy fit?

"Is the political system meeting the needs of the people?

"Most say we could do a lot better," Cinjun said.

"Yeaaaaahhhh!" Miles exploded. He talked to Cinjun, to the people in the place, to the sheltering sky above.

"I'm calling for—a *Modern Reality Debate!*" Cinjun declared.

People took Cinjun into their interest, and murmured *'A Reality Debate? A Reality Debate?'* A battle was come. A high time would be had by all.

*"A Reality Debate*—I love it," Miles roared. "That Cinjun S'mythe is such a beautiful man, what a beautiful thing to put into the world—a Reality Debate?" *Yes—it had rightness to it.*

"Yea-agh!" Miles shouted. And held back nothing. "Fortune favors the prepared mind," he said.

"A fight in the light show!" Cinjun said, on the *light*vision, speaking from his home in the City of Gold, with shelter and dream in his eyes. He was going to buy himself a mountain, and build a palace on its peak.

"A fight in the light show!" Miles said. Rolling it over in his mind. He liked it; the shape was pleasing to him.

"He's not talking about you," the Hammerhead said. "You're crazy, you know that?"

"You'll be happy to hear that I do know that," Miles said, "and Cinjun will be happy . . . to hear that he is talking about me . . . It will set his soul on fire."

*Nothing was what it seemed.*

But Miles saw a path to the *Flame.* He held his eyes on the path.

*Oh, the lightning in his eyes!* revealing *Tygers* crouched in jungles, in his dark eyes.

*The Night Sun* went on shining; the stars stayed in the sky; a river flowed; and a way of knowing formed a path of *'where it goes.'*

Maybe this was where it would go. To where a certain mountain touched the sky, to a place where there was a cold wind blowing.

*Ah, where this would go!*—No one knew—The people living alone in the city, would know a season of *Dreaming.* Where in the world would the dream go?

*Where it goes!* This was where Miles would drive it to. To where in the world the *Love* did go. To where in the world the *Dream* chose to hide.

# The Fix Is In

---

THE NIGHT SLIPPED into day . . .

At House Crimson, Cinjun and Skyler were meeting with their committee of advisors.

"Skyler," Cinjun said, "who can we get?"

"Yes, who can we get?" Skyler said.

"He must be a known," Cinjun said. "Mellons and lemons that's what I want to look at—Most battles are won or lost before the first shot is fired—He must be a good sell, but a lemon I can squeeze. Sidney, what are your thoughts?"

"We should go with an unknown," Sidney said. "An outsider."

"Sidney, stick a sandwich in your mouth, and shove it deep. Don't be daft, Sidney."

Cinjun broke his contact with Sidney and turned to the others.

"I want someone predictable," Cinjun said. "Someone who plays a straight game."

"We don't want a cowboy who wanders all over the range. That's the problem with outsiders—with goddamned sidewinders and Sound Chasers. They play a curved and warped game. We don't want that. He must play a straight game. And he must be a name."

"How about Floyd Pernell?" William said.

"Good reputation. Plays a straight game," Cinjun said. "Let's think of exciting choices like that."

William and Skyler nodded.

Cinjun held them in his look.

"I want more great ideas on how to give this the right feel—and the perfect ending," Cinjun said.

Now they saw where they were heading . . . All were now headed into the correct storm.

Into a coming sound storm of wonder and mystery—A modern storm, with a modern ending.

Into a landscape and a form of Cinjun's making. A storm filled with rich sensation and with lush, beautiful feelings . . . Yes, much would grow richly in the coming storm . . . It would be a storm that would open onto rich impressions, rich ways, and a rich future.

## A Modern Debate

He wanted a dialogue. He wanted to ask the *Big Questions.*
  To give them happy talk, strong talk, and a confident swagger.
  He wanted a debate forum.
  A rigorous debate A formal debate.
  To take us to a pure state.
  To take us to primitive inspiration packaged in modern design.
  Oh my, how exciting it would be.
  A future flow.
  An arena debate.
  A modern frontier debate.
  He was pursuing:
  A warlord forum. A red sonic.
  *A Big Generator.*
  "We have to slinghsot ourselves into the future," Cinjun said to them.
  "That's what this would be—a journey into the future.
  "I'm calling for a battle of the Big Questions," Cinjun said to them.
  *A Channelforce Debate—was come.*
  *A Pure Debate—was come.*
  A Ground-Level Debate.
  A Stone Debate.
  Ground-level voices . . .
  A street scene . . .
  Give your heart, your soul, your brains—The natives will not resist.
The natives will yield.
  Go out and talk.
  Talk to them every week.
  Give them a ground-level feel—for Heavens' sake.
  A Modern Debate.
  You are stripped bare. And the American public sees you for who you
are.
  This was about reshaping the times.
  A Ground-Level Debate.
  This was Big Red in Reality Valley.
  The Reality Debate.
  They were going to debate reality—*Real versus Unreal.*
  A Modern Reality Debate—Let's really see the modern world.
  The Roaring Reality Story—That's what we're looking for, he says.
  A reality war—To teach them reality—To fight the reality wars—

Are you real?
Step with us into formalized reality.
What everyone thinks is neat—for a reality.
A reality filled with answers—Welcome to *Answerland*—Have a look around. You'll like our answers. We have the finest answers in the world.
Join a faceless congregation—Everyone think it's real.
This is real.
The Reality Arena Debate.
The Rolling Reality Debate.
The Great Reality Debate.
The Roaring Reality Story—and the Modern Reality Debate!

Say, "I like it—*if it's what everyonee else thinks is real—for a reality.*"
Stylish imagery—a reality contrived, conspired, connected and combined to take me far away from here.
I like a reality that can take *me* far away from *me*.
That's where I'd like to be—in reality.
Who doesn't want to be part of what's real?

Come take off your clothes and swim naked in the waters—
Enjoy the feel of other naked bodies all around.
New kicks—
And new joys—
On moonlit nights.

Here was:
A great future—
A crimson future—

Here was:
Cinjun Khan S'mythe—
And . . .
The Modern Reality Debate.

# The Land of the Blind

AND NOW—THE DAY WAS SLIPPING. And now . . . slipping into night.
And now it was night. Dark, so dark. Cold, so cold.

Miles was in a darkened room somewhere.
He was standing in a night club, standing on the stage, . . . and everything around him was fading to black.
He stood in the spotlight, there in that place.
The place was called the *Mind Mill*.
It was a fun place, a night club, a very cool place to be.
*Come in and get your mind warped.* That was what you did in that room. A lot of great entertainers played that room.
They took to the stage, . . . stood in the light, . . . and amid the great fading-to-black expanse took the listeners on a journey.
Now Miles was going to take them into a mindbender—into his own brand of mindbending story.
Slowly he went into it, in slow careful strides, . . . with everything around him fading to black.
He was going to take them into a session of reality warping.

Here within this sheltering place, within this drinking hall—Miles felt his emotion building as he stood on this platform of this night-room. And he spoke to . . . this group of lively people.

"A man walked into the *Land of the Blind* ————" Miles said to these people, his voice ringing out.

"It was a nice place, a beautiful place—but a place high in the mountains, away from everywhere—and it was a place where nobody could see—a Land of the Blind—They didn't even have a word for seeing. They were set apart from the rest of the world. He told them he could see, and described what it was like to see.
" *'Can I show you daylight?'*—was his desire. *'Can I show you the world?'* That was his game.
"He was a Sound Chaser. He spoke of things out there in the world; things that he had seen. Things he had seen that were sad; things he had seen that made him hurt so bad; things he had seen that made him feel so

fine.

"He was a Sound Chaser, this man————"

*Oh, the breeze blew back his hair as he spoke.* The highest power of seeing was to see the Sound Chase. Oh to see forever leading to forever leading to forever—the Sound Chase. Beyond and beyond and beyond. To see forever leading to forever leading to forever. Time slipping—The Sound Chase. The Wãoynde.

Cutting through; crossing through; sweeping through. At play in the fields of the Sound Chase.

His dreams were not empty. His dreams were filled with life. He was a madman, don't you know.

And the mad have a biting imagination that bites hard on their madness . . . The madman's dreams are filled . . . And this madman's dreams were filled. *Oh, the breeze blew back his hair as he spoke.*

"Now," Miles said, "this was the land without Sound Chasers. When this seeing man walked into the land of the blind, how could he speak of sound chasing?————"

And how could he speak to them of the highest power of seeing?

He told them what it was like to be a Sound Chaser—They couldn't see it.

He told them what it was like to see such a thing—They couldn't imagine seeing.

They couldn't even think the thought—The thought of seeing was beyond them.

What they decided was that he was crazy—that the Sound Chaser was absolutely insane.

He made their feelings hurt so bad, with his talk—*Oh, dear god, you couln't take it!*

This was the thing about it—He made it all hurt so bad. "Oh, don't make it hurt so bad," they cried out. When he spoke, he made it hurt so bad. "Oh, no! No! No-oo-ooo!"

No, no, no. No! No-ooo-oo! His talk made them hurt so bad. His talk made everything hurt so bad.

He told them what you saw when you were a Sound Chaser. He told them what the view was when you were a Sound Chaser. And they listened. For an instant. But then they shifted their stance—

*Crack him open!* They decided that this was the thing to do.

*Take him apart!* This was the thing to do.

*Break him apart!* This was the thing to do.

*Destroy danger,* became their concern. *Destroy danger.* And the Sound Chaser described something very dangerous—an emotion-filled insanity and a tearing apart of the entire order of their world. Oh, their ordered world where everything had fit their needs.

"Oh, no! No. No-oo-ooo!"

Hearts burned with it.

Silencing him became the step to honorable victory over evil. Silencing the talk of the Sound Chaser became a good thing. The most wonderful, marvelously good thing they could do.

"He's out of his mind," they said.

"If we take out his eyes," one said softly, "he'll be fine. Because then he'll be just like us."

And now they reached the great turning point, and the great truth lay before them.

"Yes," they felt it now, "that's what we must do. Why no one likes to do it, when it is not absolutely necessary. But we'll cut out his eyes; it's for his own good."

Why if they cut out his eyes, he would be fine. He would stop seeing; stop being a Sound Chaser, and then he would be just like them. And the madness would be over.

And now the Sound Chaser saw that not one of them knew what it was like to see. Not one of them could be made to see through their blindness.

And then . . . coming at him out of a black void, out of black seas . . . he saw danger! Violent, immense danger!—

They were coming to take out his eyes.

Well, the Sound Chaser had a problem here—you see, they were going to have to *kill him* before he would stop seeing what it was to be a Sound Chaser. The only way it would ever be over, would be by *killing him.* Only then would he stop seeing what it was to be a Sound Chaser.

And now the listeners, the saviors, and the wise men carefully, very carefully, but with extremely good feeling joyfully bounded across the expanse, and crossed through the *Gates of Delirium.*

"Okay," they decided, "let's kill him, to save him."

"Okay," the Sound Chaser decided, "I'll keep chasing sounds—Stop me—You can try—Try to kill me—But death won't end it—"

Abruptly—a heckler shouted at Miles from the crowd of people—

Mister Rin Tin Tin interrupted. Mister Rin Tin Tin knew a great many things; and he knew shit when he saw it—
"Oh who the fuck are you!" Mister Rin Tin Tin said. "Who the fuck are you to carry on like this! Who the fuck are you to talk such shit!" Mister Rin Tin Tin was an enlightened gentleman with lots of schooling and book-learning that he liked to parade. He was a spectacular wise man now.
"Who the fuck do you think you are!" Rin Tin Tin said.

Miles let the man shout, and run to a point, to the point of his great cascading wisdom.

"—Who the fuck are you? Who do you think you are to me? That's what I really want to know." Rin Tin Tin said—"Come on, tell me, who the fuck are you!"
And joining in now Rin Tin Tin's friend said to Miles on the stage—"You expect us to listen to this shit!"
And then another singer sang out at the same time—"Why should we listen to this shit!"
Miles smiled, and felt their reaction. He took it on the inside. And swept his gaze to Mister Rin Tin Tin.

"What is this about?" Rin Tin Tin said. "We've been listening. What is this?"
"It's about a question," Miles said. "The question is: When did this game get dangerous? If you're inside a game, how do you see outside of it?"
"You're telling us a question?" Rin Tin Tin said. "You're not here with a joke! It's not even a fucking riddle? You're here with a question!—You can't make a show out of questions."
"Why not?" Miles said.
And Miles smiled.
Some people in the club laughed. That sent Mr. Rin Tin Tin into a deeper rage. He was on a real tear now.
"Send somebody else on!—I don't care if it's Happy the Clown, so long

as it's not this guy—I have no idea why we're listening to this."

"There's only," Miles said, "one *'why'* that I can think of.

"It was over for you before it began. And I'm telling you about what it's like when it's only just begun—"

"Aw, shit!" Mister Rin Tin Tin said. "Will you quit it! We're here to have a good time—Not to listen to a goddamn fucking question."

"How about I put the question to you another way. Are you ready? Here it is . . . It's a deep question with a trick ending . . . You're living in a darkened room . . . *Are you living,*" Miles said, "*in the Land of the Blind?*"

Rin Tin Tin looked at Miles.

"It's a good question, isn't it?" Miles said.

Miles felt his pulse quicken. He was being pushed into a state that he did not want to enter. He knew he should not say what he said next. He couldn't stop himself.

"No, no effect. You don't care in the least, do you? But maybe you'll follow this . . . How about if I put the question to you a different way again?"

Now Miles pulled himself into a state of calm. He stood on the stage and spoke with total calm.

He spoke in a simple human tone. He was a human being talking to another human being.

He had failed and was pressing deeper into failure.

It was pulling him in, and he could not stop himself from wanting to go deeper. From wanting to save it somehow. To pull victory from disaster.

"Let's say I'm a doctor. And I see you. And I see that you have cancer. And it's destroying you. The cancer is killing you.

"Now if I talk to you about your nice eyes, and how nice your teeth look, but I don't tell you that you have a cancer that is destroying you—What am I doing? What kind of sounds am I making?—That's the question there: What am I doing? . . . That's a good question, isn't it?

"Now do you care? No, not in the least," Miles said

"The question is—How do you see inside the game? How do you get outside the game to see inside? How do you see what's really happening?

"You're living inside a game. . . .

"How do you know the game you're living in is not the Land of the Blind?" Miles said.

"How do I know anything?" said Rin Tin Tin. "How do I know that I exist?"

"I'm not sure you do. Prove it to me," Miles said.

The audience laughed. Rin Tin Tin didn't like that. *Who was winning this?*

"I can feel that I'm here," Rin Tin Tin said.

"How do you know they're your feelings? Maybe they belong to someone else. Maybe you just think they're yours."

Miles smiled.

The audience laughed.

Rin Tin Tin now put on an angry face.

Mile said, "Still think you can't make a show out of questions?"

They laughed again.

"Listen," Rin Tin Tin growled, "I know what world I live in—I'm a good goddamn Christian, and I don't like what you're saying!"

"Then forgive me," Miles said.

They laughed again.

Rin Tin Tin grew angrier.

"Seeing through the game," Miles said. "I'm talking about seeing through the game. There's only one way I know of doing that.

"It's by asking questions that run opposite to the game.

"I want people to question things.

"For example, ask yourself, *'What kind of show is this?'*"

That set them laughing.

"Ask yourself, *'Why am I talking to this guy on the stage?'*—I'll leave you with that question—For you it's a very good question."

They laughed. Thought about it. And laughed again.

"I'm going to join together with the night now. So long," Miles said.

"So long screwball!" the man said.

"So long Mister Whoever-You-Are," Miles said. He crossed the platform. And left the scene.

*Well, well, well, no one was going to steal that act from him—it amounted,* Miles thought, *to a fairly marvelous failure.* But learning came from such difficulties. He was close to something. And this thing could be made to work. He absolutely had to figure out how to do it. He would make it work.

And so Miles enjoyed this particular failing, for a very sensible reason. If you want to learn to ski, you don't just go down easy slopes. One of these days, Miles was going to ski down the face of a cliff, and he wanted to be ready.

This thing could be made to work, he felt certainty building in him. A force building, building to an explosion.

His next move would be stronger. And the move after that, stronger still.

There was a fire in his belly. He could sense it. And the fire was growing.

The only question was, what would he do when they came for him; when he collided with them. At that point, he would have to have enough might in him to win. Or he would get dead.

He stepped forward, and kept going.

Traveling. The Seeker moving into tomorrow. The Seeker hurtling into forever.

Probing. Seeking and hunting all the many means and tricks of *survival.*

Loading himself with all the might there was to find.

Acquiring every form of might that anybody in this place could ever find.

Hoping that his growing might would . . . maybe, just maybe . . . give him the soaring force . . . power enough to beat back the dangers, when they came. The dangers of this forest society, that were coming for him . . . The dangers that in time would work to end him.

He did not want his life to end beneath the force of this coming stone cold assault, he did not want his life to end badly.

He was picking up this *might* . . . this power—this thing streaming wild, wild as can be—this power that might, just might save him when he came to his encounter with *Cinjun Smythe.*

## Act Two

# Wild in the Wilderness

## The Wilderness

MILES WAS ON THE STAGE. His eyes were closed. The audience didn't know what to make of him. Miles was doing nothing immediate.

His voice was drifting . . . his eyes remained closed.

"People take a deep breath," Miles said. "And I'll try to do something good to your head.

"Listen, listen, listen people. Let's go back, way back, to stone and bronze. Back to, back to, back to————"

Miles felt an alerting sensation throughout his body.

He sensed the touch of an uncompleted thing, awakening, rising. Something crouched within him. It was like a coiled spring waiting for release.

He traveled deep within himself and found an area of crashing waves. He entered it and suddenly felt the flow all around him . . . and it was rising. It exploded in waves of red, orange and yellow.

He opened his eyes. And it came out of him. Radiating to the audience. He struck like fire.

He told the tale.

"A Young Lion walks into the wilderness————"

On the far hill, he sees *An Old Lion*.

Down below, *The Others*, listening.

And the Old Lion cries,

Clothed in the colors of old lies,

'We are all equal,' the Old Lion says.

'Justice is blind,' the Old Lion says.

'You have nothing to fear but fear itself,' the Old Lion says.

And the lies come down,

Like a warm rain,

On the ones below.

All the other lions saying, "Ah-hungh!"

Not one lion questioning.

The Old Lion draws a figure, . . . *outlines* how to *think* and *act.*

While . . . the Young Lion . . . in his lonely height . . . realizes that in back of this old lion's lies is a voice that whispers, *'Don't be yourself, be us. Become a part of us.'*

This is while in glowing features up front, the beautiful, charming Old Lion promises them everything, . . . every wish is there, waiting for his command.

He promises the moon and the stars, the sun and the sky, he promises everything . . . *Sunlight streaming in his hair.*

He promises everything they're dreaming of . . . *Sunlight streaming in his hair.*

Well, they have a lot of dreams, and he can make them all come true. He promises them anything they're dreaming of . . . *Sunlight streaming in his hair.*

He promises them everything.

Roll, roll, roll, *he fills their soul.*

'Hear my song,' he cries.

'Can you feel it, now—that spring is come?

'We're standing on the long lonely lie of freedom's shore, waiting. The first flashing of Eden Estates is striding in cool ascendance here before us. Can you feel it? It's time to emerge from wintery recess; it's time to live in the sun. A strange life. A bold life beneath a warm, glowing sun. A sun touched with red. A sun favoring Crimson. And a House bathing warm in Crimson possibility.'

At that moment, . . .

The Young Lion recognizes the true *danger* in the wilderness, sees its full form and pressure—*the Old Lion is his enemy.*

Oh, the mighty Soft Bull-Mud Parade has now begun. And you could listen to its mighty engines hum.


Miles said:

"The Old Lion is playing the 'In Group' trick. He's selling them on tribal thinking———"

'The wilderness is a dangerous place. To live here, we have to live together. We must make a group, we must make a tribe.'

It's a good thing. The danger is that it always goes too far. You always reach the same point, *'We have to tell The Story of Us.'*

And the story always ends up being: *We're great!*

Now, if we're an In Group, suddenly you need an Out Group. We have to feel we're right. For that we need people who are wrong.

Now here's the question, at which point did this game get dangerous?

At the bar, one drunk turned to another. "What the hell kind of act is this?"—

"Our tribe versus them," Miles said. "Our tribe is good. Their tribe is evil ————"

It always crosses the threshold into *The Bullyashat*.

*The Bullyashat* is a belief. It is the true belief, of *Us*. Of the In Group.

What would you have to do to set up a country run by group-think gurus? You would need *The Official Story*. They would all have to work off of the same script.

You would need *The Official Bull Mud Story*.

When the old lion comes to you, he comes to you as your friend.

He brings a bucket of mud. Hard, bitter mud. He presents it on a velvet cloth.

And he says, *"This is the finest, richest, and rarest mud in all the world."*

This is *The Official Bull Mud Story*, my friend.

Now to run the Bull Mud thru the changes, you do this: all along the way you drive people into a state of grace, a state of warming *We*-feeling, *The Bullyashat*. The *Bull Satori*—Satori is a state of enlightenment. A state of knowing, and feeling what you know to be *it*, to be the *All*. The *Bull Satori* is a state in which what you believe is total bull mud. It allows you to become a hippopotamus. And to feel this is the highest form of life you can attain.

It allows you to accept rubbish as knowledge. *Balderdash*. To accept Balderdash as the highest form of knowledge you can reach. Balderdash is a punchy, powerful mode of bull-mudding. Balderdash is the highest level of Bull Satori. Of Bull S'tori.

When the young bull meets the old bull in Eden Estates, that's what the old bull tells him, by way of advice—*The Bull S'tori*.

On the sidelines, two comedians rated Miles's show. They talked over each other's lines.

"What kind of act is this?—"

"—Lame—"

"—All the who's down in whoville are supposed to eat this up?—"

"—Not even one dick joke to help it along—"

"—Before you take on the world, learn to tell a decent dick joke—"

"—Alright, that's not your style. How about a pussy joke—"

"—You don't have to take it all on. A tit joke—"

"—Something—"

"—Where's the art in what he's doing?"

# The Platform

IN THE COMMITTEE ROOM OF HOUSE CRIMSON, Cinjun wrote his platform with a committee of people.

That was not how Miles wrote his platform . . .

Miles whipped out a sheet of paper, grabbed a pencil and carved a message.

He posted it on his wall. There was nothing on his walls in the bare apartment. It was as if he didn't live there. This sign lived there.

It said:

one     Opposites
two     Attitude
three    Story

While Cinjun operated in the warmth of his inner core—
Miles erected this at his place in the wilderness.
On the outskirts of the settlements.
He lived in the wilderness manor,
At the crossroads
On the edge of town,
The outskirts of the city.
If you go there, just bring your gun
and you'll be safe.

## The Official Bull Mud Story

MILES WAS ON THE STAGE:

"The Bull Mud is a fun ride, with thrills and chills————"

Some people have been on the Bull Mud for a long time. And they forget it's just Bull Mud. A Bull Satori.

Then there are those people who come to us and say, 'It's just a ride.

'Don't be afraid, ever. Be yourself. Love yourself, and love one another.'

And we . . . kill those people.

Shut him up! We have a lot invested in this ride. We've got to stop that boy. He's gone too far out. He's gone wild.

'It's just a ride.'

We always kill those good guys who tell us that. You ever notice that? And let the demons run amok.

What's going on?

What is the moment that must never come?

A Young Lion would step up to the Old-Lion Leader and ask: "Mister Old-Lion Leader, perhaps you are seeing things wrong?"

The leader would get all hot and say, "Are you questioning my judgement!"

And the Young Lion would say, "Is your judgement so perfect that it can never be questioned? Mister Old Lion Leader, I have a question. It's a very old question, maybe you've heard it asked before. *Quis custodiet ipsos custodiet?*

"Who shall guard the guardians?"

"Who shall see that the guardians commit no offenses?"

"How may we know that they will rule rightly?"

## "How May We Know That You Would Rule Rightly?"

MILES WAS SITTING in the lobby of House Crimson.

A fellow stepped from the lift—it was Skyler, striding across the expanse with a smile.

"Miles, always a pleasure to talk with you," Skyler said, "How can we help you?"

"Can we talk?" Miles said as he rose to his feet.

"Let's talk here where it's nice and comfortable," Skyler said. And took him to the front door.

"It's good to see you Miles. You look fit. You look good. I'm happy you stopped by."

"I'm here to talk with you," Miles said.

"About what?" Skyler said.

## The Reality Debate

*"The Reality Debate,"* Miles said, "I have an idea for how to make it a great show."

"With who?"

"Listen, Skyler, I have a way to—"

"With who!"

"Skyler, I'm getting to your answer—"

"With who?"

"Myself. You're asking for a come-from-nowhere guy—"

"—True," Skyler said.

"You're asking for an *'every man' to step forward!"*

"—True," Skyler said.

"You're asking all over the place. So, all I'm saying is hear me out. Hey, look, I'll make my pitch brief, as brief as hell. It won't cost you anything to listen."

Skyler cast a gaze at Miles . . . of such penetrating force . . . and said, "Fee, fi, fo, fum, I see a Sound Chaser. Say it isn't so."

Miles held his look.

"You're a Sound Chaser," Skyler said. "Say it isn't so."

Miles said, "I can be a great help to you, if you'll hear me out—"

"You're not a proper sound chaser," Skyler said.

"A 'proper' sound chaser?" Miles smiled and laughed in a friendly way. "What the hell does that mean? . . . I'd love to hear what makes someone 'proper'?"

"Thanks for stopping by Miles. I have to go."

Skyler started walking away. The meeting was over.

*Crackpots!* Skyler thought. *Everywhere I turn, crackpots.*

Miles followed after Skyler. This was suddenly some kind of strange pursuit.

Skyler asked Miles a question—in an incidental way—he tossed it to Miles over his shoulder as he moved away, and didn't even turn to catch

Miles's reaction.

"What organization are you with now?" Skyler said.

"I'll tell you," Miles said, "a little bit about where I'm at—"

"What do you have?" Skyler asked.

"The full offices of Miles Roark International."

"Your affiliation—" Skyler was heading for the lift.

"The human race, it's filling the world. Our folks are everywhere."

"You're very amusing," Skyler said with no trace of mirth, "maybe I could work up a laugh and send it to you."

"If you're going to the trouble, make it a big one," Miles said. "Now honestly, Sky—I truly do have a good idea for you; will you hear what I have to say—"

Skyler signaled for the lift. "How would you draw a crowd?"

"By saying interesting things—"

"I understand," Skyler said. "Thank you for coming by—"

"—Please don't understand me so fast—"

"—The security guard can escort you out—" Skyler stepped into the lift.

"—Thank you for listening—" Miles said.

Skyler spoke from the lift, "—My pleasure."

## The Spark, Sparks . . . Sparks to Flame

As MILES WALKED AWAY, from House Crimson into a large plaza, he looked around, studying the territory. He looked up at the tower of House Crimson.

It was a fortress, surrounded by a chasm. Well, there was nothing else for it—it was time to build a bridge!

Inside the tower, Skyler was briefing Cinjun.

They were looking down at Miles.

"What's his name?" Cinjun said.

"*Miles Roark.* Do you know him?" Skyler said.

"Is anybody backing him?" Cinjun said.

"No, he's an outsider. A sidewinder."

"I'll have someone look into it," Cinjun said. He turned to face a man standing deeper in the room. This was Brutus, the head of Cinjun's fighting group. "See what needs to be done," Cinjuns said to him.

Brutus nodded.

# Cutting

HOUSE CRIMSON, ... the gymnasium, ... and everyone was in loose-fitting martial outfits ... sitting on mats.

Cinjun was striding among them.

Off to the side, loomed *Brutus*, a fellow with the coiled killer look, and the poise of a methodic man, who does his dirty work with gloves on. He was Cinjun's muscle and the head of his *fight group*—the group that ventured out into the land and to strange parts unknown.

He was also a very charming guy ... that was how he got away with a little murder now and again.

Cinjun said, "In all forms of strategy, you must be aware of stance. It is necessary to maintain the combat stance in everyday life and to make your everyday stance your combat stance."

"The *Way* of strategy is based on overcoming men. By victory gained in crossing swords with individuals, or joining battle with large numbers.

"Fix your intention on it."

"The gaze should be large and broad. This is the twofold gaze."

"When you take up *your sword*, you must feel intent on *cutting the enemy*," Cinjun said.

"If you know the path of the sword well, you can wield it easily.... And to wield the sword well ... you must wield it calmly."

"It's the attitude of cutting. Of striking," Cinjun said.

"Picture the attitude."

"The posture of cutting. Of cutting into the space."

"It's the attitude of striking."

"Picture the separation from others. Picture the cutting away. Picture the burning away."

"When you take this step, many will try to talk you out of it."

"You have to raise the image in your mind.
"Picture where you are going, and what you are pulling away from.
"You will have to find determination."

"Pulling away from family, from parents, from brothers, from sisters, from wives, from husbands, from friends, from lovers."

"You have to separate from the bad actors.
"You're on a higher level. On a plane of greater power. You have to cut away the bad actors."

"You have to forge new being.
"In the flames of the furnace—you must sometimes burn away your past."

"You have to put up your guard, against these bad actors.
"They will come at you in many ways.
"You have to be ready to travel on.
"To sail on.
"Do away with them from your heart and mind.
"It takes discipline. Some people must be removed. And you must know when."

"It's about getting rid of the tender spots, so that you can be stronger.
"You gain strength by overcoming these weaknesses."

"The posture of cutting. Of cutting into the space.
"It's the attitude of striking.
"Picture the cutting away, the burning away.
"You must open your heart to the Way.
"You must harden your heart against the Enemy."

"Moving onto a higher plane of reality."

"Cutting away—from the bad actors.

"Take control of your own fate. Your own journey. Your own path. Your own will.

"It's important to find your strength."

"We have to connect. Then lean forward and propel ourselves into the future."

"It's the 'Red Train'—It puts a strength in you that no one can touch.
"A drive—a mental attitude to move forward."

"Sometimes you have to take the fight to the enemy.
"You have to be willing to make enemies.
"And take the fight to the *Enemy*.
"This is the *Way*."

## The Lad

Among the listeners, a lad spoke up, expressing doubt in the *Way*.
Cinjun answered him at once.
All who listened, heard the power in Cinjun's voice. It resonated with them. They were strengthened to the Way.
Cinjun looked at the lad.

Presently, Cinjun moved into an outer hallway where he spoke with the lad in a place apart from the others. And Brutus stood nearby.
Cinjun said to the lad, "I don't feel I can help you anymore. . . . Brutus will help you leave. You can no longer be part of this."

Cinjun returned to the gymnasium.
Where he spoke, with grace and lamentation in his voice:
"He set himself apart from us. He doesn't see the beauty in the Way. He won't be able to stay with us. He doesn't have the right stuff.
"This is a place for the special, the talented. Not everybody has the stuff to make it here.
"To remain here you need to be made of the substance of fire and steel."

The boy's girlfriend was still in the fold.
Cinjun turned to her. She was pretty, a flowing voluptuous figure.
Cinjun saw great potential in her.

First, she would require domination. Which happened to be Cinjun's specialty, cultivated through long labors.

In a later moment, Cinjun took aside the young lady.

He told her, "You're very talented. You're special. I'd like you to stay here."

As for her boyfriend, Cinjun said, "He'll be fine. It's for the best. It'll be a good thing. You'll see."

She quietly cried.

He told her, "There, there darling." He kissed her cheek. And he smiled at her. He charmed her.

He had a very confident, enfolding manner that held a great magical sway on people's emotions.

He touched people, he held people. He was physical with them.

She looked at Cinjun. And met his gaze, with yearning.

She and Cinjun would presently grow closer, and warmer.

## Quinn "Flintstone" Martin

IT WAS THE DARNDEST HOUSE you ever saw. The front lawn—well, you could squeeze that—just barely—into a great lake, if you packed it tight. And that was the least noticeable part of this house. Everything about this place was immense.

Cinjun approached the front door. The huge double doors that stood strong enough to keep out an army. He heard the strains of muffled sounds that seemed to end in a loud abrupt sound. Then silence descended in folds.

Cinjun took hold of the big brass knocker latched to a lion's head and knocked.

The door came open, in a quick sweep.

The man who appeared at the door was smiling. He was filled with good cheer. Expansive . . . Enjoying the high life, in the full blossom of wealth, health, and I-don't-give-a-darn means.

Step right up, ladies and gentleman:

*Meet Quinn 'Flintstone' Martin!*

He owns the world, and its gold.

While Quinn was in the washroom, Cinjun surveyed the house.

Scouting expeditions in Quinn's manor often turned up interesting discoveries.

He glimpsed something bizarre . . . He saw a young woman tied to a bed, and blindfolded.

Cinjun didn't seem at all surprised. Quinn too had passions that were enormous; passions that needed to stroll. They knew this about each other. They were large. And their lives were large. And their passions were built to scale.

He continued down the hall.

"Do you want to have a seat?" Quinn said.

"No," Cinjun said, "I have to get going."

In the parlor room, Quinn was providing Cinjun with certain things for his operation—such portables as could be stuffed into a suitcase.

He was giving Cinjun a bronze case that—when it was opened— shone with gold and silver and the startling colors of a thousand and one portables. Gold wafers. Soostones. The little stuff that could buy a small planet.

Cinjun walked out the mammoth double doors of the manor. He stepped out into the night and went away.

Quinn led himself back into the manor and now aimed himself towards the bedroom, toward the woman. He walked down the long lushly carpeted corridor that stretched into the distance, for only about a horizon or two. Quinn spoke to the walls as he traveled.

"I suffer from boredom," Quinn said. "I am prey to the deadly lethargy that envelopes those who are sated, those who have no more desires."

Life-drag. You see, he was fighting life-drag—And what a drag it can be.

He may be king; he may possess the world and its gold. But gold won't bring you happiness when—you limit its abilities . . . Quinn opened up the bounds of his gold, to let it find him somebody to love. And then another. And another. Until his life was filled with great tender cares.

The world was still the same. But now it shone for him.

He had found himself: *Time well-spent.*

From gold well-spent.

The big fat world was his. And for him this world *happied*. It produced happiness leading to happiness, to an all of happiness. He was well settled in the happiness at the moment.

He entered the red bedroom, with the beautiful woman tied to the bed. He freed her with great tenderness. And the couple now proceeded to do something special. He continued speaking—now to the woman—as he mounted the bed:

"I am absolutely preeminent in my chosen profession. I have no more worlds to conquer within my chosen orbit—"

A woman walked through the double door dressed in a negligee—and nothing. She was stunning. Where the woman on the bed was blonde, this young lady was a brunette and filled with independent motion; she glided onto the bed, joining Quinn and the blonde.

"Alas," Quinn said, "it is too late in my life to change my orbit for another one."

A red-headed woman came through the door, glowing with sexuality. She came onto the bed.

"And," Quinn said, "since power is the goal of all ambition it is unlikely that I could possibly acquire more power in another sphere than I already possess in this one."

Other women appeared at the door, floated in, and joined their young bodies to the satin bed.

"I take pleasure now only in artistry, in the polish and finesse, which I can bring to my operations. It has become almost a mania with me to impart an absolute rightness, a high elegance, to the execution of my affairs."

The room expanded. Became intumescent, engorged.

*Woman leading on to woman, all is woman.*

And Quinn "Flintstone" Martin.

*Happiness leading on to happiness, all is happiness.*

*Something special leading to something special, all is something special.*

And Quinn "Flintstone" Martin.

He owns the world, and its gold.

"I believe," Quinn said, "that the approach to perfection which I am steadily achieving in my operations will ultimately win recognition in the history of our times.

"Each day, I try and set myself still higher standards of subtlety and polish so that each of my proceedings may be a work of art."

Red-filled, orange-splashed walls watched as Quinn rose and descended on the bed flanked by a redhead, a brunette, and a blonde.

*Meet Quinn "Flintstone" Martin.*

His crystal ship is being filled, a thousand girls, a thousand thrills.

Such is life for Quinn "Flintstone" Martin.

*He owns the world, and its gold.*

When Quinn gained the world, and its gold, he said onto the world: "Please, just good deals. Nothing pretentious. I haven't changed. A pool, a column, and a deal on the vine."

# The Bolt from the Blue

IN A TAVERN, Miles and Daphne applied themselves seriously to strong drinks.

Daphne turned to Miles. "You want to get on a stage and debate Cinjun Smythe? You want to debate Cinjun Smythe!"

"Clobber him," Miles said. "I'm going to show him god himself?"

"You mean herself. As we all know, *female* is the master race. . . . You're going to fight Cinjun Smythe?"

"I am fighting him."

"From a distance."

"I'm about to move in for the kill."

"Level with me, this is a put-on. Where are you going with this?"

"I want to show him how to talk about love. . . . He's got a great act, but I don't think he talks enough about love."

"You want to teach him love?"

"I think he's a man with a lot of love in his heart. I want to teach him how to fill his heart and soul with love. To radiate love. To be love."

"You want to teach him 'how to be love'?"

"Yes, that's my ambition."

"Anything else you want to teach him?"

"I want to teach him how to play the blues."

"And you think the reds—"

"Are too strong for him."

"And the blues—"

"Are much better for him."

"How are you going to teach Big Red to play the blues?"

"One note at a time. We'll begin with love. He needs love—the most of all things."

"You want to topple Cinjun Smythe. What's your plan?"

"I win, he loses."

"You need a helluva bigger box to stand on."

"I have to get onto the newsfeeds."

She laughed.

*"The newsfeeds!"* She rolled it over in her mind.

Then she laughed again.

"We have to get you onto the newsfeeds!"

She clapped her hands, and rubbed them together—what an act of mischief that would be! She was a prankster who saw a prank worthy of her talents.


## The Swell Old Boys

MILES WAS AT A ROADHOUSE, "The Watering Hole"—the layout was horses, a trough and a desert, cactuses and a sawdust floor, booths shaped like adobe huts.

Miles was in the "Hugs and Honeys" room.

It had a mechanical bull. A hell of a broad animal. On a red mat, which caught the people who fell off the bull, and they fell off all the time. The rest of the place did justice to the bull.

On a far platform, Miles stood. As he had entered he had swept his gaze along the seated people, and walkers-about. This place had atmosphere, he noticed. If you had a sharp knife, you could cut off a good chunk of it and take it with you for your memory book.

Miles had taken the stage.

And presently gathered a thick fold of silence around him.

And now Miles went about telling a tale . . . A little thing he was throwing together off the top of his head . . .

"The Swell Old Boys————"

The men from the syndicate.

The men from the cartel.

The men from the outfit.

The Old Boys.

Every once in a while the Old Boys put out an ad:

'Sheriff Leader wanted. Complexion shall not be unseemly.'

Up to the door, steps Mr. Whiter-Than-White.

*And the image of the thing rolled across the frontier.*

Cinjun Smythe comes to the door. He wants to rule Eden Estates. To let loose the dogs of Bullyashat—'I will take you to this old Eden Estates, that's deep in the wild frontier state of Paradise. And we will seize the main ranch house, we will seize the White Stone Mansion Under the Big Sky'—this being the feel and pretty love song of this old boy.

The money man is Quinn Martin.

Cinjun Smythe says, "I want to be your Sheriff Leader."

Quinn says, "Boy, do you know what we do! Do you know what you have to do, as one of us? Here's how the system goes . . ."

Education—The way they teach is nothing but a fraud. They teach with books—they test you, not the books. Let's say you didn't read one of their books the way they wanted you to read it, you fail the test.

Your school record—nothing but a fraud. They test you, not the need for why they have to record and grade every moving part of your schooling.

*Now some images rolled and a-rolled across this old frontier.*

The work history—nothing but a fraud. They test you, not the idea of why they have to own and run all the moving parts of your work history.

Titles—nothing but a fraud. They test you, not the ideas behind why they have to own and run all the moving parts of you and all your friend's titles.

Modern Debates—the Modern Debates they throw at you—nothing but a fraud. They own the moving parts. And they lay the fix in. We're talking nothing but a fraud.

Quinn says to Cinjun, 'Boy, we're full of our own bull mud, and how do you like that?'

Cinjun says, 'Oh, I like it plenty. See if I take your ideas, work with them a little, I could pound you out the best Sheriff Leader you ever did see.'

Quinn says, 'Boy, you're going to go far.'

Cinjun Smythe—we're talking nothing but a fraud.

I want to debate him; I'm going to debate him; and I'm going to give him a "real" battle.

# Into the Newsroom

DAPHNE WAS PURSUING Ripkin Kabob, the decisionmaker at the *Lightcaster Newsfeed*. She wanted to get on the Newsfeed. It was a conduit onto the main line, *the Wayfinder.*

Getting to Ripkin was tough. He would not respond to inquiries.

The only way to reach him was in the flesh.

So, Daphne called a *light*man and got into the newsroom that way. She stood by the *light*man until the news director walked by. Ripkin was charmed by her. She took him to a restaurant to work her wiles on him, and to exploit Ripkin's fatal flaw—Ripkin was a hopeless drunkard.

Soon, Ripkin reached the point where he was losing control and he became very delicate, . . . and here and there deliberate.

"Missus Fox, I don't care what you have! He has no following, no sponsors, no value."

"You can't blame me for trying," she said, as she gave him another glass. "Cheers!" She clinked her glass to his. She was now getting him thoroughly plowed, . . . as much booze poured down his shirt as did go down his throat. Ripkin caught himself, and made an immediate recovery.

As she drank down her own glass, she lifted a hand and helped Ripkin tip his glass back so that he swallowed every bit. They finished their drinks and put them down.

"Ahh . . ." Daphne said, "formidable, yet refreshing."

Ripkin was blotto, his eyes crossed, speech slurred, body slumped. The perfect condition for her pitch.

Now, came "the treatment"—

She put her arms on his shoulders; brought her forehead to his forehead; and talked to him in this way.

"I have a good idea. I wouldn't be talking to you unless this was the best goddamn idea you ever heard."

. . . More drinks were tossed down as they went . . .

Now she sold him on her goods.

And what she laid on him, were: glimpses of fleeting purposes.

She used some words and called them by name.

And goodness the feelings. Ah, the feelings.

This young lady, she worked him in slow, slow style.

She talked to him about the changes that life arranges, nothing but changes, of phase.

He felt himself bleeding and feeling, and coming to a tenderness, there. Very near, yet very far. Very clear. The soft strains of a tenderness there.

So strange, this talk of life-change.

He felt himself shook up. Intoxicated

Dangling in possibilities. So many possibilities. All the possibilities.

Too strange.

Mmm, yeah-ah!

He licked his chops. Began to pant. His tongue hung out. His breath began to quicken. He wanted a bone. She rubbed his belly. And patted his head.

She gave him a story. It sounded easy. Got into his skin. She was lying through her teeth.

She was telling him of a sun touched with red.

A sun leaning to Crimson.

And a House swathed in Crimson possibility.

She took him out into the streets, and the Bill Bailey on the Street. And the effect on him.

The ride. The Bill Bailey on the Street.

The talk around the campfire. The Bill Bailey on the Street.

She took him. To get it on into the inside.

*Wow! What a story,* he thought. He had to have it.

His tongue hung out. His breath came in pants. He growled. He wanted the bone. He had to have it. It had to be his now.

Before anybody else came to take it from him.

He took her ride.

He had to get it on into the inside. Thoughts of inside, filled his mind, and elsewhere regions of his bodily form.

He wanted to take a ride. And get it on into the inside.

Oh, yeah-ah! Ah-huh, yeah-ah!

"I'm going to write out the proposal on this napkin," Daphne now told him. "And we'll sign it."

She worked her charms on him as she wrote out a contract on a napkin. "It's got everything you could want. A roundup like you never had before. And a Bill Bailey on the Street, for your viewers. We want to drive up those ratings. And we will. Believe me we know how to arouse excitement."

His tongue was hanging loose. He was practically passed out. But his eyes were opened wide. Eating her. Every morsel of her. This beautiful— what was her name again—Daphne Fox. What a newswoman! He had to have her on his team. And her story. Put it on the newsfeed, it would work well. He wished she would rub his belly. And then drift downward. Where was his bowl of drink? Oh, there it was. Mmm, good drink. Lppp, liipp, lip, lip.

She had the restaurateur and a doctor witness the agreement. "Gentlemen, you are witnessing a historic moment."

Ripkin signed it. He started to crumple forward.

She subtly pulled him upright by his shirt.

"Salute them." He did. "Gentlemen ..." She gave them the pen to sign as witnesses.

They signed it and went away.

She let go of Ripkin's shirt. He folded forward, and put a dent into the table, with his chin.

She folded the napkin neatly and left.

The next day, at the *light*vision station, Daphne reviewed the terms of the napkin agreement with a now sober Ripkin.

"I what!" He was defiant.

"You signed it," she told him, as if it were a deed to be congratulated, praised, and cherished.

Ripkin wanted, mainly, to spit.

"It's a napkin!" he countered, and looked into her eyes, wondering which one to spit into.

"It's a contract," she extended the substance of the napkin.

And fastened herself to its purpose, readying herself to advance under its heavy obligation. "... And according to this napkin, you are going to pay us to produce a block for the Newsfeed!

"And we will accept the money. Further, you will not pay us cheaply, but rather to the upward extent of your ways and means. And we will accept the small fortune, ... that is our burden."

Miles interrupted, "Wait Daphne, what idiot told us we had the skill and could produce a block for the Newsfeed!"

"He did!"

"Then that's what we're going to do!" Miles said.

Miles was resolved to fulfill the promises clearly set forth in the napkin.


## Fathead Willy Meets The Black Form

---

MILES WAS DOING HIS ACT at a cocktail lounge called "The Polar Cap." The place was run by the impresario Chilly "Fathead" Willy, who was hovering in the rear of the establishment's big room, 'The Chilly Willy Room.'

Miles was telling a tale.

Cinjun Smythe is a black train, coming down the track.
Coming round the bend.
Mean old rotten train coming down the track.

Cinjun Smythe is a black storm, coming round the bend.
Black storm, sixteen skies across.
Black end, sixteen dreams long.

Sun going down!
Way out on the sea!
Here she comes, little girl going to set me free.

Train arrives. Sixteen coaches long.
Black train arrives. Sixteen coaches long.
Big black train gonna get my baby.

Black storm, sixteen skies long.
Black doom, sixteen worlds wide.
Black void, sixteen centuries long.

Going to get my baby.
Going to take my baby,
Going to get my friend.
Black doom coming round the bend.

My wild love.
My wild love.
My wild love,
Going to get my wild love.

Black destroyer, sixteen fields long.
Black forest, sixteen darknesses deep.
Black crime, sixteen scenes long.
Black night, sixteen worlds wide.

Black sea, sixteen harbors long.
Black devastation, sixteen roads across.
Black carnage, sixteen lands all told.

Black river, sixteen trenches long
Black train, sixteen realms of pain long.
Black train, sixteen lands all told.
Black cold, sixteen winds coming down the line.

"This black train is gonna take my baby," Miles said.

"She'll be gone. This mean old train is coming around the bend. This mean old evil train is gonna take my one and only friend.

"Now, mean old rotten black train—

"Do you think I'm going to let you get away with it?"

A guy in the back of the room turned to the bartender. "Hey, Miles Roark?" he said. "Who is Miles Roark?"

Chilly "Fathead" Willy was watching and listening and catching everything. He was not pleased. He was in an inferno of rage. He was on the edge of a violent explosion. He was smoldering away as Miles continued to say and do things that disturbed him all the more.

"I want to debate Cinjun Smythe," Miles said. "He won't face me. Cinjun's call for a reality debate is a trick . . . It's fixed.

"There can't be a championship fight without me.

"I'm here to tell you all; you think I'm just talking, running at the mouth, he's above my class, but you can't have a heavyweight debate without me?

"Cinjun Smythe will dodge me. He'll dismiss me, saying I'm a Sound Chaser.

"But there can be no fight without me."

Chilly "Fathead" Willy took Miles and Daphne to his office.

"What is this!" he said, "About Cinjun Smythe being a black train! Is that supposed to be an act!"

"You don't like that?"

"Why does he have to be sixteen of anything?"

"Seventeen, you think?"

"Why does he have to be sixteen rotten lengths of anything?"

"Seventeen is rough. You don't want to make him a monster . . . You don't like it do you Willy?"

"No, I do not like it, son! I do not like it at all!"

"Hmm," Miles felt out the moment. "You don't like it at all?"

Miles gave it thought.

*Why damn it all,* he realized, *Fathead Willy was right.*

"Willy, . . ." Miles said. He directed a steady gaze and took the moment into slip, into time slip.

Time slipping away.
His purpose was to search for truth.
He would let time slip.
He would go into free range.
He would feel the moment, when it came.

Willy stared at Miles.

Miles dropped back into human to human.
He slipped into no strain, no anger, no harshness.
He stood before him.
Now he spoke to him in simple human to human terms.
Now he connected in a moment of honesty.

Willy stared at Miles.

"Do you know that you're right?" Miles said plainly. "I'm hitting it too hard. You're right. How about we let the audience get it for themselves? How about I make him a magesterial form with a dark secret?"

"A what?" Willy said.

"I'll make him," Miles said, "a black magesterial form, just a plain, simple black magesterial form comin' round the bend. With one or two features, as hints.

"What the hell," Willy said, "are you talking about! A black magic form, what the hell is that? No I don't like that.

"Not a black magic, no, a black magesterial form . . . Right, well done Willy. You cut through again. Hell, let's make it a black form. A black barren form, like a fun black dirge.

"Black door, black dirge.
"Dark hearts dirge, no flowers.
"Opening on black forever.
"Black dirge, comin' round the bend."

"A black what?" Willy said. "Dirge? Isn't that for funerals?"
Willy stared at Miles.

"Black fury, sixteen cries loud," Miles said.
"And we could keep some of the really good parts from the black

train.

"Black form, comin' round the bend.

"Black form.

"Black crime, sixteen scenes long.

"Black destruction, sixteen deaths across.

"Black end, sixteen universes deep.

"Art begets art," Miles said. "Form begets form. They'll get it for themselves."

Willy stared at Miles.

It was a cold hard gaze. There was no aid and comfort for the enemy in that stare.

"What the hell are you talking about!" Willy said.

Willy continued to stare at Miles.

"For your next set," Willy said, "here are some things that I'm going to need to hear come out of your mouth. You're going to say, *'We are blessed.'* You're going to say, *'Cinjun Smythe really knows what we're about.'* "

"Yes, there's always that," Miles said.

Now Miles stared at Willy.

"It's your club," Miles said, "I'll say goodbye now."

Miles and Daphne walked out leaving Fathead Willy huffing and puffing with no house to blow down.

The scene was like no other in Willy's life.

Fathead Willy had met The Black Form.

## Screwing with the Primal Forces of Nature

RIPKIN STORMED into the newsroom, where he collided with Miles and Daphne.

"You can't say those things," Ripkin barked. "Here's what you're going to say—"

"—Rip," Miles said, "it's your company—"

"—You have to make it normal."

"No—we'll leave."

Ripkin went stark, raving mad. "Why are you here? Who sent you?"

"Take it easy. We were just going to do a piece on Cinjun Smythe's Reality Debate."

"What do you mean do? What are you up to? Who put you up to this? What kind of footage were you going to shoot? I want answers! You're fired."

As they passed Ripkin, he jumped back with a shriek. "I'm not scared of you. What are you trying to hide! Who are you with?"

"We're on our own. We're leaving."

They were dangerous people. They might have weapons, bombs, Lord only knows what. Ripkin backed away from them as they cleared out of the newsroom.

Then, courageous Ripkin shouted at their retreating backs:

"You're screwing with the primal forces of nature!"


## Brutus and the Twins

NOW WHEN DAPHNE AND MILES REACHED Daphne's apartment—they found it occupied by *three professionals*.

One was pointing a gun.

Daphne didn't give a damn.

"You're going to hold a gun to me," Daphne said, "in my flat. I don't have time for your bull mud."

She charged at him.

She ducked under his gun arm. Attacked him in a rapid up-from-under maneuver.

The other two leapt into action. One pointed a gun at Miles. One pulled Daphne off. Slammed her against the wall.

She wouldn't go down.

So he held her while the other gave her a good stiff belt.

Miles had a gun pointed to his head.

Things settled into place. Silence descended in thick folds.

The lead one stepped up to Daphne. "Well, you must be the pride and joy of your little lover boy."

Heart full of darkness, spotlight on his face, he turned to Miles.

This one in charge, Brutus, was very calm. "Now let us get down to business . . ."

"How soon we're finished," Brutus said, "depends on you . . ."

Brutus approached Miles. "My dear boy, the game of red Indians is over, quite over. You stumbled by mischance into a game for grownups. You're not equipped to play games with adults.

"It was very foolish to come out here with your spade and buckets—"

Brutus turned to Daphne. She was mounting a hell of a struggle now. Daphne was kicking and biting; scratching and punching.

She was on the floor. Brutus directed the others to step back.

They cleared a space around her.

Brutus pointed his gun.

He fired a bullet into her right thigh.

She stopped moving; looked at the leg. In a flash, she determined the entry and exit were clean. The shot went clear through.

"Now you shot me," Daphne said, "are you happy? Now get the hell out of my place." She enjoyed talking like a gun moll. This was interesting. She wanted to be a credit to women everywhere.

Now Brutus held the gun on her. The other two grabbed her by her arms.

"You goddamn coward," Daphne said, "get out of here before I send you out on a stretcher."

Brutus had his partners stand her up.

He approached her slowly. Then, abruptly, he belted her across the jaw.

She hit the floor hard; then turned toward Brutus slowly.

He gestured to her with a 'come here darling' motion.

She rose, put up her fists and staggered over. He belted her and she went flying.

She came up again.

Brutus was fascinated. "I wonder."

He pointed a gun at Miles. She went completely quiet and still.

Brutus looked at her. "I see."

He turned to Miles. "We must stop joking. Follow me in developing a cautionary tale.

"Should you continue, our next session will be a torture session.

"I will attack the sensitive parts of your body. And her body.

"I am without mercy, there will be no relenting. No one will stage a last minute rescue. There will be no possibility of escape. This is not a romantic adventure story in which the villain is finally routed. The hero is given a medal and marries the girl. Unfortunately, these things don't happen in real life. If you continue, you will be tortured into madness.

"The girl will be brought in and we will set about her in front of you.

If that is not enough, you will be killed. I will reluctantly leave your bodies. Make my way to a comfortable house that is waiting for me.

"There I shall continue my profitable career, and live in the bosom of the family I shall create.

"I stand to lose nothing. You will quit, and live. If not, the young lady and I will get together and we will have a very good time indeed."

Exit Brutus and the twins.

Miles and Daphne were now alone.

"How are you?" he asked.

"No damage that a little hospital won't fix."

"Daphne, darling, it might be a good idea for me to take it from here all by my lonesome."

"We're just getting started."

"There is no way I'm going to take a chance with your life."

"They won't be back."

"You have a fascinating way of reading a beating," Miles said.

"They were just trying to scare the hell out of us," she said. "What are they going to do kill me? I could put them in prison for that. Ignore them. They didn't have anything interesting to say."

*Foolish people are always trying to bring me down,* she thought.

*Looks like they tried to tame me; next time they try, they'll learn.*

*I was nice and chatty with them because they were just visiting. But these boys better watch out when I come undone. I'll shove these boys back into their narrow world.*

She was wild with the power. Eternally wild with the power.

# The Story that Sounded Easy

CINJUN AND SKYLER ENTERED the building, and goodness were they ever having fun thinking about the scare they put into Miles and Daphne.

Skyler liked the idea of doing damage to that bitch Daphne.

Cinjun was imagining the effect Brutus must have had on Miles.

"Ah," Cinjun said, "if he disappeared suddenly, it couldn't happen to a nicer guy."

A security guard appeared.

"Mister Smythe," he said, "there's a man in the courtyard."

"A man?" Cinjun said.

"Making trouble, all kinds of noise, and saying things about you. Weird things."

The men strode to the outer expanse of the lobby.

Outside, through the enormous picture windows, Cinjun could see: *Miles and Daphne.*

Standing there in the courtyard. Not doing much. Not doing much at all. No movement, as far as he could detect. They were holding still, in a position dead center in the plaza.

Now Cinjun began to hear the strains of Miles's voice, traveling the distance of the plaza.

Miles wasn't speaking loud. Not speaking loud at all.

He was just talking to his friend Cinjun.

"I heard a story," Miles said. "It sounded easy. But the man was lying through his teeth. This old boy was lying through his teeth."

Miles stood there.

Paused.

Then took a ride on the groove—taking it on the inside. Lending it another moment's color.

"I heard a story," Miles said—"It sounded easy. *But the man was lying through his teeth.*"

Miles stood there. Talking—to get his thoughts—and to carry them deep into Cinjun's heart.

"Let me show you," Miles said, "how you make me feel. Miles held Cinjun in his look. "And the people that you touch."

Miles stood in the summer sun . . . dangling possibilities. All the possibilities.

He did not move at all.

## Towering Figure

CINJUN HEARD MILES. Felt the possibilities. All the possibilities. And the way it was going to be.

He swept his gaze . . .

Cinjun saw Miles standing there. And a little way's back, a bowshot's throw away, a ravishing woman—Cinjun knew who he was meeting there—that was the Daphne bitch. Past this he saw some people turning, looking at Miles with interest. And that was all there was—There was nothing more to it.

Cinjun held his look for an instant, taking full measure of this scene.

"Leave him be," Cinjun said. "Make sure no one disturbs him. I want him to keep talking. I want him to talk himself out. And I don't want to hear anymore about him. When it comes time for him to leave, let him. He's not worth our time."

Cinjun strode from the scene, comfortable with the possibilities.

"Now nobody bring him any sandwiches, if he gets hungry," Cinjun said. "And if he gets tired, nobody rubs his back. And I don't want to see anybody helping him answer his fan mail. What we have here gentleman is a son of a bitch. No need to play with the bastard."

They laughed. Cinjun was the best; this was what they contemplated, as Cinjun made away from the scene in his trademark elegant, powerful strides.

He was a heap of class. It was hard to determine how a man, how one mortal man, had the strength to carry so much class. And to make it look so easy.

Perhaps, this was the thing to notice about Cinjun Smythe. . . . He told stories. . . . They sounded easy—Yes, it seemed someone had said that about him. . . . Who said it?—Who can remember—it was so long ago and so far away. And—the man who said it—well, hell, he was probably amounting to a whole heap of nothing by now.

## Let's Bring It Out in the Open

HE WAS MAKING HIS WAY into the port of Sans Souci.

This was the Sans Souci Plaza, the courtyard outside House Crimson, a wilderness sea port around which stood the skyscrapers of the Sans Souci Plaza.

*Go boat, go, go. They have no room here for someone like me*, Miles thought. *Sail, sail into these waters. Enter this port. Where they have no room for someone like me.*

He was sailing into the port, the dock of House Crimson. And above the tide was the place where they were gathering to hunt him down—Now he was coming into this place, this place of the righteous. And he was not supposed to do that. He was the hunted. Didn't he know? He knew.

He was sailing in. *Go boat, go, go.*

*Tried to tell me I was evil. Tried to trample on my soul. Go boat, go, go. Oh, oh-woah.*

*Sans Souci. I'm walking, and it ain't no dream. Go boat, go, go.*

*Sans Souci. Go boat, go, go—they have no room here for someone like me,* Miles thought, as he stood in The Sans Souci Plaza.

The Sans Souci Plaza.

It was a mood plaza, reflecting mood in the world that peopled.

The plaza told a story of the world that peopled . . . a story of the *Hunter and the Hunted.* Out there—in the world—the story ruled. The story of the Hunter and the Hunted.

He had stepped out from that story.

Now he was there in the Plaza of the Night'Sun'Sky'Sea. The Plaza of Mood Swings. Dancing the mood swing. Watch it, watch it now.

*They have no room here for someone like me,* he thought. Unwanted and unforgiven. He was prey for the hunt, and a young man who must not reach for greater being.

The Hunter and the Hunted. The story stood strong. But he would fight it—Now he was young and stood a chance against the hunter—This was why the hunted stood before the hunter. . . . This was why the hunted stood wide and open before the hunter and his forces. The hunted called for the hunt. Bring the hunt on him. *Let's bring it out in the open.*

This was the way it was meant to be. The way it had to be. . . . Now he stood a chance in hell. . . . And now he stood there with deep longing in his heart. With the longing, and a will to survive as entirely himself. He stood there, making moments come alive.

To be young . . . oh, to be fit for battle . . . He must act now. He was revealing—*need*. A silly need to survive.

He moved into the urgency with relaxed motion.

Relaxed motion, making it tender.

Miles moved with relaxed motion in the plaza outside House Crimson.

Miles stood alone with the situation—Telling Cinjun . . . who wasn't far from the scene . . . who was out there, close enough to feel it even if he didn't hear it . . . telling him something, the man ought to know. About troubles.

The subject of this day's lecture was rhythm. Soft rhythm. Soft now. So soft. You wanted to cuddle up and lie in it for days. That soft.

*It should be gentle and extended, soft and lovely,* Miles thought.

Miles stood there—Giving the moments a soft, laid back quality.

*This is soft life,* Miles determined. Not throbbing, pounding. This is pulsing, mild motion. Give it subtlety? Yes. Give it relaxed motion. Sensual, flowing, but relaxed motion.

*It doesn't have to be wrenching,* Miles thought, *or forcefully wrought.* It can ease. What's happening is big enough. It doesn't need extra pushing.

Silky.

Tenuous.

Not rampaging, but rather a mellow tone. Simple, elegant. Contained energy. Poised, reserved—He would give it those kinds of qualities.

Give it a switch up, a twist up. Release the mood into softness.

It gave Miles relaxed motion. Pulsing tender motion. He was a sensualist.

Making himself smooth in confrontation. . . . In this thing, now, he was not a molding force of character. He was light. He was flowing. He was relaxed motion. . . . He was poise. He was wild grace. . . . He floated. He danced. And his moves, were like the wind.

In the courtyard, he just went into a sensible, relaxed talk. He was not trying hard. He was not forcing anything. He was just there and talking to Cinjun. He got emotionally involved in what he was saying and let that color his tone. But it was a light and easy and tender talk. He wanted Cinjun to understand. Miles was not a jabbering lunatic.

He was talking to Cinjun—mind to mind.

Miles was present and he stood for something. And he let that work for him. Let his mere presence work in his favor. To give him force. He didn't push. He let the story of who he was, and why he was there work for

him.

And he explained. That's all. No madness involved. No strain.

It was conversation. It was talk. It was free-form expression.

No one else needed to listen. He was making his way by force of reason.

He was not compelling people. He was appealing to their thinking, to reason with him. They could come to their own conclusions. He only offered some starting points. He was not drafting anyone; he was not inducting anyone; there was nothing compulsory in any of what he was doing.

It was free expression. That came out of a great deal of thought and conviction. It carried its own force into the world. It existed on its own. He was not inventing or discovering anything; he was just allowing the flow, from him to them.

He was moving through the changes. Making his way through the changes.

"Let me show you how you make me feel, Cinjun," Miles said.

"You're asking people to give it away to you, Cinjun. Well—you've asked for feeling—let me show you how you make me feel.

"Let me show you the people that you touch————"

You talk of taking me through life change. Of taking my life into your possibilities. Let me show you how you make me feel.

I'm here to show you. I could show you. Would you like to see . . . what is meant to be? Where your too-strange talk of life-change will take you to be.

And the people that you touch.

You told a story. It sounded easy. You were lying through your teeth.

"Mm-hmmm mmm. Ooh, ooh, yeah," he said softly, in a warm cushioned tone.

Let me show you where you will take the world with your life change.

Cinjun had put out a story.

They heard the story, the people. It sounded easy. Got into their skin.

But he was lying through his teeth.

"Now bring it out from the tight spot and into the glare of daylight. Your story about a fight; how you would bring a fight, a great fight, that would be tall and handsome and would speak loud and strong.

"Well, the fight is here. The fight you asked for is here.

"And it's a *Capoeira*. A dancing, burning fight————"

And it doesn't belong to you. It doesn't belong to anyone.

It is. And it has arrived. Hear the song. The song confirms it. *The Capoeira* is here. The dancing fight is here. Step onto the dance floor.

What's in back of the sky?

I heard the story. It sounded easy. But there was more to it.

"Don't you know—it's pain—that I'm feeling?" Miles said.

The Hunter and the Hunted—Bring the hunt out. Take it out of doors. Open your doors and call me yours.

"Animal inside—leads me to the conclusion—" Miles said.

If Cinjun was going to take over, to rule the world, then Miles was going to show him that—ooh baby, baby ... *it's a wild world*—Everybody wants to rule the world, ... well, in this room, it won't be so easy.

Miles was being hunted. Now he wanted to bring it out in the open.

*Let's bring it out in the open!*

The confrontation came from being hunted—Somebody wants to take you over and destroy you ... How do you deal with it ... how do you cope with the danger ... where is the grace in the way?

Miles won't let it remain hidden behind screens.

"You've got to give it away ... *Let's bring it out in the open.* You want to take people over, try it, but try it in the open. Cope with doing it in the glare of sunlight—in a plain and apparent setting. You want to attack—make it that. No tricks!

"No more tricks, Cinjun Smythe. Let's bring it out and have a hard look at it.

"Let's dive into the swimming pool blue.

"Strip to show us all you are," Miles said.

"Let me show how you make me feel.

"So strange your talk of life change. I hear your story. Sounding easy. All the possibilities. Summer nights. Everything easy. . . . Everything perfect. Everything coming to be.

"I could show you the way that it's truly going to be.

"Let's take a look at your too-strange talk of life-change. And I will show you what it's worth. And the way that it's going to be. What is meant to be."

He didn't have any idea from one moment to the next what was happening, what he was saying, what would happen, where this was leading. What would work, what wouldn't work. He would try things.

He was breathing, and pulsing.

Miles did not know where he was going. He was attempting things.
Let it roll, baby, roll—was the feeling.
Some rolls go.
Some rolls stop.
Some pick themselves up, dust themselves off, start all over again.

"Come out of your stronghold. Ancient shapes all around you. You're making love among empty sermons. You hate to leave your sacred lair. But it's time. The fight you asked for is here————"
      You're sitting in your safehouse, saying I want a fight. Well, the fight is here.
      You're saying bring it on. Well, the battle is here.
      Can you feel it? In the darkness touching you. Can you feel it taking control?
      The wild thing is out there Cinjun. The wild thing. The wild swing. Is going to whoop you. That wild swing, oh, watch it, watch it.
      Can you feel it?
      Can you feel it?
      Can you feel it?
      Can you feel it!"

"Bring it out in the open—give it to Lady Day.
      "Let's bring this into the light————"
      Let's bring it before the *light*vision. Into the realm of worldlight, and society spotlight. Into forest city sunstreaks. Let's bring it into the light.
      Don't go breaking my heart. Cinjun, must you hide? Don't go breaking my heart. Don't throw love away. One sad goodbye doesn't mean we can't begin again.
      Let's bring it into day. You remain in my heart. Come. Join the day. And forever more stay in day.
      You've got to give it away, Cinjun. Give it to Lady Day. You've got to give it away.
      Miles had to do it now!
      Because now he was young—He could make mad dashes. Try the impossible. Do the things you're not supposed to do. He could do them now, but his strengths would wane. He had to hit them now, while he was at his most powerful. Later, he could only do less than now—Now was the time.
      He had to break on through now!
      He had to will his way through now!

Now was the time! There was no other time.

Nothing lasts but the Earth and sky. It slips away, and another minute you cannot buy. Dust in the wind.

Soon the summer would be over. The summer was almost gone; it was all tumbling away; escaping on the wind, escaping on the winds of life, leaving on winds streaming in cool rapidity—fall serenade would soon be in the air; and winter would not be far behind.

His powers would fade, and he would fall into the winter. Now, while summer was in the world, he stood at his fighting best, feeling the coursing ability. He stood and looked around . . . and wondered where he was going.

Above—the sky trembled.

# The High Window

THE TOWER OF HOUSE CRIMSON ROSE into day.

And now shooting upward through the structure, a steel liftchamber rose into enormous heights.

Within the steel liftchamber, Cinjun stood tall. Skyler stood beside him.

Cinjun settled into the center of the lift. He owned the place. He owned whatever place he happened to be in.

Now high in the structure, rode the *Octagon Office*—the domain of warrior might. A beautiful place, of streaming daylight, auburn woods, strong oaks and shorewalls. Escaping through a vast picture window, a patio terraced its way into distance.

Cinjun entered with Skyler. They came to the office. And a high view of the situation. In this place, they came to the *Command Chamber*—and a command view, at their mighty *High Window*. This was the *Octagon Office*.

Cinjun crossed to his command desk. He passed his patio door—from his high patio you could observe Miles down below. Cinjun did not pay any attention to Miles out there at all. No sight seduced Cinjun, he had seen all before. You did not take him by storm. It was not possible.

He was moving, a man in total control of his destiny.

Cinjun observed the sky out there. His destiny burned across that sky—this was the only beauty worth pause. *Beautiful today*—Cinjun thought—*yes, it was quite lovely today*. A fine day for moving, gliding, along the upward slope of his great and high destiny.

Skyler crossed the room. His gaze traveled out the window and down to Miles.

"You're making him important," Cinjun said. "He's not important. He's nothing. He's a tramp madman shouting in the middle of the street."

"We're not going to have him arrested?" Skyler said.

"The threat is a phantom. It's nothing. And left to itself, it has to go away. There is nowhere to take it—Do you understand, Skyler?" Cinjun said.

"Hmm, of course. I see what you mean.," Skyler said.

"I had thought he was smarter than the average bear. He's a man shouting in the middle of the street. Now is that any way to achieve stature? Do you move into high society by standing in the street shouting at the tallest building?"

Skyler rolled it around in his mind. It was laughable when you thought about it, when you put in the right light.

"I'm following you," Skyler said. But Skyler didn't laugh.

Cinjun smiled, he produced his golden charming smile, but you noticed there was no laugh anywhere in that smile.

"He's making a mistake," Cinjun said. "And I wish him to go on making mistakes."

Cinjun looked at Skyler.

"In contests of strategy it is bad to be led about by the enemy," Cinjun said. "You must always be able to lead the enemy about.

"You have to first recognize his school of strategy, perceive his quality, and his strong and weak points.

"See through the enemy's spirit so that you grasp his strategy and defeat him.

"With your spirit calm, attack with a feeling of constantly crushing the enemy."

## Into the Changes

"DID YOU EVER THINK ABOUT IT, Cinjun?" Miles said. "It could make you cry about it.

"Could you ever live without it, Cinjun? You've got to give it away. You're holding on so tightly. You've got to give it away to Lady Day."

Miles spoke to Cinjun up there in the tower as passing people took

Miles into their attention. And searched his talk for answers to war and pain.

Did the people think about it? They would try the changes. Taste them.

"You've got to give it away, Cinjun. You've got to give it away to Lady Day." Miles turned from the tower to the people. "What kind of champion hides in bed all morning?"

He took a picture of it for their children. They might have a look. There was a lot to see here.

Miles took it into the changes. He was the changeling. See him change.

Miles was laid back, as he spoke to the people in the plaza.

He was traveling the changes. Trying things.

He was the changeling. See him change.

He was attempting things. Trying this, trying that. Fitting changes. Taking on dimensions.

What caught the changes, he kept. The rest let slip; he let it drift away in the timeslip continuum.

He moved through the changes. He was the changeling. See him change.

He was experimenting. Some of his experiments were startling.

He did not know where he was going. If you asked him what he had just said . . . what he just did . . . he would not have the slightest idea.

He was experiencing the changes.

The people followed the changes. Tasting them. Trying them.

*This is a capoeira,* Miles thought.

He had to find the strange in the sense.

He was there attempting things. You had to give it to him—he was attempting things.

Trying them on—feats of strength. Trying them, taking a look at where they would go, where they might take him. He crashed more than he flew; he burned more than he grew.

But he stayed there—attempting things.

Experiencing forces. And hearts broken and bleeding. And the way it was meant to be.

He was moving thru experience. Moving into startling ways, heading for strange days.

He was trying different things under the sun. Reaching, probing, extending, searching, trying, moving, whirling, turning. Wearing some things out, turning to other frontiers. He was attempting things.

He heard stories . . . That got into his skin. He got shook up . . . drove, through the possibilities. Through the changes.

In the Sans Souci Plaza, Miles said, "Miles Roark is in town."

And he stood next to a fire. He stood in a fire. He stood surrounded by fire. And his heart? Burned with feeling.

Miles built it. He built the field of *Strange Days*. And then the *Strangers* came.

Streaming.

A *He,* stepped up. Then, a *She,* stepped up. Soon all the Who's in Whoville were stepping up to listen to his engine hum.

And he got on with it. Yeah.

And his heart? Burned with feeling.

He was alive today.

Oh his mind was damned messed up! Going round and round. Colors, all these colors.

But his heart burned with feeling. You see, he lived today.

He reeled in confusion, experiencing living. He was alive today.

Oh, pounding. Oh, going round and round. Colors, all these colors.

And a heart burning with feeling.

And the wind cried, all around him.

He was experiencing the changes.

He was the *Changeling*—see him change.

He sank into the changes.

He didn't give them any more than they had.

He spoke softly, casually. No differently than if he were sitting in your living room.

His approach was laid back. *Underplay the changes,* Miles thought. *Experience. Add nothing that stretches the changes.* Experience. Try coming at it from different directions. Looking for better views.

Never satisfied.

Roads ahead.

Choices to be made.

No special way.

Flying. Never rest, never be satisfied. Move into future dreams. Leave the past. Keep moving, looking for the way. Abandon reason. Know hope. And know the changes. They are come.

The seeker moved in forever. Carved its way through the changes. Leaving no story untold; denying no turbulence.

If winter took summer, that was the change. If summer tossed in storm, that was the change.

He experienced the changes. Careful with nothing. He was lost and got more lost. The trick of it was—to lose your sanity.

A tough trick to will into the world. It took him vast effort—to lose his mind. Now he never lost control; that was always the danger—the trick was to lose your senses without losing control. He worked the trick.

Tricking existence.

You would have thought he was absolutely crazy if you didn't know better. Some took an interest.

He skipped a light fandango, turned cartwheels across the floor; he did the best he could—the crowd called out for more.

They called to each other. Miles to the people, the people to Miles.

He told them tales. And they told him his worth. Some did not use kind terms. Some cuts were most unkind; they would not let him be. He moved into the next impossibility. To struggle and to hold form ... Taking it further into distance, lonely distance. He danced by.

Hang on! This was where the ride got—strange.

Miles drove on down the road. Until he came to—a fork—chose—and kept shooting down the byway to parts unknown.

Breaking thru to *strange sensation*. To strange days. To strange rains. To strange being. He was making it all—strange. They looked at this stranger—He was the changeling. See him change.

His mind tore free.

The people came. He built his big generator, and they came to listen to its engine hum.

*His mind is gone,* they noticed.

He tore a hole in space; burned across the sky. Catching a fall. Flying. His mind tore free ... of *sanity*. Tore free—and his mind shouted out loud. Tearing across the night sun sky of pained tender love dreams. Sailing on the winds of life. Leaving sanity behind for others to play with.

His was not a small mind to be held by reality. How he came to his escape? It began with rhythm. The subject of this day's lecture was rhythm. Ground rhythm. And moving through the changes of harmonies fast and furious, slow and sensual, vast and near. To ... *strange sensation*.

## Soft Insanity

TEARING INTO UNREALITY.

Not this reality. He was tearing into the one that should be. A crazy reality filled with love dreams and winds of life that swept and swept and swept on through an *All* of cool rapidity and warm slow sensation.

An *All* of sunstreaks. Leading to sunbursts. And explosions of color.

In a void—a black void—a black that was great and vast and deep and wide.

Where a seeker sailed in forever.

A dancing burning fighter—a Capoeira—exploding through green into summer and hurtling through blue into winter. Sailing through yellow into orange and red nebulas.

Sailing on the winds of life that swept and swept and swept into forever.

Giving gifts that would last forever. Wild with the power, wild as can be.

*'There is a fine madness. A far finer madness than this one.'*

Travel with me there. Run with me. Sail with me. Into the further forever. And the realms beyond forever.

He takes himself into soft insanity here.

All ride. It's all ride.

## Skyler

SKYLER—HAD STEPPED from the command floors, and found himself needing to be in the lobby, and looking out the big window at Miles.

Skyler had heard a piece of something Miles had said in the Sans Souci Plaza.

"If you're marketing shit," Miles said, "then you talk about the packaging and the things it comes with, the nice texture and color and you give it a nice sounding brand name. With vowels in the right places, next to sturdy consonants.

"And you talk about how elephants have been eating it for centuries. Because they know intuitively that it's full of nutritious bacteria that builds up your body's immune system.

"If you're selling a diamond, you just say I'm selling a diamond. You set it on a brick in a picture window, draped against black. It sparkles."

For some reason, Skyler couldn't work on the campaign after that. It made him angry. He could not put his mind to the work.

A burly guard was at Skyler's side. The guard turned his gaze from Miles to Skyler.

"Just say when," the guard said.

Skyler did not answer. The guard turned his hard gaze back to Miles.

Skyler looked at the guard. Strange, Skyler had used the same words himself once making love to a woman, as he was entering her. 'Just say when'—*Pull yourself together,* Skyler thought. *'Just say when' and you'll never have to see him again. That was what the guard meant.He wasn't saying you're so stupid that you were getting fucked.* Something was shooting Skyler's mind all to hell.

Something was making Skyler angry. He was getting angrier and angrier and angrier. And he didn't see any outlet for it. He held his anger. Tried to work through it. Forced himself to think clearly through the anger.

There was nothing to having Miles stand out there and talk. What could come of it? Nothing. Still something about it disturbed Skyler. He decided to not let it disturb him.

He was determined to put Miles in his place. The loser box.

## Penthouse Patio Planning

CINJUN STOOD ON HIS PENTHOUSE BALCONY, and looked down at Miles.

The thoughts of the *High Crimson King* were elsewhere. He turned to the sky. His thoughts took him into distance.

Cinjun was weighing the ways to deliver himself into his proper place in history, to reach his rightful position, his proper place in the course of human events.

Much was coming together. It was all so lovely.

His mood was very lovely indeed. As he enjoyed this skyview before him. And this world that he would soon own.

And he did not look down at all—to the man down below—Miles Roark—the man talking, voicing some thoughts that came in no particular order.

Drawing a course that was evidently going every which way but straight. He was a sidewinder this man below. And of no importance. No importance at all.

It seemed to be talk tinged with a touch of crazy—and that spoiled it.

This man was of no importance. His talk—was talk of no importance at all.

Cinjun's thoughts were—far away, far beyond. Having traveled on to higher ground and taken full flight into the beyond. Boldly, into the wild blue beyond.

## 'Can you imagine the hole in the world?'

IN THE SANS SOUCI PLAZA—

The Changeling and the People of the Changes.

They called out for another trick. Try something else.

Interest us, you bastard! Let's see what you can do.

Each moment demanded a new impossibility. It was like the problem a juggler faced when he had to interest an audience by juggling with nothing whatsoever in his hands. No balls, no objects. Nothing to toss into the air. Except the ride itself. He made it all ride. Miles made it all ride.

And loaded the ride with bright color.

The brightest colors he could find. He put what he had into it. And he moved.

He was floating stone free on this third stone from the sun.

As he rode this breeze of cool rapidity, turning his ride loose, he braced his being—in the now—for opposition.

And *now*, in this burning *now,* this man whose heart was burning with feeling, in this *now* you just know what has to be . . . he encounters opposition. People who *will* him to stop!

Listen to this. They will have no more of him. Listen, baby it's time to put him in a cage.

You see the people, taking their attention to it now. Setting up boundaries for him. Feeding him dead stops.

They had ways that surrounded them, filled with demands for Miles to cease. And come to sanity.

They loathed insanity. And they hated this man.

He rubbed them the wrong way. His attitude disturbed them. He would have to stop. There was nothing else for it. He must not be allowed to be this way. He must be stopped.

Terrible, for a man, to be this way. Insane. Completely and totally insane. If only somebody would shoot him.

Now that would be interesting.

Somebody should really stop him. He was too much. Far too full of himself. Arrogant. Not humble like themselves. They had the good sense to keep their hatred and rage and murderous thoughts closed off and reigned tight. You really had to be proper about it; observe the niceties. That was the thing that this monster didn't understand. He only cared to seize. To seize the day; seize the night; seize on some tricks of the tongue that made him sound as if he made sense. But he made no sense at all. None. Somebody really ought to kill him.

They began to talk of ways to end him. And people like him—*the Know It All's*. Who were not like them; they were humble and kept to themselves. Yes, he was not like them; they were nice people. And only performed nice murders.

This Miles spoke of nice beautiful things that could be gotten now without delay. It was absurd. Absolutely absurd. Everybody knew that the only paths to true beauty were through the detours of murder, carnage, bombing, slaughter, executions, military operations, invasion forces, assault squads, and other proper civilized society practices.

They didn't come easy. They didn't come the way he said, just by letting them be. If it was that easy, why weren't people happy now? Here and now. Hear it now. Near and now. It was nonsense.

If that were possible, there would be a lot of happy people in the world. Where are all the happy people?

*Show them to me.*

*They don't exist. I prove my point. Case closed. I don't think I need to say another word, but I will . . .*

And so it went.

The ticket was red and bloodied from loving arts.

. . . And the tank was flooding with love sense.

He didn't make any sense at all; he was not *of people*, people made sense.

Sense was tricky business. Not as obvious as you would think. In fact it took a lot of tricks of thought to make sense.

These people made sense. Miles—he was crazy.

And he looked like the type that was going to stay crazy.

Miles kept it hot and squeeling. The feeling that is.

While his delivery remained laid back.

He spoke softly and carried large truths.

He was crazy you know. Ask all the best people, they'll tell you.

He's crazy that boy; stay away from him. He'll wipe your mind out and fill it with obscene talk of good, clean living.

There was no way to that—without good, clean violence. Miles would learn; in time he would learn.

The learning process would begin. The ancient ceremonial phrase for it was: *a beating*—The learning process would come. Somebody would give it to him; and give it to him good.

The good people hoped Miles would die soon. Now, however long the learning process would eventually take, it was too long. He really should get dead today. They wished somebody would go over and help the boy get dead. Then he would be quiet. And that was where he should go more than anywhere else—that was more important than anything—taking Miles to silence.

He was not too obliging on that score. He kept talking.

Experiencing, trying things, breathing life into the changes.

Those god-awful changes. You could gag on them. They just kept coming.

He was the changeling. See him change.

If he kept talking, the way he was talking, he would get a beating.

And then if he kept mouthing off, he would get dead.

That was the way it had always gone. It was beautiful. Beauty being truth, and truth being beauty as a poet once observed, oh so long ago. Beauty would get him. Kill him, something beautiful. Beauty would come and end him. Something beautiful always came along.

Generally in the form of a beautiful man—like Cinjun Khan S'mythe. An ancient spirit moved in Cinjun Smythe. The people saw it, and it made them feel tender. They dreamed of Cinjun Smythe! And in their dreams, darling, they were never lonely. They loved Cinjun whenever he was inside them. They loved him for sentimental reasons. They gave him their hearts—

*Hey, wasn't this place House Crimson?*

Well, what do you know—how about that?

Yes, the word around the campfire was that this was Cinjun Smythe's place and that old Cinjun Smythe would take care of this man—what was his name again? Miles Roark, huh. A forgettable name if ever there was one.

He would never go places. Not like Cinjun Smythe. That Cinjun Smythe was something else. Now there was a beautiful person. With beautiful crimson talk of murder and carnage and other civilized society practices.

If Cinjun ever went away, can you imagine the hole in the world?

Look at this Miles Roark, will you?

He was the changeling. See him change.

Love filled with murder. This was the pulse of the world life—Not empty love like Miles proposed . . . Plain love, no taste to it at all, really—No, give me strange love over that any day, thank you.

## In an Empire of the Hunter

THE COURTYARD OF THE HIGH CRIMSON KING WAS FILLED with people and an engine that hummed, sending its vibrations, its rippling waves of energy into the people.

Somebody screamed. It was a crazy scream. There was something crazy in this air, you could feel it. But you could not hone in on it by the talk. As a matter of fact, the talk was quite tame.

In the Sans Souci Plaza, Miles said, "In an empire, a court reporter can't blast the *Emperor*, it would mean never working again. So when the *Emperor* shreds a good treaty, he says in a banner headline, '*The Breach in the Treaty Is Well Timed.*'

"Now that doesn't sound bad at all—to shred a treaty—when you put it like that. Why if you shred some human rights and some justices with the other well-timed activity, it almost sounds like you're a good, brave, courageous leader. Hell, you timed it well.

"What do you say when he murders someone? It was well committed.

"Now that doesn't sound like a bad murder at all.

"It gets tough to make it sound good sometimes, but you will be amazed at how good you can make the worst villainy sound when you give it a try. Put the accent where you want it to fall. That's how you lie with the best of them. You make the bad appear good, and the good appear better. . . . And for the truth that lies out there in the wilderness, you dig an umarked grave."

"Who the hell wants that kind of act!" Burt Higgins said. He had stopped. Looked at Miles. Looked with open eyes. And listened with ears that took in everything. Looked at Miles. And concluded. "He won't stand," Burt Higgins said. "He won't last."

But Miles would not come down. He was gone. Felt that wave, and rode it. Taking steps, higher and higher. Learning to go as he went. Experiencing freedom, life in the Sans Souci Plaza.

He was holding on to nothing.

"The *Emperor* says the Earth is flat," Miles said.

"The headline becomes, '*The Shape of the Earth Is in Question.*' It appears to be even-handed.

"If he says, '*Up is down,*' the headline is, '*Some Leaders See Up Where Others See Down! Some say up is actually down.*'"

Blue is purple.

Green is red.

Life is death.

War is love.

The days get strange when the emperor speaks.

The story gets strange when the barkers tell it.

Where does it end?

Where does it go?

You hear the story.

It sounds easy.

But the old boy—

He's lying through his teeth.

A pair of reporters were taking themselves away from the scene in a slow walk.

"It's fucking boring," reporter Karl Wentworth said, "there are no strippers. No games. You know what I mean, there's nothing there."

"Nothing interesting," reporter Morty Wallace said. "All he gives you . . . are these principles."

"Fuck him."

"What is he? The guy with the secret of the world?"

"He's on a power trip. What are we, his stooges?" Karl said, with a tone like he had broken bones for less.

"I could tell you," he said, "things that would work. Strippers, games, tricks, something. You've got to have a little bit of something to it."

"True, very true." Morty said. He wasn't afraid to call the shot.

"Ah, he upsets me," Karl said.

"It's bullshit," Morty explained.

He liked to be precise. The whole thing was terribly upsetting, made you just want to beat the uppitiness out of that Miles Roark. Cut his roses down.

"It is . . . bullshit." Karl killed it there, with his tone that brought the matter to ground, deadly stilled.

Karl was leaving the scene with no interest in what he was leaving behind. "The hell with him! The hell with his speeches, the hell with his mother, the hell with the horse he rode in on! The hell with everything that brought his family to this great country!" Karl was much impressed with his strong ability to damn things to hell this day, and suffer the consequences without fear.

"Yep," Morty said. As they started to travel away from each other.

"Strippers," Karl said, impressed by his keen sense of the possibilities, all the possibilities.

"That would work."

"Games," Karl said, tossing in something for the kids.

"That would work," Morty said, in the same high-minded professional excited tone.

"Principles and rules—" Karl said.

"That don't work," Morty said. "No day, no how."

They were parting entirely now.

"See you later partner," Karl said.

"Later partner," Morty said.

They moved from the scene, taking their massive brains with them.

---

## Pivotflow

---

PIVOT, MILES THOUGHT.

Suddenly, experiencing pivotflow.

Everything wheeled in pivots.

Separate yourself from sense. Take a ride, get it on the inside.

Crazy for sale.

*Bold*—like no crazy you ever saw.

Who would like to sample his supply?

Crazy for sale.

This crazy told of *world*—the crazy breathed through a crazy dream— like the kind that spooks you in the night. Faint as will of the wisp. But clear—and the animal was sadly serenading the moon. The C'mon Serenade, under the worklight.

C'mon.

C'mon.

C'mon now touch the world.

Cinjun tells a sane, reasonable, perfectly-accepted, completely-allowable story of: He, that is—*god* man.

Now the animal breathed in the dream and what it said was:

*'I wish to tell a story. The story of: He, that is good man.'*

Crazy for sale. Crazy story for sale. He, That Is Good Man.

# He, That Is Good Man

"CINJUN, I'M CALLING YOU out to a Capoeira. A dancing fight. C'mon! A dancing fight. Whoo-yeah! C'mon———"

That which will be, will be.

That which is, is.

He that tries, does not do it.

Let the fight rule. Let the fight take us over. Let go to the fight, Cinjun old boy.

My old friend, Cinjun. Capoeira!—Dancing fight. Let's go. Let's roll.

The fight doesn't follow your rules. The fight is here. The fight will be.

C'mon, baby.

Cinjun Khan Smythe—c'mon!

He who is good man, does not try.

The love that wants to be, well, it is.

Who says much that goes, does not go—As well as it does not go, it does not come.

You cannot fight this fight from behind soft lies, you cannot march behind a soft parade. You cannot hold on to anything.

The fight that is, will be. The fight speaks, with silent sense. T h e fight that is good, does not fall, and if one day it falls, it falls well.

Sadness walks away from this fight. This fight is a Capoeira!

This fight is not rules. This fight is not deals. This fight is not ceremonies. This fight is me. I am the fight. C'mon Cinjun. The fight that is, let it be. The fight that has come, let it come. The fight that will, is good. And if it falls, it will fall well.

Capoeira! Cinjun.

Capoeira speaks . . .

Ber-im-bau
Ber-im-bau
Ber-im-bau

The berimbau sings . . .

Che-gung-ging

Che-gung-ging
Che-gung-ging
Che-gung
Che-gung
Che-gung-ging

Capoeira speaks . . .

"He that is good man, *is,*" Miles said.
    "He who is good, does not try.
    "He who is there, does not reach.
    "That which is, will be.
    "Sadness walks, away.
    "It is. And when it falls, it falls well.
    "See, does not less. Suffer, does not let. Strive, does not need.
    "It is. It will be.
    "That which will be, is."

The berimbau sings . . .

Che-gung-ging
Che-gung-ging
Che-gung-ging
Che-gung
Che-gung
Che-gung-ging

"He that is good man, *is,*" Miles said.
    He who is good, does not try.
    He who loves, does not try.
    That which goes, goes.
    He who says much, does not go.
    He that tries, does not go.
    As he does not go, he does not come.
    He that seeks, has not found.
    He that preaches, does not know.
    He that moves strong, does not know strength.
    The capoeira that will be, is.
    He that tells much of love, does not know.
    He that forces love, does not love.

He that is a good man, does not try.
He that is good, does not fall.
If one day he falls, he falls well.

Capoeira speaks! Sadness walks away.
Hey, hey, sadness walks away.
Hey, hey, sadness walks from this place.

He who is peace, *is.*
He who *is,* does not praise.
He who wars, praises peace.
He who wars, searches.
He who searches, has not found.
He who has not found, does not know where to look.
He who has found, knows peace.
He who is peace, knows finding without search.
He who knows peace, has no need to speak of peace.
He who knows peace, knows how high peace can grow.
He who cuts it down, will never know.

Hear it now, the truth is
here and now, the truth is
near and now, the truth is
peace and now, the truth is . . .

Love is now.
. . . *love is now* . . .
Hey, hey, sadness walks away.
. . . *hey, hey, sadness walks away* . . .

Capoeira speaks! Sadness walks away.
Hey, hey, sadness walks away.
Hey, hey, sadness walks from this place.

He who does not know peace, speaks of honor.
He that is this man speaks of peace with honor, this is *victory* . . . He that lusts for victory, does not know honor.
He that is this man, who does not know honor, speaks of *mission.*
He, that is this man speaks of peace mission, this is *war* . . . He that makes his mission war, has not made it peace.

Capoeira speaks! Sadness walks away.
Hey, hey, sadness walks away.
Hey, hey, sadness walks from this place.

He, that is this man speaks of entry; this is *invasion*—He that invades
does not know welcome.
He that is not welcome, is not well come.
He that is not well come, does not rightly go.
He that does not rightly go, does not know love.
He that does not know love cannot save.
He that is this man speaks of *save;* this is *destroy*—He that destroys,
does not build.
He that does not build, does not know birth.
He that does not know birth, does not know life.
He that does not know life, does not know love.
He that does not know love, goes to die
. . . Without loving anybody.

That which is the name, is little. That which is, is much.
What is done, *is*. What is named, *is*.
Do what is good, when you say it is done.
He that says much, does not do.
He that is, does.
What is done, is.
What is, is named.

Capoeira speaks! Sadness walks away from this place.
Hey, hey, sadness walks away.
Hey, hey, sadness walks from this place.

Capoeira speaks . . .

Ber-im-bau
Ber-im-bau
Ber-im-bau

The berimbau sings . . .

Che-gung-ging

Che-gung-ging
Che-gung-ging
Che-gung
Che-gung
Che-gung-ging

Capoeira speaks ...

"He that is good man, *is,*" Miles said.
    He who is good, does not try.
    He who loves, does not try.
    That which goes, goes.
    He who says much, does not go.
    He that tries, does not go.
    As he does not go, he does not come.
    He that seeks, has not found.
    He that preaches, does not know.
    He that moves strong, does not know strength.
    The capoeira that will be, is.
    He that tells much of love, does not know.
    He that forces love, does not love.
    He that is a good man, does not try.
    He that is good, does not fall.
    If one day he falls, ... he falls well.

Hey, hey, sadness walks away ...
Hey, hey, sadness walks from this place ...
Hey, hey, sadness walks away ...
Hey, hey ...

The soft strains fading.
Time slipping, time slipping.
Miles now, taking the moment into silence.
The silence looming.
Time slipping, time slipping.

The silence stood and felt itself assaulted.
By other moments. Calls to other worlds.
And the battles of other times.
The silence felt the world taken—to the desert, to distant desert

sands.

To white dunes and slipfaces. Among this sand-splashed place, the world peopled. This world stretched before these people and called them to journey—to experience pursuit of desires. Riches—and to search out the possibilities. To take moments. To search for glory. And high purpose. And know life among the desert sands.

'*The Sultan*' spoke:

The sultan said to the old horse trader:

"Old horse trader, I wish you to bring me a black stallion that runs so swiftly that it leaves no tracks. Buy this horse for me. I wish it so."

The old horse trader said, "My sultan, I am an old man, I no longer do this work. But I know a fish monger who has a very good eye for horses. He will find your horse for you."

The next season, the sultan brought the old horse trader before him, and said:

"Old horse trader, why did you tell me the fish monger has a good eye for horses? I asked him to bring me a black stallion that runs so swiftly that it leaves no tracks; he brought me a brown mare. It is an ugly horse. A horrible horse."

"But your majesty, may I ask, does the horse run so swiftly that it leaves no tracks?"

"Yes, it runs so swiftly that it leaves no tracks."

"Then the fish monger has better eyes than I, for he sees beyond appearances."


Capoeira speaks! Sadness walks away.

Hey, hey, sadness walks away.

Hey, hey, sadness walks from this place.

## The Rundown

SUCH A LOVELY . . . loving . . . loveable grip—*the Hunter.*

And his grip reaching for the Hunted . . . and you . . . and you . . . and you . . . and you . . . and you . . .

An ancient spirit moved within Cinjun. Everyone could see it.

## The Hunter in the Red Vest

INTRODUCING THE HUNTER IN THE RED VEST. Swaying side to side, with movements like a god. There's no one like the Hunter in the Red Vest. You may meet him, you may see him—The Hunter in the Red Vest.

Oh, the wonder of the thing—the Hunter in the Red Vest. There's no one like the Hunter in the Red Vest. There never was. There never will be.

The Hunter in the Red Vest is here.

And he's telling the story. That sounds easy. Gets into your skin.

The burgundy god emperor—The strongman in the red vest.

New strongman for sale—

The Hunter in the Red Vest.

He's putting the pieces together, every movement, every moment.

The Hunter in the Red Vest speaks—

The Burgundy Parade. Care to take a sip of burgundy brew? Intoxicating burgundy brew?

The Parade—He writes it with his eyes. His eyes take everything. Take hold of everything.

He puts a spell on you . . . because you're his.

The Hunter in the Red Vest.

Breathing.

Among forest shapes.

Coming alive.

## The Parade

COME SEE THE PARADE. The parade of purposes and the parading possibilities.

Feel free to swoon when your purpose comes up.

*The Puff Parade,* Miles thought. *Puff! Puff! Puff those rings away.*

*A Smoke Parade,* Miles thought. *Puff! Puff! Puff those rings away.*
*Those smoke rings I love. Rings I know so well.*

The Puff Parade—Puff! Puff! Puff those rings away.

The Smoke Parade—smoky little rings.

Puff! Puff! Puff those rings away.

A phantom parade of love.

Blow, blow them through the air—

Silky little lies.

Those little smoke rings of lies that I love.

Puff those rings away.

Puff! Puff! Puff your cares away.

Night and day.

Blow, blow them through the air, silky little rings,

Those smoke rings I love.

## Sultan See Beyond

"STRIP AWAY BONES AND SKIN," Miles said.

Strip away the puff parade. Strip away the smoke dreams.

Strip away all.

Walk the elemental parade. Walk nature.

Now you are outside. Walk the forest wilderness. Walk all of the days. Walk all of the nights.

Walk all the pain and pleasure.

Show me what lies within. Won't you be—

*One.*

I am—one. Seeming one, be one. Being one, be one.

Be *Wāone.*

I am *Wāone.*

Be Wãone and enter the Wãoynde.

Be Wãone who enters the Whirlwind Wãoynde. The Wild Whirlwind Wãoynding Wild. Screaming Wild! Wild with the power. Wild as can be.

Be Wãone.

Hey, hey, sadness walks away.

Hey, hey, sadness walks from this place.

Oh good fellow *Soft Parade* . . . Let's knock out the front, and pound these things into some raw shapes.

Raw shapes—Showing them raw shapes and all the love in your heart. Raw, elemental beauty.

Beauty, creating the *Elemental Parade,* right before your eyes.

To show them elemental beauty. This is all he knows.

"The lies, the lies, the lies, oh, are they dressed to kill. Dressed nice. Dressed pretty. Dressed so fine.

"They shop for clothing in all the best places.

"But when they come to you with that pretty lie, see nothing but the lie."

"See merely the lie.

"Lie shapes.

"Let's pound some pretty lie shapes into raw shapes, into elemental shapes.

"Strip to show us all you are. Strip away bones and skin, strip away hide, strip away cover, strip away front, strip away put-on. Let's go to what you are. Oh, slow sad smoke parade.

"Let's have a good look. Let's have a real good look.

"Not all looking is seeing, but when they come to you, . . . you see."

## Wild in the Wilderness

"OH TO BE WILD IN THE WILDERNESS."

That's what he wants, great weddings of garden forms, producing beautiful soaring people shapes.

"I'm here to have a good time," Miles said.

"They don't want a good time at their party; nothing wild. Their party is all business. They're working some deals, that's all. Everything else stays out.

"I say, 'I want to see my people have a good time!'

"I'm driving this thing; and I'm going to drive it all over town."

"I'm not talking about throwing a revolution," Miles said in the plaza.

"I'm talking about having a good time.

"I'm talking about dancing.

"I'm talking about my people getting wicked and feeling nice.

"You know Cinjun doesn't like the way I do my thing. He doesn't get with that thing.

"C'mon, people! Let's show him what it's about!

"I'm talking about dancing. Splishing and a-splashing, a-rolling and a-strolling. I'm talking about a-reeling with the feeling. I'm talking about dancing on the living room rug. Laughing in the rain, dancing in the snow, having a good time———"

I'm talking about seeing my people have some fun. Tonight, let's have some fun, let's run. Let the wild color light up the night!

I want to feel good, I want to feel nice, that's what I'm talking about.

Oh, to be wild in the wilderness! I want to see my people have some fun.

People, people, people, I'm talking about having some fun.

How high can the people shapes grow? If you cut them down, you'll never know.

Oh, wicked fun. Be you bright, be you light, and let it fun. Oh, let it fun. Now let the world fun itself.

And oh, let it people!

The world is big now, and all grown, it can fun itself!

Oh, let it fun!

## Hey, Pachuco!

"I DON'T LIKE WHAT HE'S SAYING," Pachuco said, "it's so vicious."

He had nothing against fun, he was just opposed to it on moral grounds.

As a matter of fact, this was actually the main reason he had been hired for his job—he was an objective reporter. This was his profession. A reporter for the *light*vision.

*He's against,* Daphne thought, *the fun? He's right it could lead to funning in the streets—and cocktail hours?* Immediately, Daphne grew much opposed to strong drink. Except sometimes. After meals was still good. Before meals was also good. And during meals was good. In the morning, was fine. Afternoons, were fine. Evenings, were fine. But no other time. This talk of rampant fun had to be viewed through that prism.

"Yes, horrible, horribly vicious," Daphne said.

They stood in the plaza. Pachuco Cabeza and his *light*vision crew had arrived on the scene. They had come in response to an alert from Daphne.

Pachuco was a chief Barker, a very famous face, with an enormous show and an enormous following on the *light*vision—*Or so he hoped!*

*Or so it would be!*—Daphne assured him. No one knew him now. But he had the stuff of legend. He was only a reporter for a *light*vision station. He was hardly known in his own power station. But he would become a legend—Daphne made him feel his importance.

She gave him the treatment . . .

Her treatment . . . She put her hands on his shoulders; brought her eyes and lips close to his, until he was breathing in her body.

He drew a breath.

Pachuco looked at Daphne and studied her beautiful face.

"He's a guy talking in the street about fun," Pachuco said. "I can't encourage that kind of behavior."

"Fun in the streets?" she asked.

"Yes," he said, "where is everyone supposed to go?"

"We could have runaway fun," she said.

"That's right," he said. "I can't broadcast a call for fun. What if we have a fun riot. Or people going so 'fun,' that we can't bring them back."

She draped her arm through his. And she took Pachuco aside.

They moved away from everybody else. To a nice, cozy, intimate corner of the Sans Souci Plaza. And gazed upon the scene before them.

"I'm filled with worldly ambition," Daphne said to Pachuco. "I lust for success. And I can see what I would do if I were in your place."

"What might that be?" he replied.

"I would use stories—like this one in the street—to raise *my own profile.*"

Pachuco studied her.

"I'm not you," she said. "But if I were, I would take a story like this and turn it into a national story."

He looked at her.

"No one else is here," she said.

She turned to the plaza. He turned with her.

"You could own this story."

She turned back to him.

"You're an interesting lady," he said.

She pressed him. She wasn't about to be distracted. She said, "I would want my stock to go up. . . . The next time my contract would come up, I would want to have a slew of national stories in tow. . . . The next time a national seat would open up, I would want them to think of me, and know me as the lady who finds national stories where others miss them."

Pachuco looked around and then looked at her.

"You're a very ambitious woman," he observed.

"That's what all the men like about me," she said.

"I see," he said.

"And *women* like ambitious *men*," she said.

"There's truth in that," he conceded.

"So what might you be thinking?" she pressed.

"I could use a national story," he said. "But I don't see enough here. He's a guy standing in the street talking about fun." Pachuco Cabeza looked around, and scanned the scene with his keen reporter's eye. "I don't think there's enough here to make it a national story."

"There's more than you think," she said softly.

"How?" he asked.

"We'd like to do something special," she said.

"Something special?" Pachuco asked.

"Yes, we have something in mind that we'd like to show you."

"He's a guy in the street talking about fun."

"There's more fun to come," she said.

He narrowed his gaze.

"How about something special?" she said.

# The Swat Pow-Wow

CINJUN WENT INTO "The Swat Pow-Wow."

The executive committee commenced its activity quickly; Cinjun carried them into much pressing business.

Cinjun was drawing their attention to a grid on the board. They were seated around the broad horseshoe table.

## Swat

"Swat!—Strengths, weaknesses, attacks, threats." Cinjun was calling out the quadrants of the grid. "Let's examine them."

This was the *Swat! Session.*

They would look at their *strengths,* to be cherished; *weaknesses,* to be ended—*attacks,* that was where they might attack—and, *threats,* that was where they were under threat.

It was a see-all system, so that they might be all. And end all ungood things under the sun.

He was taking them into the rapids that streamed upwards. Taking them to higher ground. This was movement along the *Red Continuum.*

Abruptly, Cinjun heard a sound.

Distance intruded.

Cinjun saw their attention seized.

They were being assaulted by a wave of sound, from outside. They were being disturbed. They looked to the windows . . . there was a kind of screeching, squeeling hum out there.

And now they were interrupted by a greater wave of sound coming from outside. They ran to the window.

The commotion intruding was so great that they were forced to the patio. To step out on the edge of the aerie. And take in the scene from the high patio.

Now, they stepped onto the patio, streamed out to the aerial courtyard, and lined up by the parapet. Cinjun cut through them and had a look for himself.

Earlier Cinjun had stood on his patio, his aerie, and looked at Miles standing below in the courtyard. Miles was no longer down below. Now, he was directly across from them. He was mounting a skyscraper.

## The Scraper in the Sky

WHAT CINJUN SAW WERE: the canyons of the city, skyscrapers streaming up . . .

And on the mountaintop across from House Crimson . . . Miles Roark!

What he saw was Miles's look. A still, steady, relaxed gaze. Everything else swirled around the gaze. The look told what he was doing.

He was taking it into: mountaintop capoeira.

From the canyons, Miles arose. Striding. Taking the forest city.

This was high folly; this was an idiot, Cinjun thought. This boy didn't know enough to come in out of the rain.

Cinjun's gaze traveled to a sky vessel circling above. Inside he saw a *light*vision crew, and its *light*caster catching the scene below.

Cinjun looked down below.

Groundside, he saw another *light*vision crew. A reporter was interviewing Daphne Fox. . . . Here in this scene, the crew was holding the *light*caster low and angling it up. In the background, it was capturing the image of Miles climbing.

Cinjun took in the Sans Souci Plaza. It was now pulsing with a great crowd scene.

*The crowd was cheering*—not because Miles was climbing a mountain and was becoming the scraper in the sky—They were cheering for what took him to this moment. An intense passion.

Each in his way, wanted that intense passion. The passion of youth. The passion of purpose, and force. Where had it gone, each thought; many had it, and many saw it slide away.

Before them was a young man who had it, still. And for this, they cheered. Watched. And wondered.

It was an inspiration to the crowd, that was what made it disturbing to Cinjun; it was more than the theatrics, the trouble with it was—*It was emotional.*

People wanted to be up there.

To feel the being of being *Astride the Colossus.*

Oh, to do it in daylight, and even in company.

He made the crowd aware of the soaring forms, of rising, sweeping gold and purple into pale blue.

In the forest society, people forgot sometimes that the skyscrapers were merely *mountains*. That was what they amounted to. They were heaps of ore and rock taken from far mountains; brought to the city, and used to erect *man mountains*. And the thing to do with a mountain was to climb it.

Hell, just because no one did it, that didn't make it any the less sensible.

They didn't rise by themselves, the man mountains rose by the work of *mountain climbers*. Now why should men stop climbing it the moment the scraper hit the sky? Silly, wasn't it? Willy nilly silly. A beautiful sky form just sitting there, and no Miles Roark was ever supposed to climb it. Silly, really. Willy nilly silly.

Miles would have none of it—he climbed the man mountain.

And when he came to the sky, to one of his truest friends, he spoke to it. Man to sky.

The moment came, and was not designed by Miles, but by what stood below the moment. Made by the ground on which the moment stood.

Trained not to intrude, they were all trained not to intrude. All their lives, taught not to intrude.

Taught that the world did not belong to them. That the rock and ore of the world that peopled did not belong to the world. Taught that much was forbidden, that ways of walking, and ways of being, and places of going were forbidden.

Nature was chaos, and curves, and sloping forms. Wiggles and twists and great sidewinding. Twists and swirls and great sidewinding, this was the natural way.

Miles moved in the natural way.

He climbed the scraper in the sky; he was moving to become the scraper in the sky.

It was an act of emergence—And all who sought to stop him, be damned.

He was about to intrude . . . on Cinjun Smythe.

Miles's head was filled with songs.

He liked to take steps that make you feel dizzy. That take you into a frontier swirl, a wild whirlwind, wãoynding wild. Oooohhh, yes. Sunrays, speedrays and boundless skies. And a frontier swirl. That was the way to live.

Miles threw his head up, for a flash of a second, to look at Cinjun Smythe. And he breathed the scent in the air.

Cinjun locked eyes with Miles, and in the flash Cinjun saw the startling thing that was in Miles's eyes: he saw sunbeams. And *Tygers* crouched in jungles in his dark eyes.

Miles broke away.

Miles went on, following the form.

He felt, he felt, he felt, *Love!*
And he felt, . . . Love!
Love like the sun.
And streaming sunbeams.
Sunbeams coming down like rain.
Sun Rains!
And a wild whirlwind wãoynding wild. Screaming wild.
Oooh, sister! Ooooh, brother! Yeah, yeaaaaah!
He did not say a word.

The eyes of the *light*vision below were able to come in close on Miles when he looked down. And the *light*vision crew hovering in the air was able to come in close on Miles's eyes when he looked up.

He had a face lit with wild color, and in his eyes, that thing: *Tygers* crouched in jungles in his dark eyes.

This child, this goddamn child, Cinjun thought. Where were his parents?

Where were the adults to come take him away before he forced a man to drown the child?

Miles did not say a word.

## Lady Day

*The Steel Hulk,* rose into the blue sky.

Summer stretching on the grass. On the wood, stone, steel, and glass. Spears of light, carving nothing into form.

Resonant drops of sound rolling in the sunny clarity of the summer air.

He stood on the summit, his legs planted wide apart, leaning back against space.

Staring, staring, staring.

In this moment, life was good.

Oh, sweet lady of love. Sweet lady of the All. Lady Day!

She was his love, Lady Day. Her presence was here, she charged the air.

The form of the moment breathed life, and sang sweetly to the lady that swam in mystery. Sang with full-throated ease. Of summer, and spring, and springing ease.

Oh, sweet woman, he reached for her, a true friend of his.

He put his hands out to touch her.

"That guy can't stop himself! He's in love with her!" He could not keep his hands off Lady Day.

Lady Day,
She'll wash your troubles,
Your troubles,
Your troubles away!

He stood on the steel cliff, astride the structure, and looked out to the countryside, out to the long reaches of trails twisting out to shores and horizons, and beyond.

Everywhere, jumbles of bright fluttering winds.

Streaks.

And Miles forgot. Forgot everything.

There was just him and the wild whirlwind wāoynding wild. Screaming wild.

And a mad love affair with Lady Day.

In the summer evening . . .

Darkness mounted slowly up the beams of the scrapers in the sky. The last sunrays retreated.

Time slipped, time slipped.

Summer was almost gone.

Miles was able to summon the full force gale; but the waning of his powers, the end of his heaven, was ever near.

*The End* was chasing him. Hounding him in the time slipstream.

It was dark.

There was a strong wind. The feel of cold; whistling pressure.

Flow ripping the air. Nothing moving in stone corridors. In this realm, not a tree to stir. Only naked masses of stone. This was the feeling of the moment.

Miles held a news conference, a Moonlight Sonata in this.

## The Moonlight Sonata

MILES HELD A NEWS CONFERENCE, to give power to his punch. He had to show the world all the love that was in his heart. And show them a heart drowning in love dreams.

Time slipping, time slipping.

In the now … he has to let it rip, for all to see. He steps up, concentrates. Builds up, builds up. He has to bring them into slow sensation. Into a heart drowning in love dreams.

Time slipping, time slipping.

Take it into the now of the moment. He steps into the light. The beams are on him.

*Nobody else here, baby.* This wave was all his. Just him and the *light*vision. It was his to do. He had to take them into slow sensation.

It was time for soundshape. *But first, must come the feeling,* Miles thought.

He seized upon the fury of the moment, and formed a big generator. A mighty engine. And he let the engine hum.

Feeling, stretched out—past the shades and shafts of trees—shattered the night—attacked masses of stone. And cascaded on. Rending. Throbbing. Resounding. A heatwave tearing loose.

Moving.

Time slipping, time rending.

This was aimed straight for the Night Sun, the Cosmic All, and sweet Lady Day.

He threw himself into it.

Astral fields come away!

The boy took them into it, into slow sensation.

Heatwave, white lightning, when he moved, he moved everything.

He formed a big generator. Such a strange generator. Striking.

The Big Generator, cruising through the night.

Miles, moving up from under, he took it up high, until it began to crack apart, and let rip, in slow, slow style.

## Blue Sonic

*The Double Lung Scream.*
This was the beginning, an exploding *double lung scream;* white lightning, bound to drive you wild. And a heart drowning in love dreams. Drowning, dying, in slow, slow style. Dying, dying, dying.

And the double lung scream—

Extending, extending, extending.

On and on it goes. On and on. Stretching, stretching, extending.

Reaching. In slow, slow style.

He was screaming, screaming, screaming, . . . screaming, . . . screaming . . . screaming wild.

A song of longing for.

## Color Waves in Slow, Slow Style

A blue in green and a green in blue sonic. A blue sonic tearing through the night.

Red in yellow. Yellow in orange.

Deep blue in sky blue.

Green in yellow.

A blue sonic of color and range.

A blue sonic coming from his heart and soul.

Blowing across wind and sky. Mercy! What a blue sonic.

A song rich and deep and blue.

And a heart drowning in love dreams.

A blue sonic. Singing of a Pacifica Love Dream.

And now the Pacifica Love Dream.

The feeling spreading.

Riding the blue sonic.

Spreading. Floating. Spreading. Rising.

A blue sonic.

Purple in red in orange in yellow.

Rich black in dark blue in sky blue in emerald green in lemon yellow.

A blue sonic.

And out there the people taken in by the blue sonic.
  The *light*vision caught the extending.
  And the people out there felt the spreading waves.
  Felt the waves traveling past them into distance.
  A blue sonic.

## Out to the Buildings

The twilight washed off the buildings.
  They rose, thin shafts of blue—and the colors of evening and distance.
They rose in bare outlines, breaking upward.
  The forest city on the edge of the sky held out—a will to beauty, and a
raw presence.

Into this, Miles hurled the force of his being.
  The people of the *light*vision caught the extending.

On this street, where time had died, he let it fly.
  The street was cold, dark had won.
  Miles let it fly.
  A heatwave, white lightning.
  And there it was. Growing, growing, growing.
  Tearing loose.
  Out and away.

*Argh, remember!* The feeling had come. Slow sensation exploding in slow,
slow style. Up. Up. Up.
  A sound sunburst flowering. Emerging. Rising.
  *Argh, remember! Come on home. Your place is here,* it sang.
  The winds of life were coming back. Sweeping in. Taking the moment
into cool rapidity. Rending through flowering slow sensation.
  And they were there, the people who watched, they were suddenly
in the station. A place of . . . a power station, . . . and shockwaves. Of
heatwaves, and white lightning.
  And in the station, the boy. And this boy could move, everything.
  When he moved, it was a sin, so sweet and true.
  A song . . . deep and rich and blue.
  A song, . . . deep, and rich, and true.
  They lay in it for days, a Pacifica Love Dream Experience.
  The audience, they were, being tossed in waves and oceans of

experience.

*Argh, remember! Come on home. Your place is here,* it sang.

And grew.

C'mon home. You got to come on home. Ooh, c'mon home.

C'mon, Bring it on home.

Argh, don't forget, no! Come home. Come along, and come home.

The howl.

Going, going, going. A fire. Ascending. A flight of the imagination. Ascending. In slow, slow style.

The city moving away. In the vast emptiness of sky and ocean.

He saw it.

He felt it.

He let it rip.

The way he moved, it was a sin, so sweet and true. In slow, slow style.

He knew how to move, everything.

Always wanting more, he'd leave you longing for, slow, slow style.

Heatwave, white lightning, bound to drive you wild.

The way he moved, always wanting more, he'd leaving you longing for slow, slow style.

Every note of that song that he sang . . . was true. . . . It was here, and then in a flash it was gone.

A slow, slow style. Springing wild. Screaming wild. It was here, and then it was gone.

And coming out of the shockwave: *Miles Roark.*

In a slow, slow style.

Can you feel it?

Can you beat it?

It was an impressive display of insanity.

*Let's keep the crazy train rolling,* the world screamed.

## The Lightcasters

THE SCREAM AND THE BARKERS OF THE *LIGHT*VISION.

They looked at him on the omniscio.

*"He's a sound chaser. And he's showing us that he could perhaps be the strangest sound chaser we've ever seen."*

They were reporting live from a blue sonic, a blue sonata. A moonlight sonata.

"I've never seen a sonata like this."

"Strange."

"Yes, strange. It's better left at that."

"It's clinging awkwardly to time."

"It's getting trapped in cracks in the floor."

"How's he going to get this to match the legs of the table?"

"It doesn't go with the furniture."

"How's he going to bring it into the house?"

"It doesn't fit through the door."

"It's a sonata. It's a blue sonic. It's pretty. But what can you do with it?"

"Put it in your mouth, but that's all I can think of."

"It doesn't do anything."

"It's just a song."

Go try and do something with it.

You can't.

In fragments and tatters it was scattered across the night. They saw the pieces. The reflections of possibilities. But they could not see the whole, the purpose, the form.

It was meaningless to them.

But Miles just kept going—Singing his sonata. Rending his *blue and green sonic through the black of the night.*

The lightcasters talked about the use of it. What do you do with it?

You experience it, and then what? What do you do with it?

He leaves it to us. That's the problem. Why leave it to us? Who are we? Who is he? These are questions. When you hear a sonata like this you have to ask the questions?

What do you do with it?

Where's the answer? There is no answer. That's why it's nothing.

It's not proper.

It's not a proper thing at all.

In the background he kept going.

Did it draw some people?—Yes, some pieces seemed to work—Some people put on their coats and shoes and went out into the night. To see what was happening at the Sans Souci Plaza.

To source this sonata. This blue, moonlight sonata.

"I am time. I am truth" The song said.

That's what the song was saying. What were you supposed to do with it?

The lightcasters talked about the pieces. The jigsaw.
There's a piece here, a piece there.
This piece is doing this . . . and this piece doing that.
Where's the whole thing? Give us that.
Give us a past and a future. Give us the full picture. Give us everything.
Not just pieces, here and there.
We cannot be consigned to here or there, nor to this or that.
Give it all.
Talk about how the pieces are oddly and badly shaped.
How do you get the big piece into the house? How do you connect this piece to the table?
How do you connect the pieces to the furniture?
How do you use the pieces? In your life?
They're just pieces. What can you do with pieces?
Nothing.
You need connections. He leaves it to you to get the connections. He leaves it to you to put the pieces together. What kind of act is this?
He acts like the audience is the smartest thing in the world. Don't treat the audience like smart animals. Like smart beings.
Don't treat the audience like that? What are we supposed to do suck the ideas from your mind?
The sense of logic—no! He gives us the sense of—the sense of—
What is this poetry? We know the case. Poetry doesn't change the world.
When did poetry topple a tyrant? When did a poem beat the bad guys? It's never happened. It never will happen. It never can happen.
It's like he thinks a sound chaser can take on a thunder god.
The other guy laughed.
He's deranged. It's the aria of a madman.
The aria of the mad—that's what we have here. Move on folks. Nothing to see here.

They held their gazes steady in the *light*vision.
   They had determined what *was* and *is.*
   They let their wisdom go shining on.

   —oh, something was happening—

   They broke off, taking it back to Miles Roark ... "Let's go back to the conference, Roark appears to be wrapping it up."

   They cut back to Miles—Miles was standing on a riser. *I put a spell on you, I put a spell on you, because you're mine.* This was the feeling he was casting into a thick silence. He was waiting for the sky to fall down. Once it settled to a nice, quiet still repose of dead silence, he tore the silence softly. And what he said was:

   "There's a hell of a good universe, next door.
   "What do you say we take a trip over, and have a look?"

   Then Miles smiled. Or at least it seemed like he smiled. But as a matter of fact, he did nothing that he hadn't been doing already. And the son of a bitch didn't do another thing for a good long time. He stood there and smiled. If you could call it a smile.

## Cinjun Smythe—Come Out of Your Cave

"SET IT FREE, CINJUN! Set it free." He said it plainly. He didn't add anything to the words except their plain, and apparent color.
   "Why do you keep holding on so tightly? Set it free, Cinjun, set it free. Let it be, Cinjun, why don't you?————"
   You can't talk to a man with a shotgun in his hand. He thinks he knows how everything is going to be.
   C'mon, Cinjun, come out of your cave.
   Hear this Shotgun Man: C'mon out of your clubhouse. C'mon out of your warm bed, and step into the arena.
   Cinjun, let my people see you.
   Come out of your fortress, come out of your tank. Come out of your safehouse. Come out of your stronghold.
   Come out of your warm bed. Come out of your house. Come out from behind your gate, and guards. And see the world. Come see the world

Cinjun Smythe, it's out here waiting for you.

It's your turn to step up and take it.

Awake, Cinjun Smythe. Shake dreams from your head, my sweet thing. Enter the world. Enter the hot landscape.

I know you're comfortable in your bed. It's nice and warm and soft. But you say you're a champion and a champion does not stay in bed all morning.

All your ways, . . . but lead to bed.

Up and out and back to bed again.

Though you go in pride and strength,

you come back to bed at length.

Though you shout in mighty woe,

back to bed you're bound to go.

High, you toss your head,

but all your days but lead to bed.

Up and out and then back to bed again.

Let's go to the ledge, let's go to the precipice. Come my nemesis, let's go to the edge.

C'mon Cinjun, step up. It's your turn to step up and take it.

## Cinjun Makes a Move

CINJUN WAS NOT A THICK-HEADED MAN.

He saw clearly. And knew when to produce changes.

Cinjun turned to Skyler and said, "Let's send the come-from-nowhere guy back to nowhere.

"To perfect nowhere. To winning nowhere. To absolutely, beautiful, tastefully decorated nowhere. To Nothingsville. To Nobody Town."

Now Skyler descended to the courtyard, and brought himself to a point a pace away from Miles.

Miles turned and looked at Skyler with some passing interest.

"You're on, Miles!" Skyler said.

And waited for a reaction.

He didn't get anything.

This Miles was made of something dense, Skyler thought.

Miles looked at Skyler. Skyler drew a breath.

"Cinjun wants you," Skyler said, "to drink your orange juice, eat your vegetables and keep your mouth shut—Hold yourself together and if you can do that you'll get a chance to fight him—"

Skyler held his look on Miles. Miles did nothing.

"We'll get it on . . ." Skyler said. "You follow?"

Miles did nothing.

"Good," Skyler said. "Now are we clear? We'll get it on. And then he's going to ram his fist so far down your throat it will take you a week to get it out."

Miles looked at him.

Skyler prepared to leave.

"Do you want to say anything?" Skyler said. "Before we end this social."

"Yes, did you ever think you'd see a day," Miles said, "when you had so much trouble trying to say something clever in plain English?"

That was all Miles said.

It got to Skyler. Got to him something fierce. Miles didn't have to do anything else. He waited a moment and then said . . .

"Do you know what I have in mind Skyler?" Miles asked.

"What?" he answered.

"Something special," Miles said.

# Peace Pose

CINJUN UNDERSTOOD the Peace Craze that was killing the country. It would blow over.

The Peace Craze was nothing. The Love Craze was nothing. They would pass.

Love is like a cigarette . . . Has your heart aglow, burns to ashes. Ashes of regret. So much for love—it held the value of ashes, when you priced it high. Cinjun laughed.

He watched the clouds roll by.

Order was everything. Cinjun knew how to put the world in order.

It needed a good strongman in charge.

New strongman for sale. Strength that's new and fresh and bold. He would boldly go where no strongman had gone before. To god emperor and an era of peace. The kind of peace that remained stable, at the point of a gun.

Cinjun laughed again. It was amusing how fools might fall for love dreams.

Cinjun was proofed against it. Pharaoh's heart was hardened.

He would rule the known world. So let it be written, so let it be done.

He would employ master builders, and build a world. Naysayers could go live outside. He would send them to the black void.

It would all be easy, part of his moving on.

They would get gone for good. They would get dead. He saw the battlefield then. A beautiful battlefield, the most beautiful the world would ever see. And above—a Crimson Sun.

He was the most important man that had ever lived or ever shall live.

And he strode forward under a Crimson Sun to a House Crimson.

Love took you to hands and knees on the floor. Some majesty it offered. Ugly and small.

It was time to trap Miles Roark.

He was conspiring a trap for Miles Roark. He was moving with care, allowing it to take shape in the fullness of time. And when the time was ripe, he would stop Miles Roark, softly.

Softly.

He would proceed in steps. And then he would stop Miles Roark.

Softly.

Cinjun would move in deliberate, driving steps. Wise, strong, cunning steps.

Cinjun deliberate—

Miles was striking on impulse, where he might. That was evidence of enormous weakness. Cinjun would use it to stop Miles. Miles's talk was scattered, random. That evidenced weakness, he left open many strike points.

Cinjun saw the many ways to manipulate Miles Roark.

To take all the force from out of his assault.

Miles's arrows went wide. Cinjun would hit the mark, again and again. There would be no relenting, no missing, and no mercy given to his enemy.

This would end with Miles stopped and Cinjun victorious, stronger.

Battles go to the strong, races go to the swift. Speed kills your opponent, dead. Explosive power kills your opponent, dead.

Miles would get dead.

Blows had a cumulative effect. Blood would be taken, and taken, and taken. Cunning move after cunning move, it would add up.

Cinjun knew these smells. He knew these signs of battle. Now they were in his game. Playing on his field. This Miles was fighting out of his weight class. He would make Miles cry like a baby. Nothing less would do ... This was good versus evil. And Cinjun's belief sustained him. He would triumph. And destroy, so that he might build. He was fighting for peace ... and nothing less.

But Peace was a bloody business, full of death and destruction. That was Peace. But to live in peace, that was a great thing. A great gun.

Cinjun fought on the side of peace.

Peace was slaughter.

It had to be. He wished it could be different. But he had tried it, it didn't work.

Now, he would reap peace with blood and sword, and, ... uhm, ... gold. Peace was expensive.

Peace was written in slaughter and beauty, beauty with a fist.

He loved exacting peace with a good strong violent blow.

He loved breaking a nose for peace. God, he loved Peace!

Peace costs lives. Everyone knew that this Miles had crazy ideas. Dangerous ideas.

He had to silence Miles ... stop him ... in order for peace to sing its song of love and glory. Glory was the thing he sought, this Cinjun Smythe being. He would smite the wicked, and that was his glory. That was why he was the most important man in the world. The most important man that had ever lived, or ever shall live.

His peace would go marching on.

Slaughter leading on to slaughter. Bringing peace leading on to peace, in this way all would be peace.

That was the idea. Brilliant? Cinjun knew it was.

Slaughter, sad, but necessary. If only there were another way! But the ends would justify the means. Bringing peace leading on to peace, all would be peace.

That was the idea. Brilliant?

Cinjun knew it was.


## Cinjun, Speaking for the Record
*Talking fight and right and might*

---

"HE'S A NOWHERE MAN." Cinjun held himself poised, holding a *light*vision interview.

"He's heading to nowhere fast. You can keep adding zero to zero for a long time and still end up with zero."

Cinjun was determined to be orderly about it. This was about putting Miles in his place. Putting him in his box. And naming him, the nowhere man.

"I just hope he keeps well and I sure hope he shows up."

Abruptly, noise came from the corridor.

The double doors came open.

Miles appeared at the doorway.

Cinjun came on alert.

Miles stepped into the chamber, and with him Cinjun saw a flow of people. People entering. *Light*vision crews making themselves known in the throng.

Cinjun held himself in readiness.

Miles stepped into the place. One step. And this amounted to a tremendous disturbance. The mere fact that he had entered Cinjun's office was huge. Miles let that work for him. He didn't do anything more for a good long while.

People flowed in around Miles. Presently, the walls of the place became lined with a perimeter of people.

The people moved their attention to Cinjun.

And now—

Cinjun did nothing. Cinjun did a lot of nothing. He was coiled. He was on the verge of doing many things, but he held himself still. He did nothing, nothing immediate.

And the people wondered, what was coming?

Cinjun lifted a glass from the table and took a taste of his tea.

They were moving to a full-scale confrontation. He was aware of the showdown and what it meant. He was aware of what moments were coming. He was going to move in deliberate steps, with great care, assurance, poise and dignity. There was no need for him to do anything. In fact, he was more powerful if he stayed still. To not get heated, that was what he was working at. To not spring recklessly. To not waste movement. To not waste effort. To not kill Miles Roark. Cinjun was solid. That was his pose.

"You want to feel like the big man." Miles said, giving him plain, laid back talk. "Come on big man. Let's debate. It's all over. Let's get it on.

"Cinjun," Miles said, "let's get it on. You throw in yours; I'll throw in mine. Only one makes it out. C'mon, make it. C'mon!"

Cinjun burned, in a controlled rage.

Cinjun took another taste of tea. He would allow Miles the moment, because it would serve Cinjun's designs. This made it more of a grudge match. Fine.

"You want to feel like the big man. Come on big man. Let's get it on now. No more playing around."

"I'm not fond of your manner," Cinjun said.

"I've had complaints about it," Miles said, "but nothing seems to help."

"Don't let everyone know what a fool you are. Your springing-in-the-sun days are almost over; night is drawing near."

"Hell, Cinjun, let's get it on. Let's hit it. C'mon let's go."

And in the primal flow of the now—

The house guard entered the arena and carefully approached Miles.

Cinjun held up a hand. The house guard ceased their movements. He motioned for them to withdraw. They pulled back, into the mountains. Miles stood as he was; he hadn't moved at all.

The house guard stood back—ready, but away from Miles.

Cinjun rose from his chair; came to full attention, standing tall and straight, chest out, chin high, full command stance.

Something about Cinjun's approach seemed to be saying, 'Look at this upstart. Isn't he horrible? I'll show you how I deal with this kind of bastard.'

Cinjun reacted with deadly seriousness. He smiled. He was charming.

But he was deadly. Someone could get hurt. Cinjun would restore order through the force of his will alone.

Cinjun crossed to Miles, and stopped, holding Miles in a locked gaze.

"Now Miles, listen to me. We will fight at the event. Do you understand me?"

Cinjun talked to Miles now as if Miles had burst in brandishing a gun.

'Watch out Cinjun, stay away from him,' they murmured. Cinjun waved them to silence. "You made your point Roark. Is there anything else you wanted?"

Miles smiled. He was finished.

Miles turned to the *light*vision crews and smiled broadly. "I do believe we're going to have ourselves quite a little adventure."

They all laughed.

Miles turned back to Cinjun. And then turned to the crews and smiled.

That was the picture that went out around the world.

## Leaving the Sans Souci Plaza

"WHAT WAS THAT ABOUT?" His friend asked him about the changes. *. . . What is going on? What are you doing? . . .* "Why did you do that?" the friend asked Miles.

"Cinjun has been boasting," Miles said, "that he's afraid of no man alive. And, everybody is scared of him—He goes into every fight feeling strong, feeling sure of himself.

"I figured if I act crazy on him, that would scare him, because you never know what an insane man is going to do. You have to fear an insane man.

"We want it to be everything it can be," Miles said. "That's what Cinjun will make it now. When he comes at me, he'll come at me with everything he's got. He'll spare nothing."

"You mean," the friend asked, "you want him to give you trouble?"

"I want him to give me his best shot."

He was the changeling. See him change. Change taking place. Root yourself to the ground. Taking the song to keen rhythm. Taking the song into harmonic changes.

"He has everything going for him," Miles said. "I want him to feel it might not be enough." Miles was striding. "I want him to come at me with his best shot. I want him to throw everything he has at me. I want Cinjun to go after me with everything he's got, his damndest, straightest, best shot."

Miles was striding and his friend was striding at his side. They were leaving the Sans Souci Plaza.

He was the changeling. See him change. Change taking place. Root yourself to the ground.

*Fortune and fate and marshall forces*—took to the changes, and drove them into distance. Into long, lonely distance.

Movements formed, created traps. Loaded the dangers. And took the world into the unknown. Into mystery. Into sidewinding.

Some who witnessed the wild breeze, gave Miles a name. They called him *the sidewinder*. They did not fill their tone with kindness.

They ached for Cinjun Smythe to show the sidewinder the wages of sin.

Cinjun Smythe took himself to readiness. He produced a smile. Quickened his energy, and allowed his strong life force to become a House Crimson.

The sidewinder was destined to get dead in House Crimson, Cinjun thought. And Cinjun's eyes took on great life. He was about to enjoy himself. Enjoy himself indeed.

You could depend on Cinjun Smythe to enjoy himself.

He was the god emperor savior. He was their god—And he reached into the life of god. He would enjoy himself indeed.

He got into his god car, and drove into distance, into long distance.

Which he crossed with great speed. Growing in strength as he traveled. Into distance, into long distance.

He was the god emperor of the world that peopled.

Time stretched out before him, and called him to journey.

Murder by the roadside, would speak of his progress as he sowed a brave new world.

He was the god emperor of the world that peopled. And he moved into distance, into long distance.

And he moved with the sweetest movement the world had ever seen.

**Act Three**

---

# The Sound Chaser Versus the Thunder God

---

## Windsprinting

"THIS IS WHERE it comes together; this determines all that will follow."

Miles was running down the country road. Running fast. Beside him, a friend, Forsythe, kept pace. And a few paces behind them, proceeding steadily, was Scofield.

Miles was running, and tasting forever in his run. "Yes sir, this is where it all starts. Right here in training. What happens here determines all that is going to happen after."

It was early morning. Sunrise was carving through the air. Running on the air with flair. Traveling true. Settling. Then again passing through, leaving, leading down the trail.

The trail stretched out before them, carving, streaming into the country. Traveling. Broken trail so long. Into country vastness.

Now pounding rhythm coming down the open road, heading out, stepping on out. Miles was running. Running fast. Forsythe was holding his pace at a matching, burning clip.

Miles was finding the place, with the aim of staying sure and fast, pounding out a rhythm, leading down the trail.

Driving it to performance level—*Only pressure can take it to where it needs to go.*

It has to be about carrying the train off the track. Carrying the world out of orbit. It's heavy duty work. It takes tremendous will and ability.

*Don't give it up. Don't give in. No one touches all you are. Let me show you how you make me feel!* Whoa, rhythm is his business.

*Don't give it up. Don't give in.* A sidewinder windsprinting.

Miles Roark—there in this place—showing all he is. Forsythe—there in this place—working it, showing all he is.

Windsprinting is the heart and soul of the business, Miles thought.

That's what you have to be able to do. You need to be able to burst. To be a sunburst. To explode. To tear loose and go far.

Rhythm is his business.

He's got to learn how to sprint.

How to burst. How to explode through the changes.

Rhythm is his business.

Laughing, oh how the wind was laughing. Roaring. This uncommon breeze—the kind that does with hearts whatever it pleases.

Now pounding rhythm coming down the open road, heading out, stepping on out.

Wind changing, rearranging lives.

A sidewinder's windsprinting.

Wind sprints.

You have to train your body to recover under stress.

Miles was there, fixing up some rhythm cocktails.

*Rhythm is his business.* No more sleepy head. Take care of everything.

'*Don't look for me. I'll be shooting ahead.*' Remember, darling, rhythm is his business. Don't look for him. He'll be shooting ahead. Racing. Remember, darling, rhythm is his business.

Forsythe was also finding the place. But finding that he could not make it last. "I'm going to cut out for a minute or two." Forsythe said. "My doctor says it's okay to push yourself; but when it becomes a strain, you better quit."

"Your doctor doesn't know what he's talking about," Miles said.

Miles is running. *Rhythm is his business.* Rhythm that can make you go insane. Upside, inside, out. A fine devil crazy.

Got to.

Got to.

Got to.

—*Rhythm is his business.*

Got to.

Got to.

Got to—

C'mon!

Whoo! . . . Oh, yeah! . . . C'mon! Push and pull! C'mon!

Sprinting to wild rhythm. Exploding. *Rhythm is his business.*

"The doctor told me to cut out when it becomes a strain," Forsythe repeated.

"Some do—but your doctor doesn't know what the hell he's talking about. Damn your doctor! Life is a strain! You have to train your body to recover under strain. You follow?"

"No—"

"That's what you want to do, is strain. You want to run until your heart is bleeding and breaking, and no good at all. You want to run until it pains you! C'mon! Whoo-yeah! Upside, inside, out. Whoo--yeah! Got to—got to—got to—c'mon!"

Miles was running. Tasting the run. Tasting the pain. Forsythe was keeping up with him, seeing what the trip was all about.

"You want to keep running until your legs are in absolute pain. That's the way that it's meant to be."

Miles was tasting the run. Tasting all the pain. Forsythe was getting the trip.

"Hear the story; that's the way it has to be. The run has to get into your *inside*—You have to go—*you got to get it on the inside.* You have to strain. Until you're going to die, until you're killing everything; until you're going to fall out. Run until you stumble."

They were both running. Both at their limits. Both in agony. Now Forsythe knew where Miles was going with this. Forsythe was getting it on the inside—Some called it a heart attack.

"Until your heart starts coming apart; feels like you can't go another pace, can't go another step. Keep going. Feels like you're going to fall down in your tracks, then after that, you've only gotten started; that's when you've got to create the rhythm grooves. That's when you have to go to work. That's when it begins."

Forsythe—to his horror—suddenly saw where this was all leading. Against his will he was suddenly thrown into a course straight there—

Abruptly he was stumbling and stumbling forward—

He was tumbling to the ground—

Rolling uncontrollably—

Until he crashed into a tree.

And settled comfortably into ground agony.

. . . The tree wasn't hurt too bad.

"Come . . . on . . . man," Miles said . . . between gasps.

Miles danced around his fallen friend.

"Come . . . on, . . . mumbles! Don't you taste it? Aren't you starting to taste it? . . ."

"Ah . . . ah . . . ." Forsythe is now empty of breath. He can't spare enough breath to speak.

"Ah, rest easy," Miles said. "You're off to a good start. Tomorrow we'll really see what you can do. No more fooling around. Tomorrow we really do it."

And in the now—

Miles turns away. *Rhythm is his business.* He moves, whirls, cuts, runs. Ah, yeah. Got to take a ride. Get on the inside. Get it on the inside. Rhythm is his business. Got to get it on the inside.

Miles takes his run to Scofield. "Come on, Sco. Let's hit it." He runs a ring around Scofield. Scofield just keeps running along at exactly the same pace. And gives Miles a look. Miles races ahead, leaving Scofield behind, far behind.

A few horizons down the road, Miles begins to really appreciate the scenery—there is nothing else he can do!—Miles is collapsed against a tree, completely out of breath.

Now Scofield runs by—cool, steady and solid. Scofield gives Miles the same look again.

"Pace yourself kid," Scofield says. "You'll go longer"—*Rhythm is his business* too.

He leaves Miles there.

Miles holds his gaze on Scofield's departing figure—You can't 'burst' like that. That was no way to 'burst' through the changes. That's not a fine devil crazy. That's not sprinting to wild rhythm. That's not it at all.

Now Miles sees that Scofield is whipping into the distance at a steady clip, floating away with uncommon velocity.

To himself, he says, "Damn him, damn, that old man." Miles looks at Scofield in the distance rising high on the country trail leading to the top of the mountain—"Damn his arrogant ways."

Now Miles falls over, onto a pile of leaves. He has spent the last of his breath.

And Miles lies there, alone with the situation.

The wind moves some dust down the trail—passing him by.


## Cinjun Forming

---

"EVERYTHING IS SET. You watch," Cinjun said.

Now Cinjun turned it over in his mind; did a lot of holding still. His manipulations were paying off. It was harvest time.

"Just you watch." Cinjun did a lot of nothing. "You'll see."

*God emperor was his business.*

And it was an easy business for him. It suited him. All was going right

& breezy.

Now he would underplay it; that was what was left for Cinjun to do. The whole operation was in place; the wheels were turning smoothly; the big generator was humming along. He was being proclaimed a god emperor. Now he would underplay it. He would let it work all around him and play humbly within it.

Life was perfect, absolutely goddamn perfect.

Cinjun was feeling comfortable. Feeling "right." Everything was nice. Ah, yeah. Oh, so nice. He was giving Miles some space. He would make it a big, fantastic show—and then he would beat Miles down to size. It appeared Miles was not as weak as you would imagine—so much the better. Cinjun was feeling a thrill. It was aim your rifle; lock target; fire! He was getting Miles in his scope. Setting his sights. Going to shoot him. It was a nice thrilling hunt. A fox hunt and Cinjun was the lord of the manor.

"I'll tell you how we'll handle this . . ." He knew how to do this work. He had trained his body and mind. He was ready. All was right.

He was mounting a great show. It was going to be a blockbuster. Spectacular. Brilliant. Altogether excellent!

Cinjun described how they would move into the ceremony and how they would produce their effect.

Creating god feelings, god being that radiated feelings . . . that produced reverence . . . that lead to sanctity.

Keening ceremony. Sharp, brave ceremony. Keen sensations everywhere.

Part of the ceremony was setting light to Cinjun while burning Miles to ashes. Cinjun would make ash of Miles in the *after spin*.

He was going to kill. He always killed. What he worked on, was the after spin, the after battle. What was next? Who was next? He sent his energies into the pattern search and the prime projections.

The ceremony was already shaping itself as he wanted it.

He was getting some true heavy hitters for the Barkers.

It was going to be a big, large, mammoth thing.

He was in demand. Very popular. He had built it, and now they would come.

He was going to fill the biggest arena in town.

They were coming for him. Miles didn't matter at all. Cinjun just hoped that Miles could go the distance.

The difficulty for Cinjun now was to hold back. To let the forces work for him. *Don't look like you're working,* Cinjun thought. Don't look like you're in any difficulty whatsoever. Now let the forces work and stay loose within it all. Stay loose. Stay sporting.

Let the audience do the work; let the people do the work of building him up. Of enlarging his image. Let the reporters do the work; let his people do the work. Now his job was to hold back; to underplay; to be at ease within the seat of power.

God emperor was his business. And he knew how to play it.

Now everything was aligned around him; he had to hold himself back.

The way to play the god emperor was to underplay being the god emperor.

At House Crimson, they were meeting to decide how to build up the great debate.

Sidney said, "Let's make Miles sound big—'Lo! and behold, ye mighty, an immense danger!'—so that when you cut him down, you can play up the victory."

Now when Sidney proposed this thing, of making Miles an immense danger—Cinjun was immediately driven to the edge of violence—it couldn't go that way at all! It would make no sense whatsoever. He was the god emperor and he was supposed to make this nothing, this Miles Roark, a possible danger. Cinjun with all his powers and Miles with nothing and he was supposed to make Miles into a danger?

He wanted to do violence to Sidney. He became so goddamn enraged. But he held it. He controlled himself. He spoke softly. And played things on a small scale. He knew how it had to go now. He had to be the underplaying god emperor.

He just put Sidney in his place.

"I'm not going to make a mouse into a lion; I'm not going to make a stone into a tower, a rain into a tempest, a stream into a maelstrom, and an ending into a beginning.

"There's a difference between the way you play 'In the end . . .' and 'In the beginning . . .'

"Let me ask you Sidney, if you were an actor would you play the end of a story the same way you would the beginning? If you were a goddamned actor Sidney. . . ."

He looked at Sidney. It was a hard look, hard as a mountain.

"Would you play the day you met a woman, the same way as you would the day you ended the affair?

"Sidney, have a sandwich, have a soda, and watch. . . . Watch how it's done. . . . Speak when you have . . . *thought*, . . . and *matter*, . . . and *a future to claim . . . and live."*

What mattered now was the *after spin*. And looking to the future.

That evening Cinjun held a *light*vision interview and spoke about the future.

And Cinjun was charming, . . . as charming as charming could be.

# Nothing

As often happens, nothing happened . . . for a while.

The autumn leaves were coming.

The autumn leaves were coming into the world.

# Dancing to the Midnight Whirlpool

Lately, Daphne had looked around.

Got to seeing, wondering.

Lately, the look in *his eyes* disturbed her. Disturbed Daphne all to hell.

Something in his eyes. Shimmered with blue skies and the wings of her fate.

She wondered what she was seeing.

In Miles Roark.

Lately.

Daphne was thinking, got to feeling.

Her thoughts turned to Miles. She chased the thoughts away.

Desire developed an edge.

He was a monster, she thought. She was a princess, queen of the byways, she told herself. It did nothing.

Desire developed an edge.

It could not continue, she said. It did.

Desire developed an edge.

Someone else might make love almost as sharply.

She, might meet him some summer. And he might whisper in her ear. She told herself—it did nothing.

Miles, remained.

Somewhere in his look—a madness was clear—And somewhere—All the feelings you could find, all the lies that came in hot moments, all that you could see chasing you in loving moments, . . . all the love that you could find in all your life. All that could rise and fall.

She was the kind of girl who knew what she wanted. And where to go. She wanted Miles Roark.

In pieces rough and tumble. She wanted his feet upon her stage. It was elemental. Pull. Push and pull. A force so fine. A gift to last forever.

But she was not going to get weepy and willowy on him.

When she stood before him, she stood with arms thrown back. She was—defiance. And devil mirth.

Loving arms?

No, she threw him across a table when he came.

She lit the torch and burned the table night.

*Oh, well,* he smiled and came again.

He, turned to her.

She, turned to him.

They danced around each other, similar prowls.

They were friendly with sounds you would never know.

Changes falling out of the blue.

I want to make love to you!

Fascination.

I want to make love to you!

Moments running through their heads.

*The world is crazy. Only one thing I want to do. I want to make love to you! I can't stand to be here without you!*

It moved.

*I can't stand to be without you, baby. You—who's got a feeling for me.*

It moved.

The world stood crazy. Howled and wailed.

Insanity's horse adorned the night. They tumbled into an endless roll.

On the bed, deeper and deeper.

Touch!

Sense and skin!

Release and swelling seas!

Driving dreams through the changes.

Fascination for limits of love. Taking them deeper and deeper, and deeper into her. She was intoxication.

The bed beneath them.

Silk, satin, sheets, a frontier swirl. And dancing into the midnight whirlpool, the two most beautiful people in the world.

They kissed the changes that shaped their lives!

All around, rise and fall—all the lies you find, all that you can see, all was rise and fall.

They were traveling deeper and deeper.

They went.

Deeper and deeper.

Further and further.

Nearer and nearer.

Run run run.

Burn burn burn.

Soon soon soon.

They were drifting and drifting.

Farther and farther.

Nearer and nearer.

A swinging sway. Force and swirl. A force to find, a triumph to tear your mind. All deep down the river.

Care to fall in love with Daphne Fox?

Miles had.

His world was on fire, and nothing was on fire except her, she was the world, and there were no people.

No sailors on ships. Only her.

Mmhm, oohhh.

No generals on fields. Only her.

Mmhm, oohoohh.

No ground amid ocean; only sky, and her.

No pilots in the sky. Only her.

The world was stripped of people.

She was stripped of clothes.

There was only her, naked.

And shining sea motion.

Care to fall in love with Her?

She is thrill.

She is now.

She is sun.

She is moan.

She is wild love.

And his wild love, was screaming.

Uh, uh, uh, uh!
They had the world to themselves.

## Nothing Strikes Again

NOTHING HAPPENED FOR A TIME.
Time slipped. Slipped some more.
Went right on slipping.

## Probing—

BLUE NIGHT SLIPPED into blue night. Night slipped into day and day slipped into night. Time slipped. Time slipped.
The battle drew near. The fight approached.

Rhythm is his business—
Miles, is here now, getting ready for the fight.
Probing, probing, until he's feeling it.
Rhythm.
Probing rhythm.
He was searching, seeking the way.
The fight drew near.
The showdown was here.
And what would be the rhythm and the form, the shape and the motion. He was probing.

As for Cinjun . . . the effect, was his main concern.
Soon would come the battle, which Cinjun knew he would win. But what concerned him was the effect. Putting the right effect into play. Cutting how you thought about it. Cinjun was making his plans for how to make them think the right way. To see the battle the way they should.
He was working over the points he should drive home with his victory.
The collision course.
The day drew near.
And then it came. It was upon them. Combat.

What was this rhythm and this motion? Miles wondered.
Capoeira Nebula! Ah, it was a capoeira nebula.

He sensed it. Probed it.

Misty colors, vapors. A yellow capoeira, that was where they were heading. A yellow capoeira with red and orange relief . . . and exploding forms.


## The Stately Pleasuredome

IN THE FOREST CITY, amid forest field, did they a stately Pleasuredome decree. Where might you and me, see, fight on fight, fair and brave and free.

Here were people come.

And here were pleasures of Sultans and Kings, Kings and Khans—Boundless and bare.

Lone and level, the ground stretched to far away. To city and buildings and avenues and night and light.

Here were people come from alien worlds. From strange journeys in strange nights of sin and stone.

They came, from round and round.

And here were rivers come. Here—were rivers running.

The river British. River Rome. River Ottoman. The river Egypt. The river Greek. In mysterious union, here did meet.

A stately Pleasuredome for one and all! *"Step right, step right up!"* the Barker cried. Here were the passions and the tatters of the world that peopled. Such battles as knew no equals.

And here was a savage place.

A stately Pleasuredome here stood. With many pleasures to share. A million ways to spend your time. A million ways to fun most fine.

And here they came:

The team of Mahoney and McSmithers.

Pachuco Cabeza.

And the Fair Fathead Willy.

And here they came:

Cinjun Kubla the Khan Smythe.

Skyler the Larkin Malloy.

Fine and larking malicious.

And here they came: the streaming people floating in waves from all around. To the Stately Pleasuredome. Boy and girl; and friend and enemy; oh, on, they came . . . to a fight-in-the-light show. To know and grow.

To smell the blood and the cool clean country air. Of battles raging in forest city.

Step right up! Step right up! the Barker cried. "A battle of truth!" he lied. But he knew not, "For in truth it would be truth that fought tonight," they cried.

And here, was a stately Pleasuredome! *Step right up! Step right up!* the Barker cried.

And oh! the deep romantic chasm which slanted down the green hills to a savage arena, beneath demon moon haunted by woman wailing for her demon-lover—or, perhaps the other.

And here, was a stately Pleasuredome!

Step right up! Step right up! the Barker cried.

In this place did the people a stately Pleasuredome decree

Step right up! the Barker cried. Come and see; this was, and is, and well will be, the lone and only place. Oh, lone and only: The only place to be. Great shows and changes of face—that come—and race—and rend with eerie grace—startling and sad face—with sad and startling and rapid pace. Changes, and changes and changes of face.

Oh, lone and only: The only place to be. Where you can be you, wild and free. Yes, wild and free, here you can be. For in this place, did they a stately Pleasuredome decree.

And here did they revive color and splendor

Vapors leading on to vapors. Oh! the splendor!

Oh! Such splendor!

Oh! the splendor!

Hear and now.

Near and now.

Voices, hear them now.

Oh! the splendor! And the cheer! So fast and so near.

The works of man and woman fair. Beauteous and sexy wear. Suits and gowns. A place in color. Bust lines and lace. Fabulous and outrageous. Looking and clothing.

They were here.

They drew near.

They were here.

Well, for combat, dear.

To see combat. Giants fair and tall rend each other in the hall. A battle royal, grown in a stately Pleasuredome; grown immense in a measure Rome.

They came to sit and watch, and live! in a stately Pleasuredome. And know lightning life, and strife of life, and death of life, and mighty being. All was here for joy-splashed seeing.

The seeing was started.

The lights grew brighter.

The sounds were moaning.

And here the Barker cried:

"Is everybody in?

"The show—is about to begin."

## Dancing Barefoot

THE INSIDE OF THE PLEASUREDOME was an immense cavern.

In wait, among the crowd, lay: Brutus and his two associates.

Skyler was striding, leading Daphne and Miles through the throng of people. Rattle and hum all round. Skyler was leading them—in the direction of Brutus and his crew.

Daphne cast her gaze into the crowd, and her attention was caught— She fixed her stare on Brutus.

Brutus smirked. Actually, his smile was quite charming. Not really any menace in him at all. Except that he revealed a concealed gun.

Daphne's gaze stayed level as she flicked it to Skyler. She studied his reaction. He had seen the exchange. And seemed pleased.

Brutus smiled. He came forward. "Make sure you lose tonight," Brutus said. He was now a few paces from Daphne.

Skyler was much closer. She felt him breathing. Daphne turned to Skyler and saw a satisfied gleam in his eyes.

"Skyler," Daphne said, "in the time it would take you to kill one guy, I could get three guys to the morgue."

Immediately, her fist went to Skyler's nose, smashing it something awful, drawing blood.

She pivoted toward Brutus and moved into his space.

"You're going to threaten us!" Daphne said. "You're going to come here and threaten us!"

Now, everyone in the immediate area stopped. Their attention was seized, pulled fully to Daphne and Brutus and the two men. They froze, riveted, with charged alertness.

Brutus and the two guys held still, staying ready.

Miles was standing at Daphne's back. Readying himself to protect her.

Time stood still. Each player stood ready, waiting for the slightest motion in the other—except Daphne—she allowed her life force to quicken. And then moved.

Daphne flew at Brutus. As he started to react, her foot pounded a course through his jaw.

She was connection. And she was connecting with him.

Now she was spinning ceaselessly. Taking over.

She was dancing barefoot.

The other two thugs were nearby. She knocked them into positions that better suited her needs, as she went back at Brutus.

Some strange music drove her, made her come on blithely. A kick through a granite jaw there. Dancing barefoot. A fist through a man's chest here. She was dancing barefoot.

Spinning, outside of gravity.

She took over. She brought it on.

And they reaped: a full force gale.

And now—

She is whirlwind. She is stinging force. She is deadly. You see, her father had mated with a tigress, a temptress and an assassin to produce her—She sends Brutus to the floor in a hard crash—She breaks bone, rips flesh in the two associates—

She was showing them what lay within her.

It was part of her moving on.

Great effort, vast effort.

Training of years.

Sprung swiftly in her moving on.

Done, in a flow fierce and natural.

Her training, her work, work measured out in years.

She relieved Brutus of his gun.

Now she pointed the gun at the other two. One held still; the other seemed to be a little more restless—he just might show her a little more life than she expected; and teach her a lesson in violence.

"Down with the hand—" Daphne said quickly.

The man was fast, moving cunningly, weaving, making himself a shifting target, impossible to hit with precision; he was drawing a pistol and moving efficiently into a kill shot, using the faces and bodies in the crowd for cover.

Daphne fired. A sure shot as it turned out: the man's gun flew back and crashed against the wall. Miles grabbed the gun. While she took care of the third man's gun.

Then she returned to Brutus. Who was working successfully at his recovery.

"Up," she said encouraging his powerful recuperative ability.

He rose and readied himself for action. She took a crack at his face; delivered a series of blows in lightning succession.

Bam, whack, thrak, b'boom!

He might as well have been frozen in ice for all the resistance he was able to mount. He went down, harder than before. But she wouldn't stop!

Bam, whack, thrak, b'boom!

People gasped! She pounded and broke his body.

"Up," she said. "Come on, are you going to leave it there?"

But his lights were out. He was in a total bringdown. She was talking to an unconscious body.

"Up," she said. "Now is that all the fight you're going to give me? Up! Up! You're going to go to bed this early?"

Now she stopped. She looked around, scanning the crowd.

"You saw him," she said. "He had a gun."

They didn't seem to be getting it.

"Did I have a gun?" she said. "No. He had me at his mercy. Luckily I can get by on my wits."

## The Show Is About to Begin

INSIDE THE GREAT STADIUM, the seeing was about to get started.

The lights grew brighter.

The sounds were moaning.

"Is everybody in?

"The show—is about to begin."

The Barker cried, "The curtains will soon be parted! The seeing will be started!—Bright with sin—sound and fury—and its kin—Is everybody in? The show is about to begin!

"Sinning sound and sinning fury.

"All sin and all its kin, perhaps might win.

"Or would truth slip in? And truth in end, to sear and win? And truth in end, so sear as to win?

"Drawing fast and mighty and near, and in this way to win?"

The Barker spoke above the din—"Come in and sit," until the battle is writ, . . . all fin.

With fast and certain reason, we were about to go to heaven, fast, so fast and in season. Go fast, so fast, and get there in season.

The truth seemed this day, not far away.

"Is everybody in?" the Barker said.

"The show, is about to begin."


# Capoeira! The Dancing Fight

THIS WAS A YELLOW CAPOEIRA, with red and orange relief. Red and orange waves, emergences.

As Miles moved, this was what he was seeing.

You sailed in yellow . . . hunting for orange. And red! Worlds. Exploding worlds.

They were sailing deep in the yellow capoeira.

All around, swirling vapors of yellow mist.

Capoeira Nebula!

Sailing in misty colors.

All this—as Miles took his journey into: The Arena.

Miles would take the night into mystery. To take it into the mystery, was to take it into the nebula.

Miles had to take the night into the winding way. Warp and shift the form into its fullness. Into its raw existence and reach. Into the nebula.

Miles had to take them into the Wãoynde. Shift and warp the form of the moment, until they went into the Winding Way.

Miles would make the fight big. Much bigger. He pursued a fight that radiated. That formed a whirlpool Wãoynde. A worldwind, whirlwind Wãoynde.

This was a capoeira!

Miles, felt it.

And saw that Cinjun moved the night to a more formal arrangement.

No, they were into capoeira.

He that is good man, will be.

But no planning, no ceremony—Capoeira!

Floating force.

Charging.

"Che-gung-ging!" Miles said, singing out the berimbau.

He would take it into its raw shape. No soft lies, no soft parade,

Elemental Capoeira!

"Kai-bing!" Miles said.

Cinjun observed this. He considered what Miles was speaking into the night—As if they were words.

He turned from Miles and swept his gaze across the people. They had not picked up on it. It had just been a passing piece of bizarre behavior. Cinjun put it out of his mind. It was nothing.

Miles too was sensing the people all around, their energy filling the place, the form of the thing.

He, Miles came for a capoeira, a dancing fight—a Wild Whirlwind Wãoynding Wild, screaming wild!

He put everything out of his mind, except the moment, and the moment was Capoeira! Let's dance and battle in the Night Sun, my enemy, Cinjun Smythe and I. My enemy, the Dark King, and I. Capoeira! And a chance to die.

The Capoeira that dances, will be!

All that was left to Miles, was the becoming. How that would happen? He had no idea, and it didn't worry him a bit. He had wit.

In the other corner, Cinjun moved to seal the covenant set long ago between himself and the powers that sprang him. He was here to collect the world.

The men and women of the world that peopled. His mighty forces. His weapon that peopled. His military majesty.

He was here and he was about to win. He was here to write history— He had charted it on the way here—And now all that was left for him was to breathe victory in the form that had been set long ago.

Miles felt a shape and a becoming. He didn't know from form. He knew flux and change and sun streaked looks. And soaring Capoeira. A wild whirlwind wãoynding wild.

Miles drew a deep breath. He let it out ever so slowly. Drew his next, deep breath. And braced himself.

Miles would have to carry this night, carry this train, off the track. Hmmm, crash to the other shore. Fly across the sky, into the nebula. Let the nebula wash all over them.

Yes, time to carry this night away.

Carry it to where it belonged—outside of time and place.

Enter the nebula.

Enter the scape.

Enter the escape.

Enter the dream.

Enter the dreamscape.

Enter the bender.

Enter the mind bender.

Enter.

The night resisted. Everything in the place resisted. And fought, and would fight him.

He moved.

C'mon.

C'mon.

C'mon.

*C'mon Miles. No stopping. Move damn it move!* Miles's thoughts grew furious. *You saw the Capoeira Nebula. Now take the night off the track. Damn it, take this train off the track!*

Pa doo dum . . . Pa deem doo . . . da doo dum.

Listen to the wind and the mystery comes alive.

Pa doo dum . . . Pa dee doo da doo dum . . . Da de Doom. Doom. Doom. Doo doo de doom . . . de doo doop. Doop. Doop. De doo dooop doop dum—

Pa de dum! . . . Pa dee doo da de dum! . . .

Cinjun was training his eyes on Miles—he felt there was something very strange going on inside that boy.

Miles—he knew the important impulse. It was: Don't save me from myself. Don't hold on to anything. Let it go.

Into the mindbending nebula.

Into the Wãoynde. Into the mindbender. Into the dream.

To the far horizon. To the far reaches.

Into the further forever.

Take it into the beyond.

Into the wild blue yonder.

Into cool rapidity.

Miles could see that Cinjun was moving the night into a formal arrangement. A ceremony of soft strokes and fightless fighting. No, Miles would have to find a way to carry this night off the track. He must not let it grow cold—stone cold—he must not let it move into the stone cold black hold.

That is where Cinjun will take it. Where ancient and forest city forces will control it; hold it down.

Time to breathe life into it; and life was a simple form, a form of: *Anything Goes.*

Collision course, . . . and connection!

Battle joined.

The people wanting, wanting, wanting more. More and more and more.

Yes, the fight was moving to "on"!

Cutting loose.

Into the storm.

The voyage had begun.

The people lent force to the movement.

*War, put on your faces!* Miles's mind wanted to shout out loud.

Tonight we have—a battle of: *Anything Goes.* Miles's mind wanted to shout out loud.

Welcome one and all, gentle all. Tonight we present a muse of fire. A battle of fire. Within this O, we have packed two mighty forces, the Barker cried.

On one side, we have . . . Miles Roark.

On the other side, Cinjun Khan S'mythe.

Tonight, we have . . .

Miles walked away and did about the looniest thing you could do in a debate. . . . He sat down and closed his eyes.

He was probing.

Probing the night. Getting a feel for it.

As the Barker opened it up . . . Miles quietly sat down.

Cinjun turned.

The Barker glanced down at Miles.

The audience grew more alert.

For Miles, it was the experience of diving into cold water, and exploring. Feeling alive. Feeling life within him, and around him. Feeling the flow, and going with the flow. Tonight, he would swim with the currents of mood. . . . This was Miles's way of beginning the fight.

For Cinjun . . . this was like nothing he had ever encountered before. It made him mad.

The Barker stopped speaking, he was unprepared for anything unexpected to happen.

Miles spoke, picking it up where the Barker had dropped it:

"My friends, tonight, we present a fight for the heavyweight title! In olden days, debates were about words and prose, tonight *anything goes!* Tonight is about making changes go round, everything changing, everything shifting: *Anything Goes!*"

The crowd went with it. That'll work. Jolly good. Good show!

That's what they wanted: a good show.

Cinjun didn't like this one lick. What was this grandstanding? He jumped into it.

*Miles seated on the floor?* This boy had no respect.

Cinjun would play to the crowd's sentimentality. And to its dignity. Here was a major encounter—and the boy was sitting on the god-damned floor.

Cinjun moved in and took charge of the moment.

"I called this—" Cinjun said "—so that we could get into the big questions of our lives." He took his glance to Miles. "But you must understand respect, there is a way to do things—"

Miles was sitting on the ground, with his eyes closed.

Out of those closed eyes, he seemed to be seeing things.

Time to breathe life into this, he thought, and in life: *Anything Goes.*

Miles said, "There is not a way to do things. Doing, is the way."

Cinjun's eyes were on the audience. He returned his look to Miles.

"Show some respect," Cinjun said.

"Respect?" Miles asked.

"That's where we have to begin," Cinjun said.

"Respect?" Miles asked again.

Cinjun was like the strongman—who had the army, the navy, the air force, all those guns—he was the strongman—pointing, all those guns at you, and saying: Let's not . . . use force.

Cinjun was steady, taking the higher ground. "Yes, respect for rules of order."

Miles opened his eyes.

"I'm here to build a new house. I don't need rules, and rulers, I need wood."

Miles rose to his feet.

Miles swung from the audience to Cinjun. "I may respect you, but I have to hit you to win the fight.

*Where is he going with this?* Cinjun came on guard and moved into burning feeling.

"Therefore," Miles said. "I apologize for what I'm going to do." Miles shifted and moved.

"Cinjun," Miles said, "you were right when you tried to skip this session, this dance lesson. You never should have come here . . . but I'm glad to see you made it."

Cinjun smiled, so nicely, and politely, but with a look whose handle should have stuck a few stone lengths out of Miles's back.

"Cinjun," Miles said, "here's where I'm going, . . . here's what I want to know: *Will you and your friend get on down? Or are you and your friend going to let me down?*"

Now in a hush, Miles traveled. Where was he going?

Miles started toward the audience. The hush grew vast. Miles walked to where Quinn Martin was seated.

"I apologize," Miles said to Quinn. "I know you've spent a lot of money on him, but I'm going to have to take him apart. You bet on the wrong horse."

The crowd and barkers reacted with interest.

"You want a tough fight?" Cinjun said. "Fine. Let's play games. I'll be *an honorable man*, and you'll be . . . *yourself.*"

The tone and timing amused the audience.

Miles turned to Cinjun.

Miles would let Cinjun have that one. Miles revealed nothing. Miles saw a sign, a physical sign. What he saw in Cinjun was, rage. Wonderful, beautiful rage, Miles thought.

He wondered if he had ever seen anything so beautiful in Cinjun before.

## Ceremony

---

THE BARKER LAUNCHED IT with questioning, fine questioning, hurling— the open question—to Cinjun . . . Now, the question, was made tame by Cinjun.

Just close your eyes and feel the wave.

Cinjun making all questions tame. All attacks into womanly openings, which he would penetrate with His Destiny. At least this was how *Unumbatai* saw it.

Cinjun Khan *Unumbatai* S'mythe rose to *Sky God.*

And in this way spoke Unumbatai—

Cinjun Khan *Unumbatai* S'mythe. This, incidentally, was his true full name. Everything about it was true.

Vrooom, thrak, b'boom, went the engine.

Vrooom, vrooom, vrooom, went the feel.

Thump, thump, thump, went their heart strings.

Swing, swing, swing, went their feelings.

Zing, zing, zing, went their mood.

And when he smiled they went into a universal reel.

And in this way spoke Unumbatai—

The Barker had kicked off the debate with an open question. *Well,* Miles thought, *isn't that the way of it?* Handing it to Cinjun, to run with as he may. This was the way of modern civilization. The powerful were privileged to fight in fightless fighting.

The question, Miles thought, was very sporting.

Very gentlemanly.

Very softball.

Very nothing.

The Barker had said something that amounted to the cutting force and controversy of a stage cue. He may as well have said: "Mister Smythe, can you tell us anything you damn well feel like telling us?"

Cinjun reacted. The themes flowed. The big wheel went into a spin. People fell in.

And in this way spoke Unumbatai—

*He rent the night with the beautiful song of unity. . . . United we stand.*

Like a fiery sun—a sun rising—together—we are House Crimson.

The Song of Unity. It was a crowd pleaser.

The cannon of unity.

The fighter plane of unity.

The citadel and weapons and great works of unity.

The firepower of unity.

Just think what we can build with the sword of unity.

What strokes of love, when we wield the sword of unity.

Of red—crimson—purpose—fighting for Peace.

This was Cinjun's Moonlight Sonata.

Miles studied the ceremonial hosts.

A pack of Barkers.

His judgment spoke of them, as a pack of dogs, a pack of wolves. Just there to eat the carcass. Not helpful. Not adding life—*They're devouring. They're feeding—but this is not a supper.*

The Hosting Barkers—were a pack of common barkers, who sought to be important by packing other people's moments.

Miles saw them in their own themes. Saw them deep in it. It was up to their knees.

# Life and Time
## *A Box of Thunderbolts*

THE HERO WITH A THOUSAND FACES. That's what Cinjun is. When you count the faces modestly.

The powers of life, and their inflection through man and woman.

No empty spaces, for the imagination to struggle for myths.

We have a whole new realm.

And in this way spoke Unumbatai—

*New Unumbatai for sale.* Unumbatai that's fresh and bold. Unumbatai that's only a few days old. Who would like to sample his supply?

And in this way spoke Unumbatai—

The Hunter in the Red Vest become a Swordmaster—A stranger can show up and help you. We're talking not only a physical force, but a center.

Wielding this strange weapon. . . . This too strange talk of life-change. . . . A story, sounding easy. Getting into your skin. This thing communicates. *It is in a language that is talking to young people today,* the wise man says.

The Hero goes for something—everyone knows—he is not just along for the ride, not a mere adventurer.

Now the Hero in the true sense. Are you ready for it? For the themes. The achievements? Of the hero? Are you ready for—Manifestation. The landscape. The conditions. The environment. . . . Can you match the readiness of the hero?

He begins as mere mortal, ends as hero. Evoking a quality of higher character.

This man, functioning beautiful in the world, *a something* pushing it.

Bringing favorite themes, true purposes, and big wheels—where you are is—on the edge—about to embark on outlying spaces—real adventure— this is the jumping off place. You haven't been there. I have. Now I take you. To the atmosphere.

Use space.

The walls were closing in on them.

Now they were descending into the dark place.

Going in, to come out again.

Down into the depths, many fathoms deep in the Black Sea of Dreams.

He was taking them deeper and deeper into the Black Sea.

The Black Sea.
*The Black Sea of Black Dreams.*
C'mon.
C'mon.
C'mon.

Miles held himself still, taking in the view.

Cinjun stood strong before the people now, and spoke to the multitude.

And in this way spoke Unumbatai—

Water. Being. The unconscious. Darkness.

First stage in *hero adventure.* Leaving realm of light, moving to threshold. Monster comes to meet him. Will the Hero be cut to pieces? No, he may kill the dragon power. Take the power. Take the song of nature, the powers of nature, unity, the Song of Unity.

And come upon the land, bringing the Song of Unity.

Know you Unity?

'This thing up here'—Cinjun directed their attention to his beautiful charming, shining head and face and those eyes of his, those eyes, them darn eyes, wow—'this thing up here removes us from Unity. Unity is the total human being.'

This thing up here must not put itself in control. It must submit to its humanity.

We're talking about living in terms of a system.

Systems of Unity and Might. Cinjun pulled a clever, most clever stop then. Turned into Systems of Unity and Might.

We operate in our society in relation to a system.

Will the system eat you up? Or will you use the system to serve a high purpose? We don't need to change the system, we will help you to live in the system. Not make it impersonal.

Be a scholar. This is what happens in your spiritual life. Listen to its demands. Do not insist on your own program. Do not put yourself off center. This is not what your body is interested in, because you have stopped listening to yourself.

Commit yourself to a system. Obey it. The creative spirit ranges strongest within the support of a great and mighty system.

System—great and deep and wide—creating Establishment, and The Man. Listen to The Man, y'all.

The Man is a Hero.

And The Hero lurks within each one of us. The system evokes more and more and more of us.

Now let us evoke our higher nature, rather than our lower.

A terrific darkness came over them then. A strange darkness of strange sensation. Darkness—made by some magician at work somewhere.

Let's gather. Collect wood for a fire and spend the night here.

I have come to save you; I await your reply.

I'm serious about all this.

Mere human beings are not good enough. Another domain, is where we go. The adventure is marvelous.

In His Lodge, the people greet you, you feel comfortable.

The next day, you go off to—*hunt*.

Strange sounds, strange days. Evenings come.

You hear strange sounds again.

The Hunt is where you need to be. Follow your bliss. Follow The Hunter in the Red Vest—Unumbatai.

And in this way Unumbatai speaks—

Hear the voice of The Man. Pulling you out of the water. You have moved from hard ground, solid earth . . . and you are in, caught in the abyss. You are rescued now by the elevated powers.

We're talking something smashingly brilliant, my dear friends, we're talking forces out of the local field, higher powers!

If you are not eligible to join, it's going to be a demon wedding for you. It's going to be a mess.

This is a story of expressing a truth.

The edge of what can be done and the mystery transcendent of all human search. The source of life. Knowledge of mystery. Balance and harmony.

We're talking: Thinking, in terms that help people.

We're talking: Ask not what you can do for yourself, ask what you can do for others.

See positive values.

Organ*ization* raised to high art.

Organ*izing* raised to high power.

Cinjun felt His Destiny, surge.

His Destiny rose, driving to climax—

And in this way spoke Unumbatai—

Miles applauded.

Cinjun turned—interrupted—damn—it was a kind of interrupted sex—

Miles relaxed his arms, relaxed his hands, and relaxed in the moment.

"Oh," Miles said softly, "I'm sorry. I thought you were finished. I'm terribly sorry." And he looked it.

Where could this be going, Miles wondered, and how far?

Miles motioned for Cinjun to take it away again.

Cinjun drew a breath, and let this one pass. He turned to the people. Cinjun returned to the bed of the fair and strong for some more . . . involvement. He felt His Destiny surge anew.

The whole world is conscious.

Plant and animal life.

Is Consciousness something peculiar to the head? Well, it isn't. It's an organ that inflicts consciousness. There is a consciousness here in the body.

Energy is the same thing. Where you see energy is consciousness.

We come out of energy.

Now observe, a form, an aspect of the energy.

The eyes of the earth are a Force Red. The voice of the earth is a Force Red.

Okay, y'all, you raise your consciousness. That's what meditation is for.

Levels of meditation, is what we're talking now. All right y'all.

Concern for family, and nation. Important concerns. And physical conditions.

Communicate now.

How do you get that?

Now—What this too strange talk of life-change is for, is to bring us to a level of consciousness that is spiritual.

Mystery. Everything speaks to us of mystery and atmosphere.

Bring your consciousness to a higher level. Then when you come back to this one. Associate it.

Hold it on that level. Don't let it drop down.

This is simply a lower level of that.

Express *relationship*.

Anyone who has spent any time fully awake, has felt it.

Look at every single figure in the museum, in the history of our people. Be there—so much so—that . . . you climb . . . to the great bell. Go up and up. Up there. And ring the great bell.

Bong! Bong! Bong!

Brilliant, adventure, lord.

Miles wanted to show them where this room was.

Presently, he would act presently . . . for now he let time slip.

Time slipped, time slipped . . . and Miles considered where Cinjun was going. Why was this so important to Cinjun? Miles considered it. Rolling the pattern search through his mind.

Ripeness was not now. Not yet. It was near. Miles put his ear to the ground—and heard a gentle sound. A sound of revealing, revealing what he was witnessing in the wild breeze this night.

A very moving beautiful thing, Cinjun was saying. I want to go there time and time again.

Take me to informed principles. You can tell their importance by the size of the principles. They're the tallest in the city. Wow! Such dwellings.

The history of civilization, was all he was talking about.

And who can build the tallest building.

*Magnificent building. Architectural triumph.*

*A statement—We are a power center!*

Here is what you will dream tonight.

Symbolic forms. A planet of moneyflow and violenceflow.

Beautiful.

Maturation. Adulthood of the world. And how to do it.

And relating it to the cosmos.

And—oh my goodness—what a society he was talking about! It could take the planet.

Oh, to see this thing from space. A force very small, but growing very grand.

New world to come. And the people. To be one with it. Surrender yourself to it. To the journey.

Expand your view of the world.

These are the things Cinjun is saying and has been saying. This was where it was all going.

This night Cinjun would take it there. He was on his way—such a way—all through the night.

The journey formed around him . . . a journey to a House Crimson.

The promised realm. The big view. The breathtaking landscape.

Cinjun was in full form, at the top of his game. And he played.

Now he took them on a journey in the form of a story.

The world was without form. Darkness was upon the face of the deep.

The song of the deep.

Violence—Gathered thick in places. Violence—Crowding, then separating.

Violence—The spirit was moving. Violence—The ancient spirit.

In the beginning was Reflecting. This am I.

Cinjun—Takes them to the field.

The ultimate word for what was transcendant, divine: god being.

*Took them to god being.* The universe is divine.

*Mask of Eternity,* expressed. Now—move into the god emperor savior, moving in the field, coming forth in male being, Cinjun Khan Smythe.

Who has eaten of the fruits of knowledge, good and evil, man and woman, future and past. He knew everything.

Being and non being.

Realization. And the promised center. House Crimson.

Emerging from this great zone, *Cinjun Khan Smythe.*

In the full cool of evening.

Man and nature in one man, beautiful, with big fists.

An ancient spirit moved in Cinjun Khan Smythe. Everyone could see it.

A totally different way of living. Full of revelation.

Passing between god being and the world. Between the moon and the forest city.

In the full cool of the evening.

No one knew where nature ended, and this man began.

Introducing the Hunter in the Red Vest.

Open up the world! He was coming in from outside.


He had taken them out of this world. And now brought them back.

To run with him.

The Visiting Deity, at least this was the way they made him feel. With their recognition of his identity.


And with Deity always came: *The One Forbidden Thing.*

The forbidden fruit which . . . you very well know you will eat.

Knowing *The One Forbidden Thing*—was being *One.* Miles was *One.* He was Wāone. And looked the type to stay Wāone—And would not be forgiven for it.

And—now—in this night, emerging—Unumbatai—the great god being, oh sky god—came down from the sky, and said, 'Who told you that you could be *One?*'

"I did," Miles said to Unumbatai.

"How dare you be *One!*" Unumbatai thundered.

"Because I feel like it," Miles said to Unumbatai.

He spoke thus with his presence—Miles Roark—was what he said. Being and becoming was his end of the talk.

He remained One. And studied. Readied himself for when he would make moments come alive. He remained One, wild with the power, wild as can be.

Now—Life was throwing off the past, and continuing to live. The moon shed its shadow.

Unumbatai was now the next thing to the Buddha in the field of time. Throwing off death.

In this moment, being eternally alive.

A fantastic thing.

## Fantastic Things for Sale

IF YOU DON'T GET IT HERE, you don't get it anywhere.

Heroism requires you to take a journey and share it.

Now—he gives them a Crimson Teaching on the go.

Takes their interest into a Teaching on the go.

*Keep it strong, keep it pure. And get serious. About belief.* This being the lesson.

It's important to have; it's an important thing to people. People live by this.

Here's the offer. Move through the night.

Values—found. From study. So fresh.

*New values for sales.*

Values that are fresh and strong. New values for sale.

He was a great teacher of values, raising money, keeping the teaching going. *Appreciate it.* Please, we need your help—It was about more than just Peace and Love and Fun. It was about something far higher—*Murder.* In modern language.

Belief systems. *New belief systems for sale.*

Varieties of belief. Gain them. Let them act upon you on the journey to maturity.

What he invented now, was—A good way to talk about killing— When you kill—You come away with a few things that are wonderful, and make wonderful things possible.

Now it was time for you to make your contribution and get the entire set of powers.

*New powers for sale.*

Powers that are fresh and bold. Powers that are only slightly old.

*New powers for sale.*

No better time to join. A convenient time. Support the program, right here, and join us. Be proud of the part you play.

We're in Prime Time.

Are you willing? Can you feel it? Let's see the real you!

Join us. It takes only a moment, and the change we will make will last for generations. For a long stretch of time, reaching—oh, for about the size of forever.

Illumination—Realize—In time.

Don't withdraw from the world. Horror is the foreground of wonder. Come. All life is sorrowful; it wouldn't be life if loss were not involved.

This is the way it is. Nobody intended it. This is the way it is.

History is a nightmare from which I am trying to awake.

Do not be afraid. Recognize.

All of this, is as it is, is as it has to be.

The ultimate conclusion is beautiful.

Know philosophy. Know wisdom.

Participate. *I will go to War!*—Is this a private fight or can anybody get into it?

The Hero is the one who comes to participate in it.


Feel the sense of wonder. Try to understand this existence.

Feel universal being.

Don't go out there, come in here.

Resurrection. You too can feel god being.

We're talking a thing, beyond the concept of reality. This goes beyond all thought.

A line connecting you to mystery.


Buddha—was the one who woke.

Wake up to what is within us.

Heaven—that desired goal—Heaven—and Hell—are within us. All the gods are within us. All heavens, all worlds are within us. Magnified dreams. Dream manifestations of energy—forms in conflict with each other.

Energies within us, in conflict with each other.

The ground of being.

Inward we are the source. We are mystical teaching.

Let me show you a Fixed Star by which to chart your course through the spaceways.

A Myth forming life instruction. Gives you—life models.

Listen—Time—changes, and continues to change, so fast. Virtues of the past are vices today.

Godphrodite, for the women. How to be a goddess of beauty.

Godeus, for the men. God with a lot of rules and no mercy. Give me some of that old time god.

Signals.

He went up to the mountain of the world and built a palace.

He filled it with what you yearned for—Bigger Ideas. He was marvelous; there was no end to his desires. He was caught for life in life.

He was sitting on a lotus of divine energy.

Telling his story. The story that sounded easy. Got into your skin. Shook you up.

Fixed you right; fixed you nice; made you feel nice all over.

And Unumbatai spoke in this way—

"Welcome!" Unumbatai said.

The thunder was rolling on the horizon.

. . . and Unumbatai took your thoughts, to far away, to a galaxy far far away . . .

Go there now!

Think of the galaxies beyond the galaxies in infinite space.

This was the Highest Illumination—drop your thunderbolt in it.

Sit on the throne. Go ahead try it on for size. God being for sale. Beautiful new god being for sale.

God being that's fresh and bold and only a few days old.

Enter the God Palace.

Oh, the beauty of this Palace.

He touches them with his Crimson Myth.

They experience it.

'Have as much as you can of this experience,' Unumbatai says. 'Have a marvelous time. Here is the place to have it.'

Join your thoughts to these actions . . . details to follow.

Sign on below. Genesis for sale.

He was explaining the universe through story.

A coat of many colors.

With a red vest.

Touching people, making impact. Citadel forming.

And the companion book to the power of this myth—was a book called *House Crimson*—To touch you personally. With insights and the universal story. Put life into your life. Please join us.

We're pleased to welcome you.

We have the pleasure to have you be part of our world. Thank you.

He was: A marvelous teacher.

Listen, we all search for meaning; this we know.

He makes meaning. Makes it with his character. He is the meaning. Striking chords. Distributing meaning.

Is there anyone better? Anywhere? People responded. Recognized their own appetites.

Now they will back Cinjun with their bodies and of course their money.

*Oh the Power,* they thought. *Yes—Do the walk of life.*

You can depend on him for quality power. Go to him now and get yourself some power.

*New Power for Sale.* Power that's fresh and bold, and only a few days old.

*New Power for Sale.*

---

# Miles Roark
## *Stranger in a Strange Land*

---

GOODNESS, MILES REALIZED what this all was.

The showdown was nothing more than a sideshow to this; the showdown was meant to be nothing.

This was an enfolding drive. This was one long extended unseen vast enfolding drive.

He was picking up people. He was sweeping up people.

That's what this was all about.

Cinjun Khan Unumbatai Smythe was far more brilliant than Miles had appreciated.

Whirling around this fireball in space, on this orbiting form . . . rode great meanings . . . and great structures.

Cinjun was creating a great structure and pulling in people to pleasure themselves in the great painted cave.

He was offering light for inward darkness, and nightly visits of well being.

He was enfolding. This goddamned thing was one massive enfolding drive.

Space blazing crystal ship burning across the spaceways. Soaring into distance. Power springing from its internal reactor, from its massive enfolding drive.

## Enfolding

HE WAS THE STAR ATTRACTION. And the night was a Ceremony Capoeira.

He was enfolding people.

He was taking people in.

Power Ordeal.

Enfolding people.

Ceremony Capoeira.

This was the mix. Seasoned with fine talk.

This was about enfolding people! This had been clear from the start, but now the full form of Cinjun's dreambird was taking wing.

Cinjun was proving to be, not only a smooth, but also, a grand operator.

Cinjun's ploys and maneuvers were fascinating. Miles held fast, and wondered what Cinjun would do as he traveled in his ascent.

This was a capoeira, a dancing fight. They were in the Roman Arena.

All this, and for Cinjun, more—Cinjun was forming *A Crystal Ship*.

Cinjun was playing the teachings of power. He wasn't going to show his power. He was past that stage. He had sealed up his power. He didn't have to prove his power. He had to get people to believe in him and join him, that was what was absolutely necessary for Cinjun now.

He was moving to seize immortality and great being.

He was seizing the world.

Violently seizing the world.

Oh, the Beauties of violence. Thoughts to help you go with the violence. Traditions that helped. Names that helped. Stages that helped.

All this working toward—the violent. Charming, beautiful, enjoyable violence.

Relaxing in the wonder of violence.

The body reaching for power over others.

A vehicle to take control of you and you ... and you ... and you ... and you ...

Watch this thing go.

Gradually, the whole thing becomes violent environment.

Violent consciousness.

Violent being.

Murdering without effort.

What a beautiful future Murder would have under Cinjun Smythe rule.

Cinjun would turn it to the image of death.

And laying the image on some people, on some troublemakers. On some men and women that did not see life right. Did not see it through your experience.

Make them *not there.*

Get them lying down, and turning cold, and rotting. And making themselves *not there.*

Help them get *not there.*

Beautiful burials. Beautiful burying. Of burying people *Alive!* While he held up the sky.

Sacrifices for noble purposes. Noble anger leading to noble murder to save life and save the world. All being saved under this sky.

And this was were Cinjun was pulling it all. To save the world by murdering *you.*

It will all be better if we get rid of *you.*

Miles remembered now the story of the Land of the Blind he had placed on a plane of energy.

This Land of the Blind will be great once we get rid of you, because you can see. Seeing is preventing you from knowing joy filled life in blindness.

Circling round, it was circling round—to Homegrown Traitors.

Murdering the Homegrown Traitors.

---

# Strip to Show

---

MILES APPLAUDED.

"More! More! Bueno! Bravissimo! You didn't get to the part where we turn on the people—on our own people. Where we silence the artists. The people who won't play along, the Homegrown 'Traitors'. That's the best part of the trip. The part of the trip I really like. The best part, that's where you can be proud to be a part of this number."

The Barker moved in, to draw the proceedings to order. "Mister Roark, you'll have a chance to respond, once Mister Smythe has used his time."

Miles casually emerged from behind his wooden stand, moving between Cinjun and the protective Barker.

This was very stilted for a Capoeira. This wouldn't do. What was the Barker to the Capoeira or the Capoeira to the Barker? Old friend, Cinjun my old friend, what is the Barker to the Capoeira or the Capoeira to the Barker. Away, sweet Barker! Adieu.

"Cinjun, are you sure the things you say are right?"

"Yes," Cinjun said.

"Then," Miles said, "you would want the questions presented to you to be the most penetrating they can be. So that you will have a chance to get right to the root of things. And speak exactly the truth? Correct? And the truth can do no harm to you?"

"We're all here for the truth Miles," Cinjun said.

"Now who will ask," Miles said, "the most penetrating questions, your friend or your adversary? Who will ask the most dangerous questions, your friend or your enemy?"

"You want to trip me up, Miles," Cinjun said.

"But you said you're right," Miles said, "so you're not afraid of being tripped up. If you speak the truth, how can the truth trip you up? Now this esteemed gentleman is your friend. I am your opponent. Whose questions are more dangerous? Mine, correct?"

"I agree." Cinjun paused a beat for effect. "Your questions are off the wall, offbeat and off the mark. I suppose that's what you mean by dangerous. Yes, Miles I'm willing to let you ask me off—err, excuse me dangerous questions. Yes Miles let's call them 'dangerous' questions. Dangerous to which one of us we shall see."

Now the audience ate it up. A lot of them loved Cinjun Smythe, loved him so.

"Who should ask you questions?" Miles said. "I should . . . That's why we won't need a barker today."

He dismissed the pack of—err, panel of barkers—He made the lead Barker a feather in the wind, and sent him on his way.

Now Miles saw that the trail he was carving was taking on colored dimensions.

The Lead Barker happened to be a fellow by the name of *Profumo Moraz*. Oh you've heard of him. Yes, he was the great legendary Mister Profumo Moraz. The most trusted, beloved, popular man of the *light*vision. He was *that* Profumo Moraz.

Oh he was known the world over. A very famous Barker indeed. Mister Profumo Moraz. Highly respected. Highly powerful. Highly revered— Miles didn't give a damn. He couldn't have given less of a damn if he tried.

The soft strokes of Mister Profumo Moraz held nothing for Miles. Nothing of any interest at all.

But when he sent Profumo Moraz away—oh my God, what a scandal! Cinjun and everyone, the people close to Cinjun most especially, were immediately outraged. Didn't he know how difficult and what a high honor it was to have Profumo Moraz put in an appearance, attend to a debate himself? How dare Miles send Profumo Moraz from the scene in a kind of disgrace? This was damnable stuff. Mister Profumo Moraz was a legend among Barkers. This would turn many people against Miles—You did not just treat the great Mister Profumo Moraz like a cherry pit; chew him up and toss him away. Oh no.

Miles couldn't have given less of a damn if he tried.

Profumo Moraz held nothing for the capoeira. And a capoeira was come, into this place. Miles knew what to want and where to go.

*Ah, better, freer, more open*, Miles thought. *More possibilities for wheels of fire.*

Now, Cinjun was behind a wooden stand, Miles saw. Well, what was the wooden stand to the Capoeira? Or the Capoeira to the stand? The furniture made it very neat, very sporting. . . . This was not a place for furniture, Miles thought.

"Do you want to be completely open?"

"I am open," Cinjun said. He spread his hands wide.

"Do you need to hide behind things? Are you completely confident? Or do you need to hold onto things that comfort you such as the furniture? Do you need a stand?"

Cinjun's hands were still held wide. And open. "No, I don't," Cinjun said, smiling. With great charm.

"That's why today we will argue without any stands. Let's remove everything that gets between you and me."

He made the wooden stand a branch and sent the branch a-tumbling, to the woodpile.

Better.

For wheels of fire to carve through the Sun Night.

Miles was pleased.

For an instant they were eye to eye.

Then Cinjun turned toward the audience.

"Stunts are the name of his game," Cinjun said. "Let's not be fooled. I am so certain that I'm right, I'm willing to continue in this way and win on any playing field he chooses. Any proving ground will do."

Now, Cinjun was directing his look to the audience.

Miles thought, what was the audience to the Capoeira or the Capoeira to—Now wait a moment. The audience was fitting, was handsomely becoming to the shape. The world of people lent force to its seasons. The audience was a goodness. But Cinjun was sore astray.

Miles would help him see the path. See the wheel of fire between them.

Miles said, "Don't talk to them, talk to me. You want to talk to them, go ahead. When you're finished, talk to me."

# Rip Currents

AH, BETTER, FREER, MORE OPEN.

It could breathe now.

All was right.

And then, . . . moves.

Needs, . . . beginning.

Battle, joined.

Flying, to where shadows ran under the night sun in the place of the *light*vision.

Cinjun turned, looking into Miles's eyes, he saw *Tygers* crouched in jungles in Miles's dark eyes. Cinjun saw them and then they sprang. And Miles laughed.

Chilling and weird; it rubbed Cinjun the wrong way. Launched him into a blood rage. Bloodlust!

Blood in the streets. Bloody red sun of House Crimson rising.

Cinjun charged deep into the blood rage. He was in a fight to the finish with a madman. He would fell him. It would come in necessary, certain steps. It had to be a progression. He would win the audience with his war art.

Miles—he recognized the night. It was deep and rich and blue. It was deep and rich and true.

And a yellow Capoeira soared across the blue.

Now The Wonderland Band plays in the background to lend force to the seasons, to lend force to the capoeira. As in the long tradition of capoeiras, the berimbau begins the rhythm—the bass beats, sets the ground rhythm of cool rapidity, and then the drums kick . . . and the Wonderland Band is swinging away. Moving phase by phase. Lending some wild swing, some booming bass, and kicking rhythm to the substance of fire.

The audience sways with it, feeling it, going with it—yes, they like it. What the hmmm—It's a good time—This works for them—They ache for more. More and more and more. They'd like to see some more of that wild swing.

"Capoeira—Cinjun! . . ." Miles said. "Capoeira is come, capoeira is here, the berimbau confirms it."

Enter the bender.

Enter the mindbender.

Enter the fantastic voyage.

Enter fantasia.

*Ah,* Cinjun thought, *the games grow a little wilder.* Cinjun knows where to take this—to his home territory—to his mighty territory. The field of armed forces and might.

Cinjun turns to the audience. And smiles.

They love it. He's still in control. The old boy is really something—yes, that Cinjun is really something, he'll show Miles "the way of might."

Cinjun's presence fills the pleasuredome . . . he stands in silence for a breath, and then—taking the territory—he strides.

"Bring it on Mister Roark! Put on your traveling shoes we're going to take a trip. Run and dance as much as you like. And when you're finished let's get down to business like true men, let's get down to the people's business."

The Wonderland Band played a tropic rhythm, setting up a tropic corridor, a tropic splendor—and a wave, of oceans calling. Of salty air, and of going on down to cool rapidity—of taking it on down, oh yes, a rhythm that would take it on down and keep keeping it down—You know it just might fly on down to Rio, swoop into an upward glide, fly round the world, in a big old plane—fly round the world, round and round and round again—The Wonderland Band and the blue night called.

Miles smiled. "Yes, let's take a trip. A big trip. A trip the size of the world, what do you say? Shall we go. I'm ready when you are?"

"Let's take a world trip," Cinjun said. "Let's take a tour of what you're doing . . ."

## The World Trip

"WHAT YOU STAND FOR," Cinjun said, "is sneering at systems. Tearing down beliefs. You're not sure that the earth is here and men walk upon it. Beware of him. Do not let him make the worse appear the better.

"He's about tearing down everyone," Cinjun said. "Tearing down is an easy game to play. In this day and age, when our might is so important, we need somebody who understands how to work within a group and to move that group forward! To be the leader of a group!"

Miles said, "You deliver all the colors of a monotone."

"Tearing down," Cinjun said, "throwing things off balance, shaking things up is easy. Stirring. That's all an easy game to play. Chaos is easy.

Order is the hard part. Setting up order Mister Roark. What do you have in the way of order?"

"Seems to me," Miles said, "we had some pretty good systems lying around the house. Somewhere, I came across a few I liked. Yes, somewhere I read about . . . ————"

Somewhere I read of the freedom of assembly.

Somewhere I read of the freedom of speech.

Somewhere I read of the freedom of the press.

Somewhere I read of the right to protest for what is right.

Somewhere, I read it. It was written on something small, so I guess it's easy to miss.

The ideas behind it, were good.

You pool together.

You don't become a group thinking thug.

You bring together a sea of different people.

You don't make every person into the same person.

We don't live under one strongman rule. We shouldn't. We should be free to be you and me.

That's what I read somewhere. It was a pretty good thought, so it stayed with me.

I'm talking about nourishment.

I'm talking about having fun.

I'm talking about my people getting down, having some fun.

Dancing on the living room rug.

"How you talk Mister Roark," Cinjun said. "I don't hear how to run a country in anything that you're saying. My book has a plan for saving our country. What do you have?"

"What do you have," Miles said, "in that book for people who don't want to be part of your system?"

"Don't dodge the question—what's your plan?" Cinjun demanded.

"Majority rule, minority rights," Miles said. "Freedom of speech, freedom of expression. And decadent frills like public education and health care."

"I believe in the same," Cinjun said. "Not free preaching. We're not required to broadcast sneering. We're not required to listen . . . to be subjected to a jabberjaw."

"Oh, free speech," Miles said, "as long as no one hears it. Perfect.

"I'll cut to the chase," Miles continued. "I'll tell you what I'm all about. I'm about freedom of character. With me, everybody gets to become a character. With you, everybody gets to become a humanoid, a machine, a cog in the system of machines, if they're lucky; some people only get to be a piece of a machine, a piece of a people-shape. You want an assembly line. I want a kaleidoscope. What you're missing in your picture, is people who don't want to be part of your plan."

Cinjun relished the moment, the fool had handed Cinjun a winning hand. "Drop out, get high. We've gone down this road before. We've heard this story before."

"Just once," Miles said, "I'd like to hear a positive drop-out story. To hear what it's all about————"

## The Drop-Out Story

"TODAY, A YOUNG MAN ENTERED a state of relaxation in which he shut everything off.

"He realized that all matter is merely energy condensed.

"He realized we are all one.

"He lay in a field of green grass for four hours saying, 'My God, I love . . . everything.'

"The heavens parted and the sun shone through.

"He realized it doesn't always have to be about going on towards going on towards going on.

"Rest, is when your body does all the good things; it builds up everything you need for motion.

"If you're sprinting all the time, you get achy and can't sprint. If you stop sprinting once in a while to rest, you can sprint all the better.

"If you want to improve your 'on,'—you don't keep going more and more on. To improve your on, you have to shut off.

"To get really cool, you have to chill out. To get really groovy, you have to get laid back. To get really sexy, you have to release your load.

"That's what I think you have to do Cinjun is release your load. And I'm going to help you do that.

"To be a truly good warrior, you have to be a lover. Love is the answer.

"If I could melt your heart, we'd never be apart. You're frozen when your heart's not open."

# Taking It to Mighty Territory
*People Shapes and People Force*

STRENGTH, seemed now supremely important. . . . This is Cinjun's great message. This is his battle cry . . . And that's where Cinjun angles *it*—and to *all that jazz*—He wants to take it into muscle and strength. That's his territory. He's sure to win there. To smack dab in the middle of *Mighty Town*.

Miles goes with it—He'll beat Cinjun where it's hardest to do it— smack dab in the middle of Mighty Town.

Plop me smack dab in the middle. You can drop me smack dab in the middle. And I'll swing.

*Get hit in your soul. You've got to.*

Give him some of that ole' wild swing, Miles thought. See what it does? Yeah, smack dab in the middle. Here we go. Hit it! Warrior, samurai, capoeira. Cool! Let's run with it.

Miles saw the battlefield landscape spread before them now.

Ledges and rolling landscape, like a wilderness.

Natural forms for the playing field.

Turning absolutely nothing into form.

"That's what it's about," Miles said, "turning absolutely nothing into form. The secret, is that form emerges. Form follows function, and emerges. People emerge."

"You'd make," Cinjun said, "a fine fourth-rate poet." Cinjun favored Miles with a smile. "Let's stop talking about nothingness and things you can't touch. That—again—is an easy game to play. Let's talk about strength and healthy might, a force for goodness, now when it is so important, now when we are under attack by so much evil. It's a nasty world. Leading us into dreamland is an easy game. *It's a nasty world;* we have to do nasty things to protect ourselves. I'm talking about protection. I'm talking about protecting you."

"For my protection?" Miles said. "Who's going to protect me from you? That's my question for your suggestion box."

"I'm talking about fighting for peace," Cinjun said. "I'm here to show the way to peace."

"Your mind is fled and gone," Miles said, "there is no way to peace, peace is the way."

Cinjun felt good. Miles had lost, and he didn't know it yet. But it would be made clear to him.

"Tricks, Mister Roark," Cinjun said, "no more tricks. Are you here to talk the people's business, or not? You're back to tearing down, and sneering at people who lead. And now, we need leadership, we need someone who knows how to lead a group and move them forward."

"I'm talking about people shapes," Miles said. "And nature. Nature shapes. Elemental shapes. There's nothing more important in the whole wide world, not a thing more important in the whole wide world."

Cinjun shot a look at Miles. "Your plan for evil nations, for the enemies that hate us?"

"Books," Miles said.

"Books?" Cinjun said.

"Poets—" Miles said.

"Hah—" Cinjun explained.

"Jazz. Rock and roll," Miles said.

"That's your plan?" Cinjun said. "To fight dictators with books and poetry?"

"That's what they're afraid of," Miles said.

"That's the best you can do?" Cinjun said.

"That the best there is," Miles said. "That's what they always try to shut down. That's what they're afraid of. That's who they try to hold down. Haven't you ever noticed that? And that's what you're trying to hold down—"

"Now," Miles said, "I do wonder—why are you so obsessed with giving people big, mighty shafts . . .

"You know Cinjun," Miles said, "anyone who is so obsessed with guns, missiles and sticks is compensating. I think you're thinking about what you're missing. A hungry man thinks about steaks. A lonely girl thinks about men. Why are you thinking about giving people big shafts? I wonder."

"You can't see a belt," Cinjun said, "without hitting below it."

"I think you're frightened."

"Frightened of what?"

"Of what you're missing."

"I'll ask the President to pardon you, for being a jackass."

Cinjun was starting to lose it in ferocity—that was more like it—and the audience surged with the ferocity of the moment. The delightful savagery.

Good show! Bravo! Intense Savage Night.

"This is too much," Cinjun said.

Now Miles put a hand out, swept it across the audience. "Look, Cinjun. It's just right."

The people were leaping out of their seats, lunging into the air. Cheering.

Cinjun felt the people urging him. The crowd wanted to see a man get eaten by a lion.

They were screaming, and howling.

They seemed to be saying, *'Fight! Fight! Fight!'* Telling Cinjun: *'It's time—Put him out in the rain; hammer him down to size; show him who you are! Show him. Show him.'* The crowd ached—for moments of high stakes; and it sided—oh, you know, the crowd sides with the guy who takes—oh, they love a rake.

The audience was aching for savagery.

Cinjun was fighting to stay in control. To not kill him.

And the crowd wanted it, so bad. Wanted a fight in the light.

## Good Show! Bravo!

CINJUN FELT HIS IMPORTANCE.

Cinjun was an important being. So important. A being of high value. A marquee being—in headlines. A man written in headlines. A man of headlines. A man made of headlines and epic being. Conquistador, khan, mighty general. The soul of triumph—this was an important man. And this was his time.

Back slapping. Good show man. A leader. A ruler. An important man, much glory being given unto him and much to be taken, in the way of great men.

Statuesque being—Giant who walks the Earth—Striding—A Colossus. Great and grand and good and a general. Distinguished extinguisher of evil, ungood, untrue things under the battlefield sun.

Cinjun was tall bravado.

Staggering bluster.

Keen cuthroat-ery.

Miles felt *intensity*. And moving.

Into intensity and currents and storms.

The winding way. Taking it deeper and deeper, farther and farther, higher and higher, away and away. Out! To outer reaches. Into distance.

Distance! To the size of forever.

Driving into long distance, taking the size of the road to the size of forever.

Forever, . . . give or take a few steps.

To immense feelings, whose time had come.

How slow the moments did go—Time had died.

The world stopped spinning.

And now, into cool rapidity.

The winds of life came sweeping through.

Wildfire feeling, letting slip, letting slip . . . letting a lifetime slip away.

Slipping and slipping and slipping.

Time flow, river currents,

A wild whirlwind winding wild. Screaming wild.

And now—Cinjun thinking, *"What a goddamn bastard!"*

And now—Cinjun, feeling the train coming.

Miles now taking the night off the track, away—past all, to the nebula.

Let's go into the Capoeira Nebula.

Deeper and deeper, we sail. Into the yellow mist. Into the sun mist. Into the heart of the sunrise.

Sail past the nasty world, past war and peace, and might. Past us and them. Past control.

Nebula all around. Vapors all around. Misty life.

The Capoeira Nebula.

Miles was deep in the nebula now. Cinjun saw Miles emerging from yellow vapors, orange and red explosions—coming at Cinjun, a full force gale, radiating.

And it was affecting the audience, taking them into the sweep.

Danger! Cinjun thought. The man was a danger.

## Mighty Grind and the Battle Brew

How's IT GO? Not too slow. A maddening pace.

Dirty and lowdown.

They kept it low, low as can be.

*So they go*, at a maddening pace.

Keeping it low, low as can be.
You don't want to say a little too much.
You don't want to do a little too much.
When it's all going at a maddening pace.
You've got to take the place, at the maddening pace. Take it tenderly.

So many roads to choose. And it's all just begun.
So many horizons to choose. And it's only just begun.
Watching for signs, working way by way.
As the evening came, and smiled. So much ahead. So much to choose.
And it's only just begun.

Getting savage. Getting intense. This was where the feelings were going.
*Time to make it tricky. Time to make it a little tricky.* Oh, yeah. Trick It Out!
Each man held himself still now, revealing little, just letting the feelings slip, and slide, across the timeflow.
The crowd sensed the feelings; saw the physical signs of the feelings.
What the feelings might have said were myriad.
But the fighters held the feelings in control. Guided them. Guided their energies.
A capoeira was come, here and now, hear it now, near and now, A-Whack and Pow!
What they actually said to each other was simple.

Things might have been said; things were possible now.
Some of them might have gotten said.
They moved quickly now. Collision course realized!
Course realizing collision . . . details to follow.
The night moved fast now.
Tempo in time, time in tempo.
Pictures forming.

*Make elegant choices,* even in a fight.
It was about the choices you made. How you attacked the thing. All in how you attacked. *Choose wisely.*
This they knew. Each chose wisely and moved with skill.
Collision realizing itself.
*Defining moments;* define the moments; do not let the moments define

you. Do not let your enemy press you into the wrong choices, into wrong action—This was victory for your enemy—No, you had to choose wisely; at times very quickly. This was the nature of the thing. The nature of deadly combat.

Choices weighed heavily.

In free form combat.

How you pressed your advantage was important.

You had to think not just one move ahead, but many moves ahead. You had to determine a strategy, based on the difficulties. And the difficulties were shifting under your feet.

Choose wisely. *Oh, choose wisely.*

Impulse had to be directed toward a plan, and the plan had to be made up as you went.

This was the most difficult part of free form combat—the great thinking involved, the rapid thinking. Making choices on very little visibility, with damn little time. With no recovery time to be had if you slipped in your choices.

Now it moved.

The ground shifted under their feet, and the walls closed in, the ceiling came down, and the shifting ground rose in eruptions beneath them, exploding here and there in dangerous, startling ways.

This was the playing ground. This was the arena in which they fought.

In this arena, think fast. Sense everything. Be ready to react to anything—You did not know what was coming.

This was the way the crowd liked it—now seemed it rich to die; rich for someone to die.

*The deadly blows will come from unexpected places;* this they know.

Every moment is a moment of testing. As the hustle roamed deeper and deeper into this thing.

Cinjun's strategy—To go to the mighty.

Miles—He will go again to the land of the fair and strong. He wants to fight Cinjun where Cinjun is strongest, where Cinjun has every advantage.

## Mighty Sideswipes

CINJUN WAS THE MASTER OF HIS DESTINY. He would not kill him. To not kill him. To not kill him.

"You can stretch the truth," Cinjun said. "And you do."

"Use caution in your tone," Cinjun said. "I'm a fair guy. But you're moving out of bounds; you're using up my entire stock of patience."

"What's fair got to do with this?" Miles said.

"You're a champion repeater; repeat it and repeat it," Cinjun said, "until it sounds important. Because it sure isn't. Bend your mind to the problem. You ran out of things to say, but want to keep talking. So come up with anything. Then go fry your brain in it.

"Put your pieces together," Cinjun said, "create a great big work of nothing."

*Then glue it to your rear; I don't know what else it would be good for. Maybe you can sit on it for the hell of it. I'm not going to sit on it.*

I won't say it! I won't do that! He can take it from there to some moves that will put me in jeopardy. He avoided the clear traps, moved with skill. This, I must not do . . . you had to know the limits. You were expected to know limits. He bounced up against the limits like ropes.

Choices looming.

No! *Downfall,* lay along that path.

Diverging paths presented themselves. Cinjun chose.

"Put the pieces of your mind back together," Cinjun said. "Maybe you could still end up with something that works."

*Or maybe you could steal a better one from a donkey. I don't know if you want to risk working with a brain that advanced for you. Let others do the thinking, you don't have the equipment.*

Choose, in the heat of it, in the hottest point of it.

"Be careful," Cinjun said. "Don't preach. And don't pretend that you can teach."

"I'm not preaching," Miles said, "because I'm full of sin."

"Would you like," Cinjun said to the people, "to live in a lion's roar out in the world? Or sleep in a corner, and belong to a dying nation? That's the choice. That's the only choice there has ever been. Now—" he swung round on Miles, "don't pretend that you can think, Mister Roark."

Cinjun turned to the people—

"It all belongs to you out there. Not to this man standing in front of me."

"I make an impression, don't I?" Miles said. "I've tried to fix it. Nothing helps. I mourn for my impression over long winter evenings." Miles shrugged. "My only gift is that I can see—*Comedown is calling*. I can see, what will be—*Comedown is calling*."

"I'm beginning," Cinjun said, "to think you write your own dialogue. I notice it's a little thin on plot. But don't let that stop you from giving us some more. And we'll put it in an appropriate place."

*Rip this place apart. You're the boss.*

Cinjun felt his bosshood surge.

"*Comedown is calling*," Miles was saying. "Cinjun is taking it on the inside—*Comedown is calling*."

Miles, the nowhere man, was naming Cinjun the Go Scared Man. He was holding the repeating rifle of *Fear;* aiming it sure and fast at Cinjun; and firing off rounds of *'You are scared.'*

And now—the people turned to observe—

Cinjun easing the bite of it, smiling in spite of it . . . forgetting Miles while he was still burning inside his brain.

"So you're going to beat me, huh?" Cinjun said. "Remind me to get scared. I'll write it into my calendar. Leave a note on the door on your way out," Cinjun said, turning to the people, "and I'll have somebody write it into my schedule. 'Get scared of Miles Roark.'" Cinjun heard his engine. It was cooking. And now Cinjun turned his shooting looks towards Miles. And shot a look at him. "I'll see what I can do. But don't look for it too fast. I'm going to have to do a hell of a lot of work to get scared of you . . . to work up to getting scared of you . . . I don't see a way to do it quite yet. But maybe you'll yell *'boo'* some time, that should startle the hell out of me—"

"Boo," Miles said, stifling a god emperor that strove to make him rot, in a life lonely.

Cinjun held his rage in silence.

"It worked—you look scared," Miles said.

"It'll scare me for days and days," Cinjun said. He was about the farthest thing from scared you ever saw.

He was about as scared as an atom bomb.

"Straighten up and fly right," Cinjun said. "Flatten out, and do right!"

"Sit there and count the beatings," Miles said. "Go on take it easy, if you're afraid to lead."

"Do right, Miles Roark. It's time for you to do right, Miles Roark. We want to count on you. Do right!"

"Your hope is getting slender," Miles said. "Cheer on."

The world is still young. There is lots of world left to experience. Does your ending need mending? Let your end take wing. The world is full of possibilities. Sweeping wind-tossed possibilities. Oh so many possibilities.

## The Road Less Traveled

"You're afraid," Miles said.

"Now why suppose such a thing?" Cinjun said, charmingly—he was the most civilized, charming man you ever saw. And he was forcing caution to be the better part of valor.

"Because," Miles said, "you're not coming to get me. You stand there. And stand there. And stand there. You're going wrong, Cinjun. You're doing it all wrong. You're making a lot of noise. I don't see anything. Take away your noises, and what do you have. Nothing. You're going wrong, Cinjun. You're doing it all wrong."

"Use caution in your tone, I'm a fair man but—" Cinjun said.

"The talk of a coward." Miles swung round. "Is there anything to you? Is there anything to you at all? I want to see the real you. Can you see the real me, Cinjun! Can you? Whoa, can you! Can you see the real me, Cinjun?"

The audience—the people—looked on Miles with interest. They wondered if they might see the real him? They looked at him. They looked at Cinjun.

"I seem," Miles said, "to scare you a little, Cinjun. I'm going to show you to the Golden Gate. This is the *end of days,* Cinjun."

"You make me laugh—" Cinjun said.

"Do you betray what you think?" Miles said.

Cinjun looked sharp. He saw Miles's trick. He felt the turning of the world. Cinjun held himself, and thought coolly, *to not kill him.* To not kill the son of a bitch. Outside he remained smooth, a smooth ocean under the moon.

"Can we see the real you, Cinjun?" Miles said. "Come on, show us the real you, Cinjun. You can't be this scared man, can you? Strange person you are—maybe that's you—a coward living in a yellow house. Doesn't want to know trouble. Is afraid of trouble. I am true trouble Cinjun and I'm here for you. Can you see the real me, Cinjun! Can you! I'm full of life and I can't wait to show it to you. Come on, Cinjun. We want to see the real you. Will you show us the real you, Cinjun? Will you? Will you!

"I'm coming at you." Miles said. "I'm crazy god help me. But I'm all here. Can you see the real me, Cinjun! Can you see the real me!"

Miles was swirling his upper body with the flow of the emotions. Hovering, floating, lightly, easily. Swirling.

Cinjun was still. Entirely still. Breathing deep and strong. And holding his look on Miles. Holding Miles's eyes. With great force.

Miles was taking Cinjun into full force winds. He would not let it be. I am the master of all destiny, Cinjun thought. I will not kill him. To not kill him. To not kill him.

"You declared you would be taller," Miles said, "you only become what I make you. You thought you were chasing a destiny calling. You only become what I make you.

"Look here now Cinjun," Miles said, "what do you see? Can you see the real me?

"You thought force could make the changes go round? What do you see now? Where have you ended up? You're coming up against something. Let's see how your force stands against it.

"What is there to your force? Nothing. What is there to you? Nothing. I'm looking at the real you Cinjun.

"You're framed large. I'm framed larger.

"You're something. I'm something more.

"Can you see the real me, Cinjun? I'm wildfire. And I'm taking over. What are you going to do about? What are you going to do? How long are you going to let it go on? How long are you going to let it go on?"

"I'm trying to speak between lines of your oration," Cinjun said.

"It's hard," Miles said. "I'm saying a lot."

"You're saying nothing—at great length."

"Yes, I'm talking about nothing. I'm talking about you."

"Be careful," Cinjun said. "Don't pretend you can teach."

"We're on the dance floor, Cinjun. This is a capoeira. We're in a dancing fight. The fight is dancing around you. And you're afraid to take a step. Cower. Quake. Run, if you're scared. Flee if you quake. Goodbye Cinjun—if you can't take it."

"I am *One*," Miles said. "You are nothing—without your people. I am *One*.

"Where do you get your talk of force, Cinjun?" Miles was provoking a reaction. "You're a goddamn coward. You're nothing.

"While I—am *One.*"

A soft sound came at them, from a distance.

Cinjun turned. He saw a marvelous, beautiful woman now standing in the crowd of *his*—of Cinjun's—people. He recognized her. This was the girl Miles loved.

She was a scorching beauty, Cinjun observed. And she was smooth. And she was hot. And she was standing by a burning sun. She was fire. And she was the turning of a world. Turning round and round. And her emotion was hitting. And her heart? Was *burning* with feeling.

And now she was emerging from her flaming world, and she was saying, "He is one." And she laughed. "He is one." And she laughed again. "He is one." And she saw her cosmic kiss taking on dimensions—and she saw a wheel of fire carving into the Sun Night. And the wheel of fire was heading for Cinjun Khan Smythe. "Goodness gracious," she said, "great balls of fire! He is one."—No, it was not going to catch her now—she was not going to let sanity catch her now. No more sanity for her, she was her reason for reason. She stepped into her cool, and lifted the place up to better suit her mood—"He is one!" she said. She swept it into the audience now. She shot her gaze—and the look of love in her beautiful, radiant eyes, and her scorching beauty—at a fellow in the crowd—just for the hell of it. "He is one!" she said to the fellow. It did a few things to the man. One thing it did was—it startled him out of his senses.

The audience reacted with interest.

The fellow felt the turning of the world. This life wasn't good enough. He would change his life. Enter her cool. He had to enter her groove. He wanted to feel the turning of her world. In her body, he saw the kind of loving that could be so smooth. The fellow opened his jacket. Took a deep breath, and reached for her cosmic kiss. He joined into a kind of *'dance'* with this pretty girl. "He's the one!" he said. Oh, how he wanted her cosmic kiss.

A laugh nearby.

Daphne shot her gaze and shot her scorching beauty at the people behind her. "He is one," she said. And burned in a wide sweep with the look of love in her beautiful radiant eyes. Her heart was *burning* with feeling, they saw and it took their breath from them. As they felt the turning of her world, they couldn't breathe.

The look in her eyes startled the hell out of the people who fell under her gaze. None of them had ever seen a look like that. And they felt it was the damndest look they would ever see come out of a beautiful woman's eyes.

*She's crazy, god help her!* They could see the real Daphne. And from her eyes they could see rivers of flowing rain and lunging flames.

It brought some of the other tickets into a lunge; they felt the turning of her world; tickets along the sweep of her gaze, lunged from their cushioned reclines, and began to say, "He is one." They jumped into her groove.

And it was the real them!

Daphne returned her gaze to the man. She looked at this strange man who knew her now, and would long for her for the rest of his life. She flashed him the real her. "He's the face!" Daphne said to the stranger in the jacket, giving him a sultry look that always spoke to men, to the deepest part of men, to somewhere dead in their middle. And that place in this man became flushed, and flooded with blood. And yearned to bursting for her cosmic kiss. This thing in this man saw the Golden Gate. And in her body, the turning of a world so smooth, and he saw scorching beauty, and he was bursting with desire. And he had to jump into her groove. And oh God! He couldn't take it anymore! He couldn't live if he couldn't fuck her right now!

"He's the face!" the man in the jacket said—and made it real. Having no idea at all of what he was talking about. He felt the turning of her world. And with her look, he would yell out anything she damn well tossed over to him. And make it real.

A laugh nearby. A grunt. Strange sounds. People in strange worlds reacting to strange actions along strange territory.

Daphne danced deeper into the ballroom.

"He is *One!*" she said. And they all felt it, the chill divine. The men felt bursting yearning. The men looked at her. She didn't own the clothes she was wearing.

She tossed it back to Miles.

Miles turned to Cinjun.


"You're running a helluva unit!" Cinjun said. "What do you want to discuss now? What kind of color you are? What kind of flower you feel yourself to be? What's next of great consequence and meaning for us here?"

Emotion was taking Cinjun. The night was spinning.

Cinjun remained in control; he remained—high up there; high up in a towering world. He would not dive down and kill Miles in the ocean. He would stay high, above the storm. Let the tide wash and wash below. He would take it in slow control.

"I'm flying through the sky," Cinjun said, "that makes me an easy target for snipers." Cinjun began flowing across the sky. "For idiotic, do nothing, moronic snipers—now you wouldn't happen to be one of those would you Miles? I'm here to help you Miles; you do believe I'm here to help you don't you; we have to help fools. Especially ones rippling in stupidity, boiling in assinineness—who forget where the truth is. Now if you're a jackass, just say again 'you are one.'"

"I am *One,*" Miles said.

"I'll believe you. You look like one."

"Underneath your great show," Miles said, "is a frightened man. Are you a mighty warrior or a blowhard? It comes down to the dare. You're a fighter or not—I am *One.* What are you?

"You're piling it high and deep tonight, aren't you Miles?"

"And you've been laying in it for days Cinjun. My force is bigger—"

"I could shove this fist—" Cinjun said.

"—My force shoots farther—" Miles said.

"—so far down your throat—" Cinjun said.

"—My gun is more dangerous—" Miles said.

"—even your missus will think you're a hole in the ground," Cinjun said.

"—More powerful—" Miles said. "That's why you're scared and I've won."

"You haven't won."

"The last man standing is the winner."

Whoa . . . everyone is with it. It's a show-stopper moment. Bloody excellent.

"I know I'm a man," Cinjun said. "What are you?"

"The word you're looking for is, winner. You do know what that is when you're looking at one, don't you?"

"You're nothing; you seem to be able to talk a whole lot of it."

"Well, I know what nothing is, Cinjun. I'm looking at it—Run, if you're scared. Go on. Git. Go home Cinjun. If you stay you might get hurt. And I don't want to see you cry."

Cinjun produced a smile. "Very good Miles. Excellent."

The smile grew fierce. Rage carried the expression.

"Use force Cinjun," Miles said. "Use force. Let's see what you have."

Cinjun held himself still. To not kill him. To not kill him. To not lose control. To not lose control of his senses. To not let Miles carry him off the track—of sanity. Cinjun held himself. To not go mad. To not go mad.

He was the god emperor. And the god emperor had responsibilities. He could not unleash himself. The rage had to be controlled. He must not go mad. He was insane when he went berserk. He would not let himself enjoy this. He must not allow the pleasure—of killing this man.

"Lone and only you stand there Cinjun," Miles said. "Your people are wondering if there's anything to you. If there ever was anything to you. I'm wondering myself. You look like such a lost soul. Oh, you poor thing. Standing there all by your lonesome."

Miles begins to feel it now. "It's so—it moves me deeply Cinjun."

Miles starts to show him love. Shower him with love and compassion.

"You poor thing Cinjun. Oh how the night has gone for you. All your streets have turned from red to blue. Now you're looking for a better view. I feel terrible for you. You look so sad and lonely standing over there. Would you like some love Cinjun. How about it? Do you feel love. Do you feel loved—do you feel luh-uhved? Do you feel loved?

"Would that help you to be strong? We want you to be strong. We wouldn't want you to go off and kill yourself after this. And go to bed and cry with the lights out.

"We're looking at the real you now, Cinjun.

"Tell you what. I'll show you something to take your mind off your troubles. I'll show you the real me."

What had he been saying? Miles wondered. What on earth had he been saying? Suddenly, he couldn't remember for the life of him? Suddenly he felt himself elsewhere.

Perhaps the wise thing to do was pull himself together. Get himself back on track. It would have been mighty smart to take a deep breath and make it back to where "it" was—where sense and logic was. That would be what everyone else in the world would have done. That's why Miles didn't do it.

Two roads diverged in a yellow wood. He took the one less traveled.

Abruptly, everything came awake. Miles crackled with energy.

He felt it coursing through him—he was suddenly capable of anything. His entire being, crackled and produced a kind of energy. His arms and body shot it into the air—the surge cut through the atmosphere, taking it over. It filled the world.

It flowed and flooded, filling the world.

Miles crackled with energy—The energy taking shape. The feeling deep within him growing, evolving. Taking on greater and greater form. Surging outward in an explosion that took him over.

Miles crackled with energy. He felt it from the ground rising and surging through all his being and then shooting into the air. Slow sensation—taking over.

"Oh, Let Me—Show You—How You—Make Me Feel!" Miles said. In a voice that may have been a little too loud. "Argh! How You—Make Me Feel!" And in the background, maybe The Wonderland Band played the moment a little too strong, maybe too many trumpets blared. But he was One. And he saw things along this road. It reached into the Capoeira Nebula.

This was an extending of the fight, into something. He put out— *probing sensation.* He was taking in *wide sweeps.* Wildfire slipped from him. Sweeping feelings and cosmic winds swept in. The winds of life came sweeping through.

The currents grew strong.

Miles was on his way—such a way.


Love had exploded into the form.

He would use it; work its colors in among the green and fold; among the azure; against the orange and red backdrop, splashed across the yellow Capoeira.

A love Capoeira? He would see where it led. And he promptly lost his mind. The world disappeared. And for Miles, there was only the love capoeira.

Miles lost himself in the love capoeira.

The currents grew strong.

Run with the currents? Will you?

Miles was—Miles was on his way.

Some like it hot.

Some like it storming.

Some like it wild.

Miles was on his way.

He would show Cinjun the way to the storm. To wind swept, rumbling, thunderous being—There were men and women high in the forest society who had seen everything, who had seen quite enough of the world, but they had never seen anything like this. A man standing calm, and traveling the world in sweeping orbits around him.

The lights made stars shine on his smile.

Miles wasn't paying attention to anyone. He wasn't aware of anything.

His time had come. The only thing he cared about was: Did he like what he saw?

He stood in this place, calm.

Using his imagination to start a fire. And making some sounds that made changes go round. Who gave a damn about the sounds!

It was just thunder.

But the feelings, oh, the feelings!

Immense feelings whose time had come. He was using his imagination to start a fire.

The feelings swept through the streets.

In this place where time had died—the winds of life came sweeping through.

*The Pacifica Love Dream Experience.*

The audience was being experienced.

Cinjun felt it. Spreading wildfire. Swooping energy fields, emerging stars—an energy field—an emotional nebula.

Miles was making the little world—big! Making "your" little world bigger and bigger.

Cinjun had to match it.

He would not let the devil take the night. As if he was doing no wrong.

It was taking the audience into its sweep.

Madness.

Feeling.


The energy coming off Miles—goddamn him! Damn him to hell! Cinjun thought.

And Miles made it look like mere living. Miles seemed to be standing in a state of perfect calm. Framed in a state of perfect grace. And all these feelings—were flowing, and flowing. Outward. Onward. And roundward. Conspiring an armor, and flowing out again. Moving outward into the outer reaches of forever. Remembering distant memories, recalling other worlds. Flowing under. And traveling down. Sweeping up. And rising over. Rippling over canyons. And flying through the skies. Flowing into the oceans, and flowing through the skies. This was stormy. And this was calm. This was the actor. And this was the scene. He was in this water. And this water was streaming out as far as you could see.

This was the actor. And this was the scene.

Now one of the girls Miles loved was a perfect dresser. And this girl had a scorching beauty that danced across the ballroom with a face that looked quite a lot like Daphne's. But this lady was a flow of day energy. Of energy, pure and easy. She was the day trip. And she went by the name of Lady Day. And now heaven above tried to match her for perfect pure and easy grace. Miles saw her dance across the ballroom, the lights making stars shine on her smile.

Miles was the face, and she knew him.

What the hell kinds of feelings, Cinjun thought, were these he was throwing into the mix—that he was mounting? Child's feelings.

The boy was becoming a child.

He wanted to drown Miles in cold water.

The boy was growing younger before him. These were the timeslip feelings, of youth—No wisdom, no sense of the world, no order. Feelings of—*Got to, . . . got to, . . . got to get away.* Feelings of—*Got to, . . . got to, . . . got to Go.* Feelings of—*Oooh, turn me loose!*

Feelings of he can't sleep, and he lays and he thinks.

Of—Love rain on him! Rain on him. Over him. Under him. Over him, under him. Love rain on him.

Of—There's a stranger inside him some where, who stays up all night. A stranger. Who never dies.

Of—Can you see the real him? Whoa, can you! Can you! Can you! Can you see, can you see, can you see the real him!

Primitive feelings and tricks, of not being held down, of riding the breeze.

Life and play. Turning loose.

Running wild, screaming wild.

Careening wild. Stone free.

Winding wild. Stone free.

Miles was on the road to dreams.

He was on his way.

His heart drowning in love dreams. Radiating feelings, sweeping feelings across the ocean, the people ocean.

His heart was drowning in love dreams.

Whipping tails and swirling vapors, of feeling, and a young man, drowning in love dreams.

Cinjun saw the danger.

This stripling was the worst kind of bastard.

Playing to every rank stupidity he could grasp.

Leaving the world behind, Cinjun thought,—same old story,—drop out—as if to drop out was a glory.

And shouting to Cinjun out of yellow vapors that a fight was come!

That a fight was here—a blood ship upon them.

Cinjun saw *Tygers* springing all around.

Miles was firing shots directly at him. Cinjun was under fire. Exploding shells of yellow dust. Collisions and tumults.

Cinjun was under total attack.

This wildman was a wolf. This wildman was a villain. What he was playing to—

Cinjun was alone with the situation.

"Do you like what you see?" Miles said. "Crazy. Isn't it?"

He was radiating love.

Cinjun's reaction was *hatred*. Raging hatred. He didn't complicate it; it was not a mixed drink; it was pure raging hatred, every fluid ounce of it.

He didn't look on the emotion coming off Miles as a kind of beauty. He saw it for what it was. *An opiate for the masses.*

He was taking them into love. A man drowning in love dreams.

He was showing them a kind of peace. A swirling vaporous feeling of peace.

Cinjun recognized this thing. It was the peace used by the enemy. The thing used to lower their guard. To take them into a dreamy lull. Ripe for slaughter.

There were fools out there falling for it. It was taking them into its sweep. They were walking on the trail he was carving.

A road of dreams. A road of love dreams.

Miles was experiencing it. Sending it into the audience.

The audience was being experienced.

Goddamn him! Cinjun thought. Goddamn him. Damn him to hell. This stripling was the worst kind of bastard.

Taking them by their feelers into slave existence. Into losing being. Into weak chambers of languid sins. Strange nights of sins and satin sheets. Of pliant women and tender men. Weak striplings.

It would lead to bloody faces—Victory would belong to the enemy— This was where he was taking them—The goddamn bastard. Goddamn him to hell!

Cinjun would be damned if he was going to let this son of a bitch get away with it.

*"Do you feel loved, Cinjun?* Miles had said. *"Do you feel luh-uhved?"*

This fucking son of a bitch! Cinjun thought. Taking shots at Cinjun, like he could do no wrong. Where does he get his balls packed so tight? His walk so swaggered? His bullshit so thick? Where does he get that done? Cinjun saw him. Saw the real him. Studied him.

Miles had no idea what was going on, where he was, he wasn't thinking—Was Miles's voice screaming too loud? Speaking too soft?— Where was he? What was he saying? What was coming?—He had no idea in hell what was going on anywhere in the world—He was feeling—He was bleeding feelings into the world.

The Pacifica Love Dream Experience. And a man drowning in love dreams.

The audience was being experienced. They were dancing across the ballroom with him. Lights shining from the stars across their faces. And Miles was *the face*. This was what they knew. They hoped he would take them deeper into cool rapidity. Please, oh, please take us to where you're going. Heaven above laughed, trying to match this thing.

The Pacifica Love Dream Experience. And a man drowning in love dreams.

*Bring it on!* Cinjun thought. He watched Miles's feelings dance across the ballroom. He was the face. Fuck him.

Cinjun would blow his mind.

*Anywhere you want to take it*—Cinjun thought—*I'll take you apart.*

Cinjun towered.

He would destroy Miles. Shatter him. Leave nothing.

Cinjun was high up there. Whoo! He took the world into his sweep. Now—*His Feeling*—he produced a feeling that grew immense—taking the world, taking the night. He would flow further and wider, deeper and vaster than Miles Roark. Miles was just a tear in a baby's eye. Cinjun was the ocean—an ocean boiling with rage; a sky storming with rage. A world on fire. Cinjun was the actor; this was his scene; he was coming into powerful form.

Cinjun was passion. Great, flowing, passion. A rage. A red rage.

He was a House Crimson. He was one.

Ruling—that was what this was about—and warring for Peace. Miles knew nothing of how to rule a world. A world where people could be. This Miles was an absolute disgrace. And a lot of fools were falling for it.

Miles was an opiate for the masses. Dressed up better than anyone for the trick. Peace—but not true Peace—no, Miles was selling the slogan created by the enemy—the many enemies—to get people of right and might to drop their guard. Drop their all. And give this world away. Render the great systems to dust—render them lifeless, grind the great systems to dust, pulverize the great systems to inert powder. To smash and destroy and bring down the beautiful world order. And all that destruction would be done in the name of love and peace—this Miles Roark was indeed the worst kind of bastard. The worst bastard in the world. Cinjun could see it now. He had to be stopped. The most dangerous kind of enemy. One who pretended to come in friendship. Cinjun saw right through him. And knew what was necessary. Destruction. War for Peace. To destroy Miles, to smash him.

But with war art. Cinjun recovered his senses.

He would hold back, be sporting, show that he—Cinjun—was in control.

## Exploding Form

*ONLY LOVE can make the rain,* Miles thought.

Love.

Love exploded into the form.

Only love can make the storm. Only love can bring the doom that falls—in tears—from on high.

Only love could take the fight into tender sensation.

Only love could take the fight into utter madness.

Only love could set light to the Capoeira Nebula.

Only love.

The night grew hot.

Only love.

And now—

Love Explodes on the Scene!

Pow!

Pow! Cinjun holding back, watching the dance floor.

Pow! Miles moving into prowling, and rocking.

Pow! Miles winking at Cinjun, "Hey, lover boy . . ."

Pow! Miles moving into tigerish strut. And crowd feel.

A ship in the night on a lonely sea, a man leaping off a mountain into cold canyons. Feelings and waves of motion filling the expanse.

Love Explodes on the Scene!

Pow!

"Hey, here's the thing," Miles said, "she's wishing for someone to come and sweep her away.

"Here's the thing, she's got the world on a string.

"And my baby only cares for me. Hey lover boy, you ain't got nothing she needs.

"We're a ship in the night on a lonely sea. My baby only cares for me.

"Love, something to sweep her away. What can I say? It could happen. The Lady of Love. She's wishing for someone to sweep her away! What can I say? It could happen."

Miles prowling.

"Come as you are Cinjun. Here's the thing, she's got the world on a string. And here's the thing, you ain't got nothing she needs. My baby only cares for me."

"She does what she feels, as the crowd roars, she doesn't care what anyone else thinks of her."

Miles, dancing and prowling, circling Cinjun.

Miles, floating and drifting, circling Cinjun.

Shaman dance, bringing spirits on the scene, bringing the lady—

Love explodes on the scene!

Miles, taking him into the dance.

Showing him how to bring it on the scene.

Bringing the lady, bringing the rain, ooh, the cool, cool rains—

Love explodes on the scene!

It's cool all around the pool.

Miles, singing the song of the insane. Bringing it on, with the charm, of the insane.

A poet's thing for drama, the charm of the insane. Bringing it on down. Bringing it right on down—love rains—Love exploding on the scene! Whoo, yeah!

Columns of fire, vines of naked senses. Love. Watch out! Watch it, watch it now, wild swing. That wild swing gonna whoop him—Knock him on his—My! Oh, my! Watch your senses, baby!

And the lady waiting for something to sweep her away. The sweet lady, only caring for Miles. That other one, he ain't got nothing she needs.

A brand of loving, sets her soul on fire.

A brand of loving that drives her wild.

She doesn't want no other lovers, no other loving.

She wants his love, got to have his love, got to have all of his love.

The audience feeling it.

Feeling sense waves, and something lovely beyond the sea. Waiting there. Waiting for them on golden sands. Ships sailing, and somewhere beyond . . . a little something for them, each and every one of them.

Yeah, they're into it now—It's shaping into a helluva night—

Flying, like birds on high. They're all sailing into the nebula.

Into this strange night of strange dreaming.

And in the heart of a nightfall sunrise, a young man with a strange brand of loving—Miles Roark—screaming wild and slipping across time, taking them to forever. The wild blue forever.

Sailing, sailing, everyone sailing.

And now Cinjun was holding tightly to a thought—his lifeline to sanity. Insanity's horse adorned the night. It threatened to take Cinjun's mind. He held the thought strong. The simple thought, that was saving him. The thought was: To not kill this son of a bitch.

Cheap but lovely tricks—Cinjun thought—where is the true force in his hustle . . . taking them to a city where the night runs deep . . . into an unwelcome sleep, into cotton wooly living . . . dreams of being hip and sunset strips . . . taking them to one side of the town, to bright shiny lies.

They don't see the pimps, pushers, the boulevard of broken dreams and shattered forces, of corpses in fields, and blood soaked slaughter.

He was taking them into a disastrous, dirty sleep of cheap tricks.

And Cinjun was thinking, to not kill the son of a bitch, stay sporting, let his hustle roam, and then take him into endings, into shattered doomfilled endings.

Cinjun was going to stop the wild swing. Watch it, watch it now.

He had to stop him now.

The young have problems, many problems, they need an understanding heart, not this monstrous deranged eager pitiful thinking.

"How you talk!" Cinjun said.

"How you hear!" Miles said. "Listen, here's the thing . . . Take away the noises coming out of your mouth and what do you do? Nothing. You're frozen, because you're afraid. Let all the hurt inside of you die. Love is the answer, baby. Peace."

"Don't be seduced," Cinjun said. "Don't let him make the worse appear the better."

"There's no point in placing the blame," Miles said, "I suffer the same. If I lose you, my heart would be broken. Let all the hurt inside of you die. Love."

"That's where your kind always leads—" Cinjun said.

"Love," Miles said, "hides in strange places."

"To an imaginary—" Cinjun said.

"Love," Miles said, "hides in narrow corners."

"Will you stop cutting me off—" Cinjun said.

"Love," Miles said, "comes to those who seek it. The men don't know what the little girls understand—love."

"I don't like what you're saying," Cinjun said. "There's nothing in it to like."

"Then forgive me," Miles said.

"Lewd and low-down—" Cinjun said.

"Just when I thought you couldn't feel it," Miles said. "Love *comes*—when you least expect it."

"—What was that about coming?—" Cinjun said.

"Love—" Miles said "—Is the answer. La, la, la, love." Miles sailed on. "If I could melt your heart, we'd never be apart. Give yourself to me. You're frozen, when you're heart's not open. The road to peace is peace."

"How dare you!—" Cinjun said.

"—Love one another—" Miles said.

"—Why you obscene son of a bitch!—" Cinjun said.

"—Wine, love and song!" Miles said. "Love yourself! Love free or die!"

"You better straighten out and fly right," Cinjun said. "You have right now to pull yourself together."

"Okay. Let's teach people to stop fighting, . . . by beating them up."

"I'm warning you."

"Oh, I'm sorry. I'll go with your message, as the preacher said, 'Let's flock!' Nah, nah-nah-nah nah. You're a scaredy cat. Scaredy cat, scaredy cat!"

Miles puts up his dukes, starts dancing around.

"You want to go to heaven," Miles said, "you'll be there in seven."

"Love the planet," Miles said, "love your neighbor, love is the answer. La, la . . . la, la, la. La, la . . . la, la."

Now—Cinjun Holding Back

To not kill him! Stay in control, old boy. Stay, be sporting, let him work with that.

Way was leading on to way. Cinjun fought to bring the ship back to port, out of the storm.

To not kill him! To not kill this son of a bitch. Stay sporting.

## Turn It Loose

"WHOA, I'M COOKING TONIGHT," Miles said plainly and softly. "I'm on my way, such a way, all through the night, whoo! Come on Cinjun, put me out, or I'm going to burn you up.

"It feels pretty good to win," Miles said.

Cinjun held himself in an upward surge. His eyes held still in a down from over look.

His eyes were something else, Miles observed. Commanding eyes. The devil must have given him those eyes. They seemed like they could control a world. No wonder he was who he was. No wonder so many people followed him. Those were some eyes.

"Go home," Miles said.

Cinjun leaned his gaze—in.

"Walk away," Miles said.

Cinjun scowled something fierce, kept his look loose. "You couldn't handle me if I came at you," Cinjun said.

A trace of a sneer. The eyes lost nothing. They stayed in command.

His brow tightened.

"You snotty bastard!" Cinjun said.

"Turn around. If you're done," Miles said. "If you're frightened to keep going."

"I save lives," Cinjun said, "I don't take them."

His eyes narrowed, staying in control, staying in command.

His expression widened. The eyes burned. His gaze took on flaming existence.

He leaned further forward. And the eyes took on an up from under look. A look that was fierce. Those eyes commanded everything; missed nothing.

Miles felt the eyes. They locked in on him and took him over.

Holding Miles with his eyes, Cinjun shifted his weight back. His head pressed back, letting loose a wave of rage-splashed emotion.

"One drop of rain doesn't make the sun run away," Miles said. "Don't go away. Don't go breaking my heart."

Heated battle! The crowd roared. Good show! Bloody excellent! Yeah!

This had been worth the trip; this had definitely been worth the trip.

Blood, battle, shaking and rolling, bam bam, yeah! Rumble, ringside seats. Rumble tonight. The pounding was here. Go cat, go!

There's a rumble tonight, ain't a damn thing anyone can do! Rumble tonight. Yeah! Who will be the last man standing? Who will be the last man standing!

The Wonderland Band kicked up a storm, this was the heat, this was where it all got—wicked!

Ah, dirty boogie! Let's live it up! Stomping on a hot roof! Shaking loose! Out on the town! Head spinning! Shaking loose! This was not too clean. This was lowdown. The forest city, singing, you ought to slow down.

But when the wicked night gets low down you don't slow down.

You don't give it up, you keep it hot and squeeling when you take the feeling on the town, when you take her on the town!

"Give it up," Miles said. "Let me show you all you are."

Cinjun's eyes held the world in their grip. The eyes swept from side to side, taking control.

The eyes held still. Looked.

Miles felt a chill travel his spine. Those eyes could make you lose your mind. Miles could have sworn that the eyes were on fire. They had to be flames—they couldn't just be eyes. They were burning, blazing. Miles never thought he would see such blazing.

Miles turned to the audience—Good God! They were all lunging into the air. Screaming. In the outer extremities of madness. The crowd was absolutely berserk. Violence charged the air.

It wasn't Miles that had taken them to blazing emotion. It was those eyes.

He turned back to Cinjun's eyes.

Cinjun was doing nothing, absolutely nothing, but his eyes were taking over the world.

Miles stopped breathing for an instant. Those eyes were getting to him. Shaking him something awful.

What the hell was Cinjun doing? He had never seen anything like this in his whole goddamn life. Miles wasn't driving this anymore. Something was taking over.

Miles stepped back then, startled. It was as if an animal were taking over Cinjun. There was something like a wolf there. If Cinjun wasn't a wolf—then he didn't have far to go. Nature red in tooth and claw slipped into Cinjun's eyes and that too began to blaze.

And now—Cinjun moved—to dance across the ballroom.

Now Cinjun was—the face.

He was the night. He was everything. He was these people's world. They knew nothing except Cinjun being. And the Cinjun being was a flame the size of a world. An inferno the size of the whole goddamn world.

Cinjun stepped onto the dance floor.

Miles smiled.

Miles danced around him. Then stopped in front of Cinjun.

Cinjun was startling the hell out of Miles. There was a lot to notice about Cinjun now—Cinjun was fit. Hellishly fit. Steely muscles.

Rippling sinewy muscles. And the frame nature had used in making him was massive. And everything about him was developed to scale.

And now—Miles is standing here—is here, understanding what Cinjun is—

Cinjun is a mountain of power. A man who can throw "anywhere" punches—anywhere they hit a person, they break something.

He can pound an opponent to dust. He has arms, made to break other men's ribs.

And now—he is approaching Miles.

Scream and shout! The trip.

Cinjun heard the trumpets blare.

He heard the waves crash.

He heard the beasts roar.

He heard the moment forming all around, the canyons creating corridors, wind canyons. Way leading on to way.

Cinjun, coming into it, giving the audience what they wanted.

You only go around once on this big spinning planet.

This was his ride.

He came into it, came into it fully, he was now fully his own—Cinjun Khan Smythe.

And he struck.


## The Prizefight

FROM THE DISTANCE you could see—Swing and rip, and whipping vapors.

They were in the nebula, coming at each other.

A fight to the finish.

The end of days.

One will be left standing.

The music was hot, the lights were low.

Beneath the sun night, beneath the demon night that had heard one thousand voices and seen one thousand murders, they entered the feverish nocturne.

A fight to the finish.

Cinjun moved in—a mountain of force. Skilled to a peak. Rich with the possibilities of animal force.

Cinjun stood before the people, and the people observed—an *Iron Man*. Hard as steel. Strong as the mountains. Loaded with "anywhere" punches. Rough and tumble. Heavy weather taking over.

As they stepped out onto the floor, they forgot all other troubles. They had the world to themselves. They stepped lightly. They heard the hot music. They let themselves go. Cinjun let himself go first—he launched a shot that traveled with great speed, and landing with great force, crossed Miles's face. Within this, Miles let himself go, stepping lightly, moving in time with the blow, moving into a counterpunch, which landed hard on Cinjun's face. The men were locked in battle. And took the measure of each other. Searching for answers to war and pain ... They lay in it for days ...

Among the observers, some hearts were broken.

It was clear—uhm, that punching Cinjun—was about as effective as punching a mountain. He was a man not meant to be bothered by little things like punches. If you hit him with a steel bat, you just might get him to itch. But don't bother with less.

"Oh oh." Miles, Daphne and a few others got that 'oh, oh' feeling. Yes, Miles felt the feeling. It came with the chill that traveled his spine.

Miles had taken himself into something. The dimensions of his problem quickly became clear.

Miles took a few shots, proving to himself *that he was never going to win this fight*. Cinjun was solid steel. That was the nature and feel of him. Not agreeable at all to Miles's designs of surviving into old age.

Cinjun was steely death in the shape of hammering arms that had all the softness and give of steel girders.

Cinjun would fold this up—Cinjun moved in the way. Animal inside— leading him to ripe conclusions. Cinjun—listened to the wind and the mystery came alive. Delicious night. Nothing would turn him off. Animal inside—led him to the conclusion—The animal took hold. The training, the cunning, the skill, the abilities, they were all there in Cinjun's form. He felt it in his body. And more. He felt the animal taking control—leading him to ripe conclusion. He was coming to the party with all the tricks he could want.

And now—Cinjun punched Miles. It did a little something to him. Miles hurt on the inside. He felt that if Cinjun spoke harshly to him now he might burst out crying. Oh dearest hell and damnation—that hurt! He had never imagined that Cinjun could pack that kind of strength. It was a fascinating surprise.

Cinjun surprised Miles in yet another way—he favored Miles with a smile. Now, since hell and heaven were siding with Cinjun—each moving under Cinjun's guiding fists, he could afford to be generous—he gave Miles an opening.

Miles moved in. Miles counterpunched. Miles gave it a lot—aiming to rip away skin and bone.

The blow did nothing to Cinjun. Except maybe to make him smile.

Cinjun knew fist fighting—as it turned out.

Well schooled in combat—he was. He hadn't made it too well known until now . . .

Well schooled in martial arts—he was. He hadn't made that too well known until now . . .

A master of hand to hand combat—he was. And he was revealing this now. Why not let the world know?

Miles had asked to see the real him. Did he like what he saw?

Cinjun was in his element. He was comfortable working with his fists. This was almost relaxing to him. A nice change of pace.

And now—

Cinjun took total command of the ring, of the arena.

His eyes took command; locked on Miles. He would stay eye to eye until Miles lay beaten and bloodied underfoot. Cinjun understood combat. He knew everything there was to know about working with fists.

Miles moved in to test his ability.

He didn't get far. With startling swiftness, Cinjun delivered a shot to Miles—a nice solid body blow. Very clean. As smooth as good Scotch. You did not want to be on the receiving end of that—While, Cinjun did not even feel the effort of it. He could deliver a few more before the effort would even make him blink.

Miles countered. He took a shot at Cinjun. Miles was certain it was the closest thing to hitting a wall he could experience in hand to hand combat. Miles's shot rolled off Cinjun. Miles had hoped to get a blink out of Cinjun—He hadn't delivered enough to earn that.

On the sidelines, Daphne commented on the situation: "Oh, oh—Oh, dear, oh, dear, oh, dear."

Miles had to fall back—*How to go at it? How to do it? How?* His thoughts raced.

Miles was assailed by a memory. He was in an outdoor gym. He was with Scofield. It was one of their *conditioning* sessions. Scofield said, "Pace yourself, kid—Pace yourself, has many meanings. There's a science to how you wear down an opponent that's stronger than you—*heavyweight fighters usually burn down when you set a wide open opportunity to punch and punch in front of them."*

Hmmm, Miles wondered. There was something there. Some great secret. What form of capoeira was this?

He riffled through looming passages. Hmmm. Ah, it was to be a *bait capoeira*. The plan frightened Miles. Frightened Miles all too hell. Could you pull a thing like that off? Would Cinjun take the bait? Ah, you never know until you try. He played bait capoeira—hidden capoeira. He hid it in the guise of defeat, and taunted, with what appeared to be final stings.

He went with it, loose and flowing capoeira.

The plan called for Miles to tire Cinjun out by getting Cinjun to beat the life out of Miles, while Miles called out for more punishment. Brilliant, wasn't it? Well, it was the best Miles could do.

He drove Cinjun mad—until Cinjun was applying himself seriously to the work of ripping Miles's head off his body!

Miles sheltered his head . . . Gave his ribs to Cinjun.

Blow after blow. Shot after shot. The punishing beating developed.

Time slipped.

And now—Miles—was *enjoying himself!* Well, he had never been in bait capoeira before—this was entirely an experience that few ever knew. That few ever imagined.

Time slipped.

He gave Cinjun a lot of his body to beat.

He danced a lot to escape Cinjun's blows. He escaped a lot of them. Eventually Miles's dance lapsed—

Cinjun fanned his fist across Miles's jaw—

Vrooom, thrak, b'boom!

*Ah! This was trouble!* Miles noticed. He was in deep shit!

His legs were—

He hit the floor hard. *Ah, this was pain capoeira!—Agony capoeira!* Miles felt an alerting sensation. He was in the mysterious room of agony.

Suddenly, his legs were gone. Where had he put them?

He was—spilling over, down, everything falling away, all he could feel was pain.

He had to come back from this. He had to make it back from this! He had to get up! He had to bring it together! He had to make his legs work! He had to make his body work! Everything was—*pain*. Agony! Waves and waves of pain.

Miles willed his way through it.

Forced himself to function. Forced his body to work.

He got his body to work, moved back into the dance.

They danced around each other.

Miles was not going to let it end.

And now—Miles—

*Here he comes*—the people thought. *Here he comes.*

Miles broke through, this was walking agony. But he moved, forward. Walked his way out of the mysterious room of agony.

He circled around Cinjun getting his energy back. He just kept breathing. Kept breathing. Escaping blows. Ducking and weaving when he could. Learning to bruise and bleed on the other occasions.

They exchanged blows.

Time slipped.


Cinjun was turning Miles's body to dark colors.

Showing Miles how he made him feel. Through the twilight . . . oh, how Cinjun tried to make his feelings clear to Miles.

Pounding away. Turning Miles black and blue and bruised and bloody and not feeling so talkative.

Cinjun's fists were speaking, saying, 'Let me show you how you make me feel'—'Can you see the real me?'—'Can you?'

His fists were revealing their secrets. They didn't want to hold anything back from Miles. The fists were showing Miles all they had; they didn't want him to feel he was getting less than their best. The fists spoke clearly. *I'll tell you they are very easy to understand,* Miles thought. *It is so nice to have such plain talk presented so cleanly.*

Miles appreciated the privilege. This was everything he had asked for and more. Much more. He had feared death. He didn't even consider mutilation. Torture. Torment. Suffering. Pain. Anguish. And all the other trips Cinjun's fists could take him on. Nice to be surprised. The fists had so much in them. Who knew? Apparently, Cinjun did—but he had kept it to himself.

Cinjun had gone about his business of building and acquiring power without 'acting out' his power. There had been no need . . . He actually had the power! Rather than flaunting it for all the world, Cinjun had actually been doing a major job of hiding the full extent of his power. This man was superhuman. He truly was an Iron Man.

Now he was showing what he had. Miles just hoped Cinjun didn't have much more in him to show. If this was success for Miles, he didn't know how much more success he could handle before he would get very badly hurt. He would already be several seasons recovering from this encounter.

He wondered when he would know Cinjun's limit. The fists kept coming.

Miles did his best to breathe. And think. And do the other things that he had taken for granted until now.

Cinjun was beating Miles's body to hell sensation. To pain sensation. To agony feeling.

"Thank you," Miles said.

*What the hell is this bastard thanking me for?* Cinjun wondered at the thank you. Then decided he didn't want to sit on his accomplishments; he would give Miles more to thank. Now Cinjun became iron sweetness; and offered him a new blow. It was marvelous. Of course, Miles accepted it. Nothing was changing at all. Cinjun was delivering blows; Miles was taking their measure with his body.

The people watched Cinjun dance across the ballroom; the lights making stars shine on his smile. *Cinjun was dressed up better than anyone,* the people thought. And the people recalled other memories; recalled so many other beautiful moments in this world that had been so very much like this thing they were seeing now.

Cinjun was moving with great promise. To take off a head here; to remove a few ribs there; to soften that middle with pain; to reshape him. He didn't stop. He didn't want Miles to get to feeling lonely from neglect.

He took some sweet time on Miles's middle. Making sure the work was coming along just fine, making sure that it met his high artistic standards. Yes, it was growing balanced.

He was sculpting. Doing a fine job when you considered his options.

Miles kissed the warm night. Dug for his soul. There—right at the end of that fist. There was something real about the fist he could appreciate. He was getting a lot of truth. Now he sought—truth change.

Now he was twisting, turning, considering the deal being offered. Maybe he would think about it for a while.

*Attention!* Miles called to his senses, *back to the fight. Next!*

"Listen . . . Cinjun," Miles said mildly, "if this is the best you can do, I'm afraid it's not enough. I wouldn't hold back so much if I were you."

Cinjun looked at Miles. . . . Cinjun was smiling; having his way, having a lovely day.

"Are you," Miles said, "getting tired? Geez, I hope you can last the fight. I'm here to go the distance. Why don't you plan on putting in some more effort on this job. I think you can make an impression if you apply yourself." Bam! Cinjun applied himself, like that. Miles was now bleeding from *that*. "I thought," Miles said, "it was a little weak. To be honest, you've led me to expect more."

"Listen," Cinjun said, softly, mildly, pleasantly, "I'll see what I can do. I'd hate for the deal to collapse when we're both so close to the finish we were asking for."

"Well," Miles said, struggling for breath, "I'm sure if we concentrated we could move this to a grander level—something 'jungle,' does that sound good?"

"My thoughts exactly," Cinjun said. "Here we go; let's take you to the end of your air-breathing streak. You seem to have too much to spare. You're doing a whole lot of talking."

Cinjun's strategy had been, and remained, very becoming—To go to the mighty.

Miles was deeply journeyed into the land of the fair and strong. He had wanted to fight Cinjun where Cinjun was strongest, where Cinjun had every advantage. This beating was the realization of Miles's greatest ambitions—with every blow Miles was getting what he had wanted—Cinjun's best shots.

Cinjun was at his absolute best now. The only thing stealing satisfaction from Miles's perfect joy was that if Miles got much more of what he wanted, Miles would get gone—and Cinjun just kept coming up—for more, with more. There seemed no end to his vast energy reserves.

*Get him with talk?* Miles asked himself. *Get to him? Get him worked hotter and hotter still?* Or was Cinjun warmed up enough?

Should Miles continue talking to bring out the monster in Cinjun? Should he?

Should he do it? I mean, would you do it? Would you make a choice like that? And where would it lead?

It was all about the choices you made.

The possibilities rolled through his mind, flashing, in lightning patterns.

*He wasn't getting tired!* Miles observed.

The observation had meaning. That was it! He didn't seem to be tiring at all! That revealed it.

That was the reveal—the reveal was no reveal.

He was hiding what was really happening. Cinjun was a master gamesman. There were no physical signs but Miles recognized—*A Show of Force.* Cinjun had to be getting tired. Miles moved into the proof phase of his theory.

Miles felt certain. Yes, Cinjun was mounting a Show of Force. Behind it—he was weakening. Miles felt certain. He felt cozy and warm with the theory.

And took certain action, based on this. On his gut feeling of the situation.

He was alone with the situation. And chose. It was all about the choices you made.

Now he was taking it through the changes. He was the changeling. See him change. Change taking place. Root yourself to the ground.

Cinjun had not appeared to be tiring at all. There were no physical signs. He was working to—*To scare the life out of you*, Miles thought. He was playing Scare Capoeira, Miles realized. *He's playing scare the shit out of Miles Roark!*

He had been doing a damn fine job, at that.

*But think it through, Miles, see beyond appearances—Hey you, strip to show us, all you are.*

*Now Cinjun, let me show you how you make me feel!*

Cinjun played the most solid game Miles had ever seen. It was scary, how good he was.

Bam! Miles moved fully into the fight.

Miles moved into the changes.

And abruptly made clear to Cinjun that he was walking his way out of a *bait capoeira*. There was no more need for it. Now he moved with revived pace. And took the fight into this strange mystery.

Cinjun reacted, with a slight, coolly startled pause. *So, he's not as finished as we were led to believe!* Cinjun realized. *All the better! Let us give the people a show to surpass all shows.*

Cinjun felt all warmed up now. This fellow Miles was nicely readied—yes, there *was* that. Cinjun moved deeper into the feverish nocturne. Picked up the tempo of his symphony.

The two men were taking themselves to the peak of their existence.

Now Miles stepped in with a barrage of punches, finding an opening, and sideswiping Cinjun. Then finding another opening, sideswiping him. Stepping back.

Cinjun charged Miles—who sidestepped—no movements wasted. Miles whirled around.

Cinjun took the long road, wasted shots and momentum. Miles stepped in with another set of punches, finding an opening and connecting a lightning jab to Cinjun's chin—The shot connecting hard.

Cinjun blinked. And stopped. That got him.

Daphne let loose a hurrah.

Miles moved in fast—a hook to Cinjun's face. Just right. Miles felt hope spring strong within him.

Now Cinjun stepped efficiently further into the fight.

Miles wasn't playing around anymore. Bait capoeira was over. That was finished. Phase by phase, he probed the looming passages.

Now Miles was staring Cinjun dead in the eye, and out of the corner of his eye looking for openings or violent possibilities from Cinjun.

Cinjun opened up.

Miles stayed put, blocking and deflecting shot after shot. Keeping his movements minimal. Taking punishing blows from Cinjun. In this way, the fist fight moved into fullest, richest spectacle.

Cinjun looked into Miles's eyes and he saw *Tygers* crouched in jungles in Miles' dark eyes. This Miles was as stupid as a mule, he didn't know enough to dodge a death blow. Cinjun was in full form and raging peak. Cinjun slid away and brought himself to fuller life . . .

Cinjun considered moving in to mutilate Miles, to end Miles's life. People did die in fighting arenas! Cinjun thought—Cinjun saw a vision of the moment. He could make it be, easily—The audience wanted it. And Cinjun had a responsibility to give them the wings of their fate—They wanted to see a man eaten by a lion.

He would—in a sense—"murder" this man, Miles. He could mutilate his face—Cinjun knew how to do it. And he raged. Cinjun knew how to wreak lasting damage.

Miles was too dangerous. He had to be taken out. The fool had brought it on. Now let him pay the price to grow wise, if a little broken. He wouldn't be so pretty in a few minutes.

Cinjun—the strongman—took himself into a moment of readying.

A moment where he gathered himself, gathered his strength, pulled himself together, brought all of his muscles to full alert . . .

He willed himself into a heightened state. Forced his energies to quicken. Brought his pulse to an extreme. His adrenaline to an extreme. He took himself into heated sensation. And then sprang.

This was what he did to take himself into *a kill round.*

Now, he reached the ultimate moment.

And he moved forward, with new purpose.

And they watched. Watched Cinjun dance—across the ballroom—lights making stars shine on his smile. He was the face—they knew it. He was dressed up better than anyone they had seen or imagined.

He was the man they loved—wearing their fashion. Getting it to the tee. Heaven above, tried to match him for *charged being*. Ah, watch him—dance—across the ballroom—lights making stars shine—on his smile.

The strongman glided across time. Slipped across the timeslope. Slid along, fully alive. Primal force. Blazing being. Violence. Violence.

*Violence to violence, all was violence.*

What Cinjun would now give Miles—no one would ever be able to take away from Miles. This gift would last forever.

Cinjun heard the music—he relaxed—let himself go, to the moment.

*Wouldn't it be better for him to move to actually kill Miles?* Or just make him ugly?

Rich possibilities expressed themselves in his mind. He liked each idea. Maybe he could have both. He would make Miles ugly now, and he would kill him later!

He would make Miles ugly now. Later—he would kill Miles. He would make it seem an accident. For now—he would just make Miles ugly.

The kill?—Maybe Cinjun would do that himself; he liked the idea of later killing Miles.

No, then . . . no one would know who had done it. He wanted the murder to shine on him. Oh, heaven above—he wanted heaven above to shine on the murder. He didn't want anything taking the shine away from him.

He wanted to kill Miles. Now was his chance. He would kill Miles, make it look like something that just happened of its own. Cinjun would express great sorrow later. He could make a great show of it—oh, how sorry he would be. Yes, it would be marvelous.

Now, he had the murder to enjoy—he was free to murder Miles Roark!

He was free to murder. Cinjun thrilled at the thought.

It seemed so right. Yes, it was right! Murder, so pure. Murder, so rich. Murder, so shining.

He would make the moment shine.

It had been so long since a strongman had risen to power in this nation on a platform of murder. So long since a man had taken the seat of power backed up by an act of murder. The people wanted it so much. They wanted a murderer in charge.

He was a God Emperor. And now they would feel his power.

He invoked the ancient principle: *Reward, if you follow me; punishment, if you oppose me.*

He would use the power principle; prove his God Worth. Ancient spirits called to him in this ancient arena. And now—he was fully in The Pleasuredome. This was true pleasure that lay before him. He was man enough to take the pleasure. He was the most pleasant man that lived, had ever lived, or ever shall live. He was absolutely *pleasant*—supremely pleasant—in The Pleasuredome.

Now Cinjun stepped forward, *To Prove His Godhood*. And to feel his pleasure surge, along the long mighty shaft of His Destiny.

He was a supreme being. Open up World! He was stepping in form outside! He was stepping into God Emperor being!

And there was pleasure all around. The people felt it—pleasure. For the first time in a good long time, they were going to see a man get eaten by a lion.

Hurray! It had been so long. So goddamn long since pleasure was come to them. Now Cinjun carried pleasure into this place.

Ancient tradition, ancient ceremony—*Oh, what a show! this was about to become!* the people thought.

Gladiators! In a fight to the death! Could it get any better? Could it get any more—*civilized?*

Death in combat for noble purpose—was the mark of a higher order of civilization.

This thing was about to get very civilized indeed.

It had been a long time since a strongman took the seat of power through an act of murder.

He wanted the murder to shine on him. Heaven above—he wanted Heaven above to shine on the murder. How to do it?

The murder danced across the ballroom of his mind. Lights making stars shine on Cinjun's smile.

Could he have the murder! Miles had made it possible. Miles was giving Cinjun everything he needed to perform the murder and to prosper by it. It would be a brave wedding of summer mornings. It would be *good* shining for all the world to see!

It would be so perfect! Oh, he wanted it so badly, so longingly. His being yearned for it: Oh, Murder! He was the actor and this was the scene.

Murder, sweet goodly, pure, righteous, beautiful, helpful life saving Murder! Oh Farewell, My Lovely! Cinjun found the beauty laid out before him now. He saw the landscape of the futureflow.

Beauty is Truth; Truth is Beauty. And this murder had such beauty to it!

Cinjun stopped then—abruptly—in the arena.

All gazes took Cinjun into their interest.

Now Cinjun was The Rage Changeling. See him rage. Rage Change taking place. Root yourself to the ground.

Murder! Murder moment!

Murder! Murder to prosper by.

Murder! Murder to save a nation by.

Murder! Murder to take the seat of power by.

Beautiful Violent Enlightened Murder!

Who could resist?

*Only murder could bring the love!* Cinjun thought.

*Only murder could bring the love that rains—like tears—from on high!*

Murder Explodes on the Scene!

Oh, Murder shape taking form.

Only murder can make the *Love Life* that rains—like tears—from on high!

Cinjun felt all the love in his heart—all the love in the world—calling for Murder! In a cool, cool rain.

Cinjun stood on the rim of the hill; felt the chill of the night.

Cinjun stepped forward, taking the night into—higher dimensions of sanity.

*New murder for sale!*

Murder that's fresh and bold. Murder, that's only a few thoughts old.

New Murder for Sale!

Sanity sang the song, so sensible—and—soon to be so sensual.

*Sanity,* was most sane when it led to murder. Cinjun invoked the ancient principle now as he moved, and he was perfectly sane. As he moved with all the rage in the world, and a lot of love in his heart. It was about the sanest behavior you could ever observe. And Cinjun was now the most sane man in a very sane world, that peopled.

## Kill Strike

MILES—knew the moment—This was finality, this was heated death—It had come, the Black End.

Evasion? Could he escape it? Take it into something else? His mind leapt and darted. Yes, Miles recognized it immediately when it began. He was going to have to stop *a kill capoeira.* He had very little to stop it with, he surmised. He moved with the least movement, the least effort wasted. The timing of this dance was important. Here, speed would tell the tale.

Cinjun moved in for the kill.

Yes, Cinjun moved.

Miles saw passages. He chose.

He danced into an open space.

Cinjun moved in for his kill strike.

Now Cinjun was flinging away a wave of rage-loaded emotion. Rage-splashed color came off him in flowing waves. He was rage now. There was nothing else anywhere in his world. And it felt good to him. Strength flowed from the force of it. It made him intensely dangerous. Supremely dangerous. He was the edge of a blade crafted by some master swordmaker. His every motion could now produce death.

Cinjun had killed men before. His mind rolled back to the alien worlds he had inhabited. He remembered murdering the men. And he remembered how much he liked the feelings that came to him. They came to him now again. Delicious feelings. What do you know—this was turning into fun. Cinjun couldn't have had any more fun if he was coming at Miles with an axe—to hack his body to pieces. There was no need. Cinjun would brutalize him with his hands—his fists—he moved into a fine moment. It might be the finest moment of his existence. It certainly felt that way. He would make the final moment look like an accident—He was tasting the accident.

Cinjun stripped to show Miles all he was.

Cinjun moved in to show Miles how he made him feel.

Moving in the twilight, Cinjun put a thought deep into his mind, tasting it. *Miles wouldn't be so pretty in a moment.* The gift he would give Miles would last forever. The people would see Cinjun's mighty work—and know his kind to be work that stays done.

No one could touch all that Cinjun was. He was going to show Miles all he was. Show him how he made him feel.

Cinjun stepped into the kill strike. He moved to change the shape of Miles's face. Hah!

Cinjun knew he would like the new shape.

Cinjun moved in with life change for Miles.

Cinjun moved in. His *Iron Fist* moved to tell a story. Of possibilities for brutality. And the end of summer nights for Miles.

All this—passing through Cinjun. Flashing through him—as his *Iron Fist* went into motion.

The full weight and force of Cinjun's being in the strike.

And for Cinjun it was easy. Moving so easy. Dancing across the ballroom—lights making stars shine—on his smile. He was the face. His eyes were there. Ruling the world.

He was feeling slow sensation.

Miles was looking up from under. Living in slow sensation.

He saw looming passages. Riffled through motions and chose.

He moved.

The motion took him out of the range of Cinjun's *Iron Fist* for a brief moment, only a moment, it was taking Miles into a more open position.

Cinjun saw Miles opening up and trapped him.

Now Miles had a brief opening at Cinjun—a flashing instant—Miles took a ride. Took the moment on the inside. Got the moment on the inside. Extended the flash into a long moment, filled with slow sensation.

Miles and Cinjun locked eyes. As Miles's fist whipped into the world, and took over.

Cinjun's eyes were there when Miles's fist went through Cinjun's face. Took it on the inside. Got it on the inside. Went through. To a place where Cinjun's face had been.

Cinjun's face was thrown back, taking Cinjun's commanding eyes with it.

*You might want to grab your wartime coat,* Miles thought, *as you step out into the wind and sleet.* I am the face, Miles thought . . .—Hoping. Trying to be the face.

Now Miles was flowing.

Now Miles was on the inside.

Took the ride

for all it was worth.

His fist whipped into Cinjun's world again.

And now—

Miles's fist hit Cinjun's face.

Square

dead-on

and hard.

*Vroom! Thrak! B'Boom!*—The fist was forging fearsome being.

The fist was alone with the situation. It owned the ride.

Cinjun's face kissed the warm fist, digging for its soul. For a hard instant, the fist and Cinjun's face remained alone with the situation.
Filled the situation.

Cinjun—at this moment of impact, deep in this hard instant—thought, *I've been stopped—How?*

And now the fist went a-wiping—
wiping across Cinjun's entire world.
Streaming, driving, voyaging—this summer night belonged to this hard instant, and to this streaming hard fist.
The fist continued on its way, leaving Cinjun behind.

The fist was moving away from Cinjun and into tomorrow—the fist was alone with the situation.
Returning home to Miles.

Miles brought it on home.
And Miles stepped on back—

As Cinjun went into—freefall.

He went into falling sensation.

In the flow of it, he determined to *recover.*
Twisting and turning moving into *recovery.*

But suddenly he came to the end of his falling streak—hard instant—hard impact on hard tight ground.
He lay on the floor recovering.
Alone with this situation.

*Did you ever think about it Cinjun?* Miles thought. *Did you ever think what to do in this kind of situation?* Interesting, wasn't it? A lot to consider. All at once.

Cinjun trusted in his ability—as he took himself into recovery. Into strong recovery.
He lay on the floor recovering.
Alone with the situation.

*Take a picture for your children, Cinjun.* This is a moment you will remember for more than a season.

Were you coming to the end of a certain conquering streak? No. Of course not.

This was a tight spot—But Cinjun had gotten out of tighter spots.

He felt the recovery taking hold.

He took a straight course through the recovery. Feeling it in every reach of his body.

Ah-huh. Taking away the pain he was feeling. Now he was working again. Coming into the next phase. Fully Cinjun Smythe. Fully a strongman. Moving. Moving. Moving.

He wasn't going to take this lying down—So—uh, now, baby, he was moving into: *all right.* He would make everything *all right.*

Cinjun 'The Vision' Smythe moved. Taking observers with him.


## Love, Put On Your Faces

"GET UP CINJUN! They're going to think it's a fake." Miles said.

"You're going to go down from a lovetap! Come on, get up!"

Cinjun would win, of that Cinjun was certain, that was where this was heading. But this difficulty had to be dealt with.

The moment was to be attacked, by Cinjun. The burden was upon him.

The thing had been given to Cinjun, and it was his to do.

The task was his to do.

It spurred Cinjun to defiance. Cinjun operated in his old way, with his old strength. Nothing would stop him.

Press on. Move forward.

Step, right, left. Left. Right. Heart attack!

Go to the floor. Fold. Rest a while.

His present difficulty had to be dealt with.

Oh, yes, Cinjun, now contemplate your mixed emotions and inner feelings at this key point in your imperial campaign.

Cinjun proceeded in this way.

It pained Miles to see Cinjun like this, in this sad state. After all he had been to Miles, ... and it seemed like only moments ago.

And now—Cinjun down, Miles above—Miles rode the whirlwind moment.

All was in a freeze around them, verging on action, intrusion and calls to other moments. But in the moment there was only Cinjun Smythe, the most important man in the world, and his brave visitor, Miles Roark.

Now, Miles carved—Miles carved *inventions* into light, in the depths of this night darkness—now Miles was struggling, searching, probing to make everything all right.

Now Miles was moving in the native way. Every rock, tree and creature had a spirit. What you felled was a spirit gift of the Earth given to you. To be treasured, cherished and enveloped.

Spirits Parting!

Ah, Spirits—you treated spirits with special being. They were to be experienced.

Now Miles was experiencing Cinjun life, Cinjun being. And all the love you could find in summer and winter or anywhere the hell else you looked.

You had to fulfill certain rites at the close of the hunt. A spirit had been felled, and had now to be elevated.

You had to sing the blues!

And Miles knew—that you can't fool the blues! Oh, no.

See, you can fool the world, but you can't fool the blues. When you're making all the moves, it's so hard to lose—but you can't fool the blues. Oh, no.

You *can* fool the *rich*—But you can't fool the blues.

It just laughs at each lie. You can't fool the blues.

The Blues called Miles to journey—

The journey pulled on Miles heavily with its spirit demands.

You see, The Hunter has to fulfill certain passages of feeling. The Hunter has to feel the Blues. He had to actually feel the Blues! And you can't fool the Blues, it just laughs at each lie. You can't fool the Blues, oh no.

Before him—this was the Animal, whose spirit death he had brought about.

And his need of him, had to be made clear with blues-splashed feeling.

You had to show your feeling for the animal spirit that was killed in the hunt. This was Hunting Ceremony. It was very essential. It was more than respect. Miles was standing before a messenger of divine power.

Miles—the Hunter—was killing a God. Wiping him out.

And you must not make it a personal act. You are performing the work of nature.

A bluesy privilege, was being given to you.

It had to do with the power of the animal master. When the ancient ones of the distant lands sat down to a meal, they thanked god. But when moving in this land's ancient native way, there was another spirit force to be considered and felt—a native power to thank. These native people thanked the animal.

The felled animal was a power superior.

Providing relationship.

Lower relationship.

Now the Superior Animal, has powers that human beings don't have— and Cinjun had proved he had Animal Being.

So Miles—as the ancient Native Ones had—moved in one way. Be friendly with the fearsome animals' threats. And then kill some of them.

Then know, feel it in your soul, that the Animal was a giver of . . . purpose and being.

Now the journey called for Miles to carve his invention of light in the dark passage.

Cinjun Khan Unumbatai S'mythe would be many years dead before he could rise again.

Miles would have to leave Cinjun in the Capoeira Nebula.

Love, Put On Your Faces!

"There will be other nights like this," Miles said, "and I'll be standing here with someone new. But there will never be another you.

"There will be other songs to sing, but there will never be another you.

"There may be others, but they won't thrill me like you used to do.

"Tomorrow, I'll have to find a way to live the rest of my life without you.

"You taught me how to live, how to be myself.

"Now you're giving up on giving, baby. You're out of my reach, baby. You're gone.

"And there will never be another one like you.

"Now, it's time to say good night.

"Good night, sleep tight!

"Oh, Love! A world has opened up for me. A world filled with all your love."

Cinjun thought, it was bad enough that he was on the floor, he also had to listen to this talk, about Love! All this bilge, was merely the stuff, rubbish that rhymed with wit. He wasn't going to dignify it by using the word—ah, it was just shit.

The flow of the ride that had taken him here assaulted Cinjun. He was getting it on the inside.

Left, right. Heart tremble! Heart tremor! —Hit the floor.

Now the ticket was to—Hold onto the floor!

There you go! Keep that floor steady, don't let it wobble!

Perfect. Now stay still and stay a while.

You're just time away from standing up, Cinjun.

Lying down for a while could only do you good.

So let it do its good and might works.

Be floor, Cinjun, be floor, my friend.

Oh, Cinjun *The Vision* Smythe.

Gentle soldier, lie and rest.

And scheme of how to take over the world from this abutted place. Think of valor and blood. Rise and murder; slaying and slaughter from this abutted place. The many women you will have; the many men you will rule from this abutted place. Stay in bed all morning and then rise like the giant and wreak your revenge on the world that peoples.

Love has exploded and rent your mighty blood ship. Oh cruel vicious love! Love is a bomb. A vicious bomb, thrown at you by sinners. Hate love! That's the most beautiful thing you can do. Hate love for all the damage it has done. Hate love for the way it weakens men. Hate love for the way it seduces women. And let something die in you, inside.

There, well murdered!

Soon, you will rise and wreak havoc like a mighty tempest on the world that peoples.

A light and breezy murder. Very well murdered.

Cinjun lay there, alone with the situation.

As a crowd rushed in.

*Good night sweet God Emperor,* Miles thought. *Another night has passed. Time for me to get moving . . . time to move on.*

*Let's slide out the door.*

Miles Roark walked against the current of the people to—Daphne Fox. Her love was burning. He could not keep out of the flame. He felt her against him. And then—they were alone with the situation.

Love, Put On Your Faces.

He turned to look at Daphne, and the bunches and bunches of people weren't there. They didn't matter at all.

Honey, let's slide out the door.

Come on, darling, the time we have isn't long.

In a flash he was gone, it happened so soon. He was gone. And she with him.

Nobody saw him. Nobody heard from him. One writer wrote a book about him.

Time to get away from this side of life. Honey, I want you to be by my side. Me and my back-door moves. Let's slide out the door.

Come to me. The time that we have isn't long. Honey, let's take it.

No more, honey. No more of this. Let's get away from this side of life. No more, honey. No more.

Come to me, darling. Come to me, woman! Argh, let's slide out the door.

They slid out the door forgetting painful memories. It was time to move on. No more cold shots. No more, honey. No more.

They were gliding away.

Let's go.

Let's go.

People asked if he was dead. No reply.

He did the craziest thing you can do when you win—He disappeared from the scene.

And he was not to be found.

He couldn't stand the weather.

She went away with him.

She couldn't stand the weather.

The time they had wasn't long.

They were gone.

The time they had wasn't long.

Come to me, darling. Come to me, woman.

Me and my back-door moves. In the morning dawn and night.

Good night, darling. Another night has passed.

## The Beat Goes On . . .

WITHIN THE *LIGHT*VISION NETWORK, within the core feeds, within the central feed—in the command center—a call within the body of the works—

At the *Wayfinder,* a voice called out:

"Big Red is down. Repeat, Big Red is down. Gilligan is still standing."

## The Night Holds Sway

DRINKS FLOW. People dance across the night. With the stars shining on their smiles.

The big wheel spins.

And the beat goes on . . .

The beat goes on . . .

The ride goes up and down, and round and round. It has thrills and chills and it's brightly colored. Feathered against the dark night. Against the black reaches of a long dark night. The night is great—deep and wide.

Somewhere, a couple falls in love. Somewhere, a couple breaks up. Drums keep pounding their rhythms. A bass booms.

And the beat goes on . . .

The black night takes Miles. Removing all that came before—Miles is done. If it's not revolutionary, it'll have to do until the real thing comes along.

If it isn't jazz it'll have to do until the real thing comes along.

The black settles. Casting wide. Taking the world.

Time slips, time slips.

And the beat goes on . . .

Out in vast reaches of the black sea . . . jazz comes into the world. Escaping from the core of the world that peopled.

Escaping. Escaping. Escaping. Now.

## Sunbursts of Morning

ESCAPES from the black, black ocean of black dreams.

Sunbursts!

Light dreams burst into the blue sky—escaping, tearing loose of the black, black sea! Forming sunbursts.

Erupting, breaking through the strange night of stone.

Sunbursts!—Scorching beauty, your sun has risen, leaving it for all to see, if your warmth can touch your many ones. Mornings made in love understanding.

Into realms of blue and light.

Sunbursts rising from black seas.

It was the morning of the world.

The sunbursts rose from the black seas.

And filled the skies—sunbursts—forming sun dreams. The dreams grew in the air. Watered by rain, nourished by sun, the dreams grew.

Grew wild, and began wãoynding wild.

Wãoynding and wãoynding.

The sunbursts and the sun dreams began to seek, to seek in the river wild. Through the endless reaches of the *River All,* they sailed. Sailed into eternal realms. Casting their light, . . . their light descending on the day.

## Quinn

LIGHT DESCENDING from the sunbursts descended on the realm and manor of Quinn "Flintstone" Martin.

Life was quiet now. Everybody was settling back to business. Cinjun arrived for a meeting, and found Sidney in the parlor.

Quinn sauntered in. Quinn looked at Cinjun.

"We're going to take House Crimson," Quinn said, "away from you. Congratulations. We're going back to the old concept, Foundation House. Sidney will help you make an exit."

Quinn started to leave. Considered the moment. Quinn turned to Cinjun. He wanted Cinjun to be perfectly clear on where this was all going. "You bore me," Quinn said. Quinn turned from Cinjun and walked away.

Now—how would Cinjun live—without all the gifts that Quinn

Flintstone Martin gave to him!—Well, that was not Quinn's problem—He would take all the light from out of Smythe, and leave not a beam behind.

Cinjun would remain, not much else would be there to cherish.

Not much would be left that stirred or spoke, or breathed.

And now—moving things along, Quinn put the lid on the tomb, and went out to play golf!

It was a beautiful day outside. Of that he was certain—Every day is beautiful when you own the world, and its gold.

Miles Roark would be ridden from the world, the beautiful world. Of that there could be no doubt. But that was work for another day. Quinn never took his work with him. Today was meant for golf!

Golf, and then after, maybe a square meal of *women!*

Boy, that sun was just bursting out, today. Mm-hmm, it was bright out there! Blazing away out there. It was really cooking.

Quinn Martin, the man from down south, way down south, stepped on out . . . He sailed on out. Ricocheting away.

He was Quinn "Flintstone" Martin! He owned the world, and its gold.

---

# The Industrialists—
## Maybe a great magnet pulls all souls toward truth

---

THIS MILES WAS of some interest to them now.

They would go to him.

They would ride in on limousines and wide-body jets. They would come in with contracts and lobster dinners. They gathered together, forming plans for his talent. They would mold and shape it and work it into the routine.

They would go to him. Yes, they would come to him. As friends. And help him work his act into the routine.

They would find he wasn't home. Miles was with Daphne, and they were away.

Where were they? the industrialists asked.

Off to an island. They were off on holiday.

When would they return?

No one could say.

Well, how do you like that? the industrialists said. Outrageous! Crazy and outrageous!

Now they wanted him all the more.

They had to have him. He was special. And this Daphne, she was something too. Word had traveled 'round the campfire that she had felled three tall men just by dancing barefoot across their smiles.

Well, where was she?

Off to an island.

An island?

Off on holiday.

When would she return?

No one could say.

Oh, damn it! Outrageous!—They wanted her all the more.

Who was she with?

Miles Roark.

Oh, he was special. This Miles Roark was something too . . . word had traveled 'round the campfire that he had . . .

## Goodnight Grace

CINJUN'S MANSION WAS QUIET.

Cinjun turned his thoughts from the scene and drove them into distance.

*Crash to the other shore,* Cinjun thought. Cinjun considered age, and basking in darkness. And what it meant to be: Forgotten! He would be many years dead, but then he would rise again. And he would take the world!

He had: future. A lot of blaze. Oh, he would—Crash to the other shore . . . Comet flying across the sky . . . He was going to carry the world away, . . . lead it, to a House Crimson. All, would begin again. He would crash to the other shore. He would carry this train off the tracks. Crash to the other shore. His future loomed!—Freedom comes when you learn to let go. Life goes on now—Bring it on—Carry on now! Bring it on! Peace, would be worth the killing.

He was, after all, the most important man in the world. The greatest man that had ever lived, or ever shall live. And other such honors.

Burdens that weighed heavily on him. Many tasks were his to do.

It wasn't easy, but somebody had to be Cinjun Smythe.

Cinjun Khan Smythe. Emperor, regent, lover, philosopher and savior.

Cinjun would act fast, move rapidly, and lethally. His great works, were dying in waves, fainting in coils. There was no time to waste. Every breath would be directed to winning. And the bloody slaughter that need follow. Or preceed. Wherever, the bloodshed lay, he was ready. He was getting a little mixed up these days, but he would pull himself together, and wreak havoc, to build paradise.

Paradise was a bloody business.

He would hunt him down and revenge himself. The revenge would be sweet, the sweetest moment that ever lived or ever shall live. He was losing it a little bit. Not so you would notice, but he would pull himself together. Paradise, was a bloody business.

There would be time enough for love, once the killing was done.

# The Beach

Miles and Daphne were on a beach.

A surf of sunstreaks.

A sky of blue waves.

Daphne said, "Cheers!"

Daphne and Miles were on holiday . . . Raising drinks into the air.

Stretching out before them . . . white sand, surf, clear blue-green waters.

A gentle breeze.

Palm trees.

And sun.

"I'll race you in," Daphne said.

They raced into the water.

They crossed the surf. They both dove into the blue at the same time.

And crossed into the futureflow—

And—

*Oh, the places they will go!*

# Into Forever

RISE SPEED & AWAY. Time slipping, a-slipping away.

Rise speed & away. Time slipping, a-slipping away.

And the beat sailed on . . .

The sunbursts sailed on . . .

The sun dreams sailed on . . .

And among them, a Seeker moved in Forever.

In the reaches of Forever, the Seeker sailed on . . . its heading, past tomorrow and to Forever.

Meeting other seekers.

In The Wāoynding Dream.

The Relief from nightmare.

Ah, the Wāoynding Way.

Songs. Deep and rich and true. Songs. Deep and rich and blue.

Of people shapes flowing. People flowing across fields; shaping themselves in skies; forming the All into beautiful wild people shapes. Human forms and human giants. He's and She's, stone free. Each song of to be, open and true. Each song, the ancient spiritual, "Do What Is Inside of You."

And the dream sailed on . . .

Ah, the Wonder in a World that Peopled.

Ride the wind. Take to the skies.

"Why, it's *All Right*, it's all right, it's *All Ride*. Move on. In the way, of Life and Play. To See and see and see. To Fire and fire and fire. And rise ever higher."

The river forming people, the Olde Man R'hivyr, the river forming people, rolling, a-rolling along. Forming people song.

Forming The Lady of the All, The Lady of English and The Lady of Love. The All saying, 'Give me a river of people.'

And inside each, a Seeker.

Boldly going and boldly being. Giant in being, open and seeing.

'Oh let it People. Bring me giant people.'

*Be they light, be they bright, and . . . oh let it People!*

Ah, the Olde Man R'hivyr forming the river of People. Open shore and open way. Opening on Forever.

And in each a Seeker, a Seeker moving in Forever.

Rise speed & away.

Thru sunbursts—
Thru sky—
Thru air and stratosphere—
Thru outer madness—
Thru black and infinite reach—
A Seeker moving in Forever—
Running wild—
Wild with the power, wild as can be.


The End

# The Girl Made of Cool

# The Universe and
# Boys and Girls

OUR UNIVERSE IS ONE OF THOSE THINGS that happens from time to time—in the span of eternity.

Some say our universe has no edge. It is a form made of curved space-time.

It's a strange place to live in—Just about anyone can tell you that.

It seems perfectly arrayed for physical "systems"—and for us, little "systems" within the greater systems.

It results in young men and women.

In spring-time.

In the longings of youth and desire.

For some reason and confluence of events—in some indeterminate time in the past—there came to be a thing known to science and to great generals as:

*The Battle of the Sexes.*

Some say, with bold speculation, that it may be that space and time had an altogether different form before our now existent realm of creation came to be . . . What we know is sparse.

Among the very few things we do know, is that we can say—with some certainty—that at some indeterminate point, in the very distant past, for reasons unknown, conditions unknown, circumstances unknown, there came to exist the first moment of—time equals zero—of this thing now known to these scientists and generals as the first moment of—

*The Battle of the Sexes*
*& the Mystery of Love*
*& the Union of Opposites*

And within this cosmos of hot sex and cataclysmic battles, there came the stage called: *Dating. Or, getting to know someone* . . . Mind to mind, body to body, tingling sense to tingling sense. There came physical encounters, with the use of a bed and soft light—or with the use of darkness to enhance imagination.

And at some point, there came a moment where a young woman turned to a young man and said, "What is it you want from me?"

And his jaw went slack, and he started his answer with the statement "Uh ... uhm ..." And from there he did his level best to make sense.

And—ah—so it went ... and so it goes; you see many moments there were, there are, and continue to be in this battle of the sexes, in the mystery of love, and in the union of opposites.

Now moving more closely into its cosmos, we find this thing called: *Body and Soul.*

Body is the physical of sex; soul is the "storytelling" of sex.

Body is when sex gets hot and penetrating—and thrilling. Soul is when sex gets stimulating, and gets to be a *sustainable* story—and sometimes leads to marriage plans, and to wedding days and hilltop ceremonies, which then brings it all back to the physical realm, culminating in the honeymoon—which if all goes right is very physical indeed.

It's best when sex has body and soul ... Oh, yes, this we do know—about this universe, that some say has no edge, and some say we cannot know in any absolute sense—that is, in any formal state of perfect sense.

And thus what we know is ultimately nonsense.

And to be enlightened is to understand nonsense.

And thus again to be enlightened—about sex, is to understand why sex doesn't make sense—just adventure leading to adventure.

*And occasionally children.* There is that. No matter for now. This is strictly about the beginning battles in this level of warfare, human strife, heartache and never-ending difficulty. This particular unfolding is about: *One girl, one guy, and one more guy. Three in all.*

Now, some say that that our universe began with a big bang. And it is all but certain that the battle of the sexes—of boy chasing girl, boy winning girl—began with an echo of the big bang.

And in the many years and in the many ways of the battling sexes since then there have been many "small big bangs," if you will. Some very hot; some with a great deal of bang.

And now—even as we speak so socially—at this very moment many hot-blooded young men are pursuing many curvy young women with offers of further big bangs—and new forms of curved space-time that new universes create.

# The Big Bang that Wasn't

ONCE UPON A SPACE-TIME, there was . . . a nice, warm spring evening, . . . and there was . . .

*A house.*

And there was a black car pulling up to it . . . And a young couple dressed in black, set against rich, great colors . . .

Night-time colors.

Orange, red, yellow, purple.

Blue, green, indigo, violet.

Set against a deep, dark blue night sky with many stars.

It was a quiet neighborhood . . .

There was a smallish sound . . . of crunching gravel as the car wheels came to a stop.

And then a longish pause.

Broken by the metallic click of a car door opening.

The young man and woman looked beautiful, as they stepped from the car.

When she emerged, she was a smile. This girl was a walking, glowing, beaming smile.

It was the kind of smile that owned the room, or owned the scene, wherever she was.

The girls that she met in her travels thought that it was a lovely smile.

The boys that she met . . . wanted to be very close to that smile.

She was wearing a silky black evening dress. Sleeveless. Her arms and legs were gorgeous. She wore a silver bracelet on her right wrist. Her body moved with grace. Floating. She was wearing black heels.

Her eyes were shining with inner life. She glowed. Yes, this girl glowed.

He was wearing a tuxedo suit, with a black silk tie. A long, thin tie that cut a line down to his waist. There was a subtle pattern on the tie, a flow of waves. The suit was lean and gave him a tall line.

As he came out, he was struck by her. He was seeing her back in silhouette moving away from him, and he paused for a beat. *"Wow,"* he said softly to himself.

She walked as though she were coming off a fashion catwalk. There was something immensely sexy about this young woman. Her name was *Jayne Holly Wyatt.*

All the men fell for her. And quickly. Everything was 'right' about her.

She was a woman dangerously set. She had every man reeling or hanging or swaying or swooning, or moving softly through the air toward her. Every man wanted to lie down with her.

*Ridley Richardson* watched her walk toward his house. He was enthralled.

Ridley closed his eyes for a moment, before opening them and following her.

They were coming from a ballroom social.

They were both just past twenty years old. Just past twenty summers old. Both were recent graduates and they had recently met.

This had been a formal stepping out. And lovely, indeed, it had been. Filled with the thrill of the new. It had been an adult party. They were both so very young and it had been a new experience. It had been something beyond a nightclub, beyond a garden party, beyond a loft party. It had been a ballroom social. A boy-girl dance social.

It was the adult world, which—of course—was filled with crazy people. But they had all seemed quite nice at the ball.

Yes, he had closed his eyes in the moment of movement from one dream to the next.

Now he opened them and followed her as a gentleman properly would, should and does.

This was a very special evening for the young man, because he felt she was so truly special.

She was a seven-day-a-week woman. There was no higher beauty of woman.

What he felt as he entered the house with her was hope.

But there was a problem. A few important things he had said tonight about himself were . . . well, what was the word . . . oh, yes . . . lies.

Well, that was harshly put. He had been: *untrue.*

Yes, that was much nicer. He needed to tell her the truth. He took in a breath. He was finding it hard to breath. He noticed his heart was now beating all too fast. His knees were wobbly and trembling. And his hands, were of course, also trembling.

Truth was best, he thought.


Ridley and Jayne, stepped into the house, which Jayne was seeing for the first time. She looked around, observing a quite elegance.

Presently they were touring the house.

"It looks," she said, "like both bedrooms are being lived in."

"Oh, yes," he said, "I have a friend staying with me, temporarily."
This was: *untrue.*

They sat down in the living room.

"You said you're an executive at a public relations agency, right?" she asked. "Do you love it?"

"I enjoy it," he said. "It's a job, but it's commerce. And what can one find in commerce that leads to enlightenment?" He looked at her. "Actually I shouldn't say that. There's a lot you can learn from business people about leadership . . . Leadership is an important part of healthy spirituality— What fascinates me is behavior. Human nature. Relationships."

"I feel the same way," she said.

"Thanks for tonight," he said and looked into her eyes. "Thank you." He became quiet. And then said, "Do you feel like calling it a night?"

"No," she said.

They were sitting at opposite ends of the couch.

"What do you feel like doing?" he asked.

She reached across the couch and took his hand.

He gave it to her. "If I kissed you," he said, "would I be coming on too strong?"

"Is that what you're going to do?" she said.

He moved in for a kiss. Hesitated. Pulled away from her.

"I have to tell you something about myself," he said.

"Yes," she said.

"No, never mind . . . Please forget it." He moved toward her for a kiss. He put his arm on her shoulder. Touched her skin with his fingers . . . And he brought his lips toward hers, until he was a whisper away . . . Here, he stopped.

The moment became very still.

"Would you like me to open the window?" he asked.

She looked at him.

"You're okay? . . ." he said. ". . . Well, I want to tell you something about myself, . . . mmm . . . that is kind of important."

Jayne lay against the couch, and smiled. "Tell me what's going on in your head."

"I don't know how you'll take it."

"You don't have to tell me," she said.

"Let me just say one or two small things." Ridley took a breath and stood up.

"Does it really matter," he said, "that I have this house? That I'm a business executive? That I dress elegantly? I think it's bull-mud."

"You should be proud of those things," she said. "What you do says a lot about what you are. How you dress says a lot about what you are . . . You're saying a lot of good things about yourself."

"What if those things really say nothing?" he said. "What if they're just a kind of front? . . . How does a woman know the difference between a good dress and a bad dress?"

"I know what you mean," she said.

"Yes, right," he said, "when a woman wears a bad dress you notice the dress. When she wears a good dress, you notice the woman."

While talking, he was removing the tuxedo jacket. He took off his elegant silk tie and set it aside, carefully. "My point is that brilliant people don't need to dress to the hilt. They don't dress brilliant, they just are brilliant."

He opened the collar of his shirt, to reveal a white crew-neck undershirt. He tousled his hair, so that it would rest more naturally. His hair was wild and long. He pulled the sash from his waist, and he set it down gently.

"Do you really need to look like a million bucks? Do you need the *'million bucks front'*?"

"Well," she said, "most people would say you look better in the *'million bucks front'* . . . It's cool. It's *the art of cool.*"

That stopped him. He was trying to convince her. But first he was wondering if he had convinced himself yet.

"So it's a high-bang-for-the-bucks move?" he asked.

"Yes," she said.

"Ah, I see." He looked at her. "Jayne . . . I feel that you're a special person . . . I've done a few things that I don't feel quite right about. I wanted to put my best foot forward—See this tuxedo?"

"It's very nice," she said.

"It's not mine," he said.

"Oh . . . that's okay . . . everybody, once in a while, borrows a tuxedo."

"You know the house?" he said. "And that person that's living with me temporarily . . . He's the owner of the house. I'm just staying here—until I find a job."

She looked at him.

"I thought you said you're a public relations executive?"

"I could be," he said, "but I don't have the training. I'm telling you all this because I didn't want to get in so deep that you'd get a false impression of me."

She continued to look at him.

He sat back on the couch.

"So," he sighed, "I don't have a job—at this time. You can't tell that to a woman when you first meet her."

"I see," she said.

"There. That's it," he said. "Now those things shouldn't matter, I think."

"Of course not. It's so good that you've said these things to me. Most magazines tell you that *'You should see him for what he is, as opposed to what you want.'* I'm starting to see you for what you are. But listen . . . I should get going. It's getting late."

She stood up.

"What time is it?" she asked.

"I don't know," he said. "I don't have a watch."

# Walking Jayne Home

Ridley and Jayne were walking from the house to Jayne's apartment, which was close by. They were neighbors.

"So what happened to your last job?"

"I got . . . uhm, fired."

"Downsizing?"

"I influenced it in some ways when I told my, uhm, . . . boss, uhm, to go ahead and uhm, . . . fuck himself . . . He wasn't doing his job right. I was. I got caught up in an adrenaline rush. Do you know what that is? When your adrenaline starts shooting through you. Your heart beats faster. You start to lose control."

"Just like the way you were a few minutes ago, when we were about to kiss."

"Yes," he smiled, "you're right. You're very quick. That was an adrenaline rush. I wanted things to go right between us. I got nervous."

"So what happened with the boss?"

"Well, in business, honesty is not the best policy," he said. ". . . The whole thing happened, well, just a few days ago. It's got me a little startled . . . Oh, I don't want to get us into a total bringdown . . . I think it's all working out for the best. It's a positive."

"I see . . . But you had a rough patch there?"

"I said to him things like: You raging maniac, you psycho . . . I called him an insane bitch."

"But he's a man."

"Still it was true . . . You know . . . now that I think back on it, I can see he wanted a reaction from me. He was pushing me to the edge . . . Well, he got a reaction . . . Like I said though—it's a positive."

"It sounds positive."

"Yes, it's nice when people can be open with each other. Honesty is so valuable."

She looked at him.

"...Yes, I think it's working out for the best," he said.

"Were you an executive there?" she said.

"I was still gaining experience. Actually, I was still at the, uhm, junior level. But it really is for the best. I want to go into another field ... I've always been interested in the study of behavior. Not just of people, but also animals."

"What kind of money can you make as a behavior person?"

"They're called zoologists. Or primatologists. Or behavioral scientists. It's not really a get-rich-quick scheme. Then again there's always an outside chance you could make a real killing in animal studies." He smiled.

"That must really be something—making your fortune in animals." She laughed.

"It's not like being a doctor or anything," he said. "The money is not there in that way. The deal does leave a little something to be desired ... It's just something I feel a natural interest in. I'm hoping the money will come but that's not my first priority. I want to know about people. I want to know how the mind works."

"What happens if you meet a nice girl and you want to go out?"

"I'm hoping the young lady would be very understanding."

They continued walking.

"It really is beautiful out tonight," he said. He looked at her and then turned to take in the street.

She looked around. "I suppose. But it's just a street scene."

She saw houses, fences, sidewalks, lamps and cars with a little greenery here and there. Not exactly natural splendor.

"Can I show you a trick I got out of a book? It'll just take a moment." She smiled mysteriously.

He continued. "Stop here for a moment."

### Opening your visual field

They stopped walking.

"Take a deep breath," Ridley said, "and let it out slowly."

She looked at him.

"Turn and look at that tree across the street." She turned. "Now look up there and would you, please, imagine that on one of its branches there's a camera. Look into the lens. Do it with a feeling like you're the superstar of a great movie and they're filming you with that camera."

He paused for a beat to let her get started with the imaginary game.

"Look into the lens as if you're reaching for it with your eye. At the same time relax, and open up your peripheral vision."

He stopped a beat to let her take that in and then continued.

"Open your visual field. Keep looking into that lens with the center of your vision. The part that focuses and takes your attention. At the same time, open your peripheral vision so that you can see shapes and color on the outside."

She seemed to be following along and doing what he was suggesting, so Ridley continued.

"Imagine there's a feeler coming out from your eyes and going into that camera lens. Almost like there are lasers coming out of your eyes and shooting into that lens. At the same time, keep your peripheral vision so that your visual field is open. It should be almost like you have a two-way vision."

He paused. "How's it coming along?"

"I'm not sure, but I think I'm doing it."

"Now—take the things you've just done and scan your gaze along the street. Do a continuous, connected sweep. While you're relaxed, breathing easy, and keeping your visual field open. Move your attention along the street but the whole time keep your awareness of shapes and colors in your peripheral vision . . . Ready?"

"Yes," she said. Now she began looking around again.

He said, "Maybe try doing figure eights with your vision."

She did a slow figure eight with her gaze. And suddenly laughed. She did another figure eight.

Now he laughed.

"Do you notice a difference?" he asked.

She turned to him—then back to the view.

She saw lemon yellows. Spatterings of orange and red. Thick brush-strokes of emerald green. Blues—so many blues.

Dark blue streaked across the lower horizon and drew itself into black.

All around her she saw . . .

Red. Orange. Yellow.

Green. Blue.

Indigo. Violet.

She turned back to him.

"Thanks Ridley," she said. "You're right. It is beautiful out here tonight. And I wouldn't have noticed."

"It's beautiful everywhere Jayne . . . Should we continue walking?" he asked. And extended his hand in the air, pointing toward her house.

She began walking. He followed at her side.

"Where did you learn that?"

"Oh, it was in a small little green book. I forget the title."

## The Front Door to Jayne's Apartment

As they approached her door, as they walked up the stairs to the patio outside her section of apartments there was a strange, thick awkward silence.

This was one of those strange things that happens in a relationship. In veering from moment to moment, sometimes the feelings between two people abruptly grew very strange indeed.

He had lied to her, presented a false front . . . There had been moments of fun; that last bit had been memorable and affecting. But there was something very disturbing. There was something she sensed that was bothering her greatly. She held it in. And held it down.

They said goodbye awkwardly.

There was a current of disturbance. Things were in an uproar beneath this quiet scene.

She opened her door, and stepped in.

"I had a wonderful time tonight," she said, feeling it necessary to be polite.

She had crossed her threshold, and now there was a distance between them.

He felt that to step forward would be to intrude into her personal space. He kept his distance and blew her a gentle kiss.

She smiled. And gently closed the door.

### Oh, oh—that uneasy feeling

Once she had closed the door, Ridley felt something heavy and leaden hit him deep within his inner space . . . He suddenly felt that something had gone terribly wrong.

### She felt rattled

Inside her apartment, Jayne paused. She took a breath . . . She was feeling some things that were quite un-right . . . She drew her breath and continued moving.

She walked into her apartment, turned off the main light, and made ready for bed.

## The City Streets

Ridley was walking the streets, thinking.

He was talking to himself.

Tonight, he was full of foolish song.

The words of one ballad moved in a persistent winding—round and round—inside his head.

*"Lately, I find myself out gazing at stars,"* Ridley said the lyrics softly, while looking forward, and into the air before him. *"Hearing guitars, like someone in love. Sometimes the things I do astound me, . . . mostly whenever you're around me."*

He stared outward wistfully as he took in the street scenery. He had come to a ridge. Spread out before him, he could see rolling lights and streets.

*"Lately,"* he said, *"I seem to walk as though I had wings, . . . bump into things, . . . like someone in love."*

He stopped, took his gaze upward, and stared at the stars.

"Each time I look at her it happens," Ridley said to himself.

"Lately, I have trouble finding my way through things. It's almost like I'm in love. I'm feeling . . . like someone in love . . . In love."

He looked upward and outward into the upper reaches of space—there were so many stars.

# Chet Clifford
*The Charmer*

## The Chet Session

### The House, Later that Night

Ridley was talking to his housemate—*Chet Clifford.*

Chet was the actual owner of the house they lived in. He was good looking and a smooth operator.

Chet Clifford was stunning to women. He looked like a fashion model. . . . Perfect body, perfect smile, . . . perfect style.

### The  difficulty of launching into the world of adult romance . . .

They were all young, Ridley, Jayne and Chet—and Chet was the eldest.

They were, all three, recent graduates. They were all fresh out of school and entering the adult world.

Now Chet was off to a running start. To a flying start. He had quickly gotten an executive job, bought a house, and rented out one of the rooms.

He had so recently been mired in that ugly stage of life called: *"college."* It was only a few years ago, but he had since emerged full bore, and displayed a natural talent for adult warfare and adult games.

Ridley was still emerging from his university days, and from the damage that a *good* college education can cause on the human psyche.

Chet was already over his college education. He had quickly realized that all of the important things you had to know in life—in order to succeed in sexual coupling, in business partnering, and in all of life's alliances—that these important things simply were not taught properly in school. Most teachers did not know how, and the others did not dare teach the things that Chet knew.

He was now helping Ridley to step into the world of *adult business.*

### The Chet reaction

"You told her you got fired, you're unemployed, you're broke?" Chet asked.

"I laid it all out for her. I feel cleansed," said Ridley.

"Hmm . . . I think you dug a hole for yourself," said Chet.

"Why?"

"Well, you made too much of a thing. Why would you want to confess all these things to a girl unless you were going to get married? You can't make the date that serious."

"You think I played it wrong?" said Ridley.

"She lost interest in you," said Chet. "You led her into the phony front you were putting up. Then you blew your cover. She got turned off by that."

"But you're the one who talked me into putting up a front."

"The front was fine."

"Maybe."

"You'll get over it. Girls like this are a dollar a dozen. Listen, in the scheme of things, it wasn't a presidential election. But you have to remember with the next girl—*You have to put up a little front.* Something. And then not blow your cover! You've got the thing going for you, she's liking you, and then all of the sudden on a first date you tell her well it's not my tuxedo. It's like you're deliberately into self-destruction. What are you a masochist?

"You completely sank this one. You're out of a job. She must have lit up when you told her that one. It's not your tuxedo. She had to know that, right? And why didn't you tell me you didn't have a fucking watch? I would've lent you one. Then you could have told her you borrowed the watch—You would have had more to talk about!"

Ridley was taking it in—He felt that Chet possessed a voice of odd wisdom.

"You were nice, polite, honest. That's all too sweet. Women can't get into that."

"What do you mean?" Ridley asked.

"Life is not rational. You study behavior, you know that. People don't behave logically. Do you want to know the secret of getting women?"

"Do you have that?" asked Ridley.

"You have to think outside the normal."

Chet let that hang in the air a while.

"I don't get it," said Ridley.

# The Secret of Women
*"Women's studies"—for men*

"Life is not rational," Chet said. "People do not behave in a rational ordered way.

"You can't go about it rationally. It's not clinical. You can't go right down the middle. It's not straight—*It's curvy.*

"You have to be different than these other guys," said Chet. "They don't know what they're doing. They're disasters."

"Right, we're in favor of . . . success," said Ridley.

"Let's look at what you do the next time . . . when you go out dancing. . . .

"Here's how to build a night session. . . ."

# Night-Time Chet Sessions
*And how to seduce the sexiest of women*

### Setting up the room, the space-time of a dance floor
"Okay, here we go. . . . Let's get a picture of the dance floor.

"It's crowded," said Chet. "There are lots of drunks on the floor."

"We were at a charity ballroom social," said Ridley.

"I hate you," said Chet. "Okay, the drunks were in tuxedos. Now some of the people—by that I mean all of the people—wanted to do what I'm going to explain now . . ."

### The curvature of space-time
"First, you've got the picture . . . Correct?"

"It's crowded. It's a bar. . . .

"There are lots of drunks on the dance floor. . . .

"It's late at night. You're tipsy. . . .

"It's a dark room. . . .

"Slow, slinky, smooth. . . . Lots of people here. . . ."

"Now . . . the girl . . ."
"She has an inner dialogue going," said Chet.

"She wants to look fabulous. That's what you're helping her with. In your head, you're trying to get her into bed. That's where the night ends, if you do it right."

"I wouldn't say that."

"I would. Where's it supposed to end, in the kitchen? This is about getting into the bedroom."

Ridley said, "The way I think of it is this: You're polite. You make her look good. You show her a good time. You keep it simple. And then she'll want to dance with you again."

"Oh, you're saying you dance with her so you can dance with her next time? . . . It's now or never. You go for it straight away."

"Go for what?" asked Ridley.

"What they want is a real man on the dance floor. A guy with confidence. Casual, cool, comfortable. He's not worried. He's in his world. He's in control. And he's treating her like the most important person in the world."

"What kind of dance do you want it to be?" asked Chet.

"It's couples dancing—but what do you want the dance to be?"

"You're caught up in ballroom. . . . That's not it," said Chet. ". . . You want to be the guy women want to dance with late at night in a dark room, by a bar with the lights low and off in the distance.

"You want smooth dance.

"The destination is the bed. You want the dance that makes them want to go to bed. The dance with the guy they want in that bed. The smooth dance with the smooth operator.

"You want them to start thinking body-talk. . . ."

### Falling dance

"You want a *'falling dance,'*" said Chet. "You want a grounded dance. You want to be sinking into the ground with her."

### The bare essentials of seduction on the dance floor

"Here are some quick basics.

"We're just going to cover her weight, her hips, and your hands. You'll get the idea.

"It's the bare essentials. We'll do this quick. . . . And we'll go through some for-instances to make the picture clear for you. . . ."

# The Teaching Session
*The Master Class with Chet Clifford*

## Weight Changes

### Her weight

Chet put his arm around Ridley's shoulder.

"You meet a girl in a club. . . . Offer to get her a drink.

"You want to get her tipsy.

"Tipsy is social. Drunk is out of control.

"Tipsy is you're falling forward. Drunk is you're falling down. You want tipsy. Tipsy is just tipping forward. You want a forward pitch. You want her on her toes falling toward you, not on her heels falling away from you. Got it? . . . Falling forward you do in bed. Falling on the floor you don't do in bed. Are we clear?"

"All your concepts keep coming back to her bed," said Ridley.

"Yes, that's the beauty," said Chet.

### Taking her into closed position

Chet moved in closer to Ridley.

"We seem to be one woman short for tonight's class, so you'll fill in," said Chet.

Chet brought Ridley into closed dance position—face to face—in a return "slingshot" position, with Chet's hand on Ridley's back—where the woman's bra strap would be.

Ridley looked away from Chet, immediately uncomfortable.

"Look at me," Chet said.

Ridley glanced at Chet.

Chet said, "How do I seem? . . . I'm confidant. Cool, casual, comfortable."

"Yes."

"And you—You look like a nervous wreck."

"I never danced with another man before."

"I never danced with a man either—Be cool brother. We'll both live through this."

Ridley looked Chet in the eye. He tried to do what he had taught Jayne about opening your visual field. About keeping your focus and your peripheral vision floating in your attention at the same time. It worked. He was able to look Chet straight in the eye.

"Better," said Chet. "Breathe and relax."

Ridley breathed.

"Incidentally, if she gets uncomfortable at this point, you tell her, *'This is the younger style. It suits you.'* "

"Thank you darling," said Ridley.

"You're welcome my angel," said Chet. "Let's get started. . . . Feel me on you. Do you feel me?"

"Oh yes," said Ridley.

### Spins and turns

"She gets tipsy. . . . Then you take her dancing. I'll show you what I mean."

"But she's tipsy," said Ridley. "She won't be able to dance."

"Do you hear yourself talking? That's when you start spinning her."

Chet broke away.

He now pretended to be holding an imaginary girl in an open position and speaking to her:

"You tell her: *'Spinning is fun. Where are you from? From California? Oh, California girls love to spin.'*

"Make it fun. Then spin her."

He spun this lovely imaginary girl.

"She starts falling on you—Yummy! You brace her. You hold her. You stabilize her. You're a perfect gentleman—But look how close you are on her center.

"By the time Monday rolls around, you'll be waking up in her bed. Believe me."

Chet whirled the imaginary girl around and gave Ridley the sense that she was stumbling.

"You tell her: *'You're so beautiful doing this.'* . . . You explain to her: *'What you want to experience is release. That anything is possible.*

" *'There's no ceiling. People think there's a ceiling . . . of counting and steps. There's no ceiling.'*

"Then you find your way back into the set moves.

"You're continuing—until you're folded back into a connection.

"It's like the art of the hug—You do a goodbye—and then a hug again."

Chet looked at Ridley, "Now let's move to moment number two . . ."

# Hip Action

### Her hips

Chet said, "Get her tipsy. Get her spinning and turning. Then you do *'The Mess-Around.'*"

He demonstrated by bringing Ridley into a very loving *'hug'*—a very close intimate, sensual embrace.

Now Chet wedged his leg between Ridley's legs—or *'her'* legs. He put his hip against *'her'* hips.

And what Chet did next was the sensational part:

*He rotated their hips together in a circle.*

This sexual move of joined hip motion was commonly called *'The Mess-Around.'* That's what dancers called it. But in the way that Chet did it, it was hard to tell the difference between this move and just plain *'fucking'* on the dance floor.

At the end of one nice sexy, smoldering circle of his-hip-rolling-on-her-hip, he stopped.

He separated from Ridley—or the *'her'* in this scene.

He rocked their weight away from each other.

And that was how the hip-on-hip move ended.

Chet smiled with great charm.

Ridley became very disturbed.

"Chet," he said, "isn't there such a thing as *'personal space'*? Aren't you invading a woman's—I mean a stranger's—personal space? . . . You're putting your *'thing'* right in between her legs."

"You're fucking her," said Chet. "Yes, that's the beauty of the move. That's the nice idea behind it. . . . Women love guys who know how to fuck them. . . . Do you hear yourself when you ask these questions?" Chet continued. "Let's get back to work here. We're talking technique. It's a beautiful thing."

"How far in can you go?"

Chet smiled. And paused for effect.

"There's a lot to being a gentleman," said Chet. "What you tell her is: *'It's nice dancing with you today. Wow. You move very beautifully sweetheart.'* . . . She'll forget where the property lines are—She'll be having such a good time."

## Hand Connections

### Your hands

"It's like a masseuse. Never take your hands off the client—I mean the woman," said Chet.

"Show her how a guy should put a hand on a girl's hip. . . .

"Women love guys who know how to hold their hips while fucking them.

"Now, first, you play the game with her of *how to find the hips.* You say: *'Where is the hip?'* "

Chet touched his own ass. " *'This is not the hip'* . . ." He touched his own breasts. " *'This is not the hip'* . . ." Now Chet touched his own hip bone. " *'This is the hip.'* "

Now he touched Ridley's hip bone. He did it very tenderly, like a true gentleman—with just the tips of two fingers. It was a gentle touch. And then he pushed Ridley away gently but firmly. It had a very good feel to it.

### Hand connections

"Here's what you do with your hands," Chet said.

"Show her the hand connections. Demonstrate what *not* to do with your hands. . . .

"You tell her: *'What a gentleman does not do is this.'* And then you do it to her.

"You get naughty with your hands, but first you make it clear you're going to be naughty with her. Just with her. You don't do this with other women.

"Women love guys who consider them a special fuck."

He moved his hand down her body, beginning on her shoulder blade, down the middle of her back, . . . past her waist, . . . her hips . . .

Chet said, "Put your hand *almost* on her ass. Stop there. Because once your hand is actually on her ass, there's nowhere else you can go on the dance floor."

Chet finished dancing, and released Ridley. He patted Ridley's belly. And as his hand flew away, in the same sweep of his hand, he made a pistol motion and fired into the air.

He gracefully stepped from the dance floor like a lion king and moved to his throne—err, to his couch. He sat on the arm regally—instead of on the cushion.

**"There, you have a start . . ."**
"Put things together," said Chet, "in unexpected ways—That's the joy. You want her to feel the joy.

"You know your way around the dance floor.

"Think of it as a pursuit you stay with. Don't let it be the end. It's so worth it.

"You've got a great start. Get it into your body. Music is awesome. Dancing is awesome. There are so many opportunities in this city."

# The Master Class in Female Psychology
*Chet Clifford and advanced studies*

## Domination

**And the dominant male**
"Try this out next week," said Chet. "Chalk up this girl tonight to experience. You'll get better."

"But I'm not looking past her," said Ridley. "I don't want to look past her. . . . Chet, she's special."

"You want to know how to get her back? I'll tell you what it takes."

"What?"

"You have to get her respect. You have to be strong. The only way to do that is to be what women call a *'caveman.'* I hate that word because it puts the wrong image in your head. But if a guy is too nice, too cooperative then they get turned off. Strength is a turn-on. You have to take charge. Listen, in every relationship there's always the dominant one and the one who submits. She wants to be the one who submits. You don't have two decision-makers. You have the one who decides and the one who follows. Life is about dominance. It's the same in everything. In politics, you rule your land. In marketing, you beat the competition. Look at the animal kingdom. Survival of the fittest. Show me a weak ape and then show me how many mates he has. Take the worst vicious ape, he has all of the other females around him. There we have dominance again. Equality is a myth. All men are created equal. That's a pitch, that's not truth. It's damaging— let's follow that and see where we end up."

Chet looked at Ridley.

"I'm real. Are you?" said Chet. "Life is nothing but a game of dominance."

"I don't like to think that way," said Ridley.

"Think how you like," said Chet. "I'm just telling you how life works. I could lead you down the garden path where nothing I say is true. If I wanted to live like that, I'd become a politician. You know her a little bit. You've known other women. Has it ever seemed to you that what they want is a guy who they can walk all over? You've got a little bit to learn about what makes a man sexy. I'm a feminist, but it doesn't work. Women want a real man. She wants a man who can lead. Now go in there and show some personality."

"I can't order her around."

"Don't order. Just give her a taste of confidence. It's what she wants. She'd never admit it. But trust me. If you want her to like you, you need to go over there and take care of business."

"You think that's what she wants?" said Ridley.

"Of course. But she'll never admit it. People don't say what's really on their minds. When was the last time you honestly told a woman what you were thinking?" said Chet.

"I don't know. An hour ago?" said Ridley.

"Do you want to listen," said Chet, "or do you want to talk? Most people tell you the opposite of what they really want."

"I think you might be right."

"You think or you know?

"This is so mind-altering."

"You have something to say, do it now. It doesn't get any easier."

"Maybe you're right. Maybe I should fix this."

Now Chet Clifford went into the standard real man's advice:

"Go take a minute of her time for a straight talk. Lay it out for her. You'll feel better. Tell her *'I've got you under my skin,'* or whatever love song works for you. Lay it out. Then you really will feel cleansed of sin. If you want her, go get her. If you're unhappy, it's because you're unhappy. Tell her how you feel. See what she says. You're a great guy. Why wouldn't she want you? Why not go over right now and tell her? You've got it bad, and that isn't good. It's no good. Now go over there and show her all your good intentions. I think it'll work."

"Thank you Chet. I wouldn't know what to do or how to do this without you," said Ridley.

"Hey, we're friends," said Chet.

"What time is it?" said Ridley.

"You're thinking too much. Forget the time."

"Okay, I'll forget the time, but what time is it?"

"It's like 9, or so, maybe 10. Ah, you've got plenty of time. The night is young—What the hell am I saying!—It's a Friday night for Christ' sake. Don't think up reasons to fail. You can make this happen. Go do this. . . . You and me, Ridley, we're in this together. And we'll have you two together. It's going to happen. I can feel it."

Ridley walked out the front door.

Now Chet was alone.

Chet turned away from the door and moved into the living room.

What came next was a bit bizarre. It was a side of Chet and an experience that you could only call:

# The Chet Show

*Chet Clifford takes center stage and turns it all 'on'*

### Chet moves and Chet presentation

The light bounced off the walls filling the area with brilliance as though a spotlight had been directed onto Chet Clifford.

"I just gave him the best chance he could have," said Chet aloud to the room. "He's a good guy. We'll see what happens. Who knows? It's him, at this point.

"I'm a fatalist," said Chet, and his voice bore a rich resonance and a fluid tone that filled the whole room with a comfortable, friendly living room presence. "That's what I am. I'm a fatalist. Your fate is your character."

He was suddenly talking aloud—*to a large imaginary audience.*

This was a peculiarity—and a great virtue of Chet's. He had many magical qualities about him. And one of them was the way he was developing when it came to this thing—*to this imaginary audience that he always felt was before him.*

### The "audience"

*The principle Chet invoked here was: Use your imagination to start a fire—*
This was what Chet was doing now . . . He turned and began to speak to a rich, colorful, streaming *imaginary "audience."*

*The "audience" was always with him and there for him.*

This was part of the game. *This was part of being "on."* This was the modern way. And Chet Clifford was the most highly modern young man. you would ever meet in your life.

Yes, the *audience* was always there. They were his friends. Always wondering to themselves, "*Oh, what was that Chet up to now?*"

In playing to his audience, he liked to reveal a series of inner thoughts that he would never share in daily life with actual people.

You see, with his audience, he felt free to deliver unusual advice as though it were perfectly normal. Almost as if the audience was filled with people who were just like him, who carried around the same kinds of thoughts.

### The marketing show

Chet worked at a marketing agency. He was a public relations man. He was a campaign and warfare man. And he was always developing his act.

He was something like an adrenaline addict. He was addicted to marketing. In his field, he was Hannibal the Carthaginian general, he was Alexander the Great, he was Patton the field commander.

He couldn't kick it, he wouldn't kick it, he shouldn't kick it. It was him and it was heavy. It lent him the gravitas of great men, and he rehearsed his marketing constantly. His dream was to market to a sellout audience at the *Garden*—that great forum, the largest stadium within the largest city within the most powerful country on earth.

That would be the height of his soaring ambition. A great big spectacular marketing rock concert. It would just be him alone on a stage with a microphone and sharing his view of marketing greatness with his audience.

### The art of the bastard

Chet was a master bastard, and he felt he was an example to other bastards.

He loved sharing moves—moves stewed to perfection. Oh, he did so very much love the high and right honorable art—the ancient art of the bastard. He loved presenting it to his audience.

Chet would sometimes think to himself, *Most people don't want to sound like the 'voice of god,' they don't want to sound like they're talking from on high. That's just ridiculous when that's exactly what you want to sound like—what you want is a really good 'voice of god.' The god voice works.*

*And you have to practice, and develop a really strong god voice. You need it. If you don't have one, what happens when some guy comes along who does have the god voice? Why he's going to beat you cold.*

Yes, Chet was a master bastard, and he was a shining example to all the other bastards out there. . . . Now, in this moment, there was no rest for the wicked. Chet took to the stage and faced his audience of like-minded people.

"I'm a fatalist," Chet said again. "Your fate is your character."

This was how Chet stepped before his audience. This was how he opened the talk.

"This is Ridley's fate. I'll show you."

He paused for effect.

Once he had them in his grip, he walked them into the next room.

## Ridley's Bathroom

"This is Ridley's bathroom. Take a look at this."

He pointed to some towels that were hanging awkwardly. Then he pointed to the sink, which wasn't perfectly cleaned. It was rather disordered. The vanity held gels, soaps, brushes and razor blades.

"I don't have to use this bathroom but doesn't this tell you something about him? Come on, I'll show you something else."

## Ridley's Bedroom

The room was likewise disordered, filled with books and papers—which seemed to be spilling from every drawer and shelf. Apparently Ridley was a young man who studied a great many things.

"He lives in this. Go ahead take a look around."

Now Chet held perfectly still. He released his audience's attention to the environment of the room. He would let it sink into them.

When the audience at last turned back to Chet he was again in motion. He was opening the top drawer of Ridley's desk.

Chet lifted a set of green bills from the drawer, gracefully took one and replaced the rest.

Looking at the audience with a charming smile, he continued to educate them in his ways.

"I take $20 once in a while," said Chet, ". . . for expenses that Ridley doesn't otherwise cover. Once a week I have a cleaning lady come by. He doesn't chip in. This way I get the payments from him. I take 20 and I let him off the hook. I should actually take 25 but all right . . . I'm a nice guy."

He held the moment. Then continued. . . . It was a light-hearted aside, but significant for them to learn by. "You see simple acts like taking the bill come down to a question of confidence. You've got to make your confidence stronger and stronger every day. I don't like to take the poor guy's money, but your confidence is your most important asset. So when you come across a moment where you find yourself saying, '*I can't do that.*' Then you have to do it."

Now he directed them to the body of the room. "Look at all the books he has here. He's got more in storage. As if the library at the college down the block didn't have enough ink on paper for you. He's got to be a know-it-all about everything. You talk about something that happened two hundred, one thousand, two thousand years ago—it doesn't matter when—he'd like to have a view. . . . Is it important? Who knows, but it shows you something about him. He has an arrogant streak. Normally that's a very good thing, but not like this. He could learn all he wants about history, psychology, art. It doesn't mean he knows anything. Do you think ink on paper impresses me? He reads his books and goes to museums. Me—I'm real; I'm into the reality that's out there. I'm not an elitist.

"I deal only in facts—so I'm a cocky bastard," he said.

"I'm only interested in true success, and I'm ever watchful of failure."

He looked across his audience and made strong eye contact with them one at a time.

"I'll tell you some good things to learn. . . .

" '*Get there firstest with the mostest.*'—That's an important principle.

" '*The pursuit is as critical as the initial attack.*' . . .

" '*Reinforce strength, abandon failure.*' . . .

" '*You don't fight alone—you have to bring in, and use allies.*' "

"These are the kinds of concepts you want. These are the things that matter. . . . Listen, there's a lot to learn. Stick with me and you'll get it all."

He was performing what he termed a "*social job*"—teaching social jabs—teaching society punches.

And in his stance and manner he was teaching a subtle thing called "*The Ready Position*"—or what he liked to call the "gunslinger position."

As he strode, he maintained a strong, light, elegant frame. His arms were floating slightly outward from his torso. He called this carriage of his frame the "ready position." It meant: *'You can go this way, or you can go that way'*—Lots of great doings were possible, and each might happen at any moment.

He was always in the ready position. . . .

He was a walking broadcast. And Chet's attitude held out a message to the world in which he said, *"I'm on my way. And my time has come."*

## The Street

Ridley was again filled with romantic ballads.

Ridley's talks and voicings were different than his friend Chet's. They were like songs. Like the jazz songs that people sang to themselves.

Ridley was talking to a himself-outside-himself. To a "him" standing beside himself. Whereas Chet talked to a developing, growing audience.

With Chet, the thoughts were growing major. He was talking to a stadium of imaginary people.

Ridley's style was different.

## At long last love?

*Is this forever?* Ridley asked. The ballad repeated itself in his head. It was a famous ballad. Perhaps you might even have heard it yourself.

*Is this for all time? Is this a fancy not worth thinking of? Or is it at long last love?*

He was Hamlet—He had questions. He was racked by doubts. And the answers were elusive.

*Is it an earthquake or simply a shock? Is it a cocktail, this feeling of joy—or is what I feel the real McCoy—Is it for all time?"*

*Is it for all time—or simply a lark? Is it a fancy not worth thinking of? Or is it at long last love?*

# They Disturb Each Other
*The Viking Attack*

### Jayne's Apartment, Night

Jayne was on the phone.

"He seemed very genuine . . . but you're right. How could he lie like that to me? When I imagine what he was thinking of me, it really hurts. . . .

". . . You know me. I have a healthy respect for money, business, . . . and money. . . .

". . . But to pretend you have those things. I'll like you if you don't have those things."

Her doorbell rang.

Jayne opened the door and found Ridley standing there.

He saw that she had undressed and changed into her pajamas. She happened to look terribly sexy in pajamas.

"Sorry to disturb you," he said. "May I have a word?"

She looked at him.

He stepped in.

She picked up the phone.

"I've got to go dear," Jayne said. "I'll call you tomorrow, okay? . . . Goodnight. . . . Sweet dreams."

She hung up the line and turned toward Ridley.

"I was talking to her about some guy I went out with tonight and I expected him to be very sweet and very nice. He turned out to be a liar— and a dreamer. And we parted company. Little did I know that he would show up again around midnight. An interesting character, wouldn't you say? A winner. There's even more, the winner is about to say something. Okay winner, let's hear it. I'm all yours."

Abruptly, his insides went into overdrive. His heart started hammering. Adrenaline shot through him.

"Lately, I've been finding . . . uhm, . . . when you're around . . . when I look at you, . . . I, . . . uhm, am, uhm, feeling as though . . ."

He looked at her.

"I'm in love with you," he said.

She stood there.

"You just met me," she said.

"I know," he said. "Maybe I fell in love with you the moment I saw you."

"They all do," she said. "Do you have something serious to say?"

"Forgive me. It's my first time. I've never been in love with you before."

"Well, that's a good line. I like you when you're witty. But I don't kid around about being in love. It means something to me."

"I'm just getting the Zen of this. It's not what I expected."

"Surprise," Jayne said.

"I'm finding my way to the way you're supposed to do this."

Telling her he was in love was really, really hard. His adrenaline was coursing through him. He was disturbed. Pushing through extreme difficulty.

"It does happen sometimes. You can experience love at first sight."

"Yes, it happens all the time—in movies. But this is a place called reality."

"Why wouldn't I be in love with you?"

"Because we just met."

"That's how love at first sight works."

"Love is knowing someone."

"You're a girl."

"Yes."

"You're uhm, . . . made of, . . . uhm, . . . cool."

"Yes, I'm cool. But there's more to me."

"So I'll fall in love with that later. I'm pacing myself."

"I have a different theory," she said.

"Yes."

"People go insane. That happens. Sometimes people just go crazy. That happens at first sight too. And around me that happens to an awful lot of men. It's my brooding, smoldering sexuality."

"There's always that possibility."

"No, there's always that reality. It's called being a scorching beauty. You get men coming up to you saying, 'Jayne, I think you're the girl made of cool.'"

"Well, I could have said it better. Lately I haven't been myself."

"How about we make this the night we called it a day! I'm not interested."

"Oh."

All the energy in him crashed, a thousand feet into the ground. He stood, defeated.

"This is the rest of me," she said. "How do you like it so far?"

At times, the sexes get cross with one another.

They fancy one another, get cross, and then fancy again.

Or they fancy one another, get cross, and never speak again.

What we know about how it all works is very slender.


# Chet Session Two

### Chet's House, Later that Night

"You told her you're in love with her?" Chet asked.

"Yes, I felt it was too early to talk marriage. It's better to keep it simple. Slow and steady wins the race."

"She's good," said Chet. "She's really good. She's at the top of her game. She turned it all around so she could take charge again."

"Are you saying she's maneuvering?" said Ridley.

"Women can do it. They know no man can deal with it. No man knows how to take charge of a woman—except me, but then I'm special. You know, I'm tomorrow but I'm here today, what can I say?"

"What do we do next?"

"We wait for her to call. The ball is in her court now."

"What if she doesn't call?"

"Then we taught her a lesson."

"If she never calls?"

"You stood your ground. You did the right thing. Now feel good."

Ridley was in agony.

"She'll come to you," Chet said. "Don't worry. Now you play hard to get. Take it down a peg."

"What if she doesn't come to me?"

"Don't worry. It's physics. It works like a charm. I've had a lot of experience in this area. You'll have to trust me. You know I have no problem with women. I'm trying to get you to that level. How many women have I been with since you've known me?"

"None of this is feeling natural to me."

"If it was easy, wouldn't everybody in the world sleep with as many women as I do?"

Ridley went to the door.

"Chet, I can't do it this way. It's not for me. I'm going to talk to her."

He opened the door and walked out. Chet immediately ran to the door.

"Don't go over there. You don't know what you're doing! Aah, all right! Ruin it for yourself! Go ahead, ruin it."

# Ridley & Jayne—Friends & Thunderbolts

## Moments Later

### Jayne's Apartment

Ridley stood before Jayne.

Jayne's pajamas were hugging her hips, breast, buttocks.

Ridley noticed this.

As they talked he glanced at the bed. From where he stood he had an angle on her bed. The bed was part of his problem in this. Another problem was her scent, which he kept inhaling.

"I'm sorry for the way I acted tonight. Maybe we're not hitting it off as boyfriend and girlfriend but there are other things. Not every relationship between a man and a woman has to have sexual feelings involved."

He said this while looking at her breasts, her hips.

"There are other kinds of relationships between men and women. There's . . . mother and son. And lots of others."

She smiled and then went deadpan.

"You're a night owl. What time do you go to sleep?"

Ridley laughed. "Say you'll forgive me. You didn't catch me in a lie. I told you. No harm was done. I didn't trick you out of anything. I wanted to impress you. Now I feel bad because I have a high regard for you. I'm ashamed of myself. I'm taking enough punishment from myself. I don't think you want to chip in."

"Friends. We're going to be friends."

"Yes, friends."

### Thunderbolts

Ridley and Jayne were sitting and talking.

"I've been through it before," she said. "Where you think it's right, but you're wrong. When it's right, you feel the rightness of it."

"Thunderbolts," he said.

"Yes!" she said. "You feel a thunderbolt."

"It's mysterious."

"Yes, it's mysterious. You know what I mean then."

"I've felt thunderbolts."

"C'mon, when was the last time someone made you feel thunderbolts?"

"Maybe, uhm, . . . an hour ago."

"I do that for all the guys." She smiled. "You didn't really feel a thunderbolt an hour ago."

He answered with silence.

"I think," she said, "you thought you felt a thunderbolt because you wanted to feel one. You wanted someone who would make you feel a thunderbolt. And I happened to be the one standing there."

"Well, uhm, I think I know my thunderbolts." He looked up. "But I'll think about what you're saying."

# Chet Maneuvers

### Chet's House, Night

"Magic?" Chet said. "You two are talking magic. This is unreal. You ruined it. You went in and totally ruined it.

"Girls don't talk about feeling magic to guys they want to sleep with. They hide it from them. Let's play 'The Verdict' with your host Chet Clifford: The verdict is you lost. . . . You're killing me. You're killing me here."

### The control fit

Chet threw himself against the wall.

Chet was now leaning against the wall with his head buried in his hands. He was pounding the wall with his fist.

"Are you out of your mind? You just went in there and undid everything. Don't you want this girl?"

"But I don't want to take a chance on losing her."

"That's what you did. You lost her."

"How's that if we just became friends?"

Chet arched his back in agony and now directed his fit in the direction of the ceiling:

"Oh goddammit. What am I going to do with you—to get you to the light? How can I make you understand and see this thing?"

Now he talked to the wall. "How can I make you understand it's art? We're talking a pure true art. For real men." He was saying this to the wall. "How do you I make you understand? To see the beauty, the awesome splendor in a good seduction of a beautiful woman.

"And this girl Jayne is so sexy. She is just so damn beautiful and you could have been fucking her all night if you did this with some sensitivity and like a man taking a woman.

"You could have been pounding and banging her in her bed—instead you wanted to confess and talk things through.

"This isn't soul searching, this is the game of fucking women."

Ridley looked on—What the hell was this all about?

Chet turned to him. "Let's get to the heart of the matter. Do you want to fuck her?"

Ridley didn't answer.

"No," said Chet, "don't answer. You're you. I understand that. You have a different way to say things, a different way to experience these things, but I know what you want to do with her."

Chet concluded with:

"I've got to think," he said. "Give me a minute. This has a lot of moving pieces. Let me work through this. I don't believe in no-win scenarios. There's always a way to get past an ending with women.

"There are no dead ends—for men with true grit."

He walked out muttering, "Damn! This is troubling. What to do? What to do?"

Chet was on the strategic level of the great ones. He was on a tear— Chet was in the full throes of it now, as he exited the room.

### Chet's Bedroom

Chet entered the bedroom. He closed the door. And now had a talk with his private *"audience."*

These men and women in his audience were people like him. They could understand all of this. They could sympathize with his feelings here.

"So now they're friends," said Chet to the audience. "That's not the worst thing that could have happened. This may work out.

"Did you like the fit I threw? Very effective, huh? How did you like the part where I talked to the walls? It's a control technique. Very effective. I felt a strong impulse to punch one of the walls—I get these powerful sensations—but that would have been too much. You know what? Ridley isn't man enough for her. In a way it's for the best that now *I'm going to take her from him.*"

He looked at the audience. "Yes, we're talking a change of plan."

### A worthy adversary

"It's good for him. He needs a worthy adversary. To get him on his game."

"I was thinking about it as I made the speech.

*"She really is sexy.*

*"She is damn pretty.*

"You've seen her.

"I had this image of her getting fucked, and then I got this picture of me fucking her. And then I got a better idea of what to do in all this."

Chet moved about now very expressively. There was a lot going on emotionally here. Things were really heating up.

"It's rough. The world is rough for people like Ridley.

"The lesson here is that: *You have to watch out for number one.* I have to do what's best for me. And now that I think about it—*Do I want to fuck her?* I ask myself. Yes, I'd really like to fuck her.

"Oh, of course, I would never use that word with her. . . . *I would make love to her.*

"I'm very nice and gentle. I just think with what I'm seeing here that I could really be the kind of loving man she wants. She's looking for it. She's hoping to find a man who knows how to really make love to her.

"I'm realizing I'm it."

Chet let that sink in for a long moment.

"I'm going to be her next lover."

### Lesson time

"Do you want to hear the mistake he's making?" said Chet to the audience. "I'll tell it to you. A lot of people make the mistake. It's a real bear. Oh, it'll hang you up if you don't understand it.

"Are you ready for ultimate truth?"

He paused and let the audience consider the importance of it.

When the pause reached a peak, Chet broke the tension with a highly meaningful statement. Chet said:

*"An entirely virtuous person is not interesting.*

"You need color. Women love that."

"This is lesson time," Chet said. "Experience teaches you. And this is hard lesson time. I'll tell you, there's no substitute for experience in learning a thing. . . . The man who grabs a bull by the tail is getting sixty to seventy times the information of the fellow who hasn't."

### Destruction creativity

"This could totally break his heart, this could totally destroy him," said Chet. "But on the bright side he could learn something. He could be a new man once he sees where this is going now.

"There is an excitement, there is a creativity in destruction," Chet said.

"When you break something, you actually change the energy of it. For example, from glass to rubble. It's a different look.

"Smash 'em down. Tear it down. There's something in an explosion. You go, 'Wow.' "

He looked at his audience.

"Oh, good silence from you. Well done."

He continued.

"Mastering the flow—that's what we're talking about here. . . . I like things that stop the flow, make it back away or . . . make it go in a new direction.

"Think about it. You'll see what I mean. You have to master the flow with people. You have to be able to force feelings and thoughts to stop and find a new direction.

"Oh, yes, it's a great thing. . . . I like things that stop the flow and make it go in a new direction.

"And this'll be a really good thing for Ridley. He'll learn a lot of things about the flow of life."

Chet stopped. He looked up at the ceiling.

He turned back to the audience.

"Yes, this could be beautiful."

He thought about it.

". . . My God, . . ." he said. ". . . It's going to be so beautiful."

Chet left it there and exited the room.

## The Living Room

"She knocked you off the scene," said Chet.

Chet walked over to Ridley.

"Technically, this area is called 'Death.'

"You have to stop dying. It's not cool. Women don't sleep with dead men. True? Do you follow?"

Chet continued. "So how does a professional keep from getting good and dead?

"He uses allies. He has friends. . . . I'm going to step in and help you."

"How?" said Ridley.

"I'll go . . . and I'll have a talk with her . . . and I'll state your business . . . but very smoothly."

"Ah," said Ridley.

"Yes," said Chet.

"How would that work exactly?" said Ridley.

"Well," said Chet, "what I'll do is something very special for you my friend Ridley. We're pals. You two are meant to be together. I know that. I'm going to bring you two together. I want to see you two end up together. It'll do my heart some good."

"Hmm," said Ridley, ". . . on the bright side . . . I made it through. I'll live another day. I guess."

"That's right," said Chet. "That's the attitude. You're going to live another day. You now are dead. You soon will live. It's all good. You'll see. It'll be up, up and away—in no time. Very soon. We'll rally. . . . At ease soldier."

Ridley relaxed into his stance dutifully.

He held Chet's look with a level gaze.

"Thanks Chet. I'm glad for all your help. It means a lot to me. I really wouldn't know how to get through this without you. I would just be so confused. And I would blow it. It helps to get your wise, wise advice."

"Hey, we're friends. We're in this together—I mean I'm not going after her like you—I mean we're in this for you—For you two to be together."


# Invitation

*You and your smile hold a strange invitation*

### Chet's Bedroom, Day

Chet was dressing, before a full-length mirror.

He was a 'fashion model' getting into a suit. He knew his business.

The audience was, of course, watching in the background.

"Does everybody know why we're here?" said Chet.

"To hear a lecture on romantic literature," he said.

"No, no. You're going to watch Chet Clifford approach a young woman, a beautiful sexy young college graduate named *Jayne Holly Wyatt,* with lovely breasts, curvy hips and a cute personality. And you're going to learn.

"You're going to watch the Chet Clifford approach. You'll want to watch closely. Learn all you can. This is valuable. This is fantastic."

## 25 before 25

"She's going to be number 23. *Jayne Holly Wyatt.* Oh wow. You've seen her. She is really the most beautiful, the most gorgeous woman I've ever seen. I'll sleep with her—Then I have to start thinking about woman number 24.

"That's the important thing. I'm a businessman.

"She's going to be number 23. . . . You aim high in your objective, and then you go for it. . . . I'm only 24 years old. Hey, I happen to be wise beyond my years. But I've only slept with 22 women. She'll be number 23. I ought to have that done by the end of the week.

"Then I have to think about girl number 24. My goal is 25 women before I turn 25. See that's the important thing. You always want a clear goal and you want a way to measure against that goal. If you can't track your progress you don't know how you're doing.

"I set myself 25 before 25. It's a good, solid goal. Once you turn 25, it's time to settle down. You have to start thinking about your future."

He was finished dressing.

"Now it's show time," he said and he kissed himself in the mirror. "You're welcome to watch," he said to his audience.

## Chet's House

Chet and Jayne entered the house.

Chet said, "Yes, well, he is a little weird but he's a nice guy. His head is some place else. He lied about the job and all that?"

"Well he exaggerated," said Jayne.

"I haven't known him to do that," said Chet, "but it could be. A guy acts differently with a woman. I'm really surprised by what you're telling me."

"I think he's okay though," she said.

"He's a little naïve," said Chet. "That's what it is. He's a very good person but he's not totally in touch. You're a very attractive person and that threw him. Listen, I have some fresh-squeezed juice chilling. Would you join me?"

She looked at him.

Now they were each holding a glass of bright fresh-squeezed juice.

"What should we toast to?" he said.

"Success, success and, oh, how about . . . success," she said.

They connected glasses.

Chet took a sip. "He said that you're looking for a new job. I think I might be able to help. Give me an idea of what you want."

"Something I could stick with, where I could work my way up—I'm looking to build things up. I want a job with no ceiling. I'm ready to move up. And I want a place where I see nothing but sky above."

"Such as . . ." he said.

"Marketing," she said.

"And I work at a marketing agency," he said.

"Say, you catch on quick," she said.

"—Good! Excellent! . . ."

He took another sip.

"What do you do?" he said.

"Well, at the moment I'm looking for a job. . . ."

". . . Ah hmm . . ."

"I used to manage an international conglomerate with offices in fifty-seven countries but it went broke," she said.

"Ah, what a shame! I have some friends in that game. Perhaps they can be of some help?" he said.

"I'm thinking of opening up a gun shop," she said.

"I see—There's a lot of money in gun sales."

"No. Actually I don't sell guns, I just shoot them, . . . at men. . . . Actually, I'm looking for a job in the traditional sense. . . . Right now, as we speak, I'm in the reception game."

"Ah, the front desk game?" he asked.

"Yes receptionhood," she said.

"In the lobby of a company?" he asked.

"Oh, you're fast. Yes lobbyhood." She looked at him. "I also make some side money as a waitress."

"Do you know something?" he said. "I tell every young person that when you first get out of school you should spend some time in a service industry. It builds character. It's so important to develop a sense of dealing with people."

"You said 'young people.' How old are you?"

"I'm twenty-four," said Chet.

"Hmm." She took it in. She was an amateur detective always on the alert for true crime.

"How about you?" he asked. "You look younger than me."

"Yes, a few years younger, I just graduated," she said under the cross-examination.

"Oh, you're probably the same age as Ridley. He just graduated too."

"Yes, I know. But I don't hold it against him."

"Listen, I'm a big believer in networking. I do lunches, dinners, coffees with people. That's how I build business. How do you feel about networking?

"I'm all for it," she said.

"Excellent. Then let me toss an idea at you and tell me how you like it. . . . Let me suggest something—perfectly reasonable—that may sound off-the-wall but it's something you might want to consider. I work at a public relations agency—"

"—I know—"

"—Good. I'm supposed to have dinner with a major client. And I don't want it to be a business dinner. I want it to be social. So I arranged for it to be at a nice restaurant."

"And you want me to be your date."

"No. I would never ask you to pretend we're dating. We'll be completely straight. We'll let him know we're just friends."

"Why do you need me?" she asked.

"He'll be coming alone and so if I come alone, it'll just be business but I want him to let his guard down. If you come it'll be social. And we'll be doing us both a favor.

"Are you hitting on me? Is this a date?"

"No, I wouldn't tell him it's a date if it isn't a date. It's networking among friends. C'mon go with me. I'll give you some killer tips about how to network. And you'll be doing a great thing for me. If you're not there dinner is business; if you're there dinner becomes social. It'd be a favor. You toss one into the favor bank for me, and next time I'll toss a favor into the favor bank for you.

"Believe me, you're going to learn a lot about networking. I'm the best at it. And every day and in every way, I try to bring my friends along.

"You know what the secret of networking is? It's not about 'what you can do for me,' it's about 'what I can do for you.' That's how you have to think. You help others make connections and then they make connections for you.

"That's why it's great. That's why I'm so passionate about it. Doesn't that make sense to you?" he said.

"Yes," she said.

"Total sense, or perfect sense?" he said.

"Absolute sense," she said.

He waved his finger at her and smiled, "You're a naughty one. I can tell. I like that about you."

"And you look expensive. I like that about you," she said.

He laughed.

He said, "I tell everyone: You have to get out there—the view from behind your desk is a narrow one."

He was talking at a fast pace. He didn't want to give her time to think it through too deeply. All he needed was a "yes." There was everything good in it. He smiled a lot.

She was fascinated. He made an impression.

"What's the down side?" he said. "You have a nice dinner; I make a good impression; he has a good time. What's the up side? Possibly you get hired over there or maybe as we're talking we think of somewhere else you could get hired, which would be great—You'll see how good my company is and I'll have a friend in an inside position. Companies are always wondering, 'Should we keep our agency?' . . . 'Should we fire our agency?' . . . 'What kind of job are they doing for us?' . . . Having someone who could put in a good word is important. It's a crazy idea but what the hell."

She looked off into the distance, considering the idea. Then she looked up at him.

"Is that a yes?" he asked.

She smiled.

"Maybe. I want to hear a little more about this first."

She sipped at her juice and looked at him with a level gaze that did not blink.

Chet said, "I want to say something, and I'm not looking for remarks back or to put you on the spot in any way. . . . I just want to say you're a very attractive, beautiful lady. . . . I'm a man. I have to notice these things. And with you there's no way not to notice."

She held his look.

"And this wouldn't be a date?"

"Oh, of course not." He made a big show of a reaction to express his sincerity. "But if you want a date, just ask me out. I'm free next week. . . . I'm single and I'd be happy to be seduced by you, but I don't even know if you're single. Are you?"

She looked at him and held silent.

# Role Play

### An Office, Day

Chet was now visiting the office of his childhood friend, *Nathan.*

Nathan was a very straight-laced, straight-minded, orderly personality. He was a top accountant who thrived in an environment of stability.

"I need your help," said Chet. "I met this girl—"

"Since when," said Nathan, "do you need my help to make a girl?"

"This is a very special girl. I need a tailored approach with her."

"Why don't you ever try honesty?"

"I'm not here to kid around," Chet said. "You can't just conform in this life Nathan. You have to think outside the normal. I want to create an impression of strength. How do I do that? By talking strong? No."

He stood up.

"Come here. Shake my hand. But when you do it, I want you to pretend you're *the strongest man in the world.*"

Nathan shook Chet's hand as though he had some real muscle, the kind of heft that could break an arm off.

"You're doing it," said Chet, "the way a thousand other people would do it—Now shake my hand with *no effort.*"

Nathan shook Chet's hand again. This time with a light, easy, confident motion. And as he did, *Chet sank to his knees in agony,* as if his hand were being crushed by a steel vice.

They paused the lesson there.

"Wow," said Nathan.

"See that," Chet said. "My reaction makes you the strongest man in the world. You can't do it yourself. That's why I need you. I want her to feel she's with a guy that really has it going on right there." He pointed to his biceps, instead of his mind.

"I want her to see some depth.

"We'll go to dinner with this girl. I'll pay you to do this for me and you'll pretend to be a big client.

"Throughout dinner you will treat me with enormous respect and keep asking me for advice.

"Make me an authority.

"What you'll get out of it is: You'll be paid for your time. You'll get a fantastic dinner. And you'll learn how to seduce a girl, correctly. It'll be worth your while."

*Act Two*

---

# The Charming Dinner and
# The Lovely Evening
*Chet Clifford in the social element*

### A Restaurant Entrance, Night

Chet and Jayne were standing together at the main door of an elegant restaurant, as Nathan arrived with dramatic flair, escorting *a very attractive woman.*

Presently, the group was walking toward their table.

Chet took advantage of a fleeting instant of movement to whisper to Nathan. "Who is that girl you brought? Why is she even here?"

"If you invoke the strongest man in the world principle for tonight," whispered Nathan to Chet, "then I think she's necessary because how big of a client am I supposed to be if can't get a date? So I brought her."

"When did you start seeing her?"

"I'm not going out with her."

"No? How do you know her?"

"She only cost us an extra 50. And 50 is a great price considering how much more she normally makes for a performance."

"She's an actress?"

"No."

### The Restaurant

The group was being seated at a booth by the waiter.

"Business is great," said Nathan and he spread his arms wide. "Sales are going through the roof," continued Nathan, now spreading his arms upward. Then he brought them down with a passionate inward sweep. "Oh, I wish I had brought this month's sales report. Wait till you see it Chet. Phenomenal. Profits are going off the charts. It's an act of God."

"And public relations is part of the reason for that?" asked Jayne.

"A very big part. Chet is very good. His results are very good. Astonishing. We kill the competition."

"I don't know very much about public relations," said Jayne. "Maybe you could tell me what Chet does."

"He hasn't told you?"

"No."

"He should stop being so humble."

Chet tried to take over—

"We try to spread the word about what his company is doing," Chet said. "We try to get stories placed in the newspapers, television stations, radio stations around the country."

"He is great," Nathan said. "He can sell. They don't want to write about us—it doesn't matter. He sells them on it. He gets stories running on us everywhere: New York, Washington, Denver, the Mojave Desert. It doesn't matter. He sells. He's a supernova. He burns through the atmosphere."

"I'm impressed," said Jayne.

"Oh, sure," said Nathan. "He's great. His agency is the best too. Number one in the country."

"Really? Are you putting me on?" said Jayne.

"Well some might say that," said Chet.

"We're so lucky to have him," said Nathan, "especially now when we're expanding our marketing campaigns. Oh yes, he's putting together a real monster for us. We're launching a new product next season."

"Just in one city," said Chet.

"That's one plan," said Nathan. "The other plan is really big. We go nationwide right away. I want to win in the top 50 markets or nowhere. I say if you're going to take a risk go all the way. I never do anything unless it's going to be major. This new product is going to be in every store by the end of next season."

"That's impressive," said Jayne. "But as a practical matter Nathan, my goodness, what kind of budget does it take to go national?"

"You're going to see," said Nathan, "stories for it everywhere: The network news, the magazines, the newspapers—"

Suddenly Chet stood up.

"Uhm, sorry to interrupt but—" said Chet.

"—You'll see it on talk shows," said Nathan, "you'll hear it on the radio, you'll see it online—"

"Could I just show you something out front?" said Chet.

## The Restaurant's Entrance

Chet turned to Nathan.

"What if," Chet said, "I'm going out with her next season and your roll-out doesn't happen?"

"What do you think—two seasons?" Nathan said.

Chet looked at Nathan.

"Oh boy," Nathan said. "I got carried away, didn't I? I'm sorry. You know what makes me do it?"

"Stupidity?"

"No, insecurity."

"How do you figure that?" Chet asked.

"I didn't think she'd believe it otherwise."

"Just say we're launching in one city, as a test."

"But then the competition has time to analyze the product and create a counter-offensive. I think you have to go with a national roll-out—"

"You're going to get caught you idiot."

He grabbed his head, trying his darndest to resist smashing it into the wall.

"Keep it small," Chet said. And to himself he thought, *Don't kill him.*

## The Restaurant Booth

Everyone was now back at the dinner table.

"So you're looking for a job?" Nathan said.

"Yes," Jayne said.

"What are you interested in?"

"I'm looking for something with room for growth."

"Why don't you send a resume to my office. I'll see if we have anything for you—"

Chet stood up.

"—Excuse me—"

The conversation stopped instantly.

"—Could I just show you one more thing out front?"

## The Restaurant Entrance

Chet and Nathan were talking, in very discrete tones.

"How can you consider hiring her?" said Chet, keeping his voice low.

"She's a nice person," said Nathan, "a hard worker."

"Right."

"She needs a job."

"So?"

"What kind of person would I be to not hire her? She'd hate me."

"You don't have a company."

"She doesn't know that, at this point."

"What do you mean at this point? I'm not going to argue this one—"

"All right. All right. I'll just give her a business reference. How about that?"

"No reference. Nothing."

"Okay."

Chet walked away.

Nathan said to himself, "Not even a reference?"

## The Booth

Everyone was back at the table.

"Public relations is a great profession. A dream," said Nathan.

"Isn't the competition rough?" said Jayne. "And what about all the politics you have to deal with?"

"Overemphasized," said Nathan. "The happiest, most interesting people I know work in public relations. There's a little word association going on in my mind. You say *public relations* to me, I think of lots of happy people. . . . When you hustle, you have to have a hard shell. But it doesn't mean you can't be happy inside."

"If you'll excuse me . . ." Chet got up. "I'm going to the restroom."

"Do I need to come with you?" Nathan said.

"No. I don't think you need to see the bathroom."

"Right, that's what I was thinking too," Nathan said.

"I'll be right back," Chet said, shaking his head the moment he turned the corner.

## The Restaurant's Bathroom

Chet was there. The bathroom was there. A moment later, Nathan was there too—and a drink had been thrown in his face. He was wiping away the red wine, which was dripping down his face and shirt. His expression was anguished, on the verge of tears.

"What are you doing here?" said Chet.

"She threw a drink at me?" said Nathan.

"Who? Your escort?"

"No, the other girl."

"Why?"

"I'm so embarrassed. It was all my fault."

"What'd you do?"

"After you left I suggested very subtly, discretely, like a perfect gentleman I said, '*Why don't you unload Chet, I'll unload my girl and we'll get into something comfortable—like my place?'* It was just a question. Then out of nowhere she threw a drink in my face. I'm so embarrassed I can't go back there."

"You asked her," Chet said, "to sleep with you?"

"I didn't mean to."

"Then why'd it happen?"

"Insecurity," Nathan said. "I told you I'm very insecure."

"So you overcome it," Chet said, "by asking people to sleep with you?"

"If she had said yes that would have put me in a very secure place."

"You're going to apologize."

"I can't talk to her. I'm so ashamed."

"You're not going to say anything to her the rest of the night?"

"No. I'm not seeing her. I'm going home."

"You can't go home."

"I'm so embarrassed. Good night."

He started to leave.

"What about your showgirl?"

"Tell her she's got the rest of the night off."

"If you walk out that door you'll regret it. If not today, tomorrow. If not tomorrow, then soon, and for the rest of your life."

"Goodbye Chet."

They wrestled but Nathan broke free.

## The Restaurant Booth

Chet was now returning to the booth. With his head bowed, apparently making some heartfelt apologies on Nathan's behalf.

"He's flirtatious," said Chet. "In a way, it's a good quality. . . . He, uhm, . . . he just likes people."

"Oh, he's a people lover," Jayne said. "Why didn't you say so earlier?" Jayne looked at Chet. "Well, there you have it. I bring that out in a lot of people lovers."

"Yes, my career depends on that kind of people love," said the showgirl.

# The Girl, the Night & the Music

## The Living Room of Chet's House

Chet and Jayne stepped into the house.

"Try out that couch," Chet said. "Tell me what you think of it. I just bought that a few weeks ago."

She sat down. He took out a bottle of wine.

"Feel the contour of it. What do you think? It's the kind of couch that really tilts back."

She found that it was practically a bed.

He wanted to get her on her back.

She caressed the couch and slowly wiggled her bottom in the cushions, almost as though she were making love to it.

"Mmmm—oooo, yes. I love getting on top of something so soft but firm."

Chet had to stop a moment when she hit him with that line.

"Now," Chet said, "I want to hear what you think of this wine."

He poured them each a glass. "They say you should take a sip, work the wine around your mouth for a few seconds, then suck in a little air through the wine before swallowing. Or they have all sorts of other fancy ways to drink wine."

"Yes, I've heard about some of them," she said.

"I say drink it however you like. Don't let the proper be the enemy of the good."

Jayne drank a little wine. She sensually licked her lips when she was finished.

Chet looked at her tongue cross her lips.

And she said, "Like that?"

She smiled at him. And Chet got an erection—so stiff and hard that it startled him.

She just smiled at him. And looked pretty. And waited for his desire to grow and grow. Then she had a thought. . . .

"Oh, is Ridley home?" she asked. "Maybe he'll join us."

That didn't strike Chet as the greatest way to add to this moment.

But now all at once, she rose and began to cross toward the hallway and Ridley's room.

Chet popped up and stopped her.

"Uhm, that's okay. Sit and relax. Enjoy your drink. Let me go see," he said. "That'd be a blast if the three of us got to talk a little."

## Ridley's Room

Chet entered.

Ridley was studying.

"Would you mind," said Chet, "doing me a favor? Would you stay in here? I've got a girl and we're trying to get, uh, . . . comfortable. She's shy so I gave her the impression we're alone."

"How long do I have to stay in here?"

"Maybe an hour. What are you reading? Greek history? Oh, yeah, you'll overwhelm girls with that. Didn't I give you a list of things to read? Stick with the list. I love you but God your head is in the clouds. All right, I don't want you to feel worse about yourself than you already do. You have low self-esteem. Ah, it doesn't matter. You can cover that up. You know a book I might suggest to you. You might feel it's far afield but *'Secrets of the Central Intelligence Agency.'* You'll get so many good ideas on how to operate."

## The Living Room

Chet returned from Ridley's room.

"He's sleeping," said Chet. "I said come on, get up, it'll be fun but he's drained. The poor guy. He is just pooped. He studies until he collapses. He's set in his ways."

Chet refilled her wineglass.

"This wine," he said, "is not for the faint of heart, am I right? Although to the nose it's tame, more polite than forceful, it's a trick. In the mouth it shows plenty of fruit, fruit swaddled in tannins. It's a big, muscular wine that's going to take a few years to settle down."

He brought the wineglass to her mouth. She sipped it. Very romanticly.

"Mmmm . . ." Jayne said. "I love the mouthfeel—I love tasting it—and I love the feeling of having a warm liquid bursting through my lips and lunging deep into my throat."

Chet looked at her. He felt something warm shoot through his groin. And a direct thought came to him of what he would like to do with her later that evening.

But for now, abruptly, Chet said as innocently as can be: "How do you like dancing?"

Now Chet and Jayne were dancing.

He took her into a turn. Then into a closed dance position, into a social dance position.

"Jayne," he said in a gentle lover's voice, "today's dance style is a lot different than it used to be. It's a lot closer."

He pulled her in gently, sweetly, lovingly.

"And it's not because it's more sexual but it's because spaces are so much more limited. You don't have room on the dance floor to make big moves. Still it should be driving and sensual. You keep it gentle, tender. Indulgent yet with a forceful, decisive rhythm. In and out, and around."

He took her through some very sensual turns.

"Soothing, smooth. But determined."

He took her into some sweetheart cuddles and some fun ladies' turns.

"It's one of the last places where the man and woman still have the old sex roles. The man dominates and the woman submits—or follows, if you will—but with a silky give and take. That's where the art of it is."

"My, you're a good leader," said Jayne.

"Why thank you," said Chet.

"Would you mind if I lead for a while?" asked Jayne.

"You can lead?"

"Yes," she said.

"Are you a lesbian—I mean do you know how to lead the guy's steps?"

"No silly," said Jayne, "I'm going to be the guy. You're going to be the lady—And use your hips! I want us to look good."

"What?" asked Chet.

She took over.

She threw him into a dynamic move—in which she brought him into her, whirled him around, and then threw him out again.

Chet was stunned.

*"That move was good,"* said Chet.

Before he had a chance to recover, she took him into another move— Again she brought him in, and took total control, as she threw him around the room.

"This one," said Jayne, "is called the *'Lightning Bolt.'* Don't you love it? I came up with it. Isn't it fantastic?"

She completed the move with total grace and sureness.

Now she shot him a look.

"Hey, do you want to try some aerials?" asked Jayne. "That's where I toss you into the air."

"Ow!—You just pinched my ass!" said Chet.

"Heh, heh," she said. "I did—And just remember, Chet, if you ever try something like that on me—I'll slap you so hard you'll be lucky to stay conscious. No offense—But if you get fresh with me, I'll rip your frigging throat out of your lovely, handsome body."

And she laughed, a girlish charming giggle.

"Oh," said Chet.

"You don't need a lot of fancy moves," she said, "just a few good ones, done to perfection. It's always about perfection, baby. Perfection is a turn-on."

"Who taught you these moves?" asked Chet.

"Those last two, I got from Ridley."

"Ridley!"

"Yes, the night we went out. He's a good dancer. He's a little shy so he does them differently than I do, but yes the moves were his."

"I'll be damned," said Chet.

"Why?" asked Jayne.

"I was teaching him about dancing, a few nights ago."

"You? He's good."

"Oh, just about approach."

"Ah, that makes sense. You have an unusual approach."

She took him into spins, pivots—and then dipped him. It was a big finish.

*"Ooh, I'm tipsy from the drink,"* she said.

She gave the lead over to him for the next song.

They danced a little while longer and then—

—she started sighing. Taking long hot breaths.

It was a slow song. She laid her head on his shoulder.

She continued taking long, hot breaths.

He could feel her on him, and he was getting intensely aroused.

"I'm really enjoying talking with you," Jayne said. "Maybe we could take a rest and talk some more."

"Good idea," Chet said. "Let's lie down on my bed and we'll talk. Until we feel like doing something else."

# Relax Max

## Chet's Bedroom

Jayne was seeing Chet's bedroom for the first time. She entered doing a
dance and exploring the room with her body.

Chet watched mesmerized.

*My God, I... can't... think... with her around...* he thought. He really
did not have enought blood to fill both ends of his body.

She voluptuously entered the bed. *Oh my God! she's on the bed.*

And she continued moving the curves of her body in her dance.

"Are you aroused?" she asked

He was delighted. My goodness, that she would be so blunt. What
kind of wonderful was this? He joined her on the bed. He thought, *Yes,
we're going to hit the same town at the same time. Glory, glory, hallelujah.*

"Do you have a raging stiffness yet?" said Jayne.

She put her hand on his engorgement—that was flowing in upward
extension from his pelvic floor. She put her hand directly on it. No ifs,
ands, or buts. No coulda, woulda, shoulda. There was nothing moderate
about it. She was direct. She was firm. She looked him straight in the eye
and measured his reaction.

"Oh good," said Jayne. "Now, do you know what game we're playing?
Think really hard about what it is you see here."

"I think," Chet whispered, "I've played this one before. I'm very good
at it."

"No you're not," Jayne whispered in his ear. "You're actually quite bad
at this one."

She fell away from him and onto the plush mattress.

Now she stared, with a rocksteady gaze into his eyes. Her head was
beneath his. She was looking up at a dynamic angle. And she looked
terrificly sexy doing it. Everything about the light and the position flattered
her curves.

She rose onto her elbows and raised her head toward him. "I'm just a
country girl," she said through her sexy eyelashes, "and you've been trying
to take big-city advantage of me."

Chet froze and contemplated all the problems of the world in her
steadfast gaze.

She replaced her hand on his pelvis. More particularly, the area just
below his pubic arch—She held the head and the shaft of his being.

"Now," she said, "you're not going to do anything with this tonight.

You deserve a little frustration after all the moves you put on me in the living room."

She smiled, very pleased with herself.

He dropped down and kissed her.

"We will not be having sex together tonight," she said.

"I respect that. Of course. I respect everything about you Jayne. But why is that though, I might wonder?"

"It has to do with how men think. If I slept with you before getting to know you, that would mean I would sleep with other men before getting to know them. Would that make me more or less attractive?"

He looked at her. She had stopped him cold, with no effort, he thought. *Good God, she's not a pawn in the game. She's the queen of the chess board. . . . Well, how do you like that?*

Jayne was changing before his eyes.

"We're going to have a proper love affair," she said. "As the divine Dinah Washington used to say, *'Relax Max.'* . . . Yes, my pet, control yourself."

She looked at him.

"My pet Chet." And she smiled. . . .


*"Relax Max,"* she said.

"Your nerves are kinda bad there boy," she continued.

"Your heart is thumping with a crazy sound.

"Stay cool fool. Just take it easy, that's the rule.

"A kiss is no kiss without love.

"C'mon and relax Max," she said, completing the arc of it.

She was a take-charge girl. And she enjoyed taking charge of Chet's condition.

"Chet," she said now, "do you know how sometimes half the battle can be getting *'there'*?

He nodded.

"Well," she said, "this time your whole battle is going to be getting there."

He looked at her.

*"And the plot thickened,"* she said to him. And smiled.

"Slow down boy," she said. "I like to take things slow. Real slow."

"Slow?" asked Chet. "Hmm, slow sounds lovely Jayne."

He looked at her.

She had made their first love scene . . . into a scene about slowing down. . . . She had made it perfectly clear. This might very well be her pattern. He would learn, in time. He would learn. But at any rate—She was in control of the tempo. And she was a hell of an orchestra conductor.

In swift commanding strokes, she had slowed him down to a crawl. . . .

With the immediate effect being that—

It drove him crazy! He wanted her all the more. . . . Oh God did he want her now!

She knew that slowing things down could be very good for a boy, very exciting for the male of the species.

It allowed time for imagination to do its work. When you slowed a relationship down, the man's mind started to go to work. You see, story and imagination worked with great power in romance. . . . And . . . she held the power. She was *'The Girl Made of Cool'*—as her friend Ridley Richardson might say.

Chet Clifford was formally meeting . . .

Jayne Holly Wyatt. *The girl made of thunderbolt cool.*

. . . Chet looked at her. . . .

### Sex and the single career girl

They settled into the bed and lay beside each other.

"Now that we're finished with the activities for the evening," she said, "let's hear more from you. I want to hear about what you do with your days."

Chet said, "Do we really want to talk about work right now?"

"We don't, I do."

"Why is that?"

"We have to find out if there's a job for me at your office."

"Jayne, you're, uhm, . . . you're, uh, . . ."

"Unscrupulous. Ruthless," Jayne said. "A woman who wraps men around her finger and uses them."

"You wear manipulation well," said Chet. "But there's no way on earth we're going to start talking about work right now."

There was a . . . longish pause. . . .

He brought her closer, gently. . . .

### Surrender moment

He kissed her softly and delicately. She surrendered to it. It was terrific. It felt so good.

She closed her eyes and enjoyed it.

After a moment of dreamy intensity she opened her eyes and looked at him.

"You're a good kisser," she said. "How did you know the way I like to be kissed?"

"That was simple. The way you kiss me, is the way you want me to kiss you."

"Clever boy," she said.

"Why thank you Jayne. Any man can think it through."

"You think about these things?" she asked.

"All the time."

"Why is that?"

"You have to treat a lady right. You deserve a gentleman, Jayne."

He kissed her again.

He was fascinating.

Now he kissed her cheek. So softly, so tenderly, so lovingly.

He kissed her neck.

She was in ecstacy and hugged him. She ran her arms along his back. He was gorgeous. And he was wonderful in bed.

He brought his lips to hers and kissed her again.

He ran his hand along her belly toward her skirt. He was going to slip his hand into *her panties.*

She grabbed his hand by the fingers to stop him. Now she slowly but very purposefully twisted his fingers in a direction that fingers do not go. She twisted them back until he winced in pain.

Meanwhile, they just kept kissing as if nothing else was happening between them.

And she just kept bending his fingers back.

With his other hand—without breaking out of the kiss—he tried to stop her from bending his fingers any further.

He couldn't.

Her hold became more extreme.

He started moving his body back to adjust and lessen the agony. Too far back. He slipped from the bed onto the carpet.

She grabbed his arm and twisted it up his back until she was on the verge of causing him real damage.

Now she kissed him by bending over the bed and wrapping around his shoulder.

She did *all of this* as though nothing unusual was happening.

"Control—," she said, "this is about control Chet. Can you appreciate that—a woman with a high level of control over you?"

He liked the thought of it. And couldn't say why. This was strange to him. Why was this turning him on so much?

There was a strong sexual fascination between them.

And now they were done. They stopped kissing.

And just lay in the bed.

She curled up in his arms like a babe.

She was very happy and serene in his arms. She lay there. With him, at midnight, cradling her gently in his loving arms.

Things became quiet in that way.

She fell asleep.

Chet looked at her. His breathing became long, slow and deep. And he just continued looking at her.

## Chet's Bedroom, Later in the Night

### The sexy sleepover girl

Jayne was still sleeping soundly.

But now Chet was sitting in an armchair.

He turned to his audience and spoke, ever so softly, to them. They understood his predicament. They were good people. . . .

"Did you see how she teased me?" he asked in a whisper. "How she led me on? Now look at me. I'm sitting here and thinking about nothing but her body. And look at her."

He looked at her voluptuous figure.

"Isn't she marvelous? She knows how to play the game. You have to give her that. She's something else. What an act she has. And she does it all deadpan. She's hot. And she knows it. So she's playing it cool.

"I may have been wrong thinking I would go through her in one week. She's the kind of girl I could see myself being with for a spell.

"I'll be honest with you she's so on the ball, that if I don't act sharp, she might dump me. I better watch my ass."

He stopped, sighed, and stared at her. So pretty. She was so damned pretty, he thought.

## Chet's Bedroom, the Next Morning

Chet was sound asleep. Jayne was awake. She was peering out of the bedroom door. She closed it softly.

She woke Chet.

"Did you sleep well?" said Jayne.

"Yes."

"Could you check if Ridley is around?"

"Why?"

"I'm going to head home and I don't want him to see me."

"What's wrong if he does?"

"It might hurt him. I think he still may have left-over feelings for me. They're fading feelings, those kinds of feelings always fade, I know that, I know how men are, but . . . I'll tell him at a better time."

"Oh, is that what you're worried about? He likes you as a friend but he's over the rest. He's already past that. You don't have to worry about that Jayne. You don't have to worry about that at all. I'll talk to him later today. I'll feel him out. I'll let you know."

She looked at Chet lying there. He was gorgeous.


**About last night**

"I want to say something about last night," she said.

"You shouldn't try seduction games . . ." she continued.

"I see through you Chet. . . .

"Why do you play seduction games? Chet you're better than that. You're extremely attractive. I have to say, I, uhm . . . think you're very handsome."

"Thank you Jayne."

She smiled. "Yes, you're hot. There's so much about you that's terrific and turns women on but you shouldn't play games with this young lady— the lady said pointedly. You don't need it. You can get her just with—*you being you*," she said.

"This is a sincere moment, isn't it?" he said.

"Yes, it is."

"I could get to like these Jayne."

"Me too Chet, my dear."

She looked at him.

"You've got looks. You've got charm. You've got personality. Why do you pull moves?"

"Jayne, you bring out the devil in me. . . . I love that you see through me."

"Does your act really work on women?"

"You'd be surprised."

"No acting with me, got it?"

"Or what?"

"Don't make me get mean on you. Don't make me hit you with my fist."

"You are the sexiest woman in town. . . . No acting. I want to be sincere with you Jayne. . . . I make mistakes. Not because I'm really a devil but because I'm mistaken. I want things to be right when I'm with you. Help me when I go wrong, please, Jayne. Will you?

"Sometimes I do things I shouldn't. Not because I'm bad. Or that I mean to. . . . It's because I haven't thought them through. . . . Jayne please help me to think things through. . . . I want to do what's right by you. And when I stumble, please be patient with me."

"You're sexy," she said, "but the important thing is a foundation of . . ."

"Of what?" he asked.

"Of . . . friendship," she said.

He looked at her.

"Friendship?" He kept looking her. "Yes, you're right. Friendship is so important."

He stopped there.

She smiled.

"Now about Ridley . . ." she said.

# Openings

### Chet's Kitchen, Later in the Morning

Chet stepped into the kitchen. Ridley was preparing breakfast.

As he entered from the living room, Chet said, "What a beautiful morning!"

"Yes," said Ridley, "good morning. . . . Would you like some eggs?"

"That would be fantastic. I'll be right back." Chet turned around and went away.

An instant later, Chet was discreetly showing Jayne out the front door.

She dashed out, blowing him a goodbye kiss as she went.

And then Chet returned to Ridley, walking into the dining area, past a set of large day windows streaming with morning light.

"How's your morning?" said Chet. "It's a fantastic morning." Chet looked out the windows and continued talking to Ridley over his shoulder, "Oh, what a morning! My oh my, how I love this morning."

And now Chet turned around to face Ridley.

Ridley was cooking a full breakfast. And he looked up at the big day windows to glimpse that beautiful morning out there. Then he glanced at Chet.

Chet looked at Ridley. "And you're in a good mood too," said Chet.

"I feel good about my problem," said Ridley. "I see a way."

"With the girl?"

"Yes."

Chet sat down, joining Ridley at the breakfast table.

Ridley continued, "I was just doing some thinking about her."

"Ridley . . ."

"Yes . . ."

"I have an important confession to make."

"A confession? . . ."

"Ridley you're my friend so this is very difficult for me."

Chet paused and then said:

*"She's the woman I had here last night."*

"Oh . . . Did she leave after an hour?"

"No."

"I see. . . ."

"Did you sleep together?"

"Yes."

"Did you have sex with her?"

*"We made love. Over and over."* Chet said. He took a breath. He looked at Ridley. "And the truth is I really didn't feel good about what we were doing."

"Oh, I see. . . ."

And yes now Ridley did see.

This was the moment.

And it was the moment where it hit him, where it just absolutely floored him. He felt like somebody had come along and hit him with something very heavy. Just punched the life out of him.

He was dead again.

. . . And he knew . . . that he would be a long time dead this time.

After a quiet while Ridley said, *"Well, I really misunderstood things. . . . I've been a fool."*

"It's not you," said Chet. "It's me and her. . . . I blame myself. What I did is—I had mad, passionate sex with her. And I shouldn't have done that."

"Well," said Ridley, "maybe I was mistaken. Maybe I didn't have a hope. . . . And I don't have a hope now."

"No, don't say that."

"I want to face the truth. . . . I must have been out of my mind. What chance was there for me?"

"You're good looking. You're a wonderful guy. "

"You don't have to . . . I understand."

"You do?"

"If you care and you're going to make her happy—"

"But it can't be anything near the way you feel about her—"

"I have to think about what's going to make her happy. . . . If she's just not that into me. And she is into you. . . . If she cares more about being with you—then maybe she should be with you."

"Oh no, no! She's yours," Chet said.

"If you would make her happy, if you're what she wants . . . Well, I want her to be happy."

"No, fight for her. Don't let me get away with it."

"Do you fancy her?"

"Yes."

"Do you have honest and true romantic feelings for her?"

"Ridley don't let that get in your way—Yes, I have very strong, very sincere romantic feelings for her."

"You might be falling in love with her."

Chet suddenly became cheery. "That's possible," said Chet.

"Then I have to step out of the picture," said Ridley.

"You're her friend. And you should stay her friend," said Chet.

"Oh god," said Ridley. That caught him and then he caught himself and recovered. "Yes, I'm her friend. I . . . should . . . be . . . her friend."

Chet remained locked face to face with Ridley.

He draped his arm over Ridley's shoulder. And in a slingshot hold curled his arm around to softly touch the back of Ridley's head. Chet continued to stay face to face, to look him in the eye, like a father would a son.

"I'm sorry," said Chet. "I let you down. God, I'm so sorry."

"I love her so much," said Ridley, "that the only thing in my mind is her happiness. There should be nothing that comes before her happiness."

"You are such a *good guy*," said Chet. ". . . Do you notice that?"

# Ridley's New State of Being
*Walking alone along the boulevard of broken dreams*

## Several Days Later

### Chet and Ridley's Living Room, a Bright Afternoon

Ridley stepped into the living room.

He stopped abruptly. In front of him, Chet and Jayne were hugging.

Ridley watched them with an expression of suffering as he noticed how passionate their embrace was.

They both turned towards him and his expression changed—He smiled. He lifted his mood. And he beamed at them.

He acted as though he didn't have a bother in the world.

Jayne said to Ridley, "I just got a job working at Chet's company. . . . Isn't that wonderful?"

Ridley instinctively shifted his weight onto his rear leg.

"Congratulations," he said.

He caught himself falling backward and rocked his weight forward.

"That's great. I'm very happy for you."

Chet kissed Jayne on the cheek.

Ridley watched them—and inside he was now completely broken-hearted, but on the outside he played the part of a good sport.

# To Be Her Friend
*And how to do it*

### Ridley's Bedroom, Night

It was very late at night.

The world was fast asleep.

Ridley was lying awake, thinking about this girl.

And now to a "him beside himself" he spoke softly.

*"To not be in love with her,"* he said.

"To just be her friend—"

That was Ridley's struggle. To not be in love with her. To resist the overpowering romantic feelings for her

He observed his breathing, observed his spine tensing and tightening.

To release. To not be in love with her.

*"To not want her,"* he said.

"Don't be a selfish dog. Don't be a jealous dog.

"To not kiss her. To not make advances on her. To not make passes. To not think about her. To not want her—There I feel better already.

"I wonder what she's doing tomorrow. I wonder does she think of me like—Does she think of me at all?

He lay there for a moment.

"Don't focus on your needs," he said. "Don't think about kissing her. Don't think about doing things to her. Instead, focus on doing things for her. Put the focus on her. That'll make it easier. Much easier. Put her first.

"Just get through one moment at a time. And worry about the next moment, next time.

"Learn how to lose," Ridley said to himself. "Love was everything they said it would be. Now it's sweet and sad and you have to learn to lose.

He thought about that for a moment.

*"To not need anything from her.* To not be needy with her. To not pull from her.

"Don't be needy. Don't need anything from her. . . . Be her friend.

"Don't kiss her. Forget about kissing with her. . . . Be her friend.

"Maybe, she could use a friend. Her life is stressful. . . . Be her friend.

"Whooo. . . . This is rough.

"To not want. You suffer because you want, so don't want.

"So this is what clear thinking feels like? It hurts. Son of a bitch—It hurts."

# Ridley & Jayne & the Late Afternoon Sky

## A Few Days Later

### The Back Porch, Late Afternoon to Night

"How's the studying going?" asked Jayne. "It's animal behavior correct?"

"Last time it was," said Ridley. "I was thinking of becoming a zoologist for a while. I think that lasted a month. That was a rough month."

"You're off of animal studies?" she asked.

"In a way," he said. "The part I like is *man-watching*. So then I thought about anthropology. And then I thought about mankind's history."

"Ah huh," she said.

She smiled a kind smile at him.

"I understand," she said. "I love learning new subjects too."

"You do?"

"Yes. What do you want to do ultimately?"

"I don't know. There's so much."

"Yes, too much to get your head around," she said.

### Mastering world history

"I'll show you what happened, so that you can picture it.

"I started thinking about people. Do I want to study people? I picked up this book."

He went into the house. He pulled a book from the shelf. He returned to the porch and sat down.

"It's called *'Mastering World History.'* It's a small book considering the subject."

He gave her the book.

"I like small books," she said, taking it from him.

"Then you might like this. It takes world history and gives it to you in a very simple way. . . . See how, if you leaf through it, it gives you the fundamentals? . . .

"It starts with *'Primitive Man '*— Then *'Ancient History Begins in the Near East '*— *'The Early Civilizations of Asia '*— *'The Greeks'*— *'The Rise and Fall of the Roman Empire'* — *'The Middle Ages'* — *'The Barbarian Invasions'* — *'The Empires'* . . . The revolutionary wars . . . The world wars . . .

"It's a pretty good book." He looked at her. "As I went deeper and deeper into it, I found myself getting pulled in by what I was dealing with. . . . What I found fascinating was where the stories started and where they went. And now where some of them were ending up in our time, Jayne."

"But then I started following some of the offshoots. I was following the stories through science, biology, psychology, social studies, anthropology, physiology. . . . And then each of them had an offshoot. . . . And each of them was so worth looking into it. It just keeps going and going."

"So that's where you're at now?"

"Yes." He turned back to her. "It's difficult don't you think?"

She laughed.

"It's a universe. . . . It's like staring at a universe. . . ." he said. "I like what I see in it."

"And what do you see?"

"Hope," he said.

He looked up at her. Looked into her eyes. And held her tenderly with his gaze.

"Hope is a big thing. . . .

"If we can do this. If we can get through. . . . Things will be better."

She looked at him. There was a longish pause.

She looked down at the book. There was a stillness and a quiet.

They sat there together.

"There's something else . . . When you look into that . . . When you really look . . . What's interesting," he said, "is the structure, the frame of it, the fascination there, how it all works. How it all goes. . . . Do you know what I mean?"

"That there's some kind of order there?"

"Well, . . . what's fascinating . . ." he said slowly . . . ". . . is . . . that . . . it's . . . all . . . madness.

"It's absolute madness. The world is a madhouse. It's all insane. That's why it's interesting. You're looking at it. And you see all these levels of insanity and unreality. Levels you never thought could even be there."

She laughed.

"Yes, you look at the news headlines: In science, they're constantly finding things that don't make sense. You look at business—at politics—in every area there's constantly all this stuff that doesn't make sense. It's weird! Isn't it? And so you ask yourself, *'What's that all about?'* And then you start reading about it, and then you're hooked. It's got you. And it never ends. Oh, it's bloody exhausting.

"If life would make sense I'd have a lot less work. I could finish all my reading tonight, if it only made sense."

He was looking at her, . . . and she was smiling. . . . He felt that perhaps, . . . maybe it would be all right, . . . to keep talking to her . . .

"It's like a flower and the petals keep opening," he said.

"You're at one level of magnification and there are all these patterns so you go in for a closer look. And what was stuff now becomes new patterns at the next level of magnification.

"It keeps opening. The further you go in, the more it opens. It's the darndest design. And the more you look at the design the more darned wild it gets."

"Are you a thinker?" asked Jayne.

"No, I'll show you my problem."

He rose and went to the edge of the porch.

She joined him.

They stood there, looking outward, far outward . . . and upward.

"I look at the horizon," he said. "And I want to go to the next one. . . . And when I get there, . . . to go to the next horizon. . . . My problem is I'm a boy scout."

She looked at him.

He looked at her. "And when I get to the next horizon, the next beautiful, gorgeous horizon, I want to come back, and show it to you, and ask you what you think?"

"Or any girl," she said.

"Yes, or any girl—as long as she is you."

"Now you're trying to beguile me."

"I'll stop."

She was looking at him.

He was returning the look.

"So am I an original thinker? Well, I think my problem is I'm an original boy scout. It's a different problem. My problem involves more travel."

"Lots of time away from the wife and kids," she said.

"Yes, lots of maps. . . . Lots of asking yourself, 'Where the hell am I now?'"

She laughed.

"And when you're home what kind of husband would you make?"

"Same as I would a boyfriend," he said.

"Hmm. Would you be a good boyfriend?" she asked.

"I would be the best ever," said Ridley.

He smiled.

"You should be a boyfriend," she said. "You should be with someone special. I wish that for you Ridley. I hope you find her."

"Thank you Jayne," he said. "Thank you, that means a lot to me. . . . One day . . . One day she'll be there."

# Fascination

## Several Days Later

### Jayne's Apartment, Day

Ridley and Jayne were finishing a dinner together.

"What's it like working with Chet?"

As Ridley asked this, he was wondering if he could bear to hear it.

"He's a major talent. He's a superstar," she said. "No wonder he got me a job. It was just normal horse-trading for him. . . . Everyone worships him. He's a marketing wizard. . . . He might even be a genius. I was really amazed."

"Yes, I hear he's very charismatic."

It hurt Ridley in a way.

He wished he could be the charismatic man in her life.

He was her friend. . . . And he did enjoy that. He enjoyed listening to her. It was something he could do. It made him very, very happy to listen to her.

He looked at her. He didn't say anything.

She continued. "I've never seen anything like him," she said.

"He's a force of nature at a marketing agency. . . . It's more than the work he does for the marketing clients—It's the way he markets himself. I've never seen anything like it. Everybody owes him a favor, and everybody comes to him for every tricky thing. It's like he controls the whole place already. He's command grade. And he's only 24 years old."

In her mind's eye she could see him relating to the CEO.

"Murf—that's Russell Murphy—he's the CEO. Chet keeps telling him, 'You're a daddy to me.' You know what he says back? 'You're the son I never had.' That's for real. He's really become the professional son. Chet is so good at getting ahead, it's uncanny."

She continued. "At work everybody is his family. . . . His boss is his father. . . . The partners are friends. . . . The juniors are brothers and sisters. . . . Do you know what I mean?"

"Hmm, that is brilliant," said Ridley.

Just then, Chet walked through the door.

"Sorry I'm late."

He joined Ridley and Jayne. He gave a nod to Ridley, and squeezed

Jayne's hand. He was a gentleman.

"Chet always waits until the boss leaves," explained Jayne.

"Well, the man always works late," Chet said. "I work a few minutes later than him. So that I'm the last one out. . . . You have to play the game."

"How's it coming along?" she asked.

"He loves me," Chet said. "Everybody loves me."

He looked at Jayne. "Is that a new outfit? You look so pretty."

# Tenderness

### Later that Night

Ridley had gone home. Chet and Jayne were sitting alone on her couch. The lights were low.

They were looking into each other's eyes.

"I have to talk to you," said Chet, "about Ridley. . . . Do you know what's on his mind? . . . Ridley has been thinking of moving out."

"Why?"

"He wants to get an apartment of his own. He craves quiet. He studies a lot. And as much as I try to make our place a library atmosphere—there is still too much life."

"I'm sorry to hear that. I would really miss him."

"I walked in the other day. He was studying. I asked him why not at the library. They went to summer hours. . . . In my house, it's a separate wing. It's almost like someone living in a completely separate house. It's a nice space. Very comfortable. But I think for him, it's too lively. You get so much street noise. And there's me. It's not like here. . . .

"Your place is so quiet. . . . It's a perfect place to read and study. This really suits someone like Ridley. Do you ever notice that?"

She gazed around her apartment. She was thinking.

"Housing," Chet said, "in this city is very, very modern. . . . At our age, people move around all the time."

"Yes," she said, "that's true. My apartment is just somewhere I shower, change and sleep."

"That's right in a big city, you keep a lot in storage. Apartments are small. You move in and out of them. You can do it in a day. That's the way it is these days."

"I've been in five apartments in three years."

"I've lived in two places in three years," said Chet.

"Yes, the world is getting strange," she said. "Living in a big city is like camping.'"

"Camping that's exactly it. It's like a campsite. In the old days, you just picked up and moved. . . . In a way it was nice. You didn't get locked down. You had freedom."

He looked at her. She was still thinking.

"Ridley," said Chet, "is thinking of moving. . . . He's at that stage. . . . Why don't we help him out?"

"Help him move? Gosh, I like having him around. He's fun."

"Right, I have an idea."

"Oh, I can see the wheels turning Chet."

"What?"

"You're about to suggest that I move in and Ridley moves here."

"You just want to have sex," she said.

"No, of course not. I'm not even thinking that way—maybe if we were going out for a few years the idea might drop into my head."

She stroked his cheek. Blew air into his ear. Then blew air across his lips. All the while she studied him.

"Is that a yes?" Chet asked.

"We're going to stay strong," she said.

"Brilliant Jayne. You're brilliant," he said, and meant it in every way.

"How long can you stay this strong?" he asked her.

"Longer than you," she said.

"Hell, I could go another month," he said.

"I can go a year," she said.

"We could be dead in a year—I mean, so much could happen, don't you think?"

"You're growing weaker by the minute, Chet my pet."

"No, I can do it."

"What's today's date?—A year from today we'll talk about maybe sleeping together. In the meantime we can talk about life and get to know each other."

"A year?" he asked.

"It sounds reasonable, I think," she said. "Are we clear?"

"So where are we at exactly?"

"Kissing and hugging for a year," she said.

"It would be like a new job," he said. "And then after a year, maybe you get a promotion?"

"Just so," she said. "I'm glad we're both strong—It's just like running for president. You work your way through hell for a year and then, if you get the vote, you get to be president."

"There's an 'if' in there," said Chet.

"Yes, it's bloody fantastic, isn't it?" she asked.

He moaned. "Yes, strong. Isn't this a little bit strange Jayne?"

She said, "A year will go by quickly. We have so much to talk about. It'll fly by."

"Hmm."

She continued. . . . "It's discipline," she said. "We wait until the moment is right."

"It's a sexy kind of strength. It's strength of will."

Chet loved that. "Why—that's fascinating. . . . Strength of will."

Chet thought about that one.

"You know normally it's a very big deal for a woman to move in to a man's house," she said.

She looked at Chet and continued. "What if we do it for the summer?"

"How would that work?"

"Like a summer sublet. There's a lot of that that goes on around a university, every summer. . . . I'll just move in for the summer. Then we look at where we are in two months. . . . The move-in is a trial. It's testing with an exit strategy," she said and looked into his eyes. "We'll do a trial move-in and I'll be the judge. I'll come to a verdict at the end of the summer. Then we'll have a hearing. And that's when I'll do my sentencing. Now how do you like that? . . . Do you think you'll be able to live with that? Do you think you'd be able to live with my ruling?"

"You know I'll like it," he said. "Of course, I'll like it."

"Jayne, you'll help me," he said. "You'll tell me how to do what's right whenever it's in question. You're a good influence. And I want you to influence me."

"Chet," she said. And smiled. "I know the schemes you're scheming, and I know the dreams you're dreaming. . . . That was a nice thing to say. I expect great things of you."

She looked at him and said, "You have moments of brilliance. . . . Like no one else. You've got it Chet. Whatever it is, you've got it."

"I know."

"I'll move into your house, if Ridley will be fine with it. I want him to be happy. His happiness is very important to me."

## Chet's House, Night

Chet sighed. A long weary, drawn out sigh. A miserable, *'I'm in agony,'* sigh.

He did this as he sat down to talk with Ridley.

He looked anguished as all hell. This would be difficult on him. He wanted Ridley to know that.

"Ridley, I have something to say about Jayne . . . about me and Jayne . . ."

He looked at Ridley with a conerned, friendly look.

Ridley looked back at him. He was already dead. What could happen? What could make it worse?

Chet said, "What we want to do may be very difficult on you . . . and I have to tell you what's coming next . . . Jayne and I care for each other . . ."

"You want to move in together."

"You saw it coming?"

"I saw it coming. . . . But this was fast. . . ."

"Yes, . . ." said Chet surprised. "Fast."

# Beginnings & Futures

### Chet and Jayne's Living Room, Day

Jayne was moving in.
>They put down some boxes.
>He put his arms around her.
>They hugged.

### Ridley's Apartment, Day

Ridley stood in the doorway, sipping from a teacup. He was staring out at the landscape. He liked to stare at landscapes.

## Days Later

### A Hillside, Mid-Day

Chet and Jayne were on a hillside, having a picnic on a summit overlooking parklands and clusters of hillside estates.
>She was looking out at the landscape.
>Chet put his arm around her. They held each other tightly. A warm hug.
>It felt good, she thought. A hug that did not let go.

They were walking along a hill.
>"Sometimes I like to look at mansions," he said. "Eventually you have to buy one—it's the only place to raise kids. When we're talking about a mansion I think we could get a good one for a couple of million. In fact I saw one I'd like to show you."

Chet and Jayne walked around a bend in the hillside.
>"You have to look around. When you finally decide to buy one, you want to have an idea. It has to suit your personality."
>They stopped and he directed their attention to a striking mansion.
>"That's what I need to get. Something I could really be comfortable in. Where you live is very important."
>"That one is gorgeous," Jayne said.
>"That's probably a couple of million, but as long as I'm going to

spend that much on a mansion, I might as well spend a little more and get something I really like. You need a pool. And a vineyard. And acreage. I saw some Arabian horses that would knock your eyes out. You really have to have some room to raise horses."

He took a breath. "Yes, it's good to look around."

### Flying in the big steel thing

Soon they were looking by helicopter.

The mansions they needed to see were so big and secluded.

"I need a lot of land. . . . I need grounds. . . . Because I like to play polo."

He turned to her. "Do you like to play polo, honey? . . . You ever play polo, darling?"

"No I don't."

"I'm going to teach you. You're going to love it. I'm going to teach you how to play polo. You know, I came in second in the—What did I do with the trophy?"

He looked down at the ground.

"That's not large enough for a polo field," he said. "Do you like an Olympic-sized pool?"

He turned to her again. "Right now, you want to know something— I'm a businessman. Right now real estate is bad, very bad. We could get that same mansion for $2 million less."

The helicopter glided along more terrain.

The hills passed underneath.

It was a lovely day. Sunny. With blue skies. Just a perfect day.

Chet sat back. And relaxed.

He was enjoying the feel of flying.

He really liked this helicopter. It had good vertical thrust. . . . He thought about it. He did an asset list of the helicopter's virtues.

It was a beautiful craft.

He turned to the pilot and called out to him, "Hey, if you wanted to buy a helicopter like this, how much would it cost?"

When they landed, off they went. He took her to play tennis. And she really enjoyed it. He was great fun.

# Ridley & Jayne & the Breeze

## The Balcony Outside Ridley's Apartment, Late Afternoon

Ridley and Jayne were sitting in yard chairs, staring outward, sipping tea.

They were talking about life, and relationships.

"Where do your relationships come apart?" he asked her.

"Well," she said, "I'm a bad girl. I'm a very bad girl. You haven't seen that side of me. You haven't seen how bad I can get. I can get downright mean. And they say 'like attracts like.' So I enjoy bad boys. That's where the fun starts. And the danger. That's always where these things come apart for me."

"What about the idea of opposites attract?"

"Yes, opposites attract . . . then drive each other crazy."

"Or live happily ever after."

"I'm thinking about it. . . . But . . . bad girl meets nice boy. Thunderbolts ensue. I don't think it works that way for me."

"And there has to be thunderbolts."

"I think so."

"Yes, I agree Jayne. There has to be thunderbolts."

"Yes," she said.

She took a sip.

"I think . . . I think . . . I like guys that are hard to get. That might be it. I don't know," said Jayne, "I keep falling for the guys that are hard to get."

"Oh," he said.

"And when I get them. When the guy wants me, I . . . well . . . I . . .," she said, "I react . . . It gets odd." She left it at that.

"What do you like about bad boys?"

"I get turned on by masterful men."

"Are you masterful?"

"No."

"Then I think opposites attract."

They each sipped their tea.

"That's a nice tree," she said.

He was looking there too. "Yes that's a really nice tree," he said.

It was nice. They both were having a nice time. And now both were sipping their tea again.

**The Street Leading to Chet and Jayne's House, Night**

Ridley and Jayne turned to each other.

Jayne said, "Ridley, nothing can change the fact that you and I once had a good time together." And she smiled.

"Goodnight Jayne," he said with a tender smile.

"Goodnight Ridley."

They separated. And off they went.

# The Haunting

**The Gym, Day**

In the morning, Ridley had told himself that he had to put himself in motion.

Ridley spent the day exercising. He worked himself to exhaustion. Worked himself to pieces. Worked himself through one exercise after another until he couldn't breath, couldn't stand.

He had attacked the gym. And attacked. And attacked until he couldn't attack anymore.

Finally he paused and looked around. *Was it all finally burned off?* he wondered.

"That was a good workout. . . ." he said to himself. "I wonder what she's doing—*Err, stop it Ridley.*"

He had spent the day trying to burn off all of the waves of painful energy he was feeling. He had exercised like mad. It persisted, this thing.

**Ridley's Apartment, Day**

He couldn't control himself. He would be doing ordinary things around the house, and suddenly he found himself saying out loud:

*"Jayne Holly Wyatt."*

He lay down on the couch to read a book. And her face flashed before him. He put down the book and stared into space.

He made himself a cup of hot tea. He brought the cup to his lips and sipped.

*"Jayne Holly Wyatt,"* he said.

It happened there too. . . . Everything reminded him of her and everything made him think of her. Walking made him think of her. Sitting made him think of her. Not thinking of her made him think of her.

Thinking of anybody or anything in the world made him think of her.

"This has got to stop," he said. . . . It didn't.

He took his cup of tea out to the balcony. He sipped it and stared out at the trees.

He marveled at the agony of it. At the complete and totally agony of it. It was really a many-sided agony. And filled with many levels of anguish.

He wondered about the pain. . . . About how very much pain he felt and how there was just no way to stop it. It was a new side of life. It was *hell.* He was getting a chance to live through *hell.* He explored the experience. Hmm, he was getting a chance to experience *brutal pain.* So this was what *intense bone-crushing pain* was like. This was what it felt like to love a woman who did not love you.

*Well, on the bright side,* he thought, *it's better to be in love than not to be in love.* And that nice, bright thought *hurt.* Damn it all, did it hurt.

*I'm very lucky,* he thought, *when you take the broad view of it. It's a good kind of pain.*

He continued to stand there on the balcony looking out at the trees. He lifted his cup of tea through the pain. And took a sip, trying to enjoying what he could of this feeling—of this wonderful feeling that was so very much like falling off a cliff to your doom. He sipped the tea and stared out at the trees.

*"Jayne Holly Wyatt,"* he said aloud to the trees.

# A Friday Dinner

### Chet and Jayne's House, Night

It was dinnertime. . . . Jayne was on the phone.

She was calling a *secretary* from Chet's office—or what was more fashionably called a *junior associate* in the consulting professions. This beautiful young lady's name was Amanda.

"Hello," said Amanda at the other end of the line.

"Hi, it's Jayne. . . . Sorry to bother you at home. You went over to the client with Chet today didn't you?"

"Yes."

"He seems to have . . . disappeared again." Jayne tried not to sound needy. "Did he go out with Russell again?" she asked.

"He didn't call you?" said Amanda.

"No. . . . He doesn't have to. I'm just wondering."

"Well, he's probably just working on developing the Russell thing. You know Russell is thinking of starting a new division and putting Chet in charge."

"Yes, I know."

"It's in the works."

"It's a good thing."

"Yes, so it eats up hours. What can you do? . . . He'll be home soon."

"Yes right. What can you do? Okay, good night," said Jane and hung up the line.

### To not be needy
That was what Jayne was going through in this moment.

To not be a jealous dog. To not be needy.

"When you have time on your hands you start thinking thoughts that you shouldn't be thinking," she said to herself as she sat down on the couch.

"Chet is a very busy boy. I'm needing to be with him but I shouldn't. We're in two separate time continuums. He's busy. Beyond busy. I'm open and making dinner.

"Okay . . . slow down. Don't be needy. Pull yourself together young lady.

"Don't start thinking thoughts you shouldn't be thinking."

She sighed, "Oh, what the secretary must be thinking. Okay fix it. This'll be good for you."

Chet had told her, *'You're in your world. That's what people respect. They don't want to see that you're worried about anyone's reactions. You are. But you don't let on. You come on with an attitude.'*

*This is like being possessed,* she thought. *I wonder if you can get rid of this with a witch doctor? . . . No, Jayne, you just have to talk yourself out of it. Don't let him get so far into your head. You're young, you're beautiful. Every guy wants to catch you. Don't let so much become about this.*

She was thinking about these things as she called Amanda again and said, "Chet just got home, never mind. . . . You were right. Boys will be boys."

"Oh, good," came Amanda's voice.

"Thanks. Goodnight Amanda. See you next week."

"Goodnight Jayne."

## Amanda's Apartment

Amanda put down the phone. . . . And turned to Chet.

They were having drinks in her apartment.

Chet came to her. "Ready for that dance lesson?" he asked. He put their wine glasses down.

They came together into a closed dance position and slowly started dancing to strains of soft music in her living room.

And the world disappeared around them.

It was a romantic interlude, a moment between Chet and a strong candidate for woman number 24 in his life.

## Jayne's Living Room

She had told Amanda 'he just got home' almost as a throwaway. She probably got the tone right, she thought.

Jayne was thinking about other things now. Although she had to ask herself: *Why did I tell the secretary that? Ah, what does it matter? What now my love? Did I just think my love? No, I didn't.*

Odd things were bubbling up. And coming out in her.

She wanted to redirect her attention. . . . "Ridley, I'll ask Ridley to come over and we'll have dinner. . . . He'll get my mind off . . . he'll get mind off . . . sex? Why would it be on sex? Stop it Jayne. Call Ridley."

Jayne called Ridley.

"Chet isn't making it to dinner. . . . It seems a shame."

## Ridley's Apartment

"You're asking me if I want to have dinner with you?" he asked.

"Yes," came Jayne's voice.

Well, it turned out that Ridley would indeed like to have dinner with her.

Presently, Ridley made himself ready and rushed over to Jayne's place.

## The House

"You're not eating much," she said. "Don't you like it?"

"It's very good. . . . I have trouble paying attention to food and paying attention to you at the same time. . . . I'd rather pay attention to you."

She looked at him.

"We cover such great ground when we talk," he said.

"Yes," she said and smiled. "We do."

She took a bite.

"What should we cover next?" she wondered aloud.

"What do you know about posture?" he asked.

"Not much," she said. "Why? Is it an interesting subject."

"Maybe. . . . I guess it depends on how you think about it?"

"Oh. . . . Well, how do *you* think about it Ridley?"

"I don't know. . . . Your posture is your attitude. . . . It's how you say, 'I'm great. I'm wonderful.'"

She was intrigued.

"Posture is not just internal, it's also in relation to your surroundings.

"Posture is not just inner space, it's also outer space.

"It's how your body opens up to the world. How it opens to these walls, to this room, to this space . . . to the people around you."

Ridley looked at her in a bashful way. "Maybe it's not for me to say but you're tense."

She looked at him. She became still and turned her attention inward. That was an interesting observation he made. "Yes," she said. "I am tense. . . . So how do you tell that?"

"You're curled forward. Normally you're not."

She held still and listened.

"Think about the wonderful spring in your body. The spine is really a spring. Now it's designed to be an S-shaped spring but when people stress out, when they become tense they crush it down a bit into a C-shaped spring."

"What?" she asked.

"They tip it forward when it should go upward. Light and easy. Like floating upward. . . . When your spine is relaxed and extended, when you have your full height, the spine is a stretched out S. Going up to the ceiling or to the sky.

"You have three big bony masses attached to your spine.

"Your body holds weight in but 3 ways: it can sit, hang or brace. The head sits, the ribs hang, the pelvis is braced.

"When your spine is in its proper shape. It's holding those 3 weights in that way.

"Starting from the bottom. Starting where you sit. Your hips. . . . If you follow your spine up. . . . It curves inward between your hips and ribs, then curves outward over your ribs, and curves inward again at your neck. It's an S and at the top is your head, sitting on the S.

"Now when people get tense they curl everything inward. To a C shape. You curl your neck so your head tips forward and comes down towards your chest. Your shoulders curl in, your rib cage sinks and shoulders come forward. Your hips and ribs curl toward each other taking out the curve in your lower back. . . .

"It's like a cat, when he gets scared to death. Yikes! Suddenly his spine curls. . . . With people, everybody does the same thing under stress."

He stood up and came to her. "Can I just show you some small things?"

"Yes, please," she said.

He sat next to her and showed her. . . . She did what he did. . . .

### Your Hips
"Okay, roll your hip forward a little bit so that you're on your sitting bones more squarely. Now extend straight up into your ribs.

### Your Ribs and Shoulder Blades
"Take your shoulders up, then back, and then bring them down. That rolling of your shoulder blades engages your lats, your back and side muscles, and opens your chest."

### Your Head
"Tuck your chin in a little to make the top of your spine extend. Bring your head back so that your ears are above your shoulders. Imagine that the top of your head is a crown and it's being lifted up or that it's floating up. . . ."

**Your Look and Attitude**

"And lastly, the final step in this is you look outward and you open your visual field. Spot the wall over there."

She did all these things as he was saying them and doing them himself.

"Now relax in that position and tell me—what do you think? Tell me your thoughts. What do you feel?" he asked.

Her posture was much better, much more open. Now she also took a beat to become more relaxed and light. To float herself upward a little bit.

She turned to Ridley.

"Thank you Ridley," she said. "This is interesting."

"Yes, balance is a wonderful thing," he said returning to his seat. "I have to keep reminding myself all the time. It makes life so much easier and so much more fun."

She looked at him as he crossed to his chair.

She hadn't noticed it before, but he seemed to be a body floating upward.

He gracefully seated himself. His movements were so light and easy, she thought.

She laughed. Not because it was funny, but because it was cute . . . and new.

He smiled back, adoring her.

He said, "You'd be a great *Miss America*—but I'm drifting off the subject. . . ." He caught himself and continued. "Want to try something?" he asked. "Go back to the way you were a minute ago and compare."

She went back to a tight curled spine. And then opened up again and relaxed.

She laughed.

He laughed.

"Where did you learn that?"

"I saw it in a little green book once."

"And you forget the title."

"Yes, I can't remember the title."

They both smiled.

"Ridley, you're sweet," she said.

"Thank you Jayne," he said.

She ate a little.

He shifted in his seat. And took a breath.

"Hey, Jayne, I'm attending a lecture next week. . . . Would you maybe come with me? . . . You might enjoy it. . . . It'll give you something a little adventurous to do on a slow night."

"Hmm," she said and looked up. "What kind of lecture?"

# The Lecture

### A Small Classroom, Night

Ridley and Jayne were seated among a group of young people.

Presently, in came *an old man*, with a strange aura about him. This was the star lecturer. He might have been in his late eighties or early nineties.

At first he seemed to be a walking mummy. He seemed to barely be able to see, hear and walk. He shuffled into the room, and sat down to rest from his entrance.

He was a tiny man with tiny movements. But this was only what he seemed to be.

What Jayne soon discovered was that when he stepped from his seat to lecture at the podium he willed himself to become someone else. To enter a totally different state of being. . . . At that point, he came abruptly to life and became a roaring emotional bull of a man. A man filled with a beaming passion for life and discovery.

Jayne was watching him with interest. *What a cute old man,* she thought. *And how strange.*

### The lecture

Now he spoke. And when he spoke, he spoke with great color:

"Let me tell you a story—", he said. "This happened to me roughly sixty years ago—

"My professor asked me to drive him to a night class that he was teaching. He was legally blind at night and needed people to drive him. I said I would do it. And so I stopped by his house one evening to take him to this night class.

"He let me in. Then immediately started to ignore that I was there. With his back to me, he said, *'You're early. Have a look around.'* Then he sat down and started reading. He didn't say another word.

"He didn't seem to have any manners. There I was doing him a favor. But he didn't look ready and he wasn't making any attempt to get ready. He was going to wait until the last minute to hurry out. Then I would have to race to get him to class on time.

"I took a look around his living room. There were some cabinets with mementos and junk. He ignored me completely—as though I didn't exist.

"I walked through the rest of his house. It had some more old junk, some sculptures. Abstract ones. Who knew what they meant?

"I went out to his yard—more abstract sculptures! It all looked like stuff that a child could have done.

"I went back to the living room and sat down. I was getting very angry. Who was he to treat me in that way?

"He said, *'Are you finished looking?'* I said, *'Absolutely.'*—Just then he turned to me. And suddenly he had this tremendously broad, friendly smile. . . . He said, *'You're a quick looker. Let me show you what you missed.'*

"I said, *'What do you mean?'*

"He said, *'Follow me. I'm going to show you what you looked at and didn't see.'*"

"We saw some really marvelous things.

"He was *hard*. And I don't like someone to behave *hard*, when he has a guest in his house. But he had a point. Sometimes you have to forgive the circumstances and enjoy the moment. . . . I was always an observer, but I didn't always see what I was seeing."

# Weekday Chet

**The Driveway of Chet's House, Morning**

Chet was going to his car.

He was opening the driver's-side door, when he found himself saying: *"Jayne Holly Wyatt."*

He stopped. He looked around. There was no one on the street.

He paused. "Why am I saying that out loud to myself?"

Soon Chet was entering his office.

He was pulling the chair back and was about to sit when he said, *"Jayne Holly Wyatt."* He stopped in place—"Why am I saying that out loud to myself?" He shook his head.

# Sunday Chet

**Chet's House, Morning**

Chet and Jayne were sitting on the couch.

"I want to travel with you," said Chet.

"My, oh my," she said. "Do you fancy me Chet Clifford?"

"It's more than fancy." He drew a breath and released it slowly. *"Jayne Holly Wyatt. . . . I . . . am . . . I'm in love with you."*

"Well . . . I didn't see that coming."

"Neither did I," said Chet.

"I can't believe I didn't see it."

"Maybe you looked at it and didn't see what you were seeing."

# The Next Friday

## The Street, Evening Twilight

Ridley was stepping out for an evening walk when he crossed paths with Jayne on the street.

She was returning home carrying a paper bag loaded with vegetables and groceries.

"How are you?" he asked. "Looks like you're cooking again tonight."

"Yes, I love to cook. . . . Hey, I've really been thinking about what your teacher said."

"Have you?"

"He was right. On so many levels."

"Good I'm glad."

"Yes, Chet and I had a talk about it. It helped a lot."

"Huh? You and Chet. I'm not following."

She smiled demurely like a little girl.

She looked at Ridley and said in a kind of whisper, "Can you keep a secret?"

"Yes of course."

"Okay, don't tell Chet I told you this. You promise?"

"Yes, I won't tell Chet. What is it?"

"Well, when we started going together we struck a kind of romantic deal. It was my idea. I led him to believe we wouldn't have a sex life for a long time. Until it was really the right moment. Do you know what I mean? I can't believe I'm telling you this. . . . I really don't know why I'm telling you this?"

"Jayne . . . what are you telling me?"

She took a deep breath, and then blurted it out—"We've had a love life with no sex life. Do you know what I mean?

"Do . . . you . . . mean . . . the sex hasn't been good?"

"No, silly. I mean there's been . . . no sex."

Ridley fell back a step, onto his back leg.

"No?" he asked.

"No."

"Oh," he said, rocking back onto his forward leg to her.

"The truth is," she said, "I've been making him go slow. But I think it's time . . . for us . . . to have a sex life."

"What's the hurry?"

"Ridley!"

"No offense meant. I'm sorry I didn't mean to say that. It just came out. I don't know why. You're right. I'm happy for you Jayne."

"Thank you Ridley. . . . I was waiting for the perfect moment. The thunderbolt moment that I'm always waiting for. . . . Maybe waiting for that moment gets you nowhere.

"But I realized something important. . . . Sometimes the moments that you want . . . don't come in the ways you expect. . . . Unprepared perfect can happen all the time. All around you. . . . Isn't that a beautiful thought."

She hugged him.

"I hope it happens to you Ridley. I hope you find love."

"One day Jayne. One day. . . . Goodnight," he said.

"Goodnight my friend Ridley," she said. She smiled and walked away.

He walked away, slowly. . . . Very slowly. . . . Not sure where he was now meant to go.

# The Strange Moment

### Ridley's Apartment, Early Evening

Ridley stepped into his apartment.

"I'm not a jealous dog," he said. "Never be a jealous dog."

"To not blow up. To not go mad. To not lose it. To not go crazy and embarrass myself . . . in front of Jayne."

He sat down on the couch and took a very deep breath. He calmed himself.

Everything seemed to be racing. He was hearing a beating of nine thousand drums.

"Where are we? . . . Where are we Ridley? . . ."

He tried to control himself. To continue taking deep breaths. To calm himself.

"The stakes—he's upped the stakes. He ups the stakes, and then he ups the stakes again.

"This is war."

Ridley calmed himself and considered this for a moment.

"It's war . . . War. . . . War. . . . War. . . . Oh my God."

Ridley continued, "Holy shit, son of a bitch. This is street-style war. This is a street fight. I let him get a mile-long start over me.

"Ridley you son of a bitch this isn't about friendship anymore.

"This is war. It's time to woo her. It's time to see if I have a chance in hell of winning the battle. It's time to fight."

"Some people like to be chased," he said.

"Oh my God! That's it. . . .

*"Some people like to be chased.*

"She's beautiful and sweet and a wonder—and she likes to be chased. Okay Ridley, let's start chasing. . . . The first thing is to outrun Chet. . . .

"I've been standing still while Chet has been advancing for miles."

He brought himself to his full height. And then standing tall, he walked out of the apartment.

He crossed to the door and opened it wide.

"Let's go get our heads kicked in by love," he said.

And he exited.

## *Act Three*

---

# Jayne Holly Wyatt
*The Girl Made of Cool*

### Chet's House, Night

Ridley rang the bell to Chet's house.

The junior associate from Chet's office, Amanda, came to the door. It threw Ridley. He'd never met her.

"You're in the right place," she said. "I work with Chet. I'm Amanda. Come in."

"Nice to meet you. I'm Ridley. Is Jayne around?"

Chet stepped into the living room.

"Hello Ridley. We're in a little meeting. You look unsettled. Are you all right?"

"I'm fine."

"You need Jayne? She's in the kitchen."

"Oh, thank you. . . . If you'll excuse me then," he said to them.

And he went into the kitchen.

Chet and Amanda sat down on the couch and Chet whispered to her.

"That's the one I told you about. . . . I think he's having sex with her."

"Him? Really? He seemed so sweet."

"Can you believe it? And whatever happened to hiding an affair? I bet you if I asked her, *'Are you sleeping with him?'* She'd say, *'Yes.'* She's that kind of person—At least, have the decency to lie to me."

"She sounds like a bitch."

"I don't want to go that far. But I appreciate what you're saying. Why can't every woman be like you? Sweet. And simple."

He moved closer to her.

"We should go over this proposal."

Their work was laid out on the coffee table. He patted her knee.

"We'll be together soon. . . . Don't worry. . . . It won't be long. . . .

"I can't lay it on Jayne yet," he said. "It's going to make her so sad. I hate to do it. It's going to hurt her. And it's not just about me. I have to watch out for her too. Listen, her lease is for another month. Now that's not the deciding factor but if she has to move, I have to consider her situation. She has bad credit. I didn't want to say anything but she has really bad credit. . . . She owes a lot of money. Maybe I shouldn't say that. But that's part of it. There's a lot going on with her.

"Listen she knows a separation is happening. You see we're in separate rooms already. It's almost like she's just a roommate now."

"But you said she has a lease," said Amanda. "How does that work? She was your girlfriend but she had to sign a lease?"

"Oh, I can explain everything."

"Yes. . . ."

"She wanted a lease. She's independent. She wanted to pay rent. . . . Listen, I think that's a good quality about her. Don't you think? How can you fault her for that?"

"It's strange."

"Yes. Yes, it is strange. You're right. Yes. You're very right." He was trying to induce a trance in her, and get past the logic traps in this story.

"Thank you," she said. "You're so sweet. You always say such nice things."

"Well, you bring out the best in me. You have so many good qualities yourself. Do you know that? Do you notice that?"

She smiled.

## The Kitchen, Early Evening

"Are you okay?" asked Jayne. "You look red."

"It's just an adrenaline rush."

"Oh, a nice Friday night adrenaline rush," she said.

"Yes, a nice Friday fight-or-flight response."

"You just get them out of nowhere?"

"Almost . . . Jayne, do you remember how I said you were *'The Girl Made of Cool'*?"

"Yes, I do. No one plays the love scenes like you."

"Sometimes I don't have the words to express myself. I didn't then. I want to do a better job tonight. Right now. This is *part two* of my *'Girl Made of Cool'* speech. There's somewhere I wanted to go with the speech. I didn't have the words. Maybe I do now. Maybe I could just say a little if that would be all right?"

## The Question and Answer Path to Enlightenment

"How does Chet lead to your enlightenment?

"Let's talk about *'The question and answer path to enlightenment.'*"

"The what?"

"Here it is, for you."

"Go."

"Question and answer. . . .

"A question that you can't let go of, causes stresses. You keep thinking about the question. You get locked in on the question. The answer brings the release. 'Ah, I get it.' And then you don't have to think about the question anymore.

"The questions and the answers are the path to enlightenment. The question is conflict. It's tension. The answer is the release and it's enlightenment.

"So I have a question for you. . . .

"The question is, 'How does Chet lead to your enlightenment?' How does he make you more of 'The Girl Made of Cool'? "

"Oh, I see," she said. "But Chet is . . . fun. Dastardly, and naughty, and loads of fun—that's his reason for being."

"But what comes next?" asked Ridley. "You're going to have sex, but are you thinking about what comes next—what's out there? Are you thinking about Europe, and South America, and Africa, and Asia, and out to Australia?"

"I'm about to have sex and you want me to think of Australia?"

"Exactly. Yes, now you got it."

"Ridley!" She pinched his cheek. "You're adorable."

## Cosmic being

"Let's just talk a minute about cosmic being. *The Girl Made of Cool* is a cosmic being.

"She's the enlightened version of you. She's your future. I can see it.

"I know I'm sounding like a little kid. . . . But goddamn it it's true. . . . Just please stay with me and listen. . . .

"It's like an iceberg. The girl made of cool is this enormous cosmic being. We only see a little of her at any one time. But there's the whole iceberg under the surface. Right now, she's in Chet's house about to have sex with him and talking to me. But below that—"

He paused, to quickly resume, "—No, it's *body and soul*. That's what it's all about. She has body, and she's filled with soul. She has both—You see there's body. Chet has body—There's soul. I've got soul—She has both. Do you see how that works?"

"Wow, that's a hell of a cosmic being."

"That's what I was trying to tell you that night we had the fight—She's the girl made of cool. That's you."

She gave him an odd look.

"The thunderbolt sensation you're looking for is enlightenment. Let's call it that. It's the answer. The moment of, 'Ah, I get it.'—You got it? Are you following me?

She gave him another odd look.

"Let's go to the garden. . . . Let me show you something," Ridley said. "Please."

He moved toward the door that lead to the garden.

She followed.

They stepped into the beautiful meditation garden that had always been a part of the old house.

Ridley and Jayne crossed the porch and stepped into the garden.

## The Garden, Early Night

The garden was lit with an orange and yellow glow.

The fading twilight was still casting its dark bluish velvet glow across the sky.

Out in the distance were the stars, the moon, the hills. There was fertility all around her. It was the full bloom of summer.

"I'm saying too much." He took a deep breath. He released it smoothly. "I have a better way."

She looked at him.

"Are we ready?" She gazed into his eyes.

"Listen to this . . ." he said to her.

She entered a state of expectation. This was interesting. What would he say next?

He looked at her.

What next?

He did not speak. The world went quiet. Silence entered the corners. The world stopped moving on its axis. Time froze in place.

She felt quiet calm and she noticed her new state.

She looked out to the garden and then turned her gaze to him.

He was looking intently.

He smiled.

She smiled.

"*This* is it," he said. "This is what I've been trying to tell you."

"Well," said Jayne, "maybe a few words would help it. What is *this*?"

"*This* is us," he said.

He leaned back. That was how the conversation broke off.

There was a calm there. It was interesting to her.

Silence.

She spoke first, "What else?"

"You're waiting for thunderbolts—What if they happen all the time?"

"Yes, what if."

"Maybe, you've been getting thunderbolts all along," he said, "and you just didn't know. Maybe they're just garden thunderbolts, or porch thunderbolts, or small shivers of heat that you feel. . . . Maybe you looked and didn't see what you were seeing.

He continued. "Maybe you get smooth bolts. Or maybe you get cool bolts. Maybe, maybe, maybe. . . ."

She thought about it. And she said, ". . . Maybe . . ."

"I figured it out. It's not a thunderbolt. It's this . . ."

"And what is this?"

". . . Stillness."

It brought out a laugh from her. "Indeed. I will think about that."

She went to the door. "You're being wonderfully mysterious. Keep it up Ridley. I like you when you develop an edge."

She looked at him as she backed into the house.

"Good night Ridley. I enjoyed our talk. Let's pick it up tomorrow."

She softly turned and entered the house. The door fell closed lightly behind her.

Ridley stood there.

He breathed deeply.

He went to the door. It was locked. It had locked itself. "Damn."

He knocked.

Presently, Chet came to the door.

"How's it going Chet?" Ridley said.

"Well," said Chet. "How are you enjoying my garden?" He smiled.

"I forgot to tell Jayne something important."

Ridley walked into the house.

"Go ahead," said Chet, "but do me a favor wrap it up—what are you telling her the story of the rise and fall of the Roman empire? Tomorrow's another day, you know what I mean sunshine?"

Ridley walked off.

As Chet came back into the house, he and Amanda exchanged looks.

Chet nodded to her as if to say, 'Do you see what I mean about them?'

Amanda mouthed the word 'Wow.'

# Connections

## The Kitchen, Night

Ridley joined her in the kitchen.

## Connections make the size of reality

"It's the pauses!" he said. "We're good on the pauses."

"Pauses and connections. We're good on connections."

"It's about connections. That's what that was all about. Making connections. Seeing many different directions and connecting them. So that you live in a bigger reality."

"Reality is only what you're aware of," said Ridley. "That's your reality. It's not even what you are potentially aware of. It's just what you are aware of. That's your reality. ... And the more connections you make, the bigger your reality. ... Most people live in a small reality, but you have the potential to live in a huge, bloody massive reality Jayne—That's why you're beautiful."

Ridley continued. "To reach it you need moments of enlightenment."

"So that's where my question comes from. *'How does Chet lead to your enlightenment?'*"

Ridley paused and then said: "Am I sounding like less of a lunatic yet?"

## The Living Room

Chet and Amanda were sitting silently, trying to overhear Ridley and Jayne.

"I can't hear a word. Can you?" she said.

"It's no use. I don't think they're talking. I think they're hugging."

"Do you think so? Right out in the open like that."

"Some people have no shame."

Now Chet gently touched Amanda. They got caught up in the moment. He moved towards her, and she moved her lips towards him.

## The Kitchen

"The size of reality," she said.

Jayne looked at Ridley. And then she continued.

"Getting a picture of reality," she said. "That's what we're talking about?"

"Yes," he said.

"Getting a larger sense of reality," she said.

"Yes," he said.

She suddenly had a bright thought:

"Come with me. I want to show you something," she said.

### The Living Room

Jayne and Ridley emerged from the kitchen.

Chet was startled. He moved quickly to recover. He put a hand on the Amanda's forehead, to feel her temperature.

"You don't seem sick," he said.

"Maybe I just have a headache," she said.

"Gosh, I hope it passes. We're up against a deadline here."

Jayne observed this for a flashing moment and then withdrew her attention. She strode from the living room. And Ridley followed.

The instant they made their exit, Chet raised his chin high and turned to the secretary.

"Do you see what I mean?"

She nodded. She was quite appalled at Jayne's scandalous behavior.

# The Rock 'n' Roll Session
*Let me hear your body talk*

### Chet's Bedroom, Night

Jayne and Ridley entered the bedroom.

"Here we are. This is Chet's bedroom. This is Chet's bed. . . ."

Ridley's eyes traveled to Chet's massive bed.

"We're two people in love. We're going to talk and kiss. Share our love for each other. If I'm wrong, then it's intercourse, physical commerce, carnal knowledge, coitus, sexual congress."

As she talked, she demonstrated some of the sensual motions they would get into.

"Getting it on, getting your snack on, doing it like animals."

She described and demonstrated the love-making with enormous delight.

"Thrust. Penetrate. Ram. Bend each other over; enjoy each other's curves; lick each other; have a baby oil party; have a hot time in the old town; get happy as a clam at high tide."

She looked at him. "Everybody out there would love to spend tonight the same way. Will you answer one question for me?"

"I will answer any question you ever pose to me."

"Can you truthfully tell me that you don't want to spend tonight the same way?"

Ridley froze, rigid, solid, like a shock victim.

"A-ha! I'm right. I'm right. I know I'm not wrong. It's all perfectly natural. You study everything. You should know about these things. It's not dirty. Or obscene. It's a thing of beauty.

"Rock 'n' roll—This is called a rock 'n' roll session. Have you heard the expression? I've heard that is the original meaning of rock 'n' roll. And who doesn't like at least a few rock 'n' roll songs?

"You're jealous," she said. "I can see it in you, Ridley. I have x-ray vision.

"Here's what we're going to do, that's what's getting to you.

"You're jealous, because you can't get started with me—I mean with someone too."

She smiled.

"This is animal behavour. Fine young animal behavior." She was throwing him all the names for 'fucking.'

She could make a pro blush—

He was on her eyes. Her gaze. Her beautiful eyes.

"Let's get physical. Let's get animal."

"It's body talk, baby. The sleep drain. The elements of horizontal style."

"You can sit in your room and worry about things. Or you can run, live fully, and get into the fundamental things that make life so worth living. There's nothing to be ashamed about here."

She looked at him. "That's what this is about."

"There isn't anything wrong here baby. This is horizontal blues music."

Ridley was seeing her. Seeing her in close-ups on her legs, on her neck, on her breasts.

"It's a good 'going over,'" she said. And she smiled in a very sexy way.

"Jayne ... you're ... being ... cruel ..." he said.

She stopped.

"What ... What do you mean? ..." she asked.

He suddenly looked very sad and alone.

"Why would this be ... Why's it cruel ... to you? ..."

"I ... don't want to say." Ridley let out a breath and looked down at the floor. Then back at her direction.

She didn't know what to say.

"It's okay," he said. "You didn't do anything wrong Jayne. It's me. Goodnight."

He walked away.

He left.

He was gone now.

And she looked—at the empty place where he had stood.

## The Living Room

In the living room, Chet continued putting moves on the secretary.

Ridley came into the living room, to find that Chet had his hand on the secretary's breast.

Chet immediately reacted. "Jesus," he said, "how do we get that stain off? Maybe if you put some seltzer on and dab it."

Over his shoulder to Ridley he said, "You think seltzer, right?"

Ridley acted as if everything was perfectly normal. He casually waved goodbye to them, as he walked toward the front door.

"Good night you two."

As Ridley opened the front door. Jayne appeared at the far end of the hall.

"Good night Ridley," she said.

"Good night Jayne," he said.

He walked out the door.

Jayne paused a moment to look at that door. Then Jayne continued down the hall and went into her room.

Chet turned to Amanda.

Chet gave Amanda a good long look.

She took in the look.

## The Street

Ridley was striding away—in inches.

He slowed down. Then went slower still.

He stopped.

He punched a shadow foe in the air.

"Ah, damn it," he said.

He turned and walked in a wide circle around Chet's house.

*What to do?*

To do something or just do nothing. He marveled at his fate.

He saw Jayne moving in her room through the lit shade.

He went to her window.

Her curtains were closed so he couldn't see into her room.

He climbed over some bushes to her windowsill. And drew a deep breath.

He saw Jayne's shadow moving.

He tapped on the window.

Her shadow stopped.

And then she appeared at the window.

"Jayne, I'm disturbed," he said. "May I say one more thing?"

"Of course, Ridley. . . . But first, . . . I, uhm, . . . I'm sorry if I teased you. I was being naughty. I don't know. Maybe you disturb me too."

"That's okay Jayne." He leaned against the window. "Whatever you do is always okay with me."

He looked at the window. Then to her. "May I come in for a moment again?"

She nodded.

He climbed in through the window. She helped him in.

### Jayne's Room

Now they stood before each other.

She said, "Where do we go next? Are we going to do silence again. That was fun but it worked better in the garden."

He was silent for a moment.

"Well, this is a different kind of silence." He took a breath. "Jayne, here's what I think I see. . . .

"What I'm starting to see in Chet Clifford is the gravitational pull of society. And orbiting bodies.

"Bear with me please. This is another one of those thoughts, and what I'm thinking is. . . .

"He'll always be looking to get into better orbits. That's the kind of man he is.

"He's attracted toward the center. And that's where his talent is. He's very good at going deeper and deeper toward the center.

"Some of us don't move toward the center," said Ridley.

"I see," she said.

"Yes," said Ridley. "Some of us move away from the center. . . . And some are in between."

He smiled at her.

"That's what I see in Chet," he said.

She was affected by what he said.

"I've been with him an awful lot," she said, "and I don't see the same person you do."

She looked disturbed.

"Well, I worry," he said. "Make sure the things you think are in his head are really in there."

He took hold of her hand.

And slowly, slowly . . .

He kissed it.

It was a significant moment.

She was somewhat turned on by it.

She combed his hair back lovingly.

Then she quickly recovered.

"The food . . . I need to check . . . on the food."

She was actually quite flustered now. And had to break away.

## The Living Room

Chet and Amanda watched Jayne pass them and head into the kitchen.

Now Ridley entered the living room. And he was a sight. His face was red and scratched from the bushes. His clothes were spotted with dirt from climbing through the windowsill.

"Hello," he said with great cheer. "It's good to see you again. Let me tell you why I've returned."

He considered how to explain it for a moment, then noticed their looks and decided to shorten his formal remarks—They were looking at him as though his hair were on fire.

"No, you know what—I'll be back in one minute."

Ridley left to join Jayne in the kitchen.

"Do you see?" Chet whispered. "And he acts like this all the time."

"He's terrible."

"I hate to talk out of turn but that happens to be what he is. It's like letting a rhinoceros into the house. I'm not going to be judgmental but in one night he's come through the front door, the garden door and her bedroom window. I'm not going to say anything but I'm aware that this is happening."

"Where do you think he'll enter next?"

"I don't know."

Chet moved away from the secretary.

"Pardon me a moment please."

## The Kitchen

Ridley joined Jayne.

He said softly to her, "I really care about you and I want you to have the best, . . . and that's it," he said. "I fumpher. . . . I do that. . . . Tonight . . . I fumphered and fumphered and fumphered. I hope some good came out of it."

She looked at him in a very odd way this time.

She seemed to be . . . about to say something—

Just then Chet stepped into the kitchen.

"Hey, you two," said Chet. "Listen, we're finished working and Amanda's going home. Why don't you come say goodbye to her—Was I interupting?"

"Oh no," said Ridley. "Not at all. Your timing is fine. We were just saying goodbye."

"Again," said Chet.

"Yes," said Ridley, "you want to get a goodbye just right."

## The Living Room

Chet and Jayne said goodbye to Amanda who walked off.

Now Ridley came to them.

"Good night again Jayne, . . . Chet." Ridley nodded respectfully to Chet as he walked away and through the doorway.

Chet smiled. "Hey, thanks for coming by Ridley. It's always nice to see you."

Jayne waved to Ridley. "Goodnight again Ridley."

Ridley left.

They closed the door.

"What were you talking about?" asked Chet matter of factly. As a throwaway line.

"Nothing. He had an eventful day."

"Oh, is that so? God bless him. He's such a sweet guy."

"Yes, he is," she said.

She embraced Chet.

And they stayed that way a while.

# Chet & Jayne Night Sessions

### The Living Room, Much Later

They were having a candlelit dinner.

The strains of soft music were playing in the background.

It was all quite nice. Just a wonderful moment between them and they both were enjoying just being with each other.

### The Living Room, Later Still

Now it was getting quite late.

Jayne walked out of the living room.

Chet lingered to turn off the lights, to lock the deadbolt on the back door, and to close the blinds on the picture windows.

Once Jayne was gone, he spoke in an aside to his *'audience.'*

Tonight the audience was in a kind of hushed, muted state.

"Oh my god," he said, "she is going to have such a good time tonight. I'm going to make sex so wonderful for her.

"She's special. To me she's very, very special.

"I hope you're learning a little something. Watch how I make the night even more special for her. Watch the master at work.

"I'm going to take her to a breath-taking, out-of-control climax. I do it with them all. She'll be scratching and biting. She won't be able to get enough. How do I get her into that state?

"What's it any of your business?

"Nah, I'm only kidding around. You've stuck with me this long—and what—now I'm not going to tell you? Of course I'm going to teach it to you.

"Well, you might call what I'm going to do now more show than tell.

"Boy, we're going to have a good time tonight."

### Chet's Bedroom

Chet and Jayne were standing in the room with the massive, very comfortable cushioned bed.

"Let's go away together next month," he said.

"Where would you like to go?"

"East, or west, or south, . . . or north. Any of those. Which would you like?"

"Hmm," she said. "Chet, that'll be fun. I can't wait."

"I can't wait either Jayne."

They kissed.

They walked together hand-in-hand to the bed.

They sat and kissed and lay down together.

At the end of a long sweet lingering kiss, Jayne said, "That was nice."

They looked into each other's eyes.

"Chet, do something for me ... before we make love."

"What, what is it sweetheart? What would you like?"

"Tell me about the other women."

"What? What part of it?"

"It's okay with me that you've been with other women. But before we do this, I need to know. Have you been seeing any other women while we've been together?"

"No, of course, not. But we've been friends Jayne. We haven't had sex until now."

"Have you been tempted? Have you wanted to sleep with other women?"

"No, of course, not Jayne."

"There are a lot of beautiful women out there. Not one. Not even one has tempted you? The whole time we've been together?"

"No one Jayne. Just you. There's only you." And he said it so incredibly sweetly that it made him adorable. He was filled with sincere and total love for her.

"Chet ..."

"Yes ... Jayne."

"It would be okay to admit it."

He paused. Took a breath. Looked her straight in the eyes.

"There's nothing to admit. Jayne, there's only you. . . . I . . . *love you Jayne.*" He was so sincere and handsome; he was dreamy. What a handsome, loving man.

"Chet ... sweetheart ... it's okay." She stroked his head and ran her fingers down his hair. It drove him crazy. "Sweetheart, it's okay to admit it. . . . Please tell me."

"Jayne ..."

"Please sweetheart ... I want to hear. . . . Men have normal urges. . . . There's nothing to be ashamed of. . . . Nothing ever to be ashamed of. . . . Please sweatheart tell me."

He looked at her.

"Have you slept with anyone else?" she said.

He looked at her.

"Who was she, Chet" she said.

He looked at her.

"Oh, . . . Jayne . . ." he said. "It was just once, . . . it didn't mean anything and it's over now."

Now she looked at him. And he realized nothing was moving. She didn't move a single muscle except to breath.

"Chet . . ." she said. She was just looking at him now. Not moving.

*"That was the wrong answer,"* she said.

"What?"

Now silence. She wasn't moving. She wasn't saying anything. She wasn't giving him anything he could react to.

What seemed to Chet like several hours later, she said . . .

"Oh my God. You've been sleeping with another girl? While saying you love me?"

"You just said it would be okay if I admitted it."

She sat back and just nodded her head as she took it all in.

"You slept with somebody? Do you love her? You must. Why would you want to sleep with her if you didn't love her? I don't want to come between such a relationship."

"It's over between me and her."

"I wouldn't be so sure. Maybe you're in a transition phase. Give it another try. Don't drop her just like that. Forget me. Get me out of your life.

"I could never forget you. What you and I have is different—I love you."

"You slept with her and you didn't love her? Why would you want to sleep with somebody you didn't love? Where's the joy in that? Did you tell her that you didn't love her before you slept with her?

"I don't remember my exact words.

"Who was she?"

"Let's calm down and talk this through."

"We are talking this through. Who is it?"

Jayne gave it some thought.

"Your secretary?"

"Let's leave Amanda out of this. Besides what I had with her is in the past—I mean with whoever it was."

"You're sleeping with more than one person?"

"No! Just Amanda—I mean just one person—will you quit twisting this around! You're putting words in my mouth."

"Why didn't I figure it out before? You spend long hours with her. The secretary, who was just here? . . ."

She gave Chet a piercing stare—

"You didn't look like you were very affectionate, considering you slept with each other. Trying to hide something? Were you trying to fool me? Was that what it was Chet? Was that what you were trying to do Chet? Lie to me? Snow me? Very good Chet."

"Don't get worked up. It's over. This is now, that was last week. Listen she's a very attractive woman. Any guy would get involved with her. Did you see the body on her? I didn't know how strong our relationship was. I didn't know how in love with you I was. Now I know and her attraction has really dropped. From a ten she's dropped down to a three—three and a half, I swear. She doesn't compare to you—I really love you. She was a slip. I slipped with her. I didn't sleep with her."

"What's in it for her? She knows we're together so why does she do it? Let's figure this one out? Is she going to get a promotion? Am I going to walk into the office in a month and find out she's my new boss?"

"Probably not."

"You've lied to me. Used me. Why? Sex? All this just to get me in bed?"

"Do you have to hurt me? Why do you put it like that?"

"Why did you do it?"

He wouldn't tell her.

"Give me a reason."

"Maybe you need to cool down. If you go in your room for a while, I would understand. Just take a few minutes. Go in there. Or I can leave you here. Just breathe easy for a few minutes. And then we'll talk."

"I'm not going anywhere until I have the reasoning behind this—What were you thinking?"

"We'll talk about this when you calm down. Go back to your room. You'll feel better, if you give yourself some breathing time. You'll see."

They were standing now.

"Why lie to me? Why such a big lie? Why a lie so deep? Why so thick? I want to know why?"

"Who," he said, "am I really hurting? . . . Myself. My own spirituality."

"What really happened?" she said. "What was really there? . . . If you're going to be glib I'm really going to lose it on you."

"Okay, okay—just calm down."

"No—why. Tell it to me."

"You're not in a state to hear it."

She bolted forward.

Stopped herself.

She shouldn't kill him. Not until she got her confession and the truth out of him.

He said he was hers. He lied. Many men lie—but only Chet had raised it to the level of bastardy. And stripping him to his bones would be her revenge and justice done under this moon and night sky. In this place— that Chet noticed was growing very, very hot. He was sweating now. And extremely bent out of his bastard shape.

He needed recovery time. He said, "Go in your room Jayne. . . . Go . . . in . . . your room."

"Chet, don't make me hit you with my fist." Perhaps she needed a little recovery time herself. She let out a breath. There. Now an audible sigh. "Oooh, . . ." She looked him in the eye. "I am *not* going to hit you. I'm the kind of lady, . . . that . . . I don't do that."

She walked out.

He stood there. Then he heard shattering sounds.

"Krrsh! . . . Ka-krssh . . . Krssh!"

It was a sequence broken up by subtle banging and thumping sounds. Then more shattering.

There was a definite melody. For those who appreciated the musicality in such moments.

## The Kitchen

Chet found her standing there, very poised.

A set of broken dishes happened to be on the floor.

She was taking a plate, holding it out now, releasing it, letting it drop to the ground.

It shattered on the floor.

She took another plate, held it out, released it.

It shattered on the floor.

She picked up another plate.

He looked at her.

It went the way of other plates.

"I want to hear '*why*,'" she said. "I want to hear it from you. I enjoy listening to you . . . darling. I want to hear your reasoning."

"What you know, you know," he said. "Why does anybody sleep with anybody? And so what, honey! She's just another one of the bunch. I can't turn my life around in a second. I just have to get used to the fact that we're in a serious relationship. It doesn't happen overnight. I have to break my old habits. But I'm trying all the time. I'm working at it."

She proceeded efficiently, she was releasing piece after piece of his precious collection of fine china.

They were making a kind of abstract art formation on the floor. All these little broken pieces. It was quite a lovely pattern, when seen from a certain vantage point.

How receptive to the beauty Chet was, . . . well, that was very hard to tell.

He walked out.

## The Living Room

As he walked through the living room, there was the sound of shattering chinaware in the background.

## The Bedroom

Chet was back in the bedroom.

He heard shattering in the background.

Then silence, a pause.

Now new noises.

A little closer and louder.

It sounded as if she had moved into the living room.

And that big heavy things were suddenly being thrown.

He heard a loud crashing sound. Then there was banging and breaking involved.

## The Living Room

He came into the living room. She had taken some heavy objects and thrown them at some other heavy objects.

She had smashed some things. . . . She had made a quick decision, when what was happening between herself and him had escalated to a point of life and death. She knew she had to act. . . . It was better to smash "things" than to smash Chet in the face.

"Oh my God," he said—*She had smashed his television set!*

He walked over and looked. There was a stick speared through the television. His television was dead. She had killed his television. It had been a widescreen set. Such beautiful sound. So stylish. So modern. . . . Now all that was over. . . . He would have to get another television.

He had entered the living room. She was still pursuing him. And not with any intention of having some tranquil moments on the couch.

She was suddenly on the other side of the Jayne Holly Wyatt spectrum. There was no physical sign of the sweet Jayne. . . . She was now a very strong character. A tall, lean elegant lady fitted in steel and fire.

With smoldering eyes and commanding presence. Sexy as hell. But dangerous. Very dark and dangerous.

He was meeting a Jayne Holly Wyatt he had not even known existed.

She was sexy as hell. That's what she was to him. But she was out of control.

"Straighten up and fly right Jayne!" he said.

"I want to hear what you were thinking," she said.

"That was a wide screen television," he said, "with surround sound! All right I did something a little wrong, I'm not going to deny that, it was a little wrong but to make a production like this.

"I don't deserve this. I do so much for you. And what do I get for my good works? This—a broken television, is that my reward? What you did to that television set hurts me more than the television. How am I going to watch '*The Sunday Business Journal*' this weekend!

"I slept with her. Big deal. Sleeping with somebody. That's physical. Loving somebody. That's important. That's what this is about between us, but not breaking televisions! You know how I felt about that set Amanda!"

"I'm not Amanda! Amanda is your secretary!"

"Right! See what happens when you get me upset."

"I just want one thing Chet—to hear a clear answer as to why?"

He wouldn't answer.

"Tell me why."

"I'm a human being. I have my imperfections. Take me as I am, that's what love is."

He continued. "You want to hear what was going on in my head—okay. In most of the sexual experiences I had with her she was actually facing the other direction and I was thinking of you. It sounds crazy—I know—but from the back she looks a lot like you.

"Human beings are far more complicated than you imagine. I think what was happening is that I was trying to cope with my intense longing for you, by momentarily satisfying the animal part of me. I'm not proud of it but the animal part is there. And sometimes it just makes demands on me.

"I didn't want to force you to satisfy me. That would be very selfish. Listen, I don't want to marry my secretary. I don't even want to promote her. It's just that I'm a man. You and I aren't sleeping together. I had to satisfy my drive in some way. Have I made any sexual demands on you? No. Why? Because of my secretary. If it wasn't for my secretary you would bear the brunt of my animal urges.

"Let's find a way to work this all out. Amanda is a very nice, sweet person. I don't want to hurt her feelings either. Maybe we'll invite her over and you'll talk to her. She's a very wonderful girl. Maybe the three of us could just sit down and get comfortable . . ."

"You ass! "

"What? What now?"

"You bastard!"

She came towards him.

"I wasn't going to do this. But it's a woman's prerogative to change her mind."

"Go ahead smash me one," he said. He tapped his own cheek at the chin. "Go ahead smash me one," he said again.

Well, Jayne Holly Wyatt . . . She wasn't reckless. She wasn't interested in smashing his face. She became very exact. She came forward and using hip motion to make a very graceful swing, she punched him in the solar plexus—She struck him hard in the gut.

She stopped in mid-strike. She was indeed very exact. She knocked the wind out of him but did not damage him.

He sank to the floor.

He panted a bit for breath, and then caught his air again.

He looked up at her.

And when he looked up, she said down to him, "It's okay Chet. I'm finished. This feels like a fine moment to end it."

Now he had heard what she had said, and he took it in.

He absorbed it—and realized where they were now.

"Oh, I can see it now," he said. "This is not going to a good place. I'm going to break it off with you. You're the problem. You Jayne."

"This is a dead end," he continued. "I can see that right away. There's something wrong here."

He slowly rose to his feet.

"And you know what—you're the problem. You Jayne. You.

"I've tried," he said. "God knows. But I have to face the music. You know what the trouble with you is? You have an unbalanced value system. I take you to nice places to eat. I take you to meet interesting people. Those sorts of things don't seem to matter. The only thing that matters is that I slept with my secretary. And I said your name wrong once."

"This is unreal," she said.

"I'll tell you what's unreal," he said. "That now I have no television set. That's unreal.

"I've had problems with the relationship but I was in love so I overlooked things. Now I don't feel I can do anything more for you."

Jayne walked off.

And what happened next happened in a kind of whirlwind between them.

Jayne started packing clothes into a bag.

Mentally she had already left. She was just in the house packing, not even reacting. Nothing he said meant anything to her.

As he began watching this, Chet's adrenaline began to really pump.

"Did you fall in love with me?" he asked.

"It might be nice to tell you," she said. "But you're not in a state to hear it."

"And you're going to leave it there?" he said. "That is not right. This is what I get? After everything, this is what I get?"

"This is a breakup. This is how things go."

"This is a pattern with you. You've done this before."

"No, I haven't done this before."

"This is unreal. This is totally unreal. I'm a real person. Do you understand that? I'm real. Are you a real person?"

"No, I don't even exist. Forget me. Don't lose what you have with your other women."

"You're a head game. You're just a game player. You don't care whose heart you break. First you break Ridley's. Now mine—"

"Ridley's?" she asked.

"You just sleep with men," he said, "I mean you just have sex with men."

"We never had sex," she said.

"Oh, I get your game. You just don't have sex with men and then continue to not have sex with men."

"Under your scenario, I'd be a professional virgin."

"Are you?"

"I'm not a professional."

"That's only half an answer. What about the other part?"

"I don't think you'll ever find out the answer to that . . . And it might be fun to leave it that way."

"Is that what this is to you, fun and games?"

"No. . . . You're right. It's not fun, at all. It's an ending."

"Holy goddamn hell! I'm being played. I was such a good guy. I played it slow because you wanted it slow. What in the name of hell are you doing?"

She was finished.

She went to the front door with her bag.

She looked at him.

"Goodbye Chet," she said.

She walked out the door and closed it softly behind her.

He looked at it.

He walked toward it.

Walked away.

Turned completely away.

Then moved his whole body forward and with his arm made a kind of graceful swinging punch into the air.

"Argh!" he said.

He shot a lightning jab into the air.

"Grhh! Uhhh. Shwoooh . . ." He whistled a long, soft descending whistle into the air.

It all went quite.

He straightened himself to his full height. Raised his head. Looked out at something.

Now he was alone with his *audience*.

## Chet Finale

He looked around.

"Hey . . . it looks like we've got a good group here tonight," he said. "You all can understand. I lay my case out in front of you. Do you see what's happened? Do you see what she's like? You never can tell what's buried inside of some people.

"Fellows—am I right? Women—can you understand her? She's a mystery wrapped in a question.

"I am so glad I broke it off with her—as soon as she started talking about leaving me. . . . I saw where that was going right away.

"You see what she's like. She's manipulative. And you were feeling sorry for her. Admit it. You were. I was starting to feel a little peculiar about bluffing her too. On the surface she looks like such a nice person. Innocent. Loving. You never can tell what's buried inside of some people.

"She deserves what I did. Good for her.

"And don't worry about me, I'll get past this. I've made mistakes in the past. I'll make them again. The main thing is that I'm learning. You have to go through these things but I'll be fine.

"My secretary isn't that bad of a person. And she really cares a lot for me. And if not her then there's a new girl. She started working downstairs at my office. What a knockout.

"I've still got a lot of good things coming my way. I'm not down. Not by a long shot. I'll catch you later.

"Where there is hatred, I bring love.

"Where there is discord, I bring harmony.

"Where there is despair, I bring hope.

"Where there is sadness, I bring joy.

"Where there are shadows, I bring light.

"The approach I take really has to do with the future.

"I'll see you in the future," he said.

And he walked away . . . into the darkness.

### Outside of the House

Jayne was standing and staring at the house.

She slowly walked away, into the surrounding darkness.

# Heartstruck
*The "Girl Made of Cool" Speech——Part Three*

### A Park, A Beautiful Day

Ridley and Jayne were sitting on a bench.

Looking at a field and a grove of trees.

She said, "That 'Girl Made of Cool' part two speech was a show-stopper."

"Well, that's nice of you to say," he said. He went quiet for a moment and then said, "Hey, do you want to know something? I figured out how I should have made the original 'Girl Made of Cool' speech."

"Let's hear it."

"I think I missed my moment."

"No, c'mon. You can't say you figured it out and then not share it with me."

"It's not like you're a reporter. It's about you."

"I like your speeches. I'd like to hear it."

"I should have told you that I had this feeling for you. . . . It's not art. It's not clever. It's just the feeling that hit me."

He caught himself.

"Oh, never mind. It would come out silly at this point. Forget it. Sorry to disturb." He turned and looked out over the park. ". . . Do you want to get something to drink?"

"No, go ahead and tell me."

"Oh Jayne," he blushed. "Now I can't." He wiped his hand across his forehead. Looked at her. Then put his head in both hands. And drew a deep difficult breath.

"Ridley, go ahead and tell me. Please I'd like to hear your idea."

He slowly drew his head from his hands and turned his gaze toward her.

"Talking like this is so difficult," he said.

She looked into his eyes and her gaze was steady.

He looked into her eyes. Her beautiful eyes. And steadied his own gaze.

They connected. A moment of something passed between them. He began to speak.

He abruptly broke off, turned from her and leaned his whole body forward, away from her.

"I can't keep going here," he said. Then he glanced over his shoulder in her direction, in a discreet, small movement. He said "—Ah, all right ... I'll go on ... somehow. ..."

She smiled. She got it. She laughed. He was a delight to her.

She looked at his back. She slapped him playfully on the shoulder blade. "Go on."

He laughed too. And then resumed. Quite sincerely. Very genuinely. And completely from his heart. He spoke.

"Sometimes when you just *state the obvious* to a girl—that can be the most significant statement you can make.

"Maybe a good speech would be just saying what it is—If what it is, is so big, maybe you don't have to add to it.

"Because ...

"When I think of you, I feel a strange sensation.

"This is a strong sensation.

"It's not at all in the place where I would expect. It's up here."

He put his hand high on his chest.

"It feels like my blood gets warm in this area, going out to my arms. Strange. Then I thought to myself, 'What place is that?' My lungs?

"I thought that's a strange place to feel for you. In the lungs. But, wait, the lungs aren't filled with blood. Then I realized that actually the lungs are around it. So I thought, 'What's in the middle?' Then I realized what place it was—I don't know if you know your anatomy too well," he smiled a small pure smile, "so I don't know if you're following me on what that thing is. ..."

"Your heart," she said.

"Yes," he said, "that happens to be what they call it. I feel for you in my heart. ... And the arteries coming out. Into my arms up here. And also down into my diaphragm.... Or I guess a better way to say it is it feels like my heart is suddenly bigger, so that it fills my chest and arms and head. ... I didn't remember ever feeling a sensation like that. So, I'm thinking to myself, '*What do you call that?*' And then I realized what people call it. Now I know what it is." He looked at her. "You know what it's called."

"Yes, I know," she said.

"You must get a lot of that sensation from men," he said.

"Yes," she said, "but usually it's in a different place."

"I see," he said.

"Yes," she said, "usually it's different."

"And I realized something about it," he said.

"What was that?"

"I'm in big trouble," he said. He turned and looked into the distance. "I'm in big goddamn trouble."

She went silent.

"There is beauty in desire," he said. "And this was a beauty that was trouble. Beauty and trouble in one. Beautiful trouble. . . . There was something funny in that. . . . Don't you think?

He continued. "What kind of basking is this for your body to do? Basking in blood streams. In a flushed feeling. I really believe beauty is truth, truth is beauty. So I started questioning. '*What kind of beauty is this?*'

"It's a flushed feeling, so you would think that would be good and feel pleasant. And it makes you feel great but at the same time it's crushing.

"It came to me—This new feeling—*It was a 'flush crush?'* "

"*Ridley,*" she said, "do you mean to tell me that you're realizing that instead of a speech about '*The Girl Made of Cool*' you should have given me a speech about—'*The Flush Crush*'?"

And right there, that stopped him.

"Foiled again," said Ridley. "I thought I had it."

"You're just going to have to face it," she said. "Ridley, *you have an imperfect speech,*" she continued. "You're faced with an imperfect speech."

Ridley was confronted with the cold hard truth of it. He drew a breath. He let it out. He looked at her.

He said, "*Jayne Holly Wyatt.*" It was a very definite statement. He went quiet.

She looked at him.

"*Ridley Richardson,*" she said. She was every bit as definite.

They both laughed. There was something funny in his plight. It hit them both at the same time. They laughed for a while and then stopped.

"You're probably wondering," she said, "what my feeling is for you."

"Yes, I have wondered."

"Maybe," she said, "one day I'll tell you."

They looked at each other, and then they looked out into the trees of the park.

They continued looking out at the trees.

No one happened by. They had the world to themselves for a few minutes.

After a moment she said, "They're very nice trees."

He said, "Yes, they're very nice . . . They go well together. Do you notice that?"

They sat and stared at the trees.

The sun was low on the horizon in the background. It was setting. And soon night would fall. It would be a warm night. Quite pleasantly seasonable. And very comfortable if you wanted to enjoy it.

# The Gravitational Pull of Society

## Several Days Later

### The Metropolitan Museum, Afternoon

Jayne walked up to its huge front entrance.

She turned her head upward, and looked.

After a moment, she brought her gaze down to the doors.

Then she went up the steps and past the pillars of the large facade, into the lobby.

And slowly moved beyond.

### An Exhibit Hall of the Metropolitan Museum

She was traveling very slowly now. . . . Jayne was walking through the Metropolitan Museum of Art. Seeing it in a new way.

She paused.

For a long, long moment.

After a long slow while, her eyes started to move to the side. . . . There was a young man a few paces away. . . . Something about him looked very familiar. . . . A familiarity that went back years and years. That had been with her since grade school. . . . Since she was a little girl with big dreams about the future. Her future. . . . He came to her and spoke.

"Hello," he said.

"Hi." She looked at him.

"You seem," he said, "to be really enjoying this."

She looked at him.

"Me too," he said. ". . . Have we met before?" he asked. . . . And he was genuine about it. He really didn't know.

She smiled. "I know what you mean. I feel it too. It seems we've met before. Yes, it does. But no, we haven't."

"Hmm," he said.

They looked at the art.

"I'm David," he said.

"I'm Jayne," she said and smiled again.

"I like to look at the art. . . . I'm very practical. But I'm learning to appreciate this."

"Yes, me too," she said. And she smiled.

"Well, I seem to be making you smile at every turn. We're off to a good start," he said.

"David," she said, "can I ask you something?"

He looked at her and she opened up.

"Do you work for a living?" she said.

"I do," he said, ". . . uhm, but my father is an attorney. . . . There's quite a bit—well, there's a fund he set up. So if I want it, it's always there. But yes I work."

"David," she said, "if all artists had to stand on one side of the room, and all business people had to stand on the other side of the room. Where would you stand?"

He gave it thought. "Well, I would stand, in the, uhm . . . I wonder," he said.

"In the middle," she said.

He looked up at her. "Yes, in the middle. That's right."

Yes, he was exactly what she thought he would turn out to be. She smiled. She laughed.

"David, I'm glad we finally met," she said.

"Finally," he said. He wasn't sure where this was going.

"Have a good life David. I have to go," she said.

"Ah," he said, "so we leave it there."

"Yes," she said.

"Have a good life Jayne," he said.

And this was how she said good bye to Mister Perfect Gravitational Pull of Society Man.

She was different now than she had been, and she was not going back.

## The Park, Day

Jayne and Ridley—met in the park.

They looked into each other's eyes.

She put her fingers to his mouth. She didn't want him to say anything just then.

"Shush," she said, "please."

She looked at him.

"I want you to kiss me," she said.

And she continued to look at him.

"Would you like to kiss me?" she said.

He smiled a small smile.

She smiled.

"We are going to kiss aren't we?" she said.

"Yes," he said, "I would like very much to kiss you."

He stood in stillness.

"Can we, . . ." he asked, ". . . kiss with . . . our eyes closed?"

She stood, too, in stillness.

"And, . . ." he said, ". . . can we do it slowly?"

They looked at each other for a moment.

She closed her eyes.

He brought his lips close to her lips. He closed his eyes.

Slowly, ever so slowly they kissed.

They kissed for years.

She pulled away slowly. Both of their eyes were still closed.

They happened to open their eyes at the same instant, and both slowly.

"I had," he said, "an ex-girlfriend who said I should stop pulling away first when we kissed. . . . I think she was right."

"Yes, she was right."

"So that was our first kiss"—and they both happened to say it at the same time.

"Maybe," he said, "we'll do it again some time."

"Maybe," she said, and smiled.

"May I take your hand?" he asked.

She gave him her hand to hold.

He took it in his hand, very gently, tenderly, lovingly.

And they walked into the park like that.

## New Year's Eve, Horizons, and Crossing the Years

Seasons changed. . . . Before long it was new year's eve.

The snow was falling. Past the yellow lights of the lampposts. Touching down on the city's streets. Set against the dark cold of the night sky, the snow was bathed in the soft warm glow of city lights.

At the party . . . Ridley and Jayne watched the show.

Then the stage was cleared, and the dance floor was opened. The band began to play. People stepped onto the floor.

Ridley and Jayne held hands as they walked on.

They danced and flowed. The songs drifted across the dance floor and the swirling couples.

Ridley looked at Jayne. And Jayne looked at Ridley.

There was something in the way they clung to each other after they had danced a while.

Soon they were home.

They kissed.

He peeked in the mirror while she stripped her gown.

Bare.

So in love with her, was he.

Whispering tenderly.

Into the night.

Thrill of the new was here.

Slipping into dreams.

So in love with him, was she.

Will it be? An affair to last? Summer love? Thrills of first snowfalls, seasons changing. Will he? Will she? Will they be in love? So in love next new year's eve?

## The Fading Echoes of the Years

A few years later—there was this photo. Of Ridley & Jayne . . . & beaming little children.

# — The End —

# The Blue Sky World

The Blue Sky World

# The Business Age

IT WAS A STRANGE TIME in the strange blue sky world.

The era was a turning point. It was a time of traveling—from one business era to the next. From one presidency to the next. From one social age to the next.

It was an era of great progress—of business progress and invention. Humanity was rising to the next level.

It was a "let's get rich" era, following the great "war" eras.

Now, they say that: *Success at the top hides many sins all along the line.*

It hides many practices, like robbermanship and son-of-a-bitchmanship. These were prevalent in the new "let's get rich" era.

Many businessmen were heady.

The fundamentals were still the fundamentals. A kiss was still a kiss. A sigh was still a sigh.

And a good racket that returned a "two-bagger" (or better) annually— meaning 100 percent (or better)—was still a wonder to behold, a mother-of-all-rackets, a *"beauty."* ... The fundamental things applied as this time went by. ... And many pursued the modern sense of *"beauty"*—to a high standard of excellence—in this age.

The time was actually the latest in a series of "let's get rich" eras. It came hot on the heels of two other similarly high-minded eras in between recent wars. This one was different in that it propelled itself higher, farther, faster.

People were blazing through companies. The returns were all that mattered. What were your returns to your company—and what were your returns to yourself? ... And if you knew what you were doing you would weigh the returns to yourself a little more heavily. Meaning 100 percent more heavily than your company. If you could make money by burning and destroying your company, why then the choice was clear. Your duty was clear. What was in question? Nothing.

What were your returns to *you?* To *yourself?*

"Oh, dear boy, dear girl, *ask not* what *you* can do for *your company,* but ask what *your company* can do for *you.*"

Always take the high road. ... Always know *true living.* ... There is no greater virtue, no greater splendor, than that which you see staring back at you in the mirror each morning.

Do not worship the front door of your company, worship the front door of your house.

Too many moonlight kisses seem to melt in the warmth of the son.

When you give your heart, give it to—yourself. And give it completely. Or never give your heart.

The is the true art of *lifemanship*, and this is the blue sky world of the *lifeman*.

Everybody loves a successful *lifeman*. No one care for a virtuous failure.

*To be loved* or *to be unloved* that is the question.

Live in a valley green with spring, where your heart can go a-journeying.

It was a question of who you truly loved.

And in your life—who did you love?

You had to ask yourself what you meant to yourself.

Did you love yourself truly, or were you treating yourself like a passing fling.

Were you treating yourself coldly, each day of the year?

And how did you treat yourself when other people were near?

Were you polite to yourself? When you told stories about yourself were you kind? Were you glowing? Did you show them how much you meant to yourself?

Oh, dear boy, dear girl, the love that you cherish so often may perish. . . . At break of dawn, was your love there? In the lonely hours of evening, did you love yourself?

Lovemanship begins at home. The loveman who loves the loveman. And the lovewoman who loves the lovewoman.

This was the most basic idea in business—*lovemanship* underlies all *successmanship*.

Now, how to achieve successmanship? This was the next question.

To be a success, you had to become an "expert"—you had to learn how to "be" an expert, to live and breathe as an expert. To exude the air and qualities of an expert. To radiate the confidence of the expert.

It was a romantic era, but to enjoy romance with another person, you had to first be your own person.

Now how did you become your own person?

In that business age, in those modern times, sophisticated ladies and gentleman knew the fine arts—the gentleman's arts of robbermanship, scoundrelmanship, and son-of-a-bitchmanship.

History tells us that in olden days—*in the dark days before the common era*—robbermanship, scoundrelmanship, and son-of-a-bitchmanship were low-level lines of work.

But in this age—the modern age—to practice *villainmanship*, and reach *successmanship*, you needed a grooming school.

These things were now the gentleman's arts. And the gentlewoman's arts.

If you wanted to be evil, and you wanted to be a success at it, you had to do the same thing that a painter or a musician had to do—practice (stick-to-it-manship). And become better at what you did than anyone else.

Why in those days, in that modern commercial era of successmanship, it was a world of politics, of dirty deals, one after another.

It was a very complicated and competitive marketplace. To be a ruthless villain in that modern business climate you needed superior training.

You had to understand loopholes (clause-manship) and how to corrupt law enforcement officials (ownermanship); you had to know how to supervise the processing of enormous amounts of paperwork (hide-the-baconmanship).

You had to know how to recruit good accomplices. That meant you had to convert the honest to your way of thinking; you had to be prepared to overcome moral objections, to get past the almighty "No!" that was constantly going to be hurled at you. In those days, everybody started with a "No!" and it could be very daunting.

You had to cultivate your skill at lying and learn to perfect untruth to the level of art.

There were so many things to learn. It was a wonder that anybody actually succeeded. Yet there were success stories, but we needn't name names. A gentleman does not.

You had to learn the principles of the profession. The laws of the trade, as it were.

In a blue sky world, you had to go to a blue sky company.

A gentleman's blue sky company, and a gentlewoman's blue sky company, where you could learn to speak with blue sky purpose.

# The Answer

THIS WAS THE OFFICE of *Sam Bartlett,* the renowned chief executive officer. Perhaps you've heard of him? He'd recently been featured in several business magazines. He was the CEO and president of an upscale business, a high-level shop of *image experts.*

Sam was sitting at his mahogany desk, in his wood-panelled office, when he looked upward and outward.

"Scooter!" said Sam.

Scooter—a young heroic junior associate, came in.

"The report," said Sam, "wasn't on my desk at 9 a.m."

"I'm sorry, sir," said Scooter, "but I didn't have enough time to finish it."

"You had one hour," said Sam. "You got in at 8 a.m. Why didn't you have the report on my desk by 9 a.m.?"

"It takes more than an hour."

"How long does it take?"

"Five hours."

"Five hours is too long. It should only take one hour."

"But it physically takes five hours."

"We only had one hour."

"I know that, sir. That's why I wasn't able to finish on time."

"That's not acceptable."

"Sir, how should I get it all done in one hour?"

"Work smarter."

"I'm sorry I'm not following you sir. Let's say the positions were reversed. If it was your responsibility to get it done in one hour, how would you do it?"

"It wasn't my responsibility. It was yours. I needed it done in one hour. You're telling me you'd like to spend five hours on it. I can't agree to that."

"But, sir, do you have a solution?"

"No, I want the solution to come from you. Give me my options and I'll pick one."

"Well, if I go at top speed, stay completely focused and don't allow any interruptions, that's about the fastest I can go."

"If you go at that pace, how long does it take?"

"Five hours."

"Listen to this. In sex anything worth doing is worth doing slow but in business it's the opposite. Now it is conceivable that this can be done in an hour, isn't it? It's not like I'm asking you to bite off your own teeth. This is imaginable."

"It is."

"Then let's do it that way."

"Do you have any suggestions for things that I'm not doing which I could be doing?"

"No, I don't care how you go about it. I'm only interested in achieving the result. I'm not interested in excuses why things can't be done the way I need them done. When I tell you I want something to happen, I want it to become reality. You're looking at me like you're confused. Does what I'm saying to you make sense?"

"Absolutely."

"If there's anything you don't understand, ask me and I'll clear it up for you."

"No, I understand what you're saying."

"Great. Now how long is this report going to take from now on?"

"Five hours."

Sam put an arm around Scooter's shoulder and patted him warmly. Scooter smiled.

Sam lead them to the couch and they both sat down.

"Scooter, this is getting so out of hand. I want you to understand what I'm doing. I'm trying to teach you so that by working with me, you become a better person. I consider every person who works for me not only an employee but also a student. I'm teaching you to look for answers. After all that is what we sell here—answers. Clients come to us with questions and we give them answers. This is an exercise in looking for an answer. The question is how do we resolve this? Do you have the answer?"

"No."

"Do you want me to give you one?"

"Please."

"The answer is—*You're fired.* Thank you for all your help and good-bye."

Sam was used to firing people and did it with great indifference. He immediately walked toward his desk to call personnel for a replacement. Scooter leapt at Sam, landed on the floor, and grabbed onto Sam's leg.

"Oh God, no please!"

"I'm sorry," said Sam. "This hurts me. I don't make a big show of emotion, but it doesn't mean I'm not suffering."

Sam pulled his leg free. Scooter remained on the floor from where he pleaded with Sam and tugged at his jacket sleeve.

"I have worked so hard," said Scooter. "Please reconsider."

"Please don't make this difficult for me. It's not easy to fire someone, especially when they're on their knees begging."

"You do feel that I'm intelligent, devoted, and a hard worker?"

"Of course. This has nothing to do with that."

"Then can you write me a letter of recommendation?"

"It's very difficult for me to write a recommendation for someone I've just fired."

"After all I've done for you I feel that you should at least help me in some small way."

"I understand where your feeling is coming from. But if you would please do this in an expedient manner I would appreciate it. I'll have payroll cut a final check for you and two weeks severance pay. That'll be ready in an hour or two. Now isn't that fair? Two weeks pay for no work."

"Very fair. "

Sam now relaxed and became casual.

"Now if you'll excuse me forever I'm going to call personnel and start looking for a replacement."

## *Act One*

# Early Enlightenment

IT WAS A FINE BEAUTIFUL DAY in the big city. The skyscrapers looked so lovely set against the clear blue sky.

### The Office Tower and Courtyard

A crowd of office workers went happily on their way to work.

*What a lovely place to work,* thought Jack Flynn.

He broke away from the flowing crowd.

Then Jack Flynn crossed the courtyard and entered the tower's lobby.

### Sam's Office

Jack and Sam's senior associate—*Ray Raymour*—stepped through the doorway.

Sam was smiling warmly at Jack, as he moved to shake his hand.

Ray made the introductions. "Sam Bartlett this is *Jack Flynn.* Jack this is Sam."

"Good to meet you," said Sam. "Make yourself comfortable."

Ray handed Sam a resume. Then Jack and Ray took a seat on the couch.

Sam studied Jack's resume. "Forgive me. I haven't had a chance to do this."

Sam read the resume while Jack, and Ray, waited on.

Sam looked up at Jack.

"I see by your resume that you've never worked for a company like ours. You have no experience in our industry whatsoever."

Sam looked at Ray.

Jack held still.

"Do you know what we do here?" asked Sam.

"I could always use more explanation."

"We are a school for experts. We show people how to come on like an expert. And you don't really have to be an expert to do that. You see experts all over the place. Have you ever asked yourself what do they really know? Of course not; because they come across like experts. You have to do what

I'm doing now. I sound like an expert, don't I?"

"You do."

"Now please tell me why I should hire you and I want you to sound like an expert."

"I may not have the experience, . . . but I, uhm, am . . . a-uhm . . ."

"Go on."

"I guess the only thing I have to offer you over other people is that I'm willing to run longer and faster than them. I make your life easier. I do a lot more. For the same money. I don't want a penny more."

"I see."

"I wouldn't worry about the resume. I have a lot of experience I didn't put on there. If you want, I can fix you one that you'll like. Besides in my case the person is even better than the resume. I make the job my life. I'm a very hard worker. I would get totally involved in *our* job. I don't need much sleep. I can start earlier than most people. And work later. I don't take breaks. I come in at 4. Stay till 11. Do you know how much I could learn in a day like that? There's no end. The more hours I work, the more I learn. I know I'm the man you're looking for. There is no one better."

Sam liked what he heard.

"Okay, that's the answer—"

"—It would be hard for anybody to match me—"

"—Let me stop you with a hot tip. Never keep talking after you make your point. People will think you're trying to understand what you just said."

Jack nodded.

"Let me tell you about how I operate. Then I want to learn more about you. My philosophy is simple—find the right people and keep them. When you have good people you can put work in their hands and forget about it."

Sam had a deep, true, soulful look in his eyes.

"This is a business that runs on people. If I had to walk away tomorrow and choose between taking all the bricks and mortar . . . or taking the people. I would choose the people. People are the power in this business. Resources help us do the job—but what our clients experience is the people. On any given day, you can be bigger to your client than the entire organization. So for me, how I relate to my people determines whether I will succeed or not. And actually, this is where I pack a wallop. I'm very good with people. Let's take my last assistant, *Scooter,* who came to me with no experience. None. He didn't even know how to shine my boots. Some thought I was insane to hire him. I saw potential and developed it, to the point where he became an out-and-out star. Then he received an offer from the competition. I was floored. I said, 'Let me pay you more than them.' Money is never my main concern. But what's done is done. He had committed to them."

Sam was making up the facts as he went along.

"So I supported his decision. I told him any time you need a reference, come to me. Please. I said let's stay in touch—we're having lunch next week."

As Sam continued with his ridiculous self-aggrandizement, Jack listened with rapt attention—looking at Sam as if he had invented the light bulb.

Sam continued. "I'm easy to please. I'm just looking for someone I can train. I move you right up if you're not afraid of hard work."

## The Hallway

Sam and Jack stepped out of Sam's office. Sam's arm was on Jack's shoulder.

"Thank you for coming by. I'm going to make my decision in the next day or so."

Sam patted Jack on his back.

Jack walked off.

Ray and Sam watched Jack wait for the elevator in the distance.

"What do you think about him Sam?" asked Ray.

No response. Sam was thinking.

Ray said, "His brain plus four quarters would get him a dollar."

"Ray, if you knew your ass from a hole in the ground you'd talk a lot less."

"Right Sam. Very good point."

"You have to develop an eye for possibilities. If you haven't learned that from me then you haven't learned a goddamn thing."

"I agree completely, the kid could work."

"How much was he told the job pays?"

"15,000 a year."

"Let's re-think that. There's no reason to throw a boatload of money at him. He's a good kid. He'll take 14,000."

"What if he holds out for 15,000?"

"Tell him he'll get it in three months."

"What happens in three months?"

"Nothing. It's an expression like 'May your dreams come true.' He wants more money, you tell him, 'You'll get it in three months.' Then you don't have to give it to him."

## The Offices, a Few Days Later

This was Jack's first day on the job.

Now Jack was a *systems thinker,* and he had gone into the office that first day determined to learn the systems of this place.

At the start of that morning, Ray and Jack were standing by Scooter's desk, which had not been touched since Scooter was fired. And it was a hell of a mess.

Jack was staring at the desk. It was littered with files and a wide range of papers.

"I think there's enough here to get you started," Ray said. "I need to get a memo out but then I'll be free to work with you."

"Okay. Great."

Ray returned to his own desk and absorbed himself in his work. Jack began sorting through the accumulated work. Then Jack looked around.

He noticed a large filing cabinet nearby.

Presently, Jack was carrying a large stack of files to the filing cabinet.

Now this filing cabinet was a massive thing. It was a large-double doored cabinet, and existed more in the sense of a large walk-in closet than a cabinet.

There seemed to be beams of *blue sky* in the cabinet—He saw a light radiating from behind the doors. He felt himself being drawn in. What was this shining aura?

He opened the double doors. He stepped in. It was a lovely wash of light, and then he was flying through the sky.

He was standing poised. In a normal stance, but he was standing in the sky. Next to him were the slots, where you dropped the files into their appropriate positions.

He glanced up. He was entranced by this place.

There was something about standing in this filing cabinet that made him think of the great business impulses:

"Rise.

"Up, up and away.

"You can have what you desire.

"You can have it all.

"You can win.

"The sky's the limit."

Yes, he liked the feeling of blue sky opening on blue sky.

He felt it like a whisper in this place.

*Though it's best not to get carried away,* he thought. And he became practical. And industrious. He went back to his work.

Jack was a systems thinker.

He glanced through the files he had, and then the ones in the cabinet.

He looked at the binders and books in there.

There was something odd about this system and this place.

He began putting them into the sort.

*Kate Greenway* passed by outside the double doors. She paused and looked at him. Kate was a sweet, attractive young lady, who also worked in the associates area.

He looked up from within the *blue sky room* and smiled at her.

She smiled and continued to her desk where she went to work.

Jack couldn't take his eyes off her. He tried to return to the filing but his eyes traveled back to her.

Kate was sitting at her desk, sorting through paperwork.

She turned around and caught him staring at her.

He turned away.

She turned back to her own work.

Jack came out of the filing cabinet and approached her.

"Hi, you're *Kate Greenway?*"

"Right."

"I'm *Jack Flynn.*"

She smiled.

They shook hands.

"It's nice to meet you."

"Same here."

Then there was silence.

"I better get back to my filing."

He indicated the filing cabinet and then walked away. She stared after him.

Jack stood in the filing cabinet. He was dropping the files into their places.

But now something strange was happening—Kate was staring at him.

He did his level best to look graceful. He picked up his pace.

And now Kate was getting up and approaching him. She entered the small cabinet and paused beside him. Very close to him. He could smell her, and she had such a lovely scent. Then he looked into her eyes. Oh, so lovely.

She spoke to him in a whisper.

"You're doing great work."

"Thanks."

"But you're putting them in wrong."

"I'm putting them in alphabetical order."

"In the wrong cabinet. They belong there."

She showed him that there was a larger walk-in filing cabinet on the far side of the associates area. That was *The Lord Consulting Group* filing cabinet.

It had a reddish, purple, orange glow, with hints of yellow, radiating in streams from below the door. He opened it and gazed in. "Ah, I see."

"Yes," she said, "only the blue files go in the *blue sky room*. All the others go here."

"Oh," he said. "Thank you."

"You're very welcome," she said and left.

The original file colors were red, purple, orange and yellow. They now matched this room and it all made sense.

He stepped back and looked at the overall associates area. There was a red and purple wall with *The Lord Consulting Group* cabinet. And on the other side was the light, streaming, baby-blue wall with *The Blue Sky Company* cabinet.

In between there was a majestic picture window. Down below you could see clouds, and below the clouds, the streets of the city.

Jack considered the feelings in the filing cabinets, which were really on the level of rooms with distinct personalities.

The Lord Consulting Group room had a molding, thick feel—a solidity.

The Blue Sky room had a light and easy feel—as if you were floating free.

*An interesting contrast,* he thought.

Yes, he was a systems thinker, and found new systems exciting.

"Excuse me Ray," said Jack.

"You need me?"

"I'm confused about how these files are set up."

"I can clear it up for you. Our company is made up of two bodies—one large, the other small. The large one is *The Lord Consulting Group*. It's named after the person who started this business."

"Who is he?"

"She—*Lara Lord* is her name. A sharp woman. I'll show you the write-up they did of her in *'Fortune.'* She's absolutely brilliant. Anyway, the second entity is a small organization—*The Blue Sky Company.*"

"Why two different . . ."

"First off, do you understand what we do here?"

"We're a school for experts."

"Right. We have all kinds of clients: manufacturing, public affairs and so on. Most people out there want to be experts and all the others want to hire experts. Now you can't make yourself an expert, you need us. We go to companies and find out what they need. Then we tell them, '*No—what you need is an expert.*' Then we sell you to them. Now we have two types of clients, very big clients and very small clients. The Lord Consulting Group is for the big jobs and The Blue Sky Company is for the small ones. I don't have to go on I'm sure, you see how that works?"

"Why not one company for everything?"

"Well that gets into other issues."

"It seems like the easiest thing would be for it all to go under one name."

"You really don't understand branding, do you?"

"Oh no, I get it. So all the accounts are divided into larger and smaller transactions."

"It's one facet of a process."

"You said Lara Lord started this company. Does she own it? "

"No, there is no one owner. This company is owned by a bigger company. Lara works for that bigger company."

"Who owns the company that owns our company?"

"Boy the questions just keep coming don't they? That's a pretty good one."

Ray left it at that. He went back to his desk and resumed his work.

Jack was just standing where they left off, wondering if their conversation was over.

Ray said, over his shoulder, "Have I cleared up a few things for you?"

"Thanks."

"Anytime. One for all and all for one. Right?"

## Across from the Building's Motorcourt

Sam and Jack were standing across from the motorcourt.

It was like a great businessman's garden.

Once you crossed the car bay, there was a great big open expanse. The outer area was fenced in by great trellises. Within there was a field and garden, and fountains.

Sam took a deep breath as if he was suddenly in the Swiss Alps. Jack also took in a calming breath.

Sam put his arm around Jack's shoulder.

"Always remain relaxed. If I'm successful in my training with you, you'll learn to operate without tension. You'll learn to release in the neck, the back, the shoulders. You don't need tension to get work done. Tension is the enemy. I work completely without any tension whatsoever."

Sam brought his feet together, kept his legs straight, bent over and grabbed his toes. He stayed in this position as he continued talking.

Jack followed Sam's lead.

"What's your morning been like?"

"Ray showed me my desk and I cleared away the files, so Ray explained how the company is broken down."

Sam got up.

"What did he say?"

"That the accounts are divided into two groups—large and small."

"Good."

"Why don't we just have all the accounts under one banner?"

"There is a company that owns our company and that company is run by a woman named Lara Lord. She's making a fortune by us. And her purse is running very deep nowadays. That's very good for us. The reason I'm telling you this is because I want you to keep something in mind. When the people at the top do very well, the ones down below can make out too."

Jack looked at Sam.

"Can I ask you another question?"

"Never be afraid to ask me anything."

"Our company is owned by a bigger company . . ."

"Right."

". . . And then that bigger company is owned by what?"

"A financial group."

"Who owns the financial group?"

"Who cares? Does it have any effect on your life whatsoever?"

"No."

"Don't you worry Jack. You will learn plenty from me. I'm going to tell you a few things over the next few days that will have you thinking like a true businessman. And then you won't be asking me these types of questions. You'll learn about efficiency which means getting the most done in the least amount of time. These questions take up unnecessary time. . . . We should head back up."

They walked away.

"Remember—always stay loose."

## The Offices, that Night

Jack was sitting at his desk. He had stayed to familiarize himself with the company's files.

He could hear voices drifting faintly out of Speed's. Speed was another manager in the company. He was Kate's boss and he was giving her a pep talk.

Jack rose from his chair and walked towards Speed's office. He would love to join them but he was afraid to interrupt. After some anxious deliberation, Jack decided against interrupting, and walked back to his desk. Then he changed his mind and turned back towards Speed's office.

While he was doing this, in the background he could hear Speed saying:

"We build *celebrity*. We super-charge a name. We build name equity. Equity is a process. Equity is performance based. There's no raw equity in a name. You need celebrity over time. Even the advertising geniuses are admitting they can't do what we do. We're innovators—over time, we've tried one of everything. We're pioneering the craft of building buzz. The techniques are something we're inventing here. And the business world is interested in investing in them."

Jack mustered up his courage and darted into the doorway.

"Hi," he said.

## Speed's Office

Kate and Speed were huddled over some paperwork. Kate was sitting in an armchair. Speed was sitting on the floor. They didn't behave formally with one another.

"Hi Jack," said Kate.

"How are you?" asked Speed.

"I'm not bothered, I hope."

"I'm sorry. I'm not following you."

"I was just working at my desk and thought I'd say—but you're obvioubly viby—I mean visibly vizy—err, busy."

"I'm Denny 'Speed' Dalton. All my friends calls me Speed. I didn't catch your name."

Jack casually entered Speed's office with the air of a man who always knew what he was doing.

"Jack."

"I've got it now. Jack, huh. Nice. I like it. It hits you fast. That's good."

Speed was a man who exuded confidence. He did everything without hesitation. He'd been in the business for years, during which he'd seen and done everything.

Speed continued. "I'm going to have to talk and run here. I hate to do it. But I'm going to be off like a shot in less than no time. But quick as a wink, let me share what I was explaining to Kate."

As Speed delivered his monologue lickety-split, he also hurriedly gathered some work and headed for the door.

Speed continued again. "Here's our scene. . . . We're in the business of lifestyle communications. Trends bubble up and then we bring them into the mainstream. I'll tell you, this is a hip, hot shop. And we're growing. And we have the latitude to create our own culture, our own new business initiatives. It's been sanctioned by the top. You're going to see how we connect the dots and get strategic—then, how it all comes to life on the streets."

Kate caught Jack's gaze and smiled warmly.

"Of course," Speed said, "it calls for extreme service. We're on all the time. We work hard all the time. There has to be a relentlessness to make sure it will all work. Maybe that's not the best way to put it. I'm still playing with the words. But it's because I'm trying to package what we do.

"We're a lifestyle company.

"The way an operation like this works is that everyone has to be busy and billable all the time. But we have to help each other.

"We have to get you to where you want to be in all the skills. And move you along the path to righteousness and success."

He laughed and then became serious again.

"I guess I shouldn't have a talk like this on the fly. But I'll throw you the pieces now. We'll connect them later. The concept is this: we provide the playing field, the tools—our people craft their own job descriptions.

"You start with entry-level apprentice—we gauge your character, you learn the craft. In leaps and bounds, you move onto the journeyman stage—with decreasing reliance on supervisors while increasing your supervisory skills—you start to aim yourself, until you become a teacher, a mentor yourself. Until you can counsel the client on anything.

"We create a creative environment. Our environment should engender nice people."

Speed moved into the doorway.

"We're defining a workplace that serves its people. And I don't want to skip over this part of it, it's very meaningful. I know I'm firing on all cylinders here but this stuff is important to say. We want to make sure caring and understanding are at least the norm. And we try to provide training and information modules. The training thing is hopefully going to be a real benefit. We're also going to offer Get-Out-Of-Jail-Free Cards, Spot Bonuses, and a Local Office Bonus Pool. But more about that later. I'm late for another meeting, so go I swifter than the wind.

"But don't you two rush out. Stay. My office is your office. Mi casa es su casa!"

And with that, Speed walked out the door. He continued yelling though. He was a marvelous madman. He was yelling Spanish to no one in particular as his voice faded away:

"Mi officina es su officina! Mi amigo es su amigo! Mi esposa es su esposa!"

Jack and Kate were sitting on opposite ends of the couch.

Their eyes met.

Jack started to rise from the couch.

Jack said, "Maybe I should beat a path back to my kingdom."

"No, stay," said Kate.

Jack sat back down, but a little closer to her on the couch.

Jack said, "Speed seems like the kind of guy that lines things up and lays them flat. He's so . . ."

Jack made an expansive gesture with his arms.

Jack continued. "But not too much. He keeps it on the down-low. I think that's the way you have to be. You have to keep keeping it down."

Jack imitated some of Speed's delivery over the next few lines. And he was surprisingly good at capturing the guy's essence.

"He's got a bit of this . . .

Jack imitated Speed's gestures.

". . . And he's swinging a groove in this direction too . . ."

Jack imitated his expressions.

"He's a fiddler calling a tune and you want to sing right along."

"Yes, he is," Kate said. "That's him exactly."

Jack put his hand on the back of the couch.

She glanced at the arm.

He brought his arm back and put it in his lap.

"What do you think of Sam?" asked Kate.

"Oh well, I've been to a lot of places and met a lot of people. I've been to a show at the convention center, I've been to a picnic, I've even been to a rodeo but I never met anybody like him. He shoots from the hip and he doesn't miss a trick. He fires you up and he sets you on the path."

"I hope you don't blush at compliments—words come out of your mouth in a very sincere way," Kate said. "You are out-and-out real. Way real."

"Wow, as far as saying things goes, that's like shooting me a breeze straight out of Coolsville. I mean holy act of Congress, thanks."

Jack continued. "Listen I know we only just met but when something seems right I'm not afraid to act on it right away. I've been thinking about what it would be like to go out for drinks with you some time. And it seems like it would be a lot of fun."

He took a deep breath.

She seemed bewildered. It was hard to read her reaction.

Jack said, "I shouldn't have said that. Oh good God, forgive me."

He backed to the other side of the couch.

"Boy did I pour it on and I don't blame you for reacting the way you did. I meant to say I think you're someone special and I really have strong feelings for you—"

He got on his feet and backed out of the office.

Jack said, "Holy shit—I mean, oh my God. I'm so sorry. I need to go kick myself some, put myself to bed with a shovel and then start off right with you tomorrow."

He exited the office but in the wrong direction—he had disappeared to the right.

A beat and then—he walked past the doorway heading left, pretending he meant to do that. He disappeared.

"Wait," Kate said, "I didn't say anything."

Jack stepped into the doorway, looking at Kate's feet instead of her face.

"Don't feel bad," Jack said.

"How did you figure out that I'm attracted to you?"

His jaw dropped but he quickly recovered.

"Oh, I don't really want to say."

He smiled assuredly and put out his arm to lean against the doorway —like a 'Gentleman's Quarterly' cover boy. He was going to convince her there were methods to his madness.

But he was so concerned with being cool that he missed the wall and fell out of her visual frame.

Kate—reacted to a loud thud.

Jack leapt to his feet, pretending nothing had happened. He propped himself against the doorframe without any further difficulty.

Kate said, "Are you okay?"

"Oh sure, I've had worse falls than that."

Kate rose from the couch and walked over to Jack.

"You're clever, a Devil with the face of a Buddha . . . pretending that you didn't know I was attracted to you. I wouldn't say no. But how can I say yes? We can't get involved. We're working in the same office. It could get complicated."

"I wouldn't talk you into anything that isn't right for you?"

"Okay. Friends then?"

He put out his hand for her to shake.

"Friends."

They shook.

## The Office, Several Days Later

Ray and Jack were standing together.

Jack's appearance was changing. He was dressing better and his hair was more neatly groomed.

Sam came out of his office. "Ray. What ever happened to *Mr. Kalbert Kishkowitz?* I thought we had a meeting.

"Kalbert Kishkowitz? Not that I remember."

"Well," said Sam, "maybe you better set up an appointment. That man is sitting on a million-dollar piece of business."

"A million in fee?" said Ray.

"Maybe more."

Sam walked back to his office.

Ray plucked a card from his desk and walked over to Jack. "Jack, I need you to interface with this guy, Kalbert Kishkowitz. Set an appointment for him with Sam. But I don't want you to spend too much time on it. You need to be decisive and you need to be fast. We have a lot to do. I want to start getting you up to speed."

Jack dialed the number.

"Mr. Kishkowitz . . . is this Mr. Kalbert Kishkowitz?"

Kishkowitz said, "Do I have to shove a bat up someone's asshole to get some business done? Ray promised to call. When? Yesterday!"

Jack said, "I apologize for the delay sir."

"Yeah right. Let's have this fucking meeting next Wednesday?"

"I'm sorry sir but Sam's booked up on Wednesday and Thursday next week."

"You're shitting me. Ray said I could meet with him before the board of directors meeting."

"Pardon me sir. Can I put you on hold for a second?"

"Sure take your time. It's only costing me money."

"Thank you sir. It'll just take one second."

He put Kishkowitz on hold.

"Ray. He says that you were already setting up a meeting."

"Oh yeah, that Kalbert Kishkowitz. That's right. With a name like that, who can remember the man? . . . Listen, that's really important. I even wrote that down so I wouldn't forget. Hmm, I don't know what I did with that piece of paper. Well, these things happen. Fortunately, we can fix it fast. This is a perfect example of what I've been talking about. Something comes up . . . boom, you take responsibility. You make the decision and you complete the action. And you move on."

Jack picked up the phone and he overheard Kishkowitz make a remark to someone in his office. "Can you believe this? Some limp dick from business school putting me on hold. Last week it was, 'Do you want fries with that?' Now he's putting me on hold. I thought Sam was running a tight ship. This is unreal."

"Excuse me sir. I'm back."

"Hallelujah. Look, is his majesty available on the fifth? If it goes past the fifth my good friend Sam can canvass another client and kiss my ass."

"Let me check."

Jack put his hand on the receiver and turned to Ray. In the earpiece Kishkowitz could be heard carrying on in his office. ". . . Guys like this, you want to fuck their wives. . . ."

"Ray," Jack said, "the only time he can meet is on the fifth."

"What's your recommendation?" Ray asked.

"Well, I would say the fifth. But Ray it seems like we have to set it in stone. On the fifth right?"

"Jack, what do you say you move on your one and only option. We're into a crisis here. You're going to piss Curlowitz off. Besides, we have more important things to get done today."

Jack spoke into the phone. "Okay sir. We can definitely do it on the fifth."

"Thank you. You're so kind."

"Come hell or high water, you will see Sam on the fifth. Thanks."

Jack hung up the phone.

Sam came out of his office. "I'm leaving now. You have the copies?"

Jack grabbed a stack of copies and handed them to Sam, who grabbed them without even noticing who was handing them to him. "Thanks Ray."

"No problem," said Ray.

Sam left. Jack walked back to his desk.

Ray picked up a hard copy of Sam's calendar.

Ray looked at it startled. "Awww! Argghhh! God damn!"

Ray brought the calendar over to Jack.

"Looks like you screwed up," Ray said.

"What do you mean?"

"You set the meeting with Kishkowitz while Sam's supposed to be on vacation."

"What?"

"He'll have to cut his vacation in half to get here for the meeting. You shouldn't have done this."

"Ray I asked you first."

"I thought you checked his calendar."

"How could I do that? You keep the calendar on your desk—and you write all these notes in it in your handwriting that I can't read."

"And that was too far for you to walk? You can't be lazy in this business."

## The Office, the Next Morning

Jack and Kate were standing together, talking softly and discreetly about the Kishkowitz problem. Ray was listening nearby.

"I have to tell Sam," said Jack. "What's the best way to do that?"

Ray came into it then. "We've got to help him Kate. Sam is going to be a monster about this."

Kate said, "I don't see anything we can do but I'm sure Jack appreciates your concern."

"If only I could have prevented this," said Ray.

Kate doesn't realize this is Ray's fault.

At that moment Sam appeared. He was in a great mood, smiling from ear to ear. "Hello all." He waved to them and darted into his office.

Ray said, "I'll go in there and explain it. Let me handle it."

"He should get it from me," said Jack.

"No, I was a part of it. I'll smooth things out. I've worked for him a long time. I know how to talk to him."

## Sam's Office

Ray was sitting across from Sam and said, "I want to talk to you about this new kid. He's turning into a problem."

"Ray, let's get one thing straight—there is no such thing as a problem; just an issue. Occasionally a concern or a debate. Never a problem."

"I'll strike it from my vocabulary."

"No feel free to use it—when you describe the competition. If they suffer from anything that cripples their business and we are immune to it—that's a problem. When it affects us it becomes an issue."

"I always learn so much from you."

"Of course. Now what did you want to discuss?"

"It's about this new Jack. Now don't get me wrong. I like him. He's a good guy. But do you know that I have to help him with everything. And I'm a busy guy. I don't have time to do his work. But I'm stuck because he keeps making mistakes. Did he tell you what he did yesterday? Listen to this one. We're scheduling a meeting and I specifically told him, 'Make sure you plan around Sam's vacation. Check the calendar,' I said. My last words. I leave the office. I've got a number of clients to meet. I come back within the hour. Sam, he has scheduled a meeting and an important meeting I might add with you on Wednesday while you're supposed to be on vacation after me specifically saying, 'Make sure you plan around Sam's schedule.' So we're stuck. I don't know what we're going to do Sam. We're stuck."

"We're stuck?"

"We're in a situation where you're on vacation and we need for you to meet with Kishkowitz ... the million in fee. Wednesday the fifth. Right in the middle."

"Bring the kid in. Call the kid in here."

"I don't think that's necessary Sam. I think under the circmstances I could rearrange my schedule a little bit."

"Send the kid in here."

"I think I sent him out. He shouldn't be all that long Sam."

"Go get him."

"Sam I thought we could just straighten this right out and arrange something whereby we could have you have the meeting. I would change my schedule around and accommodate yours. Just sort it out right now."

"Send the kid in. Ray. Send the fucking kid in!"

## Jack's Desk

Ray walked over to Jack.

"Sam wants to see you. Be careful. He's in a terrible mood. Who knows what's gotten into him."

## Sam's Office

Sam was sitting calmly at his desk as Jack walked in.

"I'm very sorry about this," Jack said.

"Please close the door."

"I'd love to explain what happened."

"Have a seat."

"Thank you. Sam please let me tell you how this happened so you can judge the wisdom of what I did."

"I'm going to give you two weeks severance pay." Sam looked Jack directly in the eye and waited for a response. He got nothing. Jack didn't reveal what he was thinking. "I'll have a check cut and you should be free to apply 'your wisdom' in a new capacity within an hour."

"Sam, I know my mistake hurts you and if you have to fire me then I understand."

Sam couldn't believe this.

Jack continued. "It's your decision?"

Sam looked at him, . . . and then said, "I'll give you an extra week of severance pay."

Jack said, "And we'll stay friends, I hope."

Sam looked at him.

## The Hallway, at the Same Time

Kate went barreling into Speed's office.

She closed the door.

An instant later Speed came dashing out of his office, heading towards Sam's.

## Sam's Office

Sam and Jack were interrupted by a knock at the door.

Sam said, in a sweet, mild voice, "Who is it?"

From outside the door a voice said, "It's Speed. Can I talk with you?"

Speed entered the office before Sam could respond.

"Speed, let's talk later. I'm in the thick of things with Jack."

"He's taking the blame for my screw-up. I told him to book you with Kishkowitz on the fifth."

Sam froze. He took it in. And his attitude instantly changed to very friendly.

"You don't say. Well don't sweat it Speed. We all make mistakes. It's not a tragedy."

He turned to Jack. "We don't need to discuss this issue any further. Let's get back to work, what do you say?"

Apparently, the matter was dismissed. Jack and Speed turned to leave.

"Speed since this is now your issue, I presume you'll be meeting with Kishkowitz instead of me."

"Of course Sam."

## The Hallway

Jack said to Speed, "Thank you so much."

Speed said, "A little advice—whenever there comes a time for telling an unpleasant truth, figure out how to say it, imagine yourself saying it, and then, unless you're absolutely sure it's going to shoot you into a better position, don't say it. The truth is lethal, even in small doses."

## The Office, Late that Night

Jack and Kate were the only two people in the office. Kate was at her desk assembling kits. There were stacks of paper everywhere. Jack walked over to help her.

"I hope this whatchyamacallit you've got to *do*,

"Is a thingamudoo that can be done by *two.*" he said.

Kate looked at him, "I'm okay. But I love you for asking."

"I'd truly love to *stay*.

"If you had something that had to be *done*,

"And it could only be done by *one*,

"Then there'd be nothing more to *say*.

"But when you've got something like this to *do*,

"I'd be so happy to be doing it with *you.*"

He grabbed a sheet.

She said, "Then that's what we'll *do*.

"We'll go at it as *two.*" And she smiled.

They began working in unison.

"How do you feel about what happened today?" she asked.

"I think thoroughness was the lesson. I need to be thorough, through thick and thin, for better or for worse, in good times and in bad, until death do me part. I let him down and I had another think coming."

"You made a mistake; learning is making mistakes."

"He gets worked up, but it's out of worry for the company. When you get to the top, you go at it alone. And there's a lot at the top that can eat away at a body."

"Let me help you out here," she said. "When people get to the top, a lot of times they go off on a power trip. I think that's what's happening here. I think you two are playing a game and neither one of you sees it. Think about this: How can people do bad things to other people and not feel guilty later? Nobody ever thinks of himself as a villain; evil people never think of themselves as evil people; so how can someone justify victimizing other people?"

She stopped and waited for him to take it in and then continued. "He has to find flaws in the victim."

This insight into human behavior came as something very helpful to Jack. "The victim has to deserve being a victim."

"Right. If you murder an old woman for her money and you get caught, and the police ask you, 'Why did you murder that woman?' If you're really evil, you don't say, 'Because I wanted her money.' You say, 'Because she was old and dying anyway. Because she hated me. Because she beat her dog.'"

"It's not why I deserved it, but why did it mean so much to him?"

Jack sprang away and marched across the room. His blood was running hot and his breath was coming quickly.

"Exactly why are the accounts divided into *The Lord Consulting Group* and *The Blue Sky Company*?"

"Money," said Kate, "tends to pile up in mountains. Any time you see someone taking money across a valley. You have to wonder from what mountain to what mountain is he taking it. You're not going to find *Lara Lord* at the top of the *Blue-Sky-Company mountain*.

"No? Who's mountain is it? . . . That only leaves Sam."

She looked at him. "Now you've got a fix on it."

"Let me get this straight. Sam is stealing money from the company? Is he crazy?"

"Of course he's crazy. Everybody in the business world is crazy. You haven't noticed that yet?"

"Wait a second, you mean to tell me the business world is full of crazy people?"

"Yes."

"I hadn't thought of it that way. Are you crazy?"

"Yes."

"You don't look crazy."

"Thank you."

"And he's crazy."

"Yes."

"Am I crazy?"

"No. You're not. But you better get crazy if you want to fly the friendly skies. If they find out you're not crazy, they blow you out of the sky and turn you to dust."

Jack was pulsing with anger.

Kate was being infected by his energy.

"What happened to Sam's last assistant?" he asked.

"He fired him."

"Why?—No, don't tell me. I'll invent the reason."

"Any one would fit."

"Was he crazy?"

"Of course not, if he was crazy, he wouldn't have gotten fired. . . . If you can't get crazy, then act a little crazy. Just so that they're convinced you're crazy. Going with the flow, that's the name of the game."

He pulled away from her.

Now he was moving about the room very swiftly. He moved into a stream of gliding rotations. The way a whirlwind does.

Kate looked at him.

And he was changing before her eyes.

He aged years. He grew from a slight, mild-mannered Jack to a tall, sinewy, muscle-bound adult hulk.

He pounced onto the floor, like a businessman seizing opportunity.

He took one arm, and in sweeping line, arched a fist above his head and brought it into a streaking pound onto the floor. . . . He looked like the legendary Norse God of Thunder—Thor, oh mighty Thor—pounding his hammer into the ground and creating lightning all around.

He was suddenly electric and crackling with energy. That was how he looked—to Kate's beguiled eyes.

Now he rose, slowly, smoothly, sleekly, with tremendous grace. He reached his arms out into the air. He took up great space. And he turned to Kate—As he came out of his maelstrom what he said to her was:

"No, I can't do crazy, Kate.

"Crazy is not my way.

"The world has gone mad today.

"And good is black today,

"And bad is white today,

"And day is dark today,

"And night is light today,

"Crazy is not my way,

"But at long last, I've arrived at where I should be.

"Thank you. Now straight is the gate and narrow is my way."

He took a few graceful, gliding steps toward Sam's office, threw his arm into the air, arched it in a direction outward, and in a newfound voice of fire exclaimed—

"I am standing on the warpath now, baby! And I'm going to blow through him, because I'm shooting to the top and nobody's going to stop me!

Jack's blood was boiling. He couldn't remain still.

He prowled about, but there was nowhere to go. He turned around to face Kate. And now with his blood running hot, and this gorgeous woman standing within arm's reach, he lost every thought of Sam—

And *he kissed Kate.*

He kissed her mightily.

He kissed her with great tenderness.

He kissed her for a long time.

She enjoyed it.

They pulled apart and neither knew what to expect next.

Then they exploded into a tempest of kisses and caresses.

Kate said, "We can't go off the deep end here."

She pulled away from his embrace.

"We can't do this? We shouldn't."

She caressed his cheek.

She said, "Thank you. Let's just do the work and not think of how we feel until we calm down."

They separated. She went back to assembling the kits. He joined her.

Jack said, "Okay. I'm not thinking about it. How about you?"

She said, "Neither am hot—I mean it's hot in here isn't it?"

"It's a steambath."

"Neither of us wants to get in over our heads. Don't you think? I mean is it just me because I don't want to put words in your mouth."

"You don't want to say what I'm not thinking."

"Let's talk about something else."

"Throw me a subject," he said.

"Business," she said.

"Management," he said.

"Who's on top—err, I mean what's going on at the top," she said.

He picked it up. "Too much of a focus on short-term profit at the expense of long term growth."

She jumped into it. "That's it. We'll talk trends the problems with business today."

"It's all the consolidations," he said.

"All the mergers," she said.

Whoa—they halted talking there.

Now there was nothing but silence. They continued assembling the kits.

*Act Two*

---

# Middle Enlightenment

---

### Sam's Office

Sam and Ray entered.

Sam said, "You've been doing fantastic work lately."

"Thank you Sam."

"First rate. Absolutely first rate. No question of that."

Sam's tone suddenly turned somber.

"We've been approached to pitch a major deal for General Developers—GD."

"We're going to work with GD! Wow! . . . Isn't that good news?"

"Marvelous news. I look forward to the challenge. . . . We're going to make a proposal for a complete reorganization, a total overhaul for them. We'll be presenting that in ten days. And you're going to be my number one at the presentation. You'll give them the works—That's in ten days."

Ray became alarmed—Ray became *very* alarmed.

"With everything we have going, that's tight," Ray said.

Sam fired back immediately, "I don't appreciate that kind of language Ray. Don't fuck with me today Ray! I'm not in the mood for this! What do you think this is? *'Fuck with Sam Day'?*"

Ray swallowed hard.

"I'm sorry Sam. I lost my mind for a moment. I don't know what happened there. I can't explain it."

"How many hours do you sleep a night?"

"About seven."

"There's your problem. You're oversleeping. They've done studies on this. Don't be a victim of sleep."

Sam continued. "That's why you're so sluggish. This business requires speed. That's part of the training here. I've noticed your work has been slowing down over the past few weeks. That's why I keep coffee in that kitchen. We shouldn't be having these kinds of problems. I didn't address it, and I may be the one at fault there, but now it's time to face the issue head-on. It's going to be a strain on all of us. But we've got a good team in place and we'll show them what we can do when we fire off our guns."

"I learn so much from you Sam."

"That's the spirit. Now here's another issue. My first vacation day was supposed to be tomorrow."

"Oh, I'm really sorry. I know you were looking forward to this vacation."

"Thank you. But the only sensible thing to do under the circumstances is to go ahead and take my vacation."

"What?"

"This is a big job. It's important that I pace myself."

## The Offices, Later

Sam and Ray were going over the new business pitch.

Jack entered with two cups of coffee and served them to Sam and Ray.

"Did you remember to put sugar in mine?"

"Yes I did. Would you like to look at the dessert tray?"

Sam scowled.

"Look at me. Do I look like I eat dessert in the afternoon? What the fuck is the matter with you?"

Jack asked, "Sam, do you think I'd be able to work on this project?"

Sam looked at Jack. "Don't be ridiculous." He moved on to serious busines. "Do you know where the dry cleaners is?"

He handeds Jack a dry cleaning ticket.

Jack said, "The one that's two blocks up?"

Sam said, "You go out the front lobby, then travel two blocks."

Jack was attentive—and pretended he need these valuable walking instructions.

Ray interjected, "Sam, involving Jack could be an option."

"We can't take him away from his duties."

Jack said, "My accounts are on schedule. As for the special projects—I could work those out. Like maybe pick up your dry cleaning during my lunch break."

"Then that's what I'm going to have you do. Have a seat," Sam said.

## Presently

Jack was sitting in one of Sam's armchairs. He was listening attentively to Sam, who was moving about.

Sam was talking directly to Ray.

"They've provided us with a dossier."

Sam rose from his chair and approached Ray with the *dossier* about the prospective client. He took a position beside Ray and began leafing through it.

Jack happened to be on the other side. He got up and crossed to a position behind Ray and Sam, so that he might peer over their shoulders.

Sam handed Ray a card.

"This is the contact person. During my absence, she can direct you."

Ray dropped the dossier into Jack's hands. And then very carefully grouped the card with a *golden notebook* (that he carried about the office).

The sleek, modern *golden notebook* was an interesting attribute and companion object in Ray's act.

Ray's notebook was in a jacket of true gold. Inside was a folio of Ray Raymour's thoughts, such as they were.

Ray carried this golden notebook about proudly.

He was just an old-fashioned genius. He did the hard work of thinking. Then put the thoughts in his notebook.

That's how it worked with him. . . . He saw himself as brilliant. And he was sure he was. . . . In every way. . . . That's what he knew. And it felt good to know it. . . . He was also constantly letting others feel it—nearby others such as Jack Flynn and Kate Greenway. *Oh lovely Kate,* he thought to himself from time to time. One day they would get to know each other better, he thought.

## The Offices, the Next Day

Sam's office was empty and the lights were out.

Nearby Ray's voice was bouncing off the walls.

"Ohhh! Arghhh! Ahhhhh! This is going to be a lot of work. You have no idea how much."

## The Associate Desks

Ray and Jack were each sitting at their desks.

Ray said to Jack, "I really appreciate your support."

"I'm ready to start."

"All right Jack."

Jack leapt eagerly out of his seat.

Ray lifted a stack of files from his desk and handed it to Jack.

Then Ray brought over several stacks of files and dropped them all on Jack's desk.

"Excuse me Ray. Aren't these your accounts?"

"Of course."

"I thought I was going to be helping you with the pitch."

"You are. But you can't build a house without a floorplan. . . . You need a floor plan. . . . And I've got to tell you it's going to be tough. But I'll do fine I'm sure. In the meantime, you can help me best by tackling lower priority issues."

The phone rang.

Ray grabbed his *golden notebook* and a pencil. He didn't answer the phone, even though Ray was closer to the phone.

Jack stepped closer to the desk and glanced at the phone.

"That's your line Ray."

"Could you do take a message?"

Ray didn't wait for a response. He walked away and disappeared into Sam's office. Jack picked up the phone.

"Hello . . ."

## Sam's Office

Ray seated himself in Sam's chair. He opened the dossier and began composing his pitch in his *golden notebook*.

Jack appeared in the doorway and asked, "Can I help you in any way?"

"I wish you could but this is a little too complicated for you. Having said that, I would go on to say that I really appreciate the support you're giving me—"

The phone rang in the background.

"—by handling some of the trivialities while I—shouldn't you be getting that?"

Jack walked off to answer the phone.

## Later

Ray was reviewing notes that he'd written into his *golden notebook*.

He was also, at the same time, standing in the middle of Sam's office casually dancing to some soft music coming off of Sam's sound system.

Kate appeared in the doorway.

"Break it down for us Ray."

"Hello Kate. Come on in. Take a break."

Kate stepped into the office.

"That's a lovely dress."

"Aw yeah, sweet ruby Ray, tossing the compliments my way. "

"I'll be right back," Ray said.

## The Associates Area

Ray walked over to Jack.

"Do me a favor Jack—no interruptions." Ray winked at Jack. "You know how it is."

## Sam's Office

Ray stepped into Sam's office and closed the door. He gave Kate his most winning smile.

## Presently

Out in the associate's area, Jack heard strains of laughter coming through the closed door.

## Later Still

Jack was on the phone with a client.

"No, I'm sorry Ray is not available . . . I'm not sure when he will be . . . is it anything I can help with . . . all right, hold on please. I'll see if I can locate him."

Jack approached Sam's office, hesitantly. He knocked on the closed door. He heard Ray and Kate laughing inside but got no immediate response to his knock, so he opened the door—to find Ray sitting beside Kate—so close that he was practically in her lap.

"Sorry to interrupt Ray but I've got a client on the phone who needs to speak with you."

"Come in here for a second."

Jack stepped into the office.

Ray continued. "Are you familiar with a mysterious, hard-to-develop technique called *'taking a message?'*" Now Ray said, charmingly but acidly, "Perhaps if you could ever so kindly help me here, you could do that for me."

Ray stood up and stepped into the hall.

## The Hallway

Jack joined Ray in the hall. Ray pointed to Jack's desk, to suggest that Jack should go sit down, but he did it as if he was communicating with a dog, whom he wanted to fetch a stick.

Jack went toward his desk, but not quickly enough to suit Ray—who *shoved* him with some solid force from behind.

Jack spun around and *punched Ray in the jaw*. With surprising street aptitude. He hit him in exactly the perfect spot to knock him senseless, and Ray fell to the floor.

Kate stepped out of Sam's office and saw Ray trying to lift himself off the floor. He was woozy and couldn't quite do it.

"What happened?"

She turned to Jack and found him leaning over his desk, wrapping up the phone call.

She turned back to Ray.

"It's okay. I'm fine."

But in truth he was not. He was approaching Jack—but he couldn't quite lift himself off the floor. So he was crawling over.

He mustered up his strength and managed to rise into a half crouch. He then curled his hands into fists.

"Let's go tough guy."

Jack didn't move.

"Come on. Let's take it outside."

Jack not only didn't move. He didn't even seem disturbed.

Ray said, "That's what I thought." He turned to Kate as he rose to his feet. "He came up behind me and sucker punched me."

"If you consider your ass your front then I came up behind you." Jack turned to Kate. "It was in self-defense. . . . Ray got carried away and did something emotional. He's not having a good day."

"Be a wise guy. We'll see how far it gets you," Ray said.

Ray stumbled away and down the hall.

Jack and Kate were alone.

Jack said, "I lost myself. I don't know what came over me. I didn't hit him that hard. Who knew he passes out so easily."

## The Office, End of the Day

Jack was watching Ray, who was leaving for the evening, and who was entirely ignoring Jack.

"Goodnight Ray." He said this pleasantly.

Ray didn't respond, he just left.

## Sam's Office, Early Evening

He found the dossier and opened Ray's *golden notebook*.

"How can this be our business proposition? It's weak Ray."

Jack looked to the ceiling.

"It should hit them harder . . . we're general business consultants that deliver communications firepower for brands. And for the people who need to become brands."

## The Associates Area, Night

Jack dashed to his desk with the dossier. He was going to create his own draft of the presentation, starting from scratch.

"We use and push mainstream marketing science to work on your most valuable asset, which is your name and how your name is perceived. We build brand equity and brand personality."

Jack worked in a *green folder*, a simple, earthen object, and filled it with his fertile imagination.

He was a dreamer, and in this he kept the stuff of his dreams.

He was a systems thinker and in it he developed the mechanics of his systems.

He had an inventive mind that built business models and in this he kept his understanding of business designs.

He felt that every brand and every business should have a supremely clear and specific focus. And in this folder was where he worked out his ideas.

He opened it and began to imagine the presentation.

He would give it a sharp focus—and dramatic people.

Speed's vision.

Sam's sagacity.

Kate's loveliness.

Ray's deliberate deftness.

And how the qualities lent force to the company focus.

## Much, Much Later in the Evening

Jack was growing exhausted, but he was still aggressively working on the presentation.

"We develop positioning and creative themes out of that positioning focus that bring brands and people to life. We select the most powerful messages built on that focus. The ones with broad appeal. We build a message package. A creative umbrella with a central focus that unifies all messages and program elements to make the sum more valuable than the parts."

## The Offices, A Few Days Later

Sam had returned and was sorting through his mail.

Jack was working at his desk. He looked down at his hands, where he was now holding his *green folder* that contained his alternate version of the presentation.

Jack took a deep breath and then started walking towards Sam's office. Ray glanced up from his desk and watched Jack enter Sam's office.

Jack closed Sam's door.

Ray wondered what was going on.

## Inside Sam's Office, A Few Minutes Later

Jack said to Sam, "I know this pitch is very . . . it's our most critical project. And we want to present, . . . uhm, to put our best foot forward . . . Ray is of course in charge—"

"And doing one hell of a job. I understand we're almost finished with a preliminary."

". . . As I understand it, our intention, was to have me contribute under Ray's direction."

"If he feels you're too busy or the work is beyond your abilities then you can't take that personally."

"But I've been free to do the work and I feel I'm capable of it."

"What do you want me to do, spank him?"

"No, Sam. What I'm saying is I came up with my own pitch."

Jack withdrew the presentation from his *green folder* and handed it to Sam.

"That's absurd. We don't have time for you to make a second pitch."

"I already did it."

"You can't do that."

"Why?"

He got no reply to his question—Sam was now carefully examining the presentation.

"Have Ray bring in what he's got, so I can review it, then let's call a quick meeting."

## Sam's Office, Day

Sam was comparing the two presentations as Jack and Ray looked on.

"I'm getting very angry here. Let's talk about why. And I'm going to try not to kill somebody today."

He held up Ray's presentation.

"Ray, this is your presentation. It's okay. Now Jack, this is your presentation. It's better."

Sam took Jack's presentation and tore it in half.

"It's never going to see the light of day. Let this be the lesson: Ray is a senior associate. You are a junior associate. Never under any circumstances go outside the chain of command. Every time you fly over your boss's head, I will blow you out of the sky and turn you to dust. So sayeth the Lord. Understood?"

"Perfectly," said Jack.

Ray looked at Jack and then turned to Sam with a lot of love in his heart and said, "Thank you Sam."

"You're welcome Ray," said Sam.

Sam turned to Jack.

"It may have been done with *good motives*"—said Sam and made 'good motives' sound as rigid as if he was actually saying 'bad motives'—"but it was not done with *military behavior.*"

Sam continued to look hard at Jack. "I cannot command a rabble, no order no discipline. I must rebuild the battalion. Show them methods of efficiency. . . . Stay in line soldier. This is an outfit, not a ball club or a fucking playground. This is a place for adults."

His look remained locked on Jack. "When I was a child," said Sam, "I played the games of children. When I became an adult I put off childish games."

## The Offices, a Long While Later

Sam was rushing down the hall. Jack was at his desk.

"Sam, can I talk with you for a second?"

Sam didn't slow down. Apparently, the answer was *no*.

Later, Sam was rushing in the reverse direction.

Jack said, "Sam, would you be free for a few seconds?"

"Do I look available?"

## Sam's Office, Day

Jack was finally meeting with Sam.

"I didn't want to upstage Ray. I just wanted to do some good work. I'd like to learn from you how I can do that. You're a businessman; a successful, experienced, and smart businessman. And with all my heart, that's what I want to become."

Sam looked at Jack.

He said, "You could feed me more and more and then some, but let's cut to the chase Jack. You want to get ahead of the pack. And your brain is spinning, trying to come up with the game plan. I can read you. You could give me every kind of lie but I could still read you. And I've got a way to get you what you want. So let's do that. I mean we could share every variety of put-on right now but instead let's talk the truth. The truth shall set you free. When I say that, it's not just me talking, that's the Lord speaking through me. The truth shall set you free. What does that mean? Okay, let's get into it.

"You've got a head full of ideas.

"But ideas are not valuable commodities. Every fucking fool has ideas. Experience—that's precious. That's what you want and I'm going to give it to you. I'm going to let you work on some of *The Blue Sky Company* accounts."

Jack was thrown. "Uhm, . . . Sam, . . . isn't uhm, . . . *The Blue Sky Company* reserved for—"

"Say it—you've figured it out, haven't you. *The Blue Sky Company* is an embezzlement outfit."

"You would characterize it in that way?"

"A turkey is a turkey. Blue Sky is a fraud. A deceit. It's also Valhalla. You know what that is?"

"No."

"Have you learned nothing from me? Yes is always the answer. You say 'yes' and then you look it up. Clients don't pay you to not know things. I hear 'no' come out of your mouth one more time, I'm going to rip your fucking jaw off.

"Back to my point . . . in this life, you fight and fight and in the end, you want to know there's somewhere you can go . . . your own company, where you can relax and be yourself. There's nothing sadder than someone coming to the end of their life and they don't own a company.

"I had a good friend, he died that way, without owning a company, poor fellow. Nothing. Not a limited liability company, not a subchapter-s corporation, not even a sole proprietorship. He was nothing. I'll be honest with you, he didn't even need to retain his lawyer at the end, let alone his publicist. That's the way most people end up.

"Now, I know stealing is a terrible thing. I'd be the last guy to tell you stealing is good. But it is a widely used, highly accepted method of building a life.

"Behind every great fortune is a great crime. Stealing is a part of business. It's expected. And respected.

"You want to know the ways of the world. That's what you're going to learn here. You think life is a bed of roses. Life is a business. And if embezzling is part of it, that's part of it. Breaking the law—that's not part of it. If you're good, you do everything within the law. I'm not talking about stupid, low-level embezzlement. They'll catch you and they'll lock you up. We didn't get where we are by teaching that. I'm talking about real, artistic embezzlement."

Jack said, "I feel like Moses in front of the burning bush."

"Absolutely," Sam said. "And now let's take a look at The Blue Sky Company. When you examine it along these lines, you find that it's brilliantly constructed."

"I'm listening."

"The art of arts is to turn a 100 percent profit. That's what I'm achieving here. The Blue Sky Company has no costs, no overhead. Just profit. And it's all legal. Do you understand the secret principle involved here?

"What is the principle?"

"If you rob from a store you become a crook, if you steal the whole store you become the owner."

"And then no one can touch you."

"That's how to embezzle. To steal from the accounts is stupid. I'm not doing that. I'm stealing the accounts themselves."

"Sam, that is so simple and yet it's sheer genius."

"That's right. Now that you know the secret, I'm betting that you'll want in on the action. Or would you prefer to be a loser all your life?"

"Oh, I don't want to be a loser all my life. Just a third of my life."

He gave Sam an amiable smile that he did not really mean at all. Jack was going to lie to Sam. He had no intention of participating in this embezzlement scam. But if he were to tell Sam the truth at this point he would be fired immediately. Therefore, he was going to pretend that he would join Sam's plot until he could come up with a way to get out of this predicament without getting fired.

Jack continued. "I'm just surprised that you're opening up like this to me. This is a hell of an opportunity. Thank you for your trust. And thank you for the truth. The truth shall set you free. Ye shall know the truth. And ye shall turn the truth into cash."

Sam turned to Jack and said, "There's such a shortage of people with a natural feeling for this business. The schools just aren't turning out qualified people to fill the spaces that are out there—What kind of degree did you get?"

"A Bachelor of Arts. In philanthropy," said Jack.

"Those fucking colleges!" Sam said. "That's the business I should have gone into. They have the best legal excuse for robbing people blind, because 'They're teaching them.'

"They have to make their money. But if the colleges weren't such dens of burn artists, feather merchants, lip gloss dealers and banana oil salesmen it would make my job a lot easier.

"Now you see what you have to go through to get good accomplices? You have to convert the honest to the true way.

"You have to be prepared to overcome moral objections, to get past the almighty 'No!' that is constantly going to be hurled at you—everybody starts with a no.

"Don't ever let something important die at the hands of no. No means maybe. No can be a lot of fun if you're willing to work with it."

### Speed's Office, Night

It was now evening, a few days later.

Jack and Speed were meeting together. Everybody else was gone for the evening.

Speed noticed that Jack's appearance was—picture perfect. He was becoming polished.

"How does the head office feel about Sam?" said Jack.

"The head office is Lara Lord. And Lara is very fond of him."

"She is?"

"Sam makes sure of that."

"I want to let her know Sam has been implementing a customized profit participation plan."

"You want to get him fired?"

"Exactly. Let me you show you this."

Jack raised a set of documents.

"I got hold of Sam's employment agreement."

Speed reached for the documents.

"Look at the language that defines company business. It applies to the Blue Sky accounts. He's in breach of contract. What he's doing is flagrantly out of bounds and he knows it."

"If we talk to Lara it may hurt Sam, but will it help us? It'll look like a vendetta—it will come across wrong for what we want."

"What he's doing is wrong. He deserves to be outed."

"That's not enough of a reason to do this. We're not prosecutors, we're businessmen."

"Okay. The problem is . . . you want to move up in the company but you want to do it because you're for something, not because you're against someone."

"Right. If we're doing this to benefit ourselves then we have to get the results we want. She shouldn't end up handing the job to a bigger nightmare."

"Then we don't tell Lara, we tell her business affairs person—in confidence. Then he'll look like the good lawyer for nailing Sam. And Lara will be upset because she had to discover the scam. By the time it filters up to her through two or three execs it'll be a major fiasco. What do you think—yes, no, maybe?"

Speed sighed.

"Is that a yes?" asked Jack.

"We're getting within walking distance of a yes," said Speed.

## The Motorcourt, the Next Day

Jack walked over to a bank of payphones.

Back then, people dropped in coins into public phones to make calls. That was how you did things when you were outside an office.

He looked at the bank of payphones. He lifted a receiver. He looked at the phone. He touched the coin return and the silver buttons on the pay phone.

Then he went into his pocket and pulled out a *cell phone*. He dialed the number and as the phone rang, he looked at the bank of payphones. What a wonder yesterday was. That's how they did things in *the last business age*.

That's how they made a secret call in *Sam Bartlett's day*. It was another world. . . . Hmm, they were moving into the new business age now and a new century.

A voice came over the line.

Jack said, "Hello. My name is Jack Flynn. . . . I work with Sam Bartlett . . ."

On the other side of the motorcourt, Sam rushed out of the lobby toward the car lane, where a car was ready and waiting for him. Sam was heading toward the passenger side of the car when he suddenly stopped—

On a side angle—he noticed *Jack on the phone*—

Immediately, lightning crackled across the heavens and a storm erupted in Sam's mind.

In the distance, Jack noticed Sam. He waved a hello with a charming smile. Jack made some comments into the phone and then hung up.

Presently, Jack was standing beside Sam.

"I was just talking to my girlfriend," said Jack. "We've been fighting so I thought it would be best to make the call outside of the office."

"Couldn't the call have waited until after hours?" said Sam.

"Well," said Jack, "you know how it is when you have a fight with your girlfriend."

"I don't want you conducting any personal business during office hours."

"You're absolutely right. It won't happen again. Is there anything I can do while you're out?"

"I've got two shirts and a pair of slacks that need a pick-up."

Jack smiled warmly as Sam handed him a dry cleaning ticket.

### The Office, Night

Jack and Kate were working at their desks.

Everyone else was gone for the day.

"Would it bother you if I put on some music?" said Jack.

"Not at all."

Jack went to Sam's office, turned on a slow big-band song, and returned.

He put out his hand to Kate, she took it, and they began a slow dance.

"Can I pose a tender question?" she said.

"Please do."

"You and Speed have been meeting a lot lately. Are you working on something together?"

"Speed and I have been putting a few words into Lara Lord's ear."

"What are you telling her?"

"A story that's been told many times before, of a big kahuna—who is in charge of a pile of money—being led down the garden path by a charmer who speaks with a forked tongue. We didn't want to crowd his act, but we wanted to move her along in her fool's paradise—to show her the scene at the end of the road—where the fool and her money are parted."

"What's she doing about it?"

"Nothing yet. She's coming into town to drop in on him. The subject will probably come up."

"How'd she take the news? Is she angry?"

"Of course."

"Good. I wouldn't want a thing like this to backfire on you. It worries me. You're breaking an organizing principle here. You're behaving sanely. And sanity is lethal in the business world, even in small doses."

"Sanity does have its day, here and there. She's going to catch him with his hand in the cash box. It's going to be an . . . awkward . . . one could almost say uncomfortable meeting but it should work out for the best. I'd say Sam is a man very likely soon to take his leave without notice."

By this point, they had stopped dancing and were standing close together. Too close. They were getting hot for each other.

The background music went into a fast swing number.

Then she leapt onto him, wrapping her arms around his head and her legs around his waist. From there, they progressed into a whirlwind of kissing, caressing, and moaning.

They began to take off clothes.

## Speed's Office, Night

It was now raining outside the window.

In the soft glow of city lights, they made love on the couch.

They were both finding it sinful, but very lovingly romantic—

Suddenly, Kate froze.

"Wait, did you hear something?"

Jack listened.

"I heard a sound," she said.

"Not to worry. I'll check."

Jack cracked the door open and had a look.

He saw two security guards in the hallway. . . . They picked up his slacks and inspected them; then stepped a little closer to Speed's office, where they picked up Kate's blouse. They both turned in the direction of

Speed's doorway and began to move.

Jack whispered, "You can fire a person in an office. You can sign a person's death sentence in an office. But just try to make love to a person in an office, and all hell breaks lose."

## The Associates Area

Jack stepped out of Speed's office. But he did it casually, ignoring the guards. It was a perfectly ordinary evening in the office. Except that he was naked.

The guards turned, startled.

Jack casually noticed them.

"Oh hello. I'm Jack."

He extended his hand for them to shake. They didn't respond at first.

Then slowly one guard stepped forward and shooks Jack's hand. But he didn't look happy to meet him.

"I'm Shake." He pointed to his partner. "This is Bake. . . . What are you doing?"

"Oh nothing much."

Jack looked at Bake who was a very large, somber man. Bake looked even less happy to meet him than Shake.

But Jack showed no fear. He smiled charmingly at him.

Bake said, "Do you work here?"

"Absolutely. This is my office."

"Is it?" said Bake.

"Certainly," said Jack. And he was very convincingly definite about it. "You'll pardon my appearance, I was catching a nap."

"Sir, you are naked."

"Of course. But it is getting nippy here."

He took back his slacks and put them on.

"My clothes'll take away the chill. How about you guys? What are you up to?"

They just stared as he put on his slacks.

Then he took Kate's *blouse* from them and put it on. It looked very odd on him—this silk shirt, with its feminine pastel color—but it was passable, and he just smiled as them oh so amiably—As though it was a perfectly ordinary evening.

"Is it a slow night?" Jack asked.

He patted Bake on the shoulder playfully. And Bake looked at Jack's hand grimly.

Bake said, "If you ever strip down naked again, I'm going to take your head and put it into a wall."

"I understand," Jack said. "Would you two care for some coffee before you head on your way? I'll brew you a fresh pot. No?"

"I'm wise to you," said the guard.

"Now my dear Mr. Shake—"

"—I'm Bake. He's Shake."

"Forgive me." Jack smiled at him. "Mr. Bake, sleep is a very important thing.

"I have to work through the night. We have a very important presentation in the morning. I need to get some sleep. Now we're chatting here very enjoyably but I have obligations.

"I'm sure if you research the subject, you'll understand why I will now leave you gentlemen.

"When you listen to clinicians talking about the effect of sleep on the brain, about disorders of sleep and alertness, then you will conclude that the mechanisms of sleep and arousal are linked. You cannot work well until you have slept well.

"Sleep is not 'time out' from life. It is an active state essential for mental and physical restoration.

"I'm going to share a secret about the great short-sleepers of history. Do you know why they got away with not sleeping a lot? Because they napped a lot.

"Well, if you'll excuse me, I have to get back to sleep. I have to start work in about an hour and then work through the rest of the night. We have a very important presentation in the morning. Let's look forward to talking again soon."

He went back into Speed's office and closed the door—leaving the Guards to face blank space.

## Speed's Office

Jack pasted his ear to the door and listened. Kate joined him.

"I lie occasionally. I don't believe in being a compulsive truth-teller."

They waited for a few long beats and then Jack opened the door.

He saw the guards disappearing in the distance.

## The Offices, the Next Morning

A bouquet of flowers was sitting in a vase on Kate's desk.

Jack was sitting at his desk. Smiling. He had bought the flowers for Kate and was awaiting her arrival.

Kate arrived. . . . She saw the flowers. . . . She turned to Jack with a smile. Then she leaned in and smelled them.

Sam came out of his office and stopped by Jack's desk.

"What are you working on?"

"The expense reports," said Jack.

"I see," said Sam. He turned to Kate. "Kate?"

"Yes, Sam."

"Do you have a few minutes to spare?"

"Sure Sam."

"I'm trying to pick out a present for a lady friend. You know how bad I am at those things."

## Sam's Office

Kate and Sam entered, and Sam closed the door.

Sam motioned towards the couch. "Make yourself comfortable."

She sat down and he took a position beside her on the couch.

"I have to tell you something that has registered with me over the past few weeks—that you're doing a terrific job. First rate. Absolutely first rate. No question of that."

"Thank you."

"You're welcome. Now, I'm a teacher. I consider everyone who works for me a student of mine. And I'd like to teach you the lesson of how things grow. Would you like me to do that?"

"By all means, yes."

"We start, as always, with the truth. The truth shall set you free. Now when I say that, that's not just me talking. That's the wisdom of kings and queens passing through me onto you. The wisdom of moguls.

"You want to know what the truth is? The truth is what is. And what should be, is a terrible, terrible lie.

"You've been in the business world for a few years. And where are you in the scheme of things? What is your net worth? Is it more than zero, yet? You don't have to answer that. I'm sure you're still less than zero, from a financial perspective. That, to me, is very sad.

"Do you want to move ahead? You need to want to move ahead. You don't have the option of letting grass grow under your feet. That's not how it works when people are involved. When you stand still, others move ahead. When you stand still, the ground erodes from under you and you descend into the abyss. If you're not protecting yourself, then you're opening yourself up to an attack. I'm speaking in truths. I know no other way to speak to a mind that has to be turned. The truth is music—mighty, fine music—and it's calling out to you.

"How do people become millionaires? You're a brilliant, beautiful, magnificent woman. You know the answer. If a guy is earning a dollar and you want to earn a million dollars. Do you work a million times harder than him? No. You find a million guys like him and feed off each of them to the tune of a dollar.

"The world is a feeding game. We live in a mutual feeding society. I go to sleep each and every night wishing it were different, but it never will be. Man lives by eating flesh and screwing flesh.

"I've watched you closely. I know what's behind the curtain.

"You're as smart as you can be. The act you put out to the world is as wonderful as wonderful can be.

"But, I know the secret of you. Do you want me to put the secret into words? You want more and more and then some.

"Time to come out, from behind the act. Time for you to grow."

Kate's expression was inscrutable.

*Act Three*

# Final Enlightenment

## The Conference Room, Morning

Speed, Jack, and Kate were prepping the conference room for the meeting with Lara Lord. Preparations for a visit by Lara were always meticulous. She was the center of the universe at this company and more latitude could be allowed for a visit from the President of the United States than could be permitted for her.

## The Hallway

Jack exited the conference room and found Lara Lord standing before him.

She was a charismatic, attractive woman who had command presence.

She was traveling with the two security guards, Jack had encountered previously.

"Hello Lara. It's a pleasure to meet you. I'm Jack."

"How are you? Where's Sam?"

"You got here in very good time. We're still just setting up."

"Fantastic. Is Sam here?"

"Not just yet. He should be here any minute. Can I lead you to our conference room? So you can have some coffee and pastries while you wait."

Lara threw a hand into the air. That was apparently a "yes."

Jack turned and lead them away.

"How was your flight?"

"Why?"

"I was just wondering if it went well."

"We got here didn't we?"

## The Conference Room

Speed was reviewing some documents and Kate was setting up the table.

Jack arrived with Lara and her entourage.

"Well, hello Lara."

"Speed."

Speed pulled out a chair for her at the head of the table.

"We're all so sorry to drag you out here. I realize this is an enormous imposition." He turned to Jack. "Do we have an estimated time of arrival on Sam?"

"I'll go keep an eye out for him."

## The Hallway

Jack was waiting by his desk.

Sam arrived with Ray.

## Sam's Office

Sam and Ray were standing together, when Jack stepped into the doorway.

"Excuse me Sam."

"Yes."

"I'm sorry to have to tell you this . . . but Lara is here."

"Oh good," said Sam cheerfully.

Kid was surprised by Sam's manner. "She's here to discuss The Blue Sky Company."

Sam, still cheerfully, said, "Really? "

Ray started laughing. Sam joined in.

## The Conference Room

Lara, Speed, Kate, and the two security guards watched as Jack, Sam, and Ray entered.

"Lara, my dear, how are you today?"

Lara nodded to the guards and they took up positions on either side of Sam.

"Sit down Sam."

He complied.

Lara said, "We all know you are taking me for a ride. You are therefore fired."

"I am?"

"I am only here for an explanation."

"True I was running a small concern of my own in these offices."

"Why you pretentious son-of-a-bitch. Who do you think you're talking to?"

"You're right. I was stealing."

Lara did not react adversely to this.

"It's inexcusable," said Sam. "It hasn't been sitting well with me at all. I made a big mistake. But now I'm going to atone for it. For the sake of our friendship I'm going to put all that money back into the company."

"Whoopee," said Lara.

Sam and Ray each looked at her.

"You have no idea how I regret it," said Sam. "I took advantage of you, a very dear person to me. You're my mentor. I want to make it up to you."

Lara didn't do anything.

"Consider this," said Sam, "it may be very good news for you that I'm going to put all this money into the company. I took out that money over the course of years. We can put it all back slowly so that at the end of this year when you have to meet with your boss you can add an extra chunk to the profit margin. Maybe you add 10 percent. Bring it into that meeting and he's going to say, 'Very good Lara.' If he asks where it came from say, 'The Devil sent it from hell with a note that said *To an old friend.*'" He'll laugh and laugh. I know him. He has a good sense of humor. He'll get up from his chair and hug you. What do you say to the offer?"

Lara said, "I'm thinking about it."

Jack stood up.

"Let's talk about sanity for a minute. I urge you to not let a thief run your company."

"He's right," said Sam. "He's a vicious, horrible Jack but there's truth in what he's saying. I'm part thief but I'm learning to tone down that part of me. I can't promise to give up stealing completely, but I won't steal anything from you."

Jack turned to Lara. Jack was a systems thinker and now he just said what he knew to be true. He said it as plainly, and as simply as he could. "You need to stand for something," Jack said. "What do you want your business to be about? Sam can keep the company going and keep it profitable. But do you want it to be all about the money?"

Lara remained poised. She looked as if she was listening with an open mind.

The room went quiet.

She started laughing. She thought Jack made a dumb speech.

Sam courteously got her attention again.

Sam said, "I'm a requisition artist. I'm not saying no. He's going to call me a thief, all right. I like to operate by moonlight. I'm a flim-flam man. I'm a grifter. I'm also a good businessman. A clean-up artist. A make-a-haul, do-the-trick, and fill-the-bill artist. It's all one. That's what you want working for you—someone who brings home the green velvet—right?"

Lara smiled. She liked what she was hearing from Sam.

Sam continued. "Isn't this kid something else? He's the one who leaked the story of my embezzlement to your attorney."

"Oh, is he the one?"

"He has a certain style. He likes to fly outside the chain of command. And he likes to talk sanity. Let's talk sanity. Without the chain of command, where are we? Anarchy. You and I could not exist. I promised him a raise in three months. I'm not going to give it to him. He's going to fly over my head to you. If he does are you going to give him the raise?"

The room went silent again.

"No," said Lara.

"Of course not. What would you do?"

She turned to Jack.

"Fire him," she said.

"It's time to fire him," said Sam.

Jack started pulsing with anger. He was going mad with fury, but only internally. On the outside, he stayed stock still. If looks could generate heat, his eyes would have scorched Sam and Lara.

"Lara, what if I expose what I'm seeing here today?"

"There hasn't been any law broken here."

"There's a breach of contract."

"We'll renegotiate Sam's contract and make it retroactive. That'll make it a problem that never existed.

"We're making our numbers, it's legal, what else is there? Go talk to your congressman, ask him to write a bill, I'll be the first to support it. In the meantime, this is all legal."

"You can't fire me," said Jack.

"I can't fire you for racial reasons, I can't fire you for reasons of sexual discrimination. But I'm firing you for no reason. There's no law against that. You see how the system works."

Jack was really burning up now. He fought to not lose control as he slowly walked out of the conference room and gently closed the door.

Lara turned to Sam and smiled. All was forgiven. They both stood up and hugged like best friends.

"You're a character," said Lara to Sam.

## Jack's Desk

Jack was emptying his desk of his personal possessions while a security guard monitored him.

Speed stepped out of the conference room. And Speed wasn't at all flustered. He shook Jack's hand.

"Well," Speed said, "I guess this is goodbye. You've got to hand it to Sam. He pulled a winning move."

"Speed I don't think this is funny."

"Oh cheer up Jack. You'll find another job in no time."

"I'm sure we both will."

"Oh, I already have."

"What?"

"I got an offer from the competition. I was going to stick around here if we could make the restructuring happen but now I might as well move on."

"Do you suppose you have a position there for me?"

"Of course. I'll try to find something there for you."

"Thank you. How can I get in touch with you over there?"

"Oh, that's okay. I'll get a hold of you."

Speed walked away.

"I just realized something," said Jack.

"What's that?" asked Speed.

"You don't care about anybody. You just put on an act."

Speed laughed.

"Everybody puts on an act. An act is the way to live. Good luck my friend."

"Help me out with one thing—is everybody in the business world crazy?"

"Absolutely. I thought you knew that already. Take care, Jack. I'm sure I'll be seeing you around. You've got too much might and main to meet your end on this field of combat. . . .

"And when these unlucky deeds I relate,

"I shall speak of you as you are; nothing extenuate,

"Nor set down aught in malice, then must I speak

"Of one that loved not wisely but too well.

"Good day, sir. Enjoy the weather. It's beautiful outside. Blue skies, nothing but blue skies."

Speed left.

Now the others stepped out of the conference room.

"Let's have dinner together tonight," Lara said to Sam.

Lara glanced over at Jack. Jack met her gaze and there was something sad in his expression.

Lara turned back to Sam.

Sam stepped between them.

Sam said, "You have a lot more to learn than anyone can teach you. Don't get me wrong. I personally like you. But you're not right for the business world. You're a troublemaker. You have a bad attitude. You don't know what cooperation means. You're a loser kid. You're a fucking loser. You need to recognize that you don't fit into this business. Or any business. You would drive it into the ground. You would put people into bankruptcy the way you think.

"Wise up before it's too late. One day, you're going to get married, you're going to end up the same way—fired. You're going to get fired from your marriage. You're going to start a family, you'll destroy the kids. You won't be a good parent.

"And I'll give you something else to think about—you're not liked. In this whole place you don't have one friend. I'm telling you this for your own good. Get a clear vision of who you are and where you are on the ladder. You're on the bottom. I think you're getting the picture.

"You have to recognize when you're not wanted and we don't want you because of the aforementioned. And I would leave before people actually start to get angry."

He has the two big security guards behind him.

Lara cut in. "Let's have Shake and Bake here facilitate his departure, that way you and Ray can walk us out."

Lara directed the guards to stay with Jack.

Everyone else left except Kate, who took a position by her desk.

Jack was doing his best to not be overcome by the humiliation of it all. He gathered his personal possessions as the security guards stood ominously at his side.

He looked past a security guard at Kate, who was standing a dozen feet away. Their eyes met. He had to say goodbye to her.

He walked toward her but was followed immediately by the larger security guard, Bake. Jack stopped and with a vulnerable plaintive whisper asked—

"I only want to say goodbye to her. Do you think you could just stay on this side of the room for a minute?"

"No."

Jack sighed. How much more humiliating did this have to get?

He walked over to Kate and the guard trailed closely behind him. Jack pulled Kate into a goodbye hug as the guard hovered beside them. Jack kept her in the hug as he whispered in her ear.

The guard must have felt left out because he separated them.

Jack said, politely to the guard, "Come on. Do we really have to do it this way?"

"Eat shit."

Jack stared at him, blankly. How do you respond to "Eat shit"?

He turned to Kate. "What are you going to do now?" he asked.

"Oh, I'm staying here for a little while," she said.

"Really? What about your problems with Sam?"

"Don't ask me why but Sam's actually going to promote me."

Jack was speechless.

He turned toward Sam's office.

He got an image in his head:

*Sam's Office, Day*

*He saw Sam and Kate sitting side by side on the leather couch. Jack felt himself suddenly a presence in that room he saw in his mind. And both of them facing him.*

*Sam said, "The truth shall set you free. The truth is what is. And what should be is a terrible, terrible lie."*

Jack turned back to Kate. Now he understood.

She was not who he had imagined her to be. He had clothed her in the colors of his longing but now he saw her—differently.

He became overwhelmed with a sense of loss. He didn't know what to say, all that came out was:

"That's fantastic."

He looked up at the ceiling and then back down at Kate.

Jack continued. "Congratulations."

Jack stepped back. Apparently he was going to leave.

"Well God, good luck," said Kate.

"You too," said Jack.

"I don't know what to say."

Kate's expression was inscrutable.

Jack said, "You've made a big mistake. But I'm not going to be judgmental. You must have had your reasons. I hope you can live with them. I think it's a shame what you've turned yourself into. I'm not going to call you a bitch. But I have to be honest with you. I'm a little disappointed. You've lost your soul. I hope you can live without it."

Kate was still inscrutable. Maybe she was starting to regret what she did. Maybe not. She didn't say another word.

Jack turned to the guards.

The guards wondered what was happening now.

Jack scanned around the room.

He dashed to his desk and grabbed a piece of paper. He looked at it very intently and then:

"This is it. The evidence I need," said Jack.

He turned to Shake and Bake.

"This paper proves what I've been alleging. It's all illegal. And gentleman you are complicit in the act. I am, therefore, placing you under a citizen's arrest."

The guards were bewildered.

They approached Jack. Cautiously. Like they were ready to beat him to the ground but they wondered if there was any truth to what he was saying.

Jack did not move.

Jack said calmly, "This paper proves that a crime has been committed in my presence. And a private citizen—when he witnesses a felony—has the right to arrest wrongdoers.

"But have no fear, you will be turned over to a policeman without unnecessary delay.

"Now, you have the right to say nothing.

"Once in police custody, you will have the right to retain and instruct counsel without delay.

"Ultimately you will be brought before a judge and the question of bail determined.

"If you do not have a lawyer, I recommend you consult the local telephone book for a lawyer referral service number, or a complete list of lawyers in the yellow pages under 'Attorneys.'

"All right. I need you gentleman to step back."

The guards stopped and looked at each other. Did he really expect them to obey?

Jack continued. "Gentleman I do not have the time nor the inclination for this. I need you to step to that side of the room."

"How dumb do you think we are?"

"I don't think you're dumb gentleman. Now you need to move to that side of the room until the police arrive.

"Fuck you."

Bake raised his fist.

Jack said, "Put down the fist! A citizen's arrest is a constitutionally protected right under the ninth amendment as its impact includes the individual's natural right to self-preservation and the defense of the others. If you prevent me from completing my arrest, then I'll arrest you for violating my ninth amendment rights and then you'll really be in deep shit."

The guards slowly stepped back. Hesitantly.

"You gonna tell us this is a for-real bust?" asked Bake.

Jack turned toward the hallway.

Jack said, "Stay where you are gentleman. "

The guards were now in a position from which they could not see the hallway. So they stepped towards Jack to get a peep in that direction. Jack turned back to them.

Jack said, "I need you to not move. Don't make me tell you four times."

The guards froze.

Jack darted down the hallway and disappeared.

The guards looked at each other for a spell. What should they do?

They cautiously inched forward until they could get a view of the hallway.

The hallway was completely empty. Jack was gone.

## Motorcourt, Day

Sam, Lara, and Ray were converged by the curb, beside Lara's limousine.

Sam was bidding farewell to Lara. His back was turned and he didn't see Jack approaching. Jack ran over to Sam and tapped him on the shoulder. Sam turned around.

Jack clenched his fist—he was about to punch Sam.

He had a clear shot at Sam's jaw but he hesitated.

Time stood still for a beat and then Jack decided against punching Sam. He unclenched his fist.

Sam turned back to Lara and ignored Jack, as if he was completely inconsequential.

Jack kicked Sam in the behind. This sent Sam flying into Lara and they both tumbled onto the pavement. Sam and Lara look into each other's eyes. And it was a romantic moment. It was love.

Jack, with enormous dignity, tucked in his shirt, combed his hair back with one hand and then patted one hand against the other, as if shaking off loose dirt. He slowly turned around. He was going to walk away with some dignity.

Ray leapt into Jack's path. Now Ray was going to be the hero. He lifted a finger into the air and pointed it menacingly at Jack's face.

"You and me," said Ray.

He bellowed these three words as if he was the voice of God. He was all confidence and bravado.

But the theatrics didn't stop there. He left his finger hanging in the air for a long moment. Then he slowly clenched the hand into a fist.

Ray continued. "You were lucky last time but this time I'm going to teach you the meaning of the word pain."

"You mean pain-in-the-ass," said Jack.

Ray got into a boxer's stance and approached Jack.

Jack stood still and calmly waited for Ray to step forward. The moment Ray got within reach, Jack punched him in the jaw and Ray instantly crashed to the floor. Unconscious.

Then the guards arrived.

The guards approached Jack ominously. They were going to toss him a beating.

"Gentlemen," said Jack, "you don't want to do this. You'll feel guilty later. And I don't want you to suffer."

But these guards didn't seem worried. They just wanted to beat him all the more because they didn't like speeches.

They started the beating. Lara and Sam, moved back a few paces for clearance room.

The guards beat him casually, as if they were baking a cake. They sprinkled a little kick here and a little punch there.

They were pretty methodical but one of the bodyguards hit the other by mistake.

Shake said, "Oh shit, I'm sorry Bake."

Bake said, "That's all right. Let's get back to work."

They were talking to each other throughout.

"What time have you got?" asked Bake.

Shake showed Bake the time.

"Okay," said Bake, "after this we each take our breaks. Son of a bitch."

Bake kicked him in the balls twice and then dropped his knee on Jack's crotch. Jack's head popped up and got clocked by Shake.

Shake said, "So remember I was telling you I went out with this girl. Holy shit, she got me so upset. Every time I think of her, everything I look at, I just see her."

Boom! They hit Jack.

"You just gotta get over her," said Bake.

"I'm going to get over her," Shake said. "Fuck her."

Shake lifted Jack's head by the hair and gave him three sharp, quick jabs to the face.

"That bitch," said Shake. "She didn't know what she had with me. I'm sensitive, you know that."

"You're a good man. Honest, bro."

Then they stopped.

"All right. This looks good enough."

Then these two "artists" of beating stepped back in sync.

Jack rose from the ground very slowly. He turned to the guards and smiled warmly.

Jack was happy. He didn't have the emotions that a person would typically have in this situation. He was not depressed. He was relieved. He was thinking, *I've graduated.*

He didn't play up any of his pain. He acted more like he was punch drunk.

Jack said, to the guards, "Thank you gentlemen. I'm so glad you were here. I was really getting out of line. Who knows how far I would have gone? Incidentally I couldn't help noticing you guys do a very good job. I had no idea. When we first started into the beating I thought you guys didn't know what you were doing. But then I started to see the results. Gentlemen, I may need your services someday. Do either of you have a business card?"

The guards were stone-faced.

Lara and Sam were looking at Jack.

Jack now addressed them. His tone was not hostile in any way. He smiled and said . . .

"I am become enlightenment; a seer of wheels within wheels."

To them, he didn't make any sense.

Jack continued. "It was a pleasure meeting all of you. I had a rip-snorting good time.

"Ya'll are good people. I feel warmer toward ya'll than I do toward my own kinfolk. I came to you with nothing and ya'll been paying me enough to buy two meals a day. I tell you what, I just got a whoopin but I ain't hungry. I feel pretty good."

Over his shoulder to the guards, he said:

"And by the by, I can't thank you enough for everything you've done for me here today. Ya'll done taught me to be a man. You whooped the tar out of me, but real proper."

He turned back to Lara and Sam.

"And ya'll taught me the meaning of good manners and courtesy. Ya'll made me feel real good by accepting me into your offices. I'm sorry it all has to end here. I just hope that the next guy you find can fill your heart the way you have filled mine with joy everlasting. Now if you'll excuse me, I really need to go to a hospital. Oh now, let's not try to talk me out of it. I should get going before I lose consciousness."

Now Jack walked away.

It was not steady going. He was dizzy. But he did his best to look coordinated and dignified.

Lara and Sam watched him.

Jack stumbled, regained his balance, and then kept going.

Lara and Sam continued watching.

Jack turned around and blew his enemies a big goodbye kiss.

Jack said:

"I'm off to do my thing.

"Going to swing it.

"Swing it, swing it, swing."

With that said, Jack walked off.

Lara started laughing.

Sam smiled.

Lara put an arm around Sam.

"What was that line about?" asked Lara. "That didn't make any sense at all. What is he going to swing?"

"It breaks my heart," said Sam. "I think he's lost touch with reality."

"How could you hire that psychotic?"

"He started off as such a nice kid. I don't know what happened to him. It's impossible to find good associates."

"There's the truth. Well, I should get going."

She moved toward her limousine.

Lara said, "We were talking about something before that no-account varmit showed up."

"Whatever it was, we can talk about it later."

They took the next few steps to the limo, walking hand-in-hand. It was turning into a love story.

Lara said, "Let's try to live it up tonight and not let that flaming queer louse up a perfectly beautiful day."

Sam kissed Lara on the cheek, very tenderly and lovingly.

Lara brought her lips to his. And they kissed.

Lara climbed into the limo. Sam closed the door and the limo drove away.

Sam joined Ray, who had regained consciousness. He helped him to his feet, then the two men along with the security guards walked back into the building.

The motorcourt was now very quiet. Very peaceful.

And it was indeed a perfectly beautiful day. The motorcourt was bathing in the golden glow of a loving sun. The trees and plants that ringed the court area, were basking in the rich colors of a spring bloom, and a soothing breeze was playing upon the leaves.

Some pedestrians passed through.

## The Front of the Office Tower

Jack was walking away from the office building.

Across the great tree-lined garden area.

Into the park . . . and the rambles.

## The Park

He strode through the rambles and came out of the other side.

He crossed a bow bridge over a narrows in the lake.

He joined the long scenic walking path stretching across to the horizon.

He was heading off to recover, but he suddenly was very happy.

He was feeling better.

Cheery.

As he crossed the place he leaped forward. He followed his momentum into a turn and kept going across.

He was traveling in a direction that took him to a terraced lawn, leading upward to a stone pavilion.

He paused on the terraced hill to enjoy the view.

He felt it now—You had to force things to be simple.

The world made things into:

Chaos.

Disorder.

It forced you to lose focus.

You had to force life to be simple.

He came to a spot on the terraced green hill, open and level.
    He angled into a dynamic posture.
    He stood in *a ready position.* One leg behind the other.
    His weight was angled forward. His center of gravity held low.
    He stood poised on the balls of his feet.

He jumped.
    He landed.
    He jumped. He went high.
    He landed.
    He jumped higher. And higher.
    He jumped higher still.
    He jumped into a ten-foot rise. He landed, poised.
    He jumped much higher.
    He landed in a ready crouch. *The international ready position.*
    He jumped higher.
    He jumped higher than the small buildings lying along the backdrop
of the city.
    He landed poised and ready.
    He jumped and he went higher.
    He jumped higher than the office tower.
    He looked straight out. He was not looking down.
    His arms were out in a dance frame. Wings spread before him.
    He came down into a landing. Crouched. Poised. Ready to jump
again.
    He jumped and went much higher.
    He jumped. This time he was aiming his momentum into the clouds.
    His jump rose and rose.
    His jump took him far above the city.
    As he shot into the clouds he was looking straight outward.
    Like a dancer in full flight he was "spotting" the horizon line.
    Now coming through the clouds he rolled himself into a great big
ball—and kept flying upward.
    In that cannonball shape he continued hurtling upward, at great
velocity.
    He was shooting upward.
    His whole frame went into a flip. Then he opened. Spread wide. And
came gliding down.
    Coming down through the clouds he could see the city spread below

him.

He was getting it all. He was seeing the wide view.

He looked down at it all.

*'That's life,'* he said.

He looked down from the sky, onto the world.

He looked at life.

And he knew that when he went back down, he would go down his own road. This was what he wanted now, his own road.

His own road.

His own road.

Life spoke to him in all its colors.

*Find your own road,* life said. *Make it your own. Find your own road.*

He would find his own road.

Then, he came down.

He descended.

And landed.

He landed, poised. Crouched. In a dynamic posture. His weight on the balls of his feet. His arms out. Balanced. In the international ready position.

He held still. Looking straight out he spotted the horizon.

He looked along the horizon line that stretched behind the office tower.

He came out of this thing now. He exhaled. Relaxed. Released.

He came out of it in a slow, moving graceful shape of motion. And he came to his full height.

He stood now with his full weight on his right leg. His left leg held out before him poised. And his arms floating outward from him in a gunslinger position—The international ready position.

He smiled. And relaxed. Released more. He was free.

Now he was spotting the horizon and he noticed a figure moving from the direction of the office tower toward him.

She was coming out of the rambles.

She was walking toward him.

It was a woman. Walking straight and sure toward him.

It was Kate. And she was looking quite lovely.

She was hip motion. And long legs. And a lovely frame moving toward

him.

Her motion was gracefully level. There was no rise and fall she was moving in a line toward him. Her hips were powering the motion. Her hips swayed. Left. Right. Left. Right.

She was moving toward him.

She had crossed the bow bridge.

And set on the path toward him.

It was a long distance. Almost like crossing a dessert.

Jack held still. His eyes were spotting outward. Seeing her. Taking her in. Watching her walk toward him.

It took a long while. It was a distance. But in time she crossed it.

Now she came to him. She entered his space. And paused very close to him.

They looked at each other.

They stood there a long while.

*"I'm sorry,"* she said. Life was tearing at her. . . . So very, very much was tearing at her.

*"I am so, so sorry,"* she said. "Sometimes, I get mean. I get very mean. I hate being mean."

*"Kate,"* he said.

*"Jack, I'm sorry. . . . I'm . . . so . . . sorry."*

He looked at her.

"Please forgive me," she said. "I did something very wrong, and now I want with all my heart to make it right. . . . I'm not who I thought I was. . . . Now I'm me. The real me. . . . And I'm so very . . . very sorry."

He took her hands into his, . . . and brought her toward him.

They kissed.

They hugged.

She took a good look at him now. "Are you okay?" she asked.

"I have good news," he said.

"Good news?"

"Yes, they've just turned me into *the comeback kid.*" He laughed.

She smiled.

"I'll go somewhere else," he said, "with what I've learned, and I'll start over. I'll do better next time."

"Don't let them own you," she said.

"What do you mean?"

"Don't let their problems own you."

"Oh."

"You're not finished here yet," she said.

"What do you mean?" he asked.

"Don't rush to *next time*. You're still in *this time*," she said. "Before you go on to be the comeback kid—Have you really lost here? It's not who wins the battles, it's who wins the war."

"Wow," he said. And looked at her amazed. "You have real courage."

"I do," she said. "You're going to be a success Jack. I know you will be. I believe in you. I trust you. . . . I think you have a war to finish."

He looked at her.

"Actually, we have a war to finish together," she said.

"Together," he said.

When they came together they felt it.

Sometimes two people together are more powerful than the two on their own.

It was two coming together in a bond of very simple force.

These two were now to dream together.

She was feeling what he had felt. They had to force things to be simple.

'Together'—was a nice word.

They saw things together. Things that they did not see separately and on their own. Yes, sometimes two people together are a lot more powerful than two people on their own.

"Now," she said, "let's get the recovery part of our day done, and then I think we should have some good strong drink. . . . Do you like single-malt Scotch whiskey? . . . We have a lot to talk about, you and I, . . . Mr. Jack Flynn."

"I believe we do, . . . Ms. Kate Greenway," he said.

They smiled, and began to walk away from an eventful day, to brace for a more eventful tomorrow.

# Enlightenment & the Scene of the World

HIGH ATOP ONE of the city's most graceful and spectacular skyscrapers, Jack Flynn had arrived—for a meeting.

He entered the offices of a chief executive officer, a rather world-famous one, by the name of John Manning.

"Hello, I'm Jack Flynn."

"John Manning."

They shook hands. And Manning noticed Jack's grip. There was something there. He looked at Jack's face. Yes, there was presence there.

"Sit," Manning said.

They sat in two armchairs, beside the chief executive's couches. It was quite an office. John Manning was a billionaire many times over. The office was simple and graceful, but had loads of accommodations for conducting business in a comfortable setting.

"This is about Lara Lord?" asked Manning.

"About *Sam Bartlett,*" Jack said. And paused.

Manning smiled. This young fellow was smart. He was waiting to get a reaction from Manning that he could read before even beginning.

"Sam Bartlett?" Manning asked.

Jack nodded slightly.

Manning said, "I know the name." Manning looked away. Out at the wide view of the city. "Let me see. Sam Bartlett. I've read about him. . . . I remember meeting him. . . . Lara acquired his company for us a while back."

Manning turned back to Jack. "It's an image firm. . . . A school for experts."

Jack nodded.

Manning said, "Are you from there?"

"I worked there until recently."

"What happened?"

"I was fired."

"I see."

Jack paused for a beat. It was a balanced pause. Not too long, not too short. He was giving Manning enough connection to get a flow moving and at the same time giving him the sense they were equals. They were separated by about forty years of business experience and several billion dollars in personal worth, but Jack felt they were equals, and Manning was beginning to sense that.

Jack gave Manning a good strong gaze. Now without blinking, without moving except to breathe, he continued. "To me, the most beautiful thing in business is to have a sense of *the fundamentals*. I have a story to tell you about the fundamentals within your business. . . . Now I know I'm jumping past seven layers of chiefs and vice presidents—of important divisions—to tell it to you. Normally that's not done, but I think you'd like to hear this story. . . . Can I tell you my story?"

"Yes," said Manning. He looked at Jack who had now settled into a graceful pause once more. "What did you say your name was, again?"

"Jack Flynn."

"Jack—I'd like to hear your story very much."

## The Skyscraper's Courtyard

Kate was waiting down in the building's tree-lined courtyard.

She saw Jack Flynn emerging from the lobby.

He stopped. And raised a graceful fist into the air for—victory!

. . . And then he smiled. . . .

She jumped into the air.

Then ran toward him.

And jumped on him.

They kissed.

And then Jack Flynn and Kate Greenway walked into the city, hand in hand.

They would jump into the future, together.

They'd only just begun to live, in the blue sky world.


— The End —

# The Storytelling Book

Act One

# Front Matter

# The Love Lead, and the
# Fire Book of Changes

---

THERE ARE many kinds of love stories. Some are hardly recognizable as such.

This is *a love story.*

This is an essay story about storytelling. And storytelling is a way of thinking.

This is a fight book for storytellers. It's an essay story about the love of the fight.

It's about a way of fight thinking, a course of study, a body of thought, and an attitude to the practice of the art.

It's a fight book, a storytelling "fire" book.

This is about: *How to direct a story.*

This is about what you can learn from the masters. . . . And how you can build an "indestructible sense of wonder" by going to the root of the problem in directing a story.

This is about: *How to give a story its direction by using "opposites" to common thinking.*

This is about: How to tell stories that move people and audiences.

It's a "How to . . ." book, in the sense of how to achieve your objectives.

We will look at hidden, inner principles, and then we will look at classic examples of how these principles were applied by star performers and masters of the art of storytelling.

The style will follow the theme of our love story.

This will be about me talking to you, the reader, and about the inner principles we all can use to fight our troubles in a brutal world.

# Branding

I WRITE love stories that are about: *Attitude.*

I write stories about people fighting for a theatrical sense of life—against a brutal world.

People fighting for a sense of love and wonder, against a strange, dangerous and mysterious world.

People who are able to build "an indestructible sense of wonder."

### Love Stories

I write love stories that are also comedies about the insanity of our modern world, offbeat funny love stories that look at how crazy our world is. What a madhouse it all is.

It's about connecting opposites.

It's about love stories set in a crazy world. Love set against insanity.

On one side is love, cosmic awe and wonder. On the other side is insanity, unreality, brutality.

### The Theme

The whole book is about one theme, one idea—It's a book of lessons about one thing. The stories are about the lessons, and the essay is about the lessons.

And that one thing is: attitude.

### Troubles

The aim is to help you: Survive your troubles, understand your troubles, do something about your troubles.

It's a message I want to get out.

I can talk about my own stories and characters, my own writing, but it's in the spirit of the John Lennon line that says: *I talk about what I do as a way of showing what we all do. I'm not telling you how to do it. I'm talking about how we all do it.*

The aim is: Improving what we all do.

### Entertainment that Instructs

A good story is entertainment that instructs.

It reflects reality. It holds up the mirror to reality.

Life is change after change after change.

Over the course of years you become a different person.

You become a character. You become more of something or less of something.

If you're able to build a theatrical sense of life . . . it changes not just you, but how you communicate and reach people.

Communication is storytelling. You learn to present ideas.

Good storytelling is a vehicle for conveying attitude.

## Amid All the Craziness

Each of the stories in *The Fire Book* is a love story but a special kind of love story; each is a comedy about the insanity of our modern world.

It's about how crazy politics is, how crazy romance is, how crazy the business world is.

Three stories. Three comedies. Three fun, offbeat looks at our world.

And the stories are about people looking for a sense of cosmic awe and wonder amid all the craziness.

## Opposites and the Sense of Wonder

It's about connecting things and making connections that others are not.

## Catching Ideas and Fitting Them Together

It's about how to build an indestructible sense of wonder

How to achieve a high state of being

It's about colorful dreamscapes. It's mosaics. It's putting fragments together into vistas. It's like the night sky. Some patches are billions of years older than other patches. Together, they make the night sky.

It's like a garden. Different parts grow at different times, but when you look at it on any one day, it's a garden.

The attitude lives in the moment, which is really a constellation of moments.

## The Message of the Fire Book

The theme and the message of the book is that the most important thing in life is: attitude. A kind of fire attitude—And I'm going tell you what I mean in this essay.

It's a book of life lessons in attitude.

It's a book about attitude. The love stories and the essay are all about attitude.

**People Facing a Brutal World**
This is about people facing a brutal, difficult world.

Tennessee Williams wrote about the theme of: *fragile people in a brutal world.* Usually through the character of the forlorn woman.

This is the opposite of "fragile people in brutal world." They overcome fragility. They fight against fragility.

They are surrounded by difficulties. Beset all around by troubles. They arm themselves with talent and fight back.

# The Lessons

The stories are about lessons.

The characters go through love stories with life lessons about how our crazy world functions.

The journey is constructed around the lessons they learn.

The three areas are: Story, Attitude, and Presentation.

### The Characters Learn Lessons
The characters go out and learn lessons. They start with an ability; they learn the lessons in how to use their ability, to achieve their objectives—And you, the reader, can learn from their experiences if you like.

There are three areas for training, three areas you can improve yourself in.

The characters do things. And by watching what they do, we get lessons about life and our own lives.

### Abstract
Here's a summary of what I'll be talking about in this essay; I'm going to be talking about three important lessons and how they apply to you.

### Lesson One: Story
The secret of all good storytelling is: *Opposites.*

It's about *presenting opposites* to common thinking, presenting opposites to the normal thinking of your audience.

Creativity is about connecting things. You have to see angles and connections that others are not seeing.

Life is a cobweb. The lines cross at funny angles.

Storytelling is about your thinking. You have to train yourself to see departures from common thinking. To recognize patterns in people's thinking, and where the departures, the connections, the relationships are that they are not seeing.

Our friend *the opposite* is always there. It's the engine inside the body. It operates at the center of it all. It's like the beat in music. To dance you have to sense the beat. To tell a story you have to sense where the opposites are hidden.

### Lesson Two: Attitude

You must have an attitude on everything you say.

You must be an actor or an actress. You must have a vision and a feeling on everything.

The essential feature of a strong act is a strong attitude.

When you perform in front of an audience, you perform in a heightened state. You cannot perform at the same energy level that you live with. You perform in an energized state.

Whether you're performing for a live audience or for a camera, you have to act out the attitude and the thinking. Not just go through the motions, but rather actually be feeling the emotions to such an extent that they affect your breathing.

You have to be "breathing the feeling." Breathing it like "breathing fire."

You don't act with the body, you act with the spirit, with the will. Then you let that affect your body. Acting is done in your feelings. Then what you do with your body is the expression of that.

### Lesson Three: Presentation

The audience thinks in terms of scenes. So it's important to understand how to present scenes to them.

How to walk them through the structure, scene by scene.

The third lesson is about: Directing the story, directing the audience's attention.

That's the push and pull with the audience—it's the question and answer.

That's what you lead them through.

Just as in dance you lead through push and pull, through tension and compression in your touch.

The problem is: How do you move your audience?

See it as person-to-person conversation. Use question and answer mechanics. Get into their minds. Open up questions. Then give them answers in the form of opposites.

The problem is: Presenting your story, in a way that gets your message across and moves your audience.

You're communicating "an act." You're communicating a doing. You're not just showing something to them that as it were "sits" in front of the audience.

It's about doing something to the audience. Doing something that will get the reaction you want.

# The Actor and the Actress

### The Outcome Is Character

You present a persona. A single, special character. You will put yourself into focus.

You'll be giving them "you."

You'll be giving them an interesting persona that is all you. You won't have to take on a character. Or to be somebody else—Instead, you'll be giving them "you."

You'll be giving them "your act"—in a way that moves them, and gives them a chance to see their world in a new, fascinating way.

It's like becoming Michael Caine in acting. He doesn't take on an immense stage persona. People like his "you-ness."

Character is the life journey. That's what you get out of it, over the course of years. You develop your talent. You develop *a persona* that is totally you. You don't have to be anybody else.

You become a character that works. You will have pathos. You will move them.

And then the ultimate end is that you'll be able to let go of your act. The mechanics will be second nature. . . . The mechanics will fall away.

And like Archie Leach who became Cary Grant—you will be the character you created. You won't have to be somebody else. Cary Grant once said: *"I pretended to be somebody I wanted to be, and I finally became that person. Or he became me. Or we met at some point."*

Like great old film actors, like Anthony Hopkins or Helen Mirren or Judi Dench when they come on the screen, you can drop into the moment. You can get into the Zen of it—Without being somebody else. . . . It'll be you.

## Persona

You'll be giving them a persona. An attitude.

Reflected in that will be them—What's inside their heads. What problems they face.

That's the climax. You'll be showing them "being." Fascinating being.

In which they will see parts of themselves.

You'll be giving them something they can't get anywhere else. Glimpses of truths about themselves.

## The End

It's about: "Being the artist."

Having an artistic sense of life.

Building an indestructible sense of wonder and life.

How to see yourself as you really are and show them as they really are. That's what they'll like. They will see their world in it. The mirror to nature.

Love and insight—How to see yourself by looking at others.

How to be yourself. And for them: To see themselves by looking at another person reflecting them.

## Being You

It's not about *becoming* you. It's *being* you—Not going to a *future* that never comes. Going to a *now* that you must live in—How do you ride the fragments and chaos of the journey?

It's Zen and the art of storytelling—That's what it is.

It's like Zen and the art of archery. You practice archery. In the end, you become the archer. You live it.

It's talent development. You're taking a given talent you have and bringing it to life—It's a way to develop your innate sense of wonder into an attitude. Into a driving force. That can take you through the different "now" moments of life.

Living and experiencing the now—but with a deep and great sense of wonder.

It's a way to experience "being you"—with a sense of wonder.

We're all destined to be ourselves. You can't be someone else—This is about how to make that a good journey for yourself. A powerful journey. An important journey.

You don't take on a character, you become a character.

You don't take on something outside yourself and walk into it.

You find a person inside yourself and you become more of that person.

Be an original, everywhere you go.

Let your voice take you places.

Let your character take you places.

And as Dr. Seuss put it, "Oh, the places you will go."

Act Two

# Storytelling

# Opposites

All storytelling is based on opposites.

The secret of all good storytelling is: *opposites.* Connecting opposites.

It is about *presenting opposites* to common thinking, presenting opposites to the normal thinking of your audience.

The mainspring of all good storytelling is: opposites. It's connecting opposites. It's unity of opposites.

Or to put it another way: Opposites produce story appeal.

It's a balancing act. It's about balancing opposites and connecting opposites. About hiding opposites and revealing opposites.

Our friend the opposite is at the root of storytelling.

It's the engine in the body.

He operates at the center of it all. Just as the beat does in music.

To dance, you have to sense where the beat is. To tell stories, you have to sense where the opposites are hidden.

### Hiding in Plain Sight

The main secret of storytelling is hiding in plain sight.

It's always right there. That's the irony.

That's why in *"The Sound Chaser Versus the Thunder God"* I have a scene titled *"The Mainspring of the All That There Is"*—in which my character talks about how the secret is right out there for all to see, if they look.

Opposites.

### All Enlightenment Is Connections

All enlightenment is connections.

Even let's go so far as to say that our life itself is an enlightenment.

It comes from an ovule. And a sperm. And it's only when they hit each other, when they make that *connection,* that everything starts to happen.

It's the same thing with thoughts.

It's the *connections* that constitute enlightenment.

It's when you see two ideas fit together. And—boom—it becomes a whole new thing.

That is it. It's the experience of enlightenment. And it's based on connections.

## All Storytelling Is Enlightenment

All storytelling is enlightenment.

All enlightenment is about connecting opposites.

Enlightenment is seeing into nature. And storytelling is holding up the mirror to nature.

But you can only perceive relationships. You can only perceive things in relation to other things.

If everything were black, could we perceive black? Could we perceive color?

Zen masters bring up a good point when they say: If everything were blue, could we perceive blue? How would we do that?

## The Center of It All

Important things bear repeating:

*All storytelling is based on opposites.*

I just want to state my theory again, because I believe this is the hardest concept to grapple with and absorb fully. I'm going to keep coming back to it because it underpins everything.

It is the absolute. It is the cosmic base of all storytelling. It's the eternal in the art, and the art in life.

*All storytelling is enlightenment. All enlightenment is about connections.*

Storytelling is all based on making connections that others are not making, and connecting opposites. Connecting what we might call "opposables."

Originality is seeing it. Not making it. It's seeing it. How new worlds are made from old worlds.

It's fitting ideas together that seem to be in opposing places in the audience's mind.

It's seeing the relationships that make the opposing ideas fit together. Seeing relationships that are hidden from others.

And when—*Boom!*—you suddenly see it, that's enlightenment.

## Defining Opposites

Now by opposites, I mean things that are opposite to common thinking. Opposite to common existence. Opposites to the normal. Opposites to the way that it always goes.

## Creating Contrasts in Storytelling

The strongest contrast you can create is an opposite.

The strongest contrast to white is black. Isn't it?

When Rembrandt painted his portraits in order to make his people glow he set them against darkness.

## The Design Principle

A good principle of construction to follow is an acting principle that says in preparing for any scene you look at the situation and then you ask yourself: "How would a thousand other people do this?" And then you don't do that. You do the opposite. You use an opposite of what normal thinking expects to happen.

An actor at an audition must stand out from ten other actors competing for the same part.

What it takes to rise to the test is a valuable lesson, and an eternal principle that we all may use in our own work.

## The Dance of Opposites

The secret of storytelling is to create *a dance of opposites,* a symphony of opposites.

With question-and-answer mechanics.

With conflict-and-resolution mechanics.

With mechanical forms that are in themselves opposites. Danger and rescue. Stress and the release. Tension and harmony.

In life, the dance of opposites is always there.

## Theatrical Opposites

The central thought here is this: You want to make connections for people.

Life is a cobweb. The lines cross at funny angles.

The "opposites" in storytelling are the funny angles in life. We want to be able to see them and that's where the storyteller helps us.

## New Worlds Are Made from Old Worlds

New worlds are made from old worlds.

It takes two to make a new idea.

It takes two; it's a team effort.

As Alan Watts once said, "It takes two to make love, to make an argument, to do anything. That's the yin and yang."

It takes two to make a story.

You have to fit together at least two ideas.

You need to fit together something normal and something opposite to the normal.

The center of the action is—opposites.

Connecting opposites. Uniting two opposites—to create something different than simple common sense.

## Classic Examples

Three classic examples are:

1. Man bites dog.
2. David versus Goliath.
3. The reversal of the sexes.

Examples are everywhere. In the news headlines we see examples of opposites all the time:

1. In science, we have the person who once was blind but now can see. The person who once was dead but now can walk.
2. In politics, we have a parallel: the politician who lost big and now is "back from the dead."
3. In business, we have the story of how failure breeds success. How sometimes you gain by losing, and you lose by gaining.

## Cosmic Opposites

A good place to start is by looking at "cosmic opposites."

### Theatrical Opposites and Caveman Stories

Our brains have not changed much in 100,000 years. We still have the brains and impulses of cave men and women from 100,000 years ago. We're filled with primitive impulses, and primitive behavior.

It's about theatrical stories. How we're living through ancient stories. Through caveman and wilderness stories. And it's about how to see the patterns.

## The Progression of Opposites

In music, you chart the harmonies and the progression of chords.

In storytelling, you chart the progression of opposites.

Let's go back to simple, caveman times.

## Character Opposites

You start with basic identity. Who you are. And how you act.

What leaps immediately to mind is "the reversal of the sexes"—A woman behaving like man. Or a man behaving like a woman.

Along similar lines, you have: adults behaving like children. Or children behaving like adults. If you go to a kindergarten graduation ceremony, you see five-year olds performing like grown-ups.

Others character opposites are:

1.  The bumbling expert — Done to perfection by Peter Sellers as the bumbling inspector Jacques Clouseau. He acts like the world's foremost expert in crime scene investigation, even when what we see happening at the crime scene—is that he's getting his testes accidentally caught in a mechanical claw. . . . The bumbling professional. It's fun watching him do something that a professional should never do.
2.  The cowardly hero — The cowardly lion. Or its opposite: the mouse that roars like a lion.
3.  The crooked judge.
4.  The innocent villain — As in "Streetcar Named Desire" where Stanley Kowalski says: What did I do wrong? I only raped your sister.
5.  The happy warrior — As in George C. Scott's portrayal of General Patton.

## Complex Human Beings We Can't Figure Out

What makes it fun, is seeing: Two bodies occupying the same space at the same time.

Two opposite lives embodied in one person.

Two ideas in the same place.

A coward in a hero.

A bungler in an expert.

A king inside a commoner—This was the Jackie Gleason "Ralph Kramden" character.

### The Arrogant Loser

The arrogant loser is a character-opposite that seems to fill our world.

We see him everywhere, and in all walks of life.

The know-it-all fool. The educated idiot. The arrogant, egotistical fool who thinks he's great but he's wrong about everything.

Sometimes he's our doctor. Sometimes he's our professor. Watch out for him. When he takes on the role of teacher or advisor, he's dangerous. The story can become quite ugly, quite quickly. And if we're not watchful, we may not know what hit us.

### Partners and Teams

Moving out from identity we go to: coupling, partners, duos, teams and so on.

Here we have examples such as:

1.  Strange bedfellows — It's two opposite people, with one big contrast between them. Two opposite people in two opposite worlds, that must live through a situation together—Two worlds enter one world; that's the idea—As in the film "Terms of Endearment" with the Jack Nicholson playboy character and the Shirley McLaine prude character.
2.  The blind leading the blind — As played to perfection by Laurel and Hardy.
3.  The idiot in charge, or the lunatic in charge.
4.  The small person in charge of the big person.
5.  The little boy seeking the big girl. Or the folksy boy seeking the worldly girl.
6.  The skinny man who adores the big wife.
7.  The artist dealing with the square.

### Situations

This brings us to situations—a series of happenings and plot turns:

1.  The confidence man and the sucker. Or the conman conning the conman.
2.  Mistaken identity — As in Hitchcock's "North by Northwest."
3.  "The last person to know" something that is obvious to everyone—That is to say someone discovering something that shouldn't take any discovering to see.
4.  The sane man entering the lunatic asylum.

5. The unwelcome houseguest.
6. The shotgun wedding.
7. The wrong party acting injured.
8. The wrong person getting the medals.
9. Building a bridge to nowhere. Or "the onward rush to nowhere."
10. Making much ado about nothing. Or its noble variation: Finding heaven in a wildflower.
11. Applying logic where there is no room for logic—For example, try applying logic and common sense to the stories of Superman, Batman, or Spiderman. Try asking why things happen the way they do in their origin stories and it will get very funny very soon.

# Opposites in Scenes

### Opposing Forces
Two forces in opposition to each other. That's the basis of scenes between people.

A conversation is not a scene. A scene is a battle of wills.

The people are generally in opposition.

### Battle of Opposites
A scene is a contest of wills and a battle of opposites.

Here are some examples:

1. The insiders versus the outsiders. The in-tribe versus the out-tribe.
2. The battle of the sexes. Boy versus girl.
3. Man versus nature. Man versus wild. Man versus monster, dragon, tiger, whale, beast.
4. Man versus sport.
5. Man versus war.
6. Man versus world.
7. Man versus fate — Here I'm reminded of the Arthur Miller line: *"I'm a fatalist. Your fate is your character."*—So a variation of this is the theme of most classic tragedies: Man versus his own character.

# The Brutal World

---

Finally we come to the brutal world. Opposites on the scale of society and the cosmos.

We live in a big bad brutal villainous world.

We live in a wild, wicked, strange, dangerous and mysterious world.

This is the theme of the stories I write, and how talented people are able to build a theatrical attitude in the face of the brutal world.

Examples are:

1.  Law and Order — The sinful reformer. The corrupt sheriff. Low deeds in high places.
2.  Life and Death — The casual killer. The charming villain. The banality of evil.
3.  The Sense of Wonder — The unity of opposites. The sense of nonsense. The logic of the illogical. The mystery in everything that we see, hear, touch, feel and think.

### All Storytelling Is Based On Opposites

We end where we began. With our mysterious friend the opposite.

He exists everywhere. He is at the center of it all.

When we look into any story what we see is a pattern of opposites.

All storytelling is based on opposites.

The secret of all good storytelling is: opposites.

# Attitude

There has to be an attitude on everything you say.

This means that there has to be an acting feeling on everything you say.

### A Sense of Attitude

It's important to develop a sense of attitude. The essential feature of a strong act is a strong attitude. You have to perform in a heightened state.

### Performance Energy

Operate at performance level. The energy level you perform at is not the energy level you live at.

You cannot perform at the energy you live with. . . . And the trend in the modern world is to strip away feeling. To make things mechanical, technical, numerical, digital. The world is always working to shut us down.

To perform, you have to bring yourself to an energized state.

You have to "turn your headlights on."

### You Have to Develop a Sense of Attitude

When you stand before the audience, you have to feel that you're a leader, almost in the sense of the leader of a movement. You have to find and build "command presence." Because you're telling them things they would not know if you were not telling these things to them.

You're the one that's setting the show; you're in control. It's in your hands.

They must feel that this show is in your control, and everything you say is really important for them to hear. You're in your world, and that is what they respect. They don't want to see anybody who is worried about their reaction.

You want a reaction from them. But it shouldn't seem that it matters to you. That's is not the important thing.

### The Importance of Being Important

You've got to give them something they can't get anywhere else.

## The Story Is Presenting You

You have to approach it as if: It is not you presenting the story, it's the story presenting you.

You're there to communicate a message. The story is a way to do that.

Shift the center of gravity when you perform. It's not that the Earth revolves around the sun. It's that the sun revolves around the Earth.

Use an "importance principle" or "arrogance principle" or an "ego principle."

The principle to follow is simply: It's not you presenting the story, the story is presenting you—Your attitude is the star attraction.

What you're saying has to feel important.

You need an attitude of attack.

Your attitude gives force to your presentation.

"You need to know this, and you're not going to get it anywhere else."

When you're speaking to them: Be forceful. Or perhaps a better term is: "force-filled." Radiate a force field. Drive it into them. Into the world. You're there to fight a brutal world. Show the world all the fight you have in you.

## Create a Value Theme

You assign values with attitude.

Your message may not have an apparent (or inherent) value. You have to give it value. Otherwise, we may not see it. You have to give it importance in the way you present it.

## The Attitude—Is the Acting Part of It

Use objectives. Emotions.

Acting feelings, which are larger than normal feelings. Heightened feelings.

The story is the message part, the "what's it all about" part.

This is the feeling, the heart and soul of a thinking body.

## Acting Feelings

You want heightened feelings inside of you.

But when they come out, you should focus them to person-to-person size.

Like modern actors do. Bring them into a person-to-person communication frame. Like a close-up in front of a camera. The camera detects everything.

Small glimpses. Small reveals. Small outlets.

But inside a large world of emotion.

That's modern acting.

Being able to come to full life in the moment—That's the idea.

The mechanics fall away. The emotion and the full feeling is there, underneath. And you exist in the moment. You—as it were—ride the moment. And you don't have to do a hell of a lot to move the moment along. You can just feel. And keep the feeling going as you think and talk.

Expression will come out of that. But coming to full life with the attitude is the important part.

It's "the thinking body"—in the moment. In the now.

It's the grace of it. The cool fire. The fire can be just radiating warmth, to the walls and beyond. Radiating on a person-to-person level.

Inwardly it's coolness. In the sense of equanimity. . . . And it's: Lengthening. Expansiveness. Lightness and ease.

The thinking body—in motion. In the moment.

## The Principle

The principle here is this:

There has to be an attitude on everything you say.

# Presentation

The audience thinks in terms of scenes.

So a presentation should be set in terms of scenes. That's the secret of presentations: scenes. And the secret of scenes is: direction.

### Directing Attention

The great art is to capture and hold attention.

This involves knowing what we might call "the audience desire." What they like to see.

It involves knowing what makes for a *problem*.

It involves giving it direction. Giving it a good lead, for the audience to follow.

It's also very much about the art of how to raise questions in their minds.

And it's about three-act structure.

### The Question and Answer Theory

My theory of presentation and staging scenes says that: You have to raise a question in their minds. A question causes stress.

### The Pyramid

If I took a pyramid and turned it upside down—if I could balance that, for a moment—you're going to feel ill at ease looking at it. Because there's a tension in the scene.

Here's what's going on:

A pyramid, for example an Egyptian-style pyramid with four triangles on a square base, or a tetrahedron—is incredibly stable when sitting on its base.

But when you set it on it's apex (the point of a triangle) . . . you get a set of opposites. You get stability in a very unstable position.

We know something is going to happen. So we have a question. We'll look to see the answer.

Will it stay there or will it fall? Once either happens the question is resolved.

The tension lies in the moment, in that moment where you set it down to balance it on its point instead of its base. Naturally, everyone would look at it and wonder: What's going to happen next? . . . You've opened a question. They're interested. They want to see the answer.

### Question and Answer Mechanics—and the Storyline

Where is your story going?

It has to end in a place that's opposite to where most normal thinking would go.

The story follows the path of "the storyline"—or what the big-time press calls "the narrative."

Where is your story going? Now think of the story as a question and an answer. A question that raises a stress and an answer that releases the stress.

What I say is that the answer has to be opposite to the "normal answer."

### A Question You Can't Let Go Of

A question that you can't let go of, causes stresses. The answer brings the release. "Ah, I get it." And then you don't have to think about the question anymore.

### Story—The Question and Answer Path to Enlightenment

Stories are always structured around creating stress that produces tension and then releasing the tension through resolution. Through an answer to the question that produced the stress.

Stories are a quest for an answer to a question that causes stress in the audience's mind.

### Three Act Structures

In the three act structure—*you raise the stress, you heighten the stress, and then you resolve the stress.*

There's a beginning, a middle, and end.

Here's the American Revolutionary War told as a three act built on stress and the resolution of stress:

1.  The Americans fought the British.
2.  The fighting grew difficult, the Americans persisted.
3.  The British lost.

## Danger and Rescue

Danger and rescue—you're showing them how to escape or how to overcome a problem.

## Fill a Need

They want to see a reflection of their lives. Answers to their questions. Resolution to their conflicts. You want to get them involved in the tension of looking for a resolution to a conflict.

Present a stressful question. The stress makes them want to know the answer, to see a resolution to the open thing in their mind.

You have to get them involved in the tension of looking for an answer to a question—to a stressful question that you raise.

## Putting People in the Story

Generally you do that by putting someone in the story—You make a connection. Love 'em or hate 'em, they care about somebody now.

They want to fall in love with somebody in the story. That's a basic human desire in the audience.

## They Want to See Troubles, Difficulties, and Suffering

They want to see someone enduring greater difficulties than they are. They want to see something that takes them away from their troubles.

They need a relief from their suffering by watching someone else go through greater difficulty.

We like to sit back and watch people suffer through bigger problems than our own.

Comedy is based on suffering. In comedy, we laugh at a character having a real problem. We recognize problems we're familiar with. . . . We want to see you suffering. The idea is watching other people in pain. In difficulty.

## Discovery Session

Every story is a discovery session.

A story is a reflection of life and what we know about life. A story is a "knowing." The word "story" traces back to the word for "knowing."

I think this is the simple way to look at what a story is. . . . And simple is best.

A story is a mirror, and when we tell a story we hold a mirror up to nature. . . . We can hold a an exact mirror or we can hold a very distorted mirror. But always a story is a rendering of reality.

## A Portrait of a Body of Thought, a Body of Knowledge

A story is a portrait of a knowing. Just like when an artist paints a portrait, he is drawing a picture of a person's face. A story is an artist's rendering of a knowing. The storyteller is drawing the shape of a "knowing." He is telling a "knowing" to get it into your head.

## To Hold the Mirror Up to Nature

You are holding up a mirror to nature.

It's Hamlet's advice to the players: "To hold as 'twere, the mirror up to nature; to show virtue her own feature, scorn her own image, and the very age and body of the time his form and pressure."

## Every Story Has to Be a Discovery Session

A story is a knowing. To present a new story, you have to present a new knowing.

Every story has to go somewhere. This is the appeal of story.

You cannot just present a keen grasp of the obvious. Every story has to go to a new destination.

## The Thought Train

You create a thought train.

Now the train of thought chugs down the track and it has to go somewhere. If the audience gets ahead of the train and sees where it's going you're done, you're thwarted. It's too normal.

So the trick is to derail the train, to make the train jump suddenly onto entirely new tracks.

To be an artist, you must be an innovator. And to innovate you have to fuse "opposites."

The "train of thought" analogy is useful because the story has to have rhythm and tracks to travel (or beats). A story needs tempo and turns.

## Reveal Leading to Reveal—Give People Angle Shots

In using this model: the train of thought—each thought is a separate car in the train.

The principle of "reveal leading to reveal" goes this way. In revealing the story: Do it car by car, landscape by landscape, stretch by stretch. Don't start with a helicopter shot from high above where you reveal all the world.

Or you can start with the cosmic and move to the earthly, but do it through angle shots, through reveals.

This is the opposite of what in journalism is called the "inverted pyramid" style of storytelling. In that, you reveal everything at the start and then fill in the parts.

This is different. This is the dance of the seven veils. Reveal one thing at a time.

### Giving It a Lead

That can be another way of thinking this concept through, of 'giving it directionality.' Because that's what a good director and his or her 'good direction' gives to a story—a good lead for the audience to follow.

### Inertia

The first part of creating directionality is creating "inertia." Mental inertia. This happens in the mind of the audience.

Sometimes people will call this setup, but I prefer we dive into this concept as inertia. It's about putting an object in motion. You begin by putting a story in motion in the audience's mind.

You create an interest, or a connection. They want to follow. Then you lead them in the direction of your pursuit.

### Direction of Motion

Directionality, can also mean giving it a thrust, giving it a leadership stance, giving it an attitude. All these are ways of looking at it.

A direction of motion is what we're talking about.

Where does your story go? Where does it end? And what's the impact?

### Three-Act Structure

Every story is a journey with a beginning, a middle and an end.

You start, you go, you end.

For example, the Julius Caesar line: "I came, I saw, I conquered."

Boy meets girl. Boy loses girl. Boy gets girl.

Every story walks the audience through a journey of answers.

### The Principle

The audience thinks in terms of scenes.

Act Three

# Character

# Focus

---

Attitude becomes character.
You become what you think.
You become what you feel.
Adventures in wonder. You become what you think.

### The End
That's the result. You will present a character.
A story person.

### How to Build an Indestructible Sense of Wonder
It's about how to build *an indestructible sense of wonder.*
A sense of wonder that grows and grows throughout your life.
Beauty is truth, truth beauty.
In the course of your life, you think yourself onto a higher plane.
That's the journey.

### Storytelling to Build Brands—A Theme in My Stories
A brand is a character and a character has to stand for a quality.

### Focus Is Perception
Focus is a perception. It's what we connect to the performer.
In the audience's attention—in the audience's world of awareness—
what does this person stand for?
That's focus.
You want to stand for something. Because that makes you interesting.
That makes you memorable.
So it goes back to the idea of enlightenment.
My theory says: "All enlightenment is connections."
And what is the thought they should connect with you?
It's a very good question to ask yourself.
And a very good answer to have.

Focus is a perception in the audience. It's the concept we give to the performer.

1.  Einstein's focus was to show us that we live in a relative universe.
2.  Charlie Chaplin's focus was the gentleman tramp.
3.  Cary Grant's focus was the elegant gentleman. The acrobat of the drawing room.
4.  Marilyn Monroe was the girlish sex-bomb.
5.  James Dean was the young rebel.
6.  Jack Nicholson's focus was a wolfish madman.
7.  Clint Eastwood—the cool, indestructible gun-slinger.
8.  John Travolta—the confident street guy.

More examples include:

1.  Alfred Hitcock's focus was suspense films.
2.  Stephen King's was horror stories.
3.  Steven Spielberg's is sentimental family entertainment.
4.  The U.S.A.'s focus is freedom.
5.  Barack Obama's 2008 campaign focus was change.
6.  Bill Clinton's 1992 campaign focus was change vs. more of the same.
7.  New York's focus is big business.
8.  Los Angeles's focus is show business.
9.  San Jose's focus is the high-technology business.

## "What Fight Do You Want to Lead On?"

Who are the people that you would like to be among?

People who can see the big picture?

People who can see a bigger reality?

What is the banner under which you will march to the fight of your life?

## Critical Thinking

Instead of being a positive thinker or a negative thinker, how about being *a critical thinker?*

That means looking at reality and asking "Why?"

To me, that's the role of storytelling: *critical thinking.* The kind of thinking that takes you onto a critical path. That gives you direction and leads you to purpose.

## The Ending

The ending is about: How to become *a great character*. One that is you. It's not about becoming someone else, or someone you make up.

The idea is: To be a star, that is you.

It's about: How are you getting to a happier place?

What is the larger picture?

My theory says: Put things together for the people.

What is the larger meaning?

My theory says: Make meaning for people.

Become a character.

Listen to others, trust yourself.

This is the art of being you. No one does it better.